The Reckoning

Also by Yrsa Sigurdardóttir

Last Rituals
My Soul to Take
Ashes to Dust
The Day Is Dark
I Remember You
Someone to Watch Over Me
The Silence of the Sea
The Undesired
The Legacy

The Reckoning

Yrsa Sigurdardóttir

Translated from the Icelandic by Victoria Cribb

MINOTAUR BOOKS
NEW YORK

THE RECKONING. Copyright © 2015 by Yrsa Sigurdardóttir. English translation copyright © 2018 by Victoria Cribb. All rights reserved. Printed in the United States of America. For information, address St. Martin's Press, 175 Fifth Avenue, New York, N.Y. 10010.

www.minotaurbooks.com

The Library of Congress Cataloging-in-Publication Data is available upon request.

ISBN 978-1-250-13628-2 (hardcover)
ISBN 978-1-250-13629-9 (ebook)

Our books may be purchased in bulk for promotional, educational, or business use. Please contact your local bookseller or the Macmillan Corporate and Premium Sales Department at 1-800-221-7945, extension 5442, or by email at MacmillanSpecialMarkets@macmillan.com.

First published in Iceland under the title Sogid by Veröld Publishing

Previously published in Great Britain by Hodder & Stoughton, an Hachette UK company

First U.S. Edition: February 2019

10 9 8 7 6 5 4 3 2 1

This book is dedicated to Mjása and Pilla

– *Yrsa*

Pronunciation guide
for character names

Æsa – EYE-ssa

Dadi – DAH-thi

Einar Adalbertsson – AY-nar ATH-albertsson

Erla – ED-la

Fanney – FANN-ay

Freyja – FRAY-a

Gudlaugur (Gulli) – GVOOTH-lohgur (GOOL-li)

Gudmundur Lárusson – GVOOTH-moondoor LOWR-usson

Heida – HAY-tha

Huldar – HOOL-dar

Jón Jónsson – YOHN YOHN-sson

Karlotta – KAHR-lotta

Kolbeinn Ragnarsson – KOLL-baydn RAG-narsson

Orri – ORR-ree

Sigrún – SIK-roon

Sólveig Gunnarsdóttir – SOHL-vayg GOON-nars-DOHT-tir

Thorvaldur Svavarsson – THOR-valdoor SVAH-varsson

Thröstur – THRUST-oor

Vaka – VAH-ka

Yngvi Sigurhjartarson – ING-vee SIG-oor-HYART-arson

September 2004

Prologue

The school building cast a chill shadow over the empty playground. Beyond it, the sun was shining. As they entered the shadow the few passers-by clutched their coats around them and quickened their pace until they emerged into the warm sunlight again. Over there the day was still, but here in the school grounds an icy wind was blowing, stirring the swings in the corner into life. They rocked slowly back and forth as if occupied by invisible children. Bored children, like Vaka. Worse than the boredom, though, was the cold. It stung her cheeks, and made her toes ache. Every last bit of her was frozen. Sitting on the stone steps only made matters worse because her new padded jacket wasn't long enough to cover her bottom. She wished she had listened to her mother and chosen the longer one, but that had only been available in dark blue; the waist-length one came in red.

Vaka shifted the school bag on her back and wondered if she should move into the sunlight. Then at least she would be warm while she waited – though still lonely, of course, and bored of having nothing to look at. But the shadow cast by the school extended so far that if she moved out of its gloom, she was afraid her dad would fail to see her and drive away again. No, better put up with the cold than risk that.

A car the same colour as her father's drove past, but Vaka saw that it was the wrong make, the wrong man, and her spirits fell again. Could he have forgotten her? It was her first day at the new school, so perhaps he would assume she'd be walking home as usual.

For the hundredth time she felt a stab of longing for her old home. The only thing that was better about the new place was her room, which was larger and way cooler than the one she'd had in their old flat. Everything else had changed for the worse, including school. The other kids, especially. She didn't know anyone. In her old class she had known everyone, had even known what the other girls' pets were called. Now a crowd of new names and faces were jostling in her head and she couldn't begin to put them together. It was like the memory game that she never won unless her mother deliberately played to lose.

Vaka sniffed. How long would it take her dad to realise that he should have come to collect her? She looked up at the main building in the hope of spotting someone, but the windows were dark and there was no sign of movement. Another gust of wind stung her cheeks and she shivered. Getting to her feet, she walked up the steps to the entrance. There must be a grown-up inside, someone who would let her use the phone. But the door was locked. Knocking did no good; the thick wood muffled the sound. Lowering her fist, she gazed up at the big door in the faint hope that it would open anyway. Nothing happened. She might as well sit down again. Hopefully the steps wouldn't feel as icy as before.

All thoughts of the cold were banished from her mind when she turned. At the bottom of the steps stood a girl Vaka recognised from her new class. She hadn't heard her approach. Perhaps she had been tiptoeing, though Vaka couldn't for the life of her imagine why. It wasn't as though she was likely to bite, or they were enemies. They didn't know each other at all, though Vaka remembered her clearly. It was impossible not to. She had two fingers missing: the little finger and ring finger of one hand. The girl had sat alone in the front row and seemed very quiet. At first Vaka had thought it must be her first day too, but the teacher hadn't introduced her like she had Vaka, so

4

that couldn't be right. When the pupils were allowed to talk to each other in the lessons, the girl hadn't said a word. During break she had sat on the sidelines, staring into space, like Vaka on the steps just now. Her expression had remained blank even when two boys started chanting a nursery rhyme that Vaka remembered her granny reciting: 'Little finger, little finger, where are you? Ring finger, ring finger, where are you?' Vaka thought this was unbelievably mean but none of the other kids turned a hair. In the end she had looked away, not daring to interfere. She was new, after all.

'It's shut.' The girl gave a shy smile that vanished as quickly as it had appeared – perhaps it had only been a trick of the light – but Vaka was left with the impression of a pretty face. 'They always lock up when school's finished for the day.'

'Oh.' Vaka shuffled her feet, not knowing what to say. She had never been very good at making friends or talking to strangers, and it was the first time that day that anyone had tried to draw her out of her shell. 'I wanted to use the phone.'

'Maybe you could use the one at the shop. It's not far away.' The girl pointed down the street. She was wearing mittens to hide her maimed hand.

Vaka swallowed and answered awkwardly: 'I haven't got any money.' Her mother was supposed to give her pocket money on Fridays but she always forgot. Usually it didn't matter but there were times, like now, when it was a pain. As bad as Dad forgetting to pick her up. Grown-ups were useless at remembering things.

'Oh.' The girl looked sad. 'Me neither.' She opened her mouth, then changed her mind and closed it again. Unlike Vaka's jacket, which had been bought with room for her to grow into, the girl's anorak was far too small; the sleeves were too short and she couldn't even zip it up properly. She wasn't wearing a hat either and her tangled hair whipped around in the wind. In spite of the dry weather, she was wearing a pair of old, faded wellingtons. In contrast, her brightly coloured mittens looked clean and new.

'It's all right. I'll wait.' Vaka tried but failed to smile. It was hard having to wait in uncertainty like this. She was cold and hungry. If Dad had come at the right time she would have been sitting in their new kitchen by now, enjoying a slice of toast. She could taste the melted butter and jam, and this only made her hungrier.

The girl shifted from foot to foot. 'Would you like me to wait with you?' She didn't look at Vaka as she asked this but off to one side, at the empty playground. 'I can if you like.'

Vaka had no answer ready. Would it make things better or worse? The choice was between sitting alone and getting cold or trying to find something to talk about with this girl whose name she didn't even know. Yet despite being only eight, Vaka knew that there was only one right answer to some questions. 'Yes, please. If you feel like it.' When the girl turned towards her with a beaming smile, she added: 'But I'll have to go as soon as Dad comes to pick me up.'

The smile faded and the empty expression returned. 'Yes, of course.'

Mindful of how the boys had teased the girl and how lonely she seemed, Vaka tried to make amends. 'Perhaps he could drive you home too?' The moment she had blurted this out, she regretted it; she'd often heard her parents moaning about the price of petrol. She didn't want to ask her father to drive miles out of their way, especially when they had so little money left after buying their new flat. 'Is your house far away?'

'No. I live just back there.' The girl pointed at the school, presumably referring to the row of houses that Vaka had noticed when she had wandered around the back of the building during break. They were separated from the school by a high fence, on the other side of which all kinds of rubbish had collected: disintegrating, faded packaging; bits of paper; plastic bags and withered leaves. Vaka didn't like litter; it was disgusting, but as this was one of the few places in the playground where the boys' cruel chanting couldn't be heard, she had gone over to the fence and stared through it, ignoring the mess.

She had studied the houses, feeling thankful that her parents hadn't bought one of them. They looked as rundown and shabby as the fence; their paint peeling, their gardens like jungles. She glimpsed a rusty old barbecue standing in a patch of tall weeds; it looked as if plants were growing out of the little grating in the lid. Grubby curtains hung crookedly at the dirty windows. In some places a blanket had been used instead; in others, old newspapers or sheets of cardboard. Unsettled by the sight, Vaka had turned away and gone back to the other children, who behaved as if she didn't exist.

The street did have one advantage, though: it was close to the school. Perhaps she could use the girl's telephone? It would only take a few minutes to walk there and her dad wouldn't have time to go far if he arrived while she was gone. Plucking up her courage, Vaka asked: 'Hey, could I maybe use the phone at your house?'

She was disconcerted by the frightened look that greeted this request. 'At my house?' The girl gulped and dropped her eyes. Staring down at her mittens, she fiddled with her maimed hand. 'Shouldn't we just wait here? Your dad must be coming soon.'

'Yes, maybe.' Vaka shifted her school bag again. It seemed to grow heavier and heavier on her shoulders, as if weighed down by all the minutes she had been waiting. 'If I can use your phone, you can come round and play at my place afterwards.' Vaka guessed the girl would be grateful for an excuse to go out if she lived in one of those horrible houses. Perhaps that's why she had reacted so badly to Vaka's request. Perhaps she didn't want anyone to see her room.

The girl seemed to be having trouble deciding how to answer. 'OK.

But you'll have to be really quick. And only if we can go round and play at yours afterwards. You mustn't make any noise, though. Dad's probably asleep.'

Vaka nodded, highly satisfied with this outcome and also with having made friends with someone from her class. Of course she would rather have got to know one of the other girls, especially the fun, popular ones, but they had cold-shouldered her, obviously having no need of more friends. Perhaps this girl would turn out to be all right, in spite of her missing fingers. At least she wasn't mean.

But as they set off, Vaka began to have her doubts. Remembering the shabby houses, she suddenly felt a powerful reluctance to enter any of them. It would have been better to wait on the freezing steps. It was too late, though. They had left the school grounds and were approaching the houses, walking in the sunshine now.

Yet instead of growing warmer, Vaka felt colder with every step.

Vainly she sought for an excuse to turn back without hurting the girl's feelings. Her new friend was also silent, apparently just as conscious that every step brought them closer to their destination. They didn't exchange a word until they found themselves standing on the cracked pavement outside one of the houses. Vaka ran her eyes over the front, careful not to move her head so the girl wouldn't notice what she was doing. It looked like the most rundown place in the whole street.

It had two floors and was clad in rusty corrugated iron that hadn't seen a lick of paint in years. The front garden was as scruffy as the ones Vaka had seen that morning. A tricycle lay on its side among the dandelions, chickweed and scrubby bushes, as rusty as the house itself. Almost all the windows were cracked and no attempt had been made to hang better curtains on the side facing the road. As if that wasn't bad enough, the front door was hanging crooked on its hinges. This was a bad place.

Vaka racked her brain to think of a reason why they should turn back but it was too late. The girl looked at her sadly and said: 'Come on. This is my house. Don't make any noise and be quick. Then we can go round to yours and play. Can't we?' Anticipation shone from her colourless eyes and Vaka had no choice but to nod.

She followed the girl, feeling as if her school bag were full of rocks, her heart heavy in her chest. Every step was an ordeal. She felt as she always did when she was doing something she knew would end badly. Like the time her parents had held a party and she had tried to carry too many plates in one go when laying the table. The instant she lifted the pile she had known it was too heavy but she had done it anyway. And every single plate had smashed. That was exactly how she felt now.

The girl paused with her hand on the doorknob. 'Come on. Remember, you've got to be quick.' It came out almost in a whisper, as if there were a monster lurking inside who mustn't know they were there.

Vaka nodded apprehensively and took the final step to the door. Next moment she was inside. Out of the sunlight into the dark. She was met by a reek of cigarettes and a sour smell that made her wrinkle her nose. The girl closed the door behind them and the darkness became even blacker. Perhaps that was just as well. It would hide the mess inside, and the girl wouldn't be able to see Vaka's look of disgust.

'The phone's upstairs. Come on,' the girl whispered, almost too quietly to be heard. As Vaka's eyes adjusted to the gloom, she noticed that the girl kept glancing from side to side. She beckoned impatiently when Vaka didn't immediately react. She had taken off her coat but only one of her mittens.

Vaka tore her gaze from the mitten that hid the missing fingers and stepped warily into the hall. As she did so the floorboards creaked overhead. The girl's head jerked upwards. Her face was twisted with terror.

Vaka went rigid and felt her eyes growing hot, as if she were about to burst into tears. What was she doing here? She gave a little moan but it hardly made any sound, in spite of the silence in the house. This was a terrible mistake. Worse than the plates. Gripped by panic, she couldn't think properly. The only thought in her head was that she didn't even know the girl's name.

Hafnarfjördur Police are appealing for help in finding a missing girl. Vaka Orradóttir, 8, was last seen at 3 p.m. this afternoon, leaving her school in Hafnarfjördur to go home. She is described as small and slim, with shoulder-length light brown hair, and wearing a red, waist-length padded jacket, a red woollen hat, jeans and pink trainers. Vaka is believed to be still in the area. Anyone who has information on her where-abouts is asked to contact Hafnarfjördur Police on 525 3300.

Chapter 1

Huldar dropped the bundle of photocopies on his desk. There was hardly anything else on it apart from a small collection of half-empty coffee mugs. These days he mostly got the assignments that no one else in CID wanted, like this business with the school. It would probably end up as a station joke, like him – the departmental manager who fell from grace. Nowadays he sat in exile at the back of the open-plan area, from where he could barely glimpse his old office.

He took care never to look in that direction. Personally, he couldn't give a damn about his tumble down the promotional ladder; it was the way his former underlings treated him, as though his fall were infectious, that really got to him. He had assumed his relationship with his colleagues would revert to how it had been before his short-lived promotion, but that was way off the mark. Their silences when he approached and their whisperings as he walked away were so intolerable that there were times when he actually wished he were back in charge.

But this feeling never lasted long. Almost immediately he would recall how much he had disliked the position. The endless forms, the reports, the meetings and all that pointless red tape; if he'd been warned beforehand what the job entailed he would never have said yes. But, sadly, information had been in short supply at the time. The whole process had been condensed into a single sentence: *How'd you like to be promoted?* The management had been under pressure to appoint someone to head up a major murder investigation, and since most of the senior detectives had been forced to step aside in the wake of a series of scandals, the choice had fallen on Huldar almost by accident. Instead of university degrees or the kind of credentials used in other sectors, a police officer's suitability for leadership was generally based on age or length of service. These offered easily comparable figures. After the recent upheaval, Huldar suspected they had opted for the next most convenient marker – height. He was convinced that the powers that be had spotted his head sticking up above the crowd. He would have done better to have ducked or sat down. Then he would still be doing his old job, somewhere in the middle of the pecking order, not stuck on the bottom rung.

Yet Huldar bore no grudge against those who had offered him the chance. He could easily have turned it down. Nor was he angry with those responsible for his demotion. Having him in a prominent position would never have worked in the long run. He had screwed up the murder investigation in such spectacular style that it would have been hard to repeat. The only comparison he could think of, when trying to explain it to one of his sisters, was if a surgeon were to come running into an operating room with his scalpel raised aloft, ready to perform emergency surgery, only to trip and accidentally cut off the patient's head.

The worst part was that he had brought Freyja, the director of the Children's House, down with him. The Child Protection Agency, unable to forgive her for shooting a man at her workplace, had relegated her to the position of ordinary child psychologist.

Really, they should both be grateful they weren't tramping the streets in search of a job.

Not that gratitude was uppermost in Freyja's mind. On the rare occasions their paths had crossed following the fateful events at the Children's House, she had scarcely deigned to look at him. She was seething with anger and there was no doubt that it was directed at him. Huldar grimaced at the memory. He had still entertained hopes they could get together, despite an awkward beginning, an uneven middle section and a catastrophic finale. He had only himself to blame; their first encounter had set the tone and it was astonishing that he had managed to get back in her good books at all, even if the truce was short-lived. Burnt by his previous encounters with women while out clubbing, he had posed as a carpenter the first time he met Freyja and spent the night with her under false pretences. Few women he met were attracted to cops. To make matters worse, he had fobbed her off with his middle name, Jónas. Later, when their paths crossed during the murder inquiry that was to put both their professional reputations through the shredder, the whole sordid deception had been exposed: carpenter Jónas had been forced to introduce himself as Huldar from the Police Commissioner's office.

Still, what had happened once could happen again. Maybe he would get another chance. The thought cheered him.

He smiled at the young policeman sitting opposite. The youth returned his smile shyly, then dropped his eyes to his computer again. The screen couldn't show much of interest; he had joined CID so recently that he was even lower in the ranks than Huldar – as low as it was possible to get. But although the rookie was currently the only person in the department who enjoyed less respect than Huldar, that state of affairs was unlikely to last long.

'Rushed off your feet?' Huldar was careful to keep the mocking note out of his voice. The boy was absurdly sensitive. It wouldn't hurt him to toughen up a bit, but someone else could take responsibility for that. Huldar had enough on his mind without worrying about detectives who were still wet behind the ears.

'Yes. No.' Above the monitor the young man's forehead turned bright red.

'Is that a yes or a no?'

'No. I'm not rushed off my feet. But I've got plenty to do.'

'You know, there are advantages to our having little or nothing to do. From the public's perspective at least.' Huldar sat down and pulled over the documents. The sooner he sorted out this nonsense, the better. He curbed an urge to sigh as he skimmed through the childish handwriting on the top page. *In 2016 there will be no need for cars. Instead there will be little helicopters that run on solar batteries. A cure will be found for cancer and all other serious diseases. No one will die until they're a hundred and thirty. Iceland will still be the best country in the world! Elín, 9–C.* The signature was accompanied by two hearts and two smiley faces. It was the first time he could remember encountering a smiley face in his line of work.

'Would you swap your car for a solar-powered chopper?' Huldar pulled aside a couple of slats in the blinds and peered out of the window. The grey winter daylight would hardly provide enough energy to allow a helicopter to take off, let alone stay aloft.

'What?' From the young man's tone, he seemed to regard this as some kind of test.

'Nothing.' Huldar didn't have the energy to explain. He had gone to a bar with some mates last night, stayed up too late and had one too many beers. Either the boy hadn't heard about the case Huldar had been given, or he was too slow to make the connection.

'Do we have access to a helicopter?'

'Yes.' Huldar immediately regretted this answer and corrected himself. 'No. We don't have a chopper. I've just got to read these predictions about the future written by a bunch of school kids ten years ago. This is one of them – that we'll travel around in solar-powered choppers. Probably not the stupidest idea I'll come across while slogging through them.'

The young man rolled his chair sideways so he could see Huldar's face. His name was Gudlaugur but he was always known as Gulli at the station, in spite of his protests. No doubt he would remain Gulli until he had proved himself as one of the team – if he proved himself. Not everyone lasted the course. 'Why do you have to do that?'

'Because they found a weird message among them and the head-teacher contacted the police.' Huldar handed Gulli the photocopy of the helicopter letter. 'At the time their school was twinned with a school in the States, and one of their joint initiatives was to bury a time capsule in the playground. The idea was to dig it up ten years later and compare the kids' predictions about the future. All the year nine children wrote down what they thought Iceland would be like in 2016, then their letters were put in the time capsule. So far so good, except that one of them seems to have taken it into his head to predict some murders. My job is to try and track down the author so the psychiatrists can decide if he constitutes a threat. Personally, I doubt it, but I've got to look into the matter anyway.'

'Who does he say he's going to kill?'

'A whole list. He mentions six people. Actually, he doesn't give their names, only their initials. And in two cases only one initial.' Huldar leafed through the papers in search of the offending letter. The school had given him photocopies of the others but the original of this one. The secretary had made a face as she handed it over, then looked relieved that it was now somebody else's problem.

Gudlaugur watched him flicking through the pile. Huldar couldn't deny that it was a nice feeling to have a colleague show an interest in what he was doing for once. It was quite a while since that had last happened. Pity the case was such a waste of time.

'Why not just talk to the relevant pupil? It can't be that difficult to track him down.'

'The letter's unsigned.'

'What are you going to do, then? Find out who didn't put a letter in the time capsule? Compare the handwriting to old homework?'

'Something like that. There's one more letter than there were pupils in year nine at the time, which suggests that the writer submitted two. So I need to compare the murder letter to the others from the capsule. Shame the kids all had such bloody awful handwriting. The boys, at least.'

'Was it a boy?'

'I assume so, considering how messy the writing is. Or maybe a girl who wrote with her left hand.'

'Any fingerprints?'

Huldar laughed. 'Yeah, right. Like I'm going to get permission to run the fingerprints off sixty-five letters by a bunch of teenagers through the lab. For that I'd need at least one corpse. And preferably all six.' He pulled out the threatening letter and read it to himself again. *In 2016 the following people are going to die: K, S, BT, JJ, OV and I. Nobody will miss them. Least of all me. I can't wait.* No smiley faces or hearts here.

'So you reckon all these people are still alive?'

'I'm reasonably sure, though as I've got nothing but initials to go on I can't be a hundred per cent positive.' Huldar passed Gudlaugur the letter. 'The school secretary says no one with these initials has been murdered in the last ten years. She did add that one man whose name began with a K had been killed in 2013, but the person responsible has been convicted and wasn't a former pupil or the right age. Of course I'll have to check for myself, but even a school secretary should be capable of running through the short list of people murdered in this country.'

Gudlaugur said nothing until he had finished reading. Then he looked at Huldar with an unfathomable expression. His face was still soft, his nose and cheeks were strewn with freckles and there wasn't the slightest hint of five o'clock shadow on his jaw. He must be in his late twenties, only a little older than the anonymous letter-writer would be today. 'There's a Wikipedia page.' Gudlaugur blushed again, which made him look even younger. 'On Icelandic murders.'

Huldar raised his eyebrows. 'Maintained by you?' he asked, a little scornfully.

'No. I just wanted to draw your attention to it. You can save time by checking the names of all Iceland's murder victims there.'

Huldar regretted his momentary lapse into mockery. He'd do better to befriend the young man – he could do with a few allies at work. But there was no time to make amends. Out of the corner of his eye, he saw Erla bearing down on them, wearing her coat. He sent up a fervent prayer that she wasn't about to drag him out of the office with her. He'd only just come in and the storm that had been forecast was already starting to show its claws. But it just wasn't his lucky day.

It was the forty-fifth area of low pressure to rage over Iceland that winter. Each one seemed more violent than the last. You'd have thought the weather gods had entered into an abusive relationship with the island and revelled in giving it a regular battering. As if in support of this idea, a gust blew a wet leaf smack into Huldar's face. It stuck, cold and slimy, to his cheek. When he raised numb fingers to his face, the leaf stuck to his hand instead. He shook it vigorously and the leaf spun away across the garden.

'Found anything?' Erla was struggling to keep her balance. Her long black police parka was acting like a sail and she turned side on to the wind, understandably reluctant to fall flat on her face in front of him. Their interactions had become rather strained since he'd been demoted and she was given his job. The awkwardness was entirely on Erla's side: he didn't bear her any grudge. Someone had to do the job, so why not her? To his mind she was a bit crude and tactless for the role, but perhaps that was part of the reason she had been chosen. The police were under pressure to promote more women, and with Erla they got the best of both worlds: a woman who behaved every bit as loutishly as her male colleagues.

'No. Can't find a thing. Nothing untoward, anyway. It's just an ordinary garden with the usual junk.' He nodded towards a battered trampoline securely tethered at the other end of the lawn. It had clearly been a while since any child had bounced on it; the fabric had rotted away until only the metal frame and a few springs remained. Huldar rapped the top of a rusty barbecue, but didn't bother to draw Erla's attention to the hot tub as she couldn't miss it. No one could fail to see how ordinary the garden was. 'It must have been a prank, don't you think?'

'A prank?' Erla surveyed the garden as an excuse to avoid Huldar's gaze. From under her hood she watched Gudlaugur poking around with a pole in a leafless bush in search of goodness knows what. A few withered leaves, like the one that had plastered itself onto Huldar's face, whirled up into the air. Erla turned back to Huldar, careful to focus on his chin, not his eyes. 'I can't see what's so fucking funny.'

Huldar shrugged. 'No. Me neither.' He was having a hard time seeing the amusing side of being tricked into going out in this weather. The joke certainly wasn't calculated to generate any warm feelings towards the prankster. On the way there Erla had told them that a message had arrived shortly after midday, addressed to her, stating that there was something in this garden that might be of interest to the police. The letter was anonymous and contained no further details. 'Should we maybe call it a day?'

Erla met his eye at last and Huldar realised he'd have done better to have kept his mouth shut.

'No. We'll bloody well look harder.'

'OK. No problem.' Huldar stretched his lips into a smile that was gone almost instantly; it was hard to pretend he didn't mind being forced to stay out here. He watched Erla's progress. She was unsteady on her legs in the gale but clearly determined to get the better of it. He turned back to the decking and peered around for potential hiding places. It would have been easier if they'd had a clue what they were looking for.

There was a rattle from the hot tub and Huldar saw the heavy lid lift slightly, then bang down again. Over the howling of the wind he heard the creaking of the fastenings. There was a small door in the casing of the tub, which Huldar had not yet investigated, so he walked over to it under the watchful eyes of the house-owner upstairs. The man, whose name was Benedikt, hadn't taken too kindly to their visit, seeming unable to grasp what exactly was going on. It seemed unlikely that he had anything to do with the anonymous message; astonishment that genuine would have been hard to fake. He looked like someone who had recently retired, one of those domineering old gits used to being listened to, the type who had trouble adjusting to the fact that those days were over.

Huldar waved and smiled again. All he received in reply was a frown and a gesture that probably meant he should leave the hot tub alone. The guy couldn't be thinking Huldar was planning to jump in; no doubt he was more worried about what would happen to the lid if the fastenings were tampered with. Huldar, who had no intention of touching them, nodded to him reassuringly.

The only things behind the little door were a pump and some pipes. When Huldar poked his head inside to make sure there was nothing lurking behind the tangle of pipes, he banged it hard on the wooden casing, which emitted a creak of protest. This was turning out to be a complete wild-goose chase. If he ever got his hands on the person who'd written that letter, it would be tempting to give them a lump like the one that was now forming on his head. One punch would hardly matter. His reputation was already mud.

Huldar closed the door and straightened up. He rubbed his sore head as he surveyed the dusk-filled garden. They had combed it pretty thoroughly, more thoroughly than the front garden. He hoped Erla wouldn't get it into her head to search that again. The old man had stood at the window, yelping at regular intervals that they were to be careful of the flowers, which was a bit of a joke, given the time of year. Only bare stalks could be seen.

Huldar swept back his hair. The wind responded by whipping it over his forehead again. A pointless waste of time, like every other aspect of this job. Where should he look next? Huldar walked around the garden, trying to spot a likely hiding place. Erla and Gudlaugur were wandering around in a similarly aimless fashion, the young man still with his pole in the air. Huldar went back and perched on the hot tub, relishing the warm steam escaping from the gaps around the lid.

There was nothing of interest here.

The letter must be a bad joke – unless someone had got here first and removed whatever they were supposed to be looking for. Perhaps some parents had found drugs in their teenager's room and wanted to hand them over to the police without getting their child into trouble. The teenager could have followed and retrieved the stash after they had left. Far-fetched. Very far-fetched. It would be much simpler for the parents to flush the drugs down the toilet than put themselves through all that hassle.

Without warning, the wind dropped and the hot steam rose up

Huldar's body until it was playing over his face. It carried a faint whiff that he recognised. The iron tang of blood.

Leaping to his feet, he unfastened the lid. There was an urgent banging on the window upstairs.

It took Huldar a moment or two to work out what the things floating in the tub were, but once his brain had processed the strange messages it was receiving, he took an involuntary step backwards, losing his grip on the heavy lid. The wind, seizing its chance, hurled it back so violently that the hinges gave way. The lid began to scrape back and forth on the decking, dangling from a single fastening. But when Huldar glanced up to see the owner's reaction, the old man's face registered not rage but disbelief.

Disbelief and horror.

Huldar hurriedly grabbed hold of the lid and battled to drag it back into place. He yelled to Erla and Gudlaugur for help. Another blast snatched at it. His arm muscles ached as though they were on fire. But he couldn't tear his eyes away. He felt a sudden heart-felt wish to be back dealing with the trivial little school matter.

For there, floating in the red-stained water, were two human hands.

Chapter 2

Things had been quiet at the Children's House for several days now and this morning was no exception. Freyja had been the last one in and the front door hadn't opened since, while the phone in reception remained stubbornly silent. It was as if winter had sapped all the energy from the country's child abusers. Fed up though she was with the endless cycle of storms and thaws, Freyja was ready to forgive the weather if it really was having that effect. She'd seen too many broken children, listened to too many grim descriptions of mistreatment, not to be grateful. All the world's storms were welcome here, if this was the outcome.

A gust rattled the window, as if instantly taking her up on the invitation. Freyja sighed. She wasn't looking forward to the inevitable hassle of scraping her windscreen and offered up a silent prayer that for once the heater in her wreck of a car would work. The thought made her shiver. To warm herself up, she reminded herself that winter had its plus sides. As long as the weather was this bad at least she had a break from the pestering of her friends who couldn't hear of a hill within ten hours' hike of Reykjavík without wanting to drag her up it.

'Freyja. I'd put away any breakable objects, if I were you. Looks to me like you've got a visitor.' Elsa, the centre's new director, was standing in the doorway of the cramped little office that Freyja had been allocated after her demotion. The woman, who was around fifty, had been head of a department at the Child Protection Agency before taking over from Freyja after the debacle. It wasn't considered appropriate for a person who had shot someone to be director of the centre. Even though it was in self-defence. Her bosses had feared a media backlash; that doubt would be cast on her fitness for the role, not least because her brother Baldur was in prison. Fortunately, the agency's worst fears had not been realised, but by then she had lost the job she loved.

'What? I'm not with you.' Her numbness gave way briefly to surprise, but that wouldn't last long. Before she knew it she would be staring listlessly at her screen again, brooding over her fate. Was this to be her life from now on? Was she fated to end up as a dispensable little wheel in the social services machine? Or not even a wheel, just a tiny cog? Her low spirits had nothing to do with her new boss. Elsa was all right, and made an excellent director. No, it was simply that her career, now at a much lower level than she was happy with, was stagnating. The shot she had fired would go on echoing in the Children's House for years to come. Lately she had toyed with the idea of returning to university and making a fresh start in a different field, though which one she didn't know. She couldn't picture herself as a geologist or an accountant. Her talent lay in gaining insights into the minds of children and adolescents, not in analysing rocks or spreadsheets.

'He's just parked outside. Your friend, the unlucky cop.'

'Huldar?' Freyja instinctively made a face. 'He's not my friend. Quite the opposite. He must be here to see someone else.'

Elsa tutted. 'I doubt it.' She raised a skeletal arm to point out of the window. 'That is him, isn't it?' The woman couldn't weigh more than seven and a half stone. She didn't have an ounce of extra flesh to mask or soften her expression and her face appeared unusually animated as a result. She tried to disguise her skinny frame in loose, hippy dresses, but occasionally even these clung to her. A severe haircut only enhanced the impression of a prisoner on hunger strike, particularly when she wore orange.

Freyja took a quick peek outside. There was Huldar, fighting to close the door of a squad car against the wind. 'Oh, Christ. I don't want to talk to him.'

'If he wants to talk to you, you won't have much choice. Assuming he's here on official business. I don't need to remind you how important it is to maintain a good relationship with the police.' From Elsa's expression it was plain that Freyja didn't have any say in the matter.

The director made herself scarce before Freyja could raise any further objections, leaving her sitting there, praying that Huldar had come to see someone else. She heard the front door open, then the sound of Elsa's and Huldar's voices approaching. Before she could finish her prayer they were standing in the doorway, her boss dwarfed by the policeman's strapping frame. He looked exactly as he had the last time she saw him: tired and haggard. Oddly enough, it suited him. She knew him well enough by now to realise that it was his habitual state. Even in court, dressed in a suit, he had given the impression of needing to go straight home to bed.

Black shadows under his eyes; stubble; shaggy hair.

It irked Freyja that this was her type, the weary but upstanding man who wouldn't waste time in bed yawning. At least he hadn't, in her experience, though it had only been a one-night stand. But that was his fault for being such an idiot. An idiot – but unbelievable in bed. Before she got carried away with these thoughts, she reminded herself that he was to blame for her present predicament; he had been in charge of the case that had cost her her job.

'No need to introduce you two. Freyja, see if you can help him.' No mention of what this entailed. Elsa turned and left them to it.

Huldar grinned awkwardly. He wasn't as angry with her as she was with him. In fact, he wasn't angry at all, judging by his constant attempts to renew their acquaintance. Since she had fired that gun they had been thrown together far more often than she liked. They had both been called as witnesses in the trial of the man Freyja had shot and, subsequently, in the much shorter trial of her brother Baldur for possession of an unlicensed firearm. He'd had twelve months added to his existing sentence. Freyja found this the hardest thing to bear, though Baldur himself had taken it on the chin. 'It'll give me more time to think,' he had told her. What it would give him more time to think about, Freyja didn't dare to imagine. Perhaps Baldur's lack of resentment was because she had at least tried to lie about the origin of the gun, claiming she'd found it lying about. To give him credit, that bastard Huldar had backed her up, saying untruthfully that he hadn't a clue how the weapon had come into Freyja's hands. It hadn't done any good, though, and being beholden to him only made her more resentful. The presence of Baldur's fingerprints on the gun had sealed his fate, and she herself had narrowly escaped being charged with perjury. That had been another factor in the decision to demote her.

'Can I come in?'

'Yes, do,' she said coolly.

'Could I maybe sit down too?'

In the same cool tone she repeated: 'Yes, do,' and watched him make himself comfortable. 'How can I help you?'

'You may well ask.' Huldar laid a sheet of paper on the desk. Observing the untidy scrawl, Freyja reflected that she could have guessed Huldar would have terrible handwriting. 'I could use the insights of a child psychologist in this case I'm investigating.' He smiled the same wry smile that had lit up his face when he stood in the doorway. 'And you're the only one I know.'

'I see.' Freyja decided to leave it at that. The less she said, the better. She didn't want to give him the impression that she was up for a friendly chat.

'Yes, so . . . Before I begin . . . How are you, by the way?' He held her gaze without blinking. A large part of the bastard's charm lay in the way he gave her his undivided attention, his air of distraction suddenly gone. No doubt he was like that with all the women.

'Fine. Great.' She didn't return the courtesy by asking how he was.

'And your brother?'

'Fine. Great. What was it you wanted to ask?'

Her curt replies didn't seem to bother Huldar. He merely smiled again, then explained: 'I've got a note here written by a fourteen-year-old, most likely a boy. I need to know if it's anything to worry about.'

'Let me see.'

Huldar handed her the paper. She read it, then handed it back. 'How long ago was this written and in what circumstances?'

'Ten years almost to the day.' He told her the story of the time capsule. Freyja listened without interest.

'I'm afraid I can't help you. This doesn't give me enough to go on. Though I don't think you need lose any sleep over it. Lots of teenagers fantasise about killing their enemies one day, but virtually none go on to act it out. You'd need to know the background – if the teenager was angry when he or she wrote it, perhaps because of something the people on this list had done that day, there's little cause for concern. The letter-writer will have got it out of their system. If, on the other hand, the kid had been nursing this hatred for a long time, that would be more worrying. It's unlikely, though. It would take a lot to motivate someone to hold on to hatred like that for a whole decade. An awful lot.'

'So there's hope you'll forgive me one day?' Huldar smiled ruefully.

'I said it would take an awful lot, not that it was impossible.' The smile was wiped off his face and Freyja immediately regretted her words. The truth was that it was hard to go on being angry with someone when they were sitting right in front of you. Much easier when you were alone, brooding on your grievances. 'All the same, if I were you I'd try to trace the individual in question. I don't suppose anything will come of it, but at least you'll be able to dismiss the matter and move on to other cases. I assume the police have more than enough on their plate.'

'No, actually. The weather's affected the crime rate. We've got one major inquiry on the go – a pretty macabre case – but I'm not on the investigation team. It was only by pure chance that I was involved in the early stages. I'm no longer entrusted with anything important.' This time Huldar's smile was intended to convey the message that he really didn't mind, but its lack of conviction merely betrayed how much it rankled.

Although Freyja knew the feeling only too well, she didn't say so. If she allowed the tiniest chink in her armour, before she knew it all her defences would be down. She did need a shoulder to cry on, though – someone to listen while she wailed about losing her job; someone, above all, to understand. And that person was sitting opposite her. Her girlfriends were useless; they pretended to be sympathetic but the moment they opened their mouths they gave themselves away. In their opinion, she had only herself to blame. It had been her decision to sleep with the carpenter Jónas, who had turned out to be the cop Huldar; her decision to make it up with him despite clear indications that he was trouble; her decision to take the gun into work so she could hand it over to him; her decision to pull the trigger. It had been nobody else's fault. So she should just accept what had happened, stop whining, and come along to their hot yoga class. The only person who might have been willing to listen was her brother Baldur, but she couldn't bring herself to complain to him; however self-inflicted his problems were, it just wouldn't be appropriate. In the end it was his dog, Molly, who turned out to be Freyja's best confidante. Despite a tendency to yawn, make faces and roll away during Freyja's monologues, at least she never criticised her or came up with stupid suggestions.

But before Freyja could give in to the temptation to open her heart, Huldar continued: 'Anyway, I'm sure that's of no interest to you, so I'll stick to the point.'

Freyja couldn't help smiling inwardly. He had unwittingly blown his chance of making peace during this visit. And she would make damned sure he didn't get any further opportunities.

'I've got another letter that looks as if it was written by the kid, presumably on the same day. But I'd like your opinion. Do you think it could be by the same person?' He passed over another photocopy.

'Well, the handwriting's similar. But the contents are different. I'm no judge. Don't you have any experts in the police?'

'Yes, for what it's worth. I was actually hoping you might spot something in the wording that would suggest it was the same boy.'

Freyja skimmed the roughly scribbled text. *In 2016 there'll be a nuclear war. It'll be cold in Iceland but better than in all the other countries where everyone will die. Instead of going to jail, prisoners will be sent abroad. And they'll die too. Thröstur, 9–B.* 'It could be the same person. It certainly betrays the same negativity. Were the other letters this pessimistic?'

'No. Well, one or two, but nothing like this. Lots of them predicted that Iceland would win the handball world championships, or went on about weird and wonderful modes of transport, or green energy, that kind of thing. Or about what kind of food we'd eat in the future. Luckily most of their predictions haven't come true. I'm not particularly keen to start dining off insects and seaweed any time soon.'

'Have you asked the school about this Thröstur?'

'No. Not yet. I wanted to hear your opinion first. I felt there was no need to alarm them with the possibility that one of their former pupils might turn out to be a serial killer. So there's no cause for concern?'

'No, I don't think so. If it is the same boy, he must have been upset for some reason when they handed in the letters. That would explain the negativity. I doubt it's any more serious than that.'

'Good.' Huldar showed no sign of leaving, though the conversation appeared to be over. 'That's good.'

'Yes, it is.' Freyja gave what she hoped was a sarcastic grin. She had made up her mind to say no more, when, struck by a sudden thought, she added: 'I assume you've checked that no one with those initials has died in suspicious circumstances?'

'Yes, of course. It's early days but nothing like that has happened so far this year.' He drew the photocopies back towards him and rolled them into a tight wad. 'But 2016 has only just started. Who knows what'll happen? Hopefully not nuclear war, though. Thanks for your help.' He smiled again and stood up.

Freyja watched him go with a feeling of regret that she didn't care for. She had next to nothing to do and Huldar had at least enlivened a dull day. When he turned in the doorway she presented a carefully blank face, trying to look as though she was glad to see the back of him. 'Was there anything else?'

'Yes, actually. Would you be willing to meet the letter-writer with me once I've found out who he is? If he's still a bit unstable, you're more likely to pick up on the signs.'

Freyja answered without stopping to think. 'OK. It wouldn't hurt to make sure.'

Huldar looked pleased and Freyja realised she didn't have the energy to bear a grudge for ten years. But before she had time to pursue this thought any further, Huldar blurted out another question, seemingly inadvertently. 'What kind of person would chop off another person's hands?'

'What?' She was so taken aback she thought she must have misheard.

'Who'd be capable of chopping off another person's hands?'

'That depends. Was the victim alive or dead at the time?'

'Alive, most likely.' The pleasure had vanished from his face.

Freyja replied without even thinking. After all, she wasn't aware of any research she could cite to back up her conclusion. 'A madman. Someone seriously deranged.'

Chapter 3

This time the e-mail contained no words, only an attachment labelled *betrayal.jpeg*. It was from the same sender as the others: reckoning@ gmail.com. The first one had arrived shortly after midnight on New Year's Day. There was no question it was from an Icelander. Although short and to the point, the messages couldn't have been written using a translation program. After each one Thorvaldur had developed a knot in his stomach that no amount of gin and tonic could soothe away. He knew because he'd tried.

Even the first message had unsettled him, though at the time he'd assumed it must be a mistake. *Have you made a will?* The opening sentence had given the impression it was spam; he'd received any number of these messages over the years and was always amazed that anyone was idiotic enough to fall for them. What kind of person would make a will in response to an e-mail? But then he'd read further: *You've seen your last firework display. Go ahead and celebrate the New Year with champagne. There won't be any more once you're in your coffin.*

He had long since finished celebrating when he opened the message on New Year's Day, in the grip of a crippling hangover.

The e-mails that followed had contained more in the same vein. Threats about his impending death – rather premature, in his opinion. He was only thirty-eight, his life not even half over, and he had no intention of dying before his time. It was ridiculous to be so shaken by this nonsense. He wasn't used to it. As a rule nothing rattled him: he was never frightened at the cinema, never moved to tears, and had never yet encountered the roller-coaster that could set his pulse racing.

Therein lay the problem. Being afraid was so alien to him that now he'd let this absurd nonsense get under his skin, he didn't know how to stop feeling anxious. If only he'd been in a better state when he opened that first e-mail, he wouldn't be sitting here now with a sick feeling in the pit of his stomach, incapable of simply binning the message and its attachment. That bloody hangover was to blame for triggering this stupid attack of nerves.

One consolation was that the sender couldn't know the effect the messages were having. Thorvaldur had resisted the temptation to reply to them, though the urge to send back a stream of abuse had been overwhelming at times.

Reckoning. The clue must be in the name. But he had no reason to expect a reckoning because he'd never harmed anyone. Not personally. Of course, it was inevitable, given that he was a prosecutor, that some people might feel they had a score to settle. Any number of them, come to think of it. Which was unfair, as they had only themselves to blame for their problems. But the possibility couldn't be ignored.

Yet the messages never gave any hint of being from a current or former prisoner. There was nothing to suggest a link to a court case. Besides, his twelve-year legal career had taught him that the wrath of the convicted tended to be directed elsewhere – at their accomplices, witnesses, the police or judges, whereas prosecutors got off pretty lightly on the whole. The criminals didn't seem to grasp how much power resided in the job. The power to prosecute or not. To decide which law to apply. Whether the defendant should receive a token

34

sentence for assault or a long spell in prison for attempted murder. To decide who should be charged with being the ringleader and who the accessory. Just as well none of them had the brains to work this out.

Unless the e-mails were being sent by someone who had realised? Someone who had suffered from one of these decisions?

No. Unlikely. In the eyes of those he had prosecuted he was merely an insignificant lackey of the justice system. A misapprehension, yes, but a very convenient one.

'Shouldn't you be in court?' One of the young clerks stuck his head round the door; a boy who had assisted Thorvaldur on numerous occasions but whose name he couldn't for the life of him remember.

Thorvaldur tried to appear normal and relaxed. The last thing he wanted was for word to get around that something had happened to fluster him. He had a reputation for never losing his cool and he wanted to keep it that way. Clearing his throat, he gave the boy his customary look of disdain. 'The case was postponed. The judge is ill. He rang to tell me I wouldn't be needed.'

'Wow. Did he call in person?'

'What do you think?' Thorvaldur made no attempt to conceal his irritation.

'Oh, I don't know. I thought they had secretaries for that kind of thing.'

'It depends who they're dealing with. You wouldn't get a call like that yourself.' Thorvaldur didn't do the boy the courtesy of looking at him as he said this. Let him blush. 'Would you mind closing the door after you? I'm rather busy.'

The door closed unnecessarily loudly, without actually slamming. The boy was no fool, though he had a lot to learn.

The e-mail was still open on his screen, the attachment still there, a picture file with the disagreeable name: *betrayal.jpeg*. Could the messages be from an old girlfriend he'd hurt? His ex-wife? Surely not. He didn't make a habit of treating women badly – to be honest, he didn't have many opportunities to do so. Since the breakdown of his marriage to Æsa, the mother of his children, he had buried himself in work and made no attempt to go out looking for women. He had little taste for trawling the city's bars, and still less for the drunken slappers, with their slack mouths and glassy eyes, who were all he seemed to attract. On the rare occasions he met a woman he liked the look of, his interest was never reciprocated. The din in those places drowned out all conversation, so there was little point in trying to persuade them that what he lacked in sex appeal, he made up for in success. He still cherished the dream of meeting the right woman one day, but that hope had faded during the year and more that had passed since Æsa walked out on him.

The thought of Æsa automatically stirred up bitter memories of their break-up. He felt hard done by – not financially, because he'd been cunning enough to keep the flat in his name and take responsibility for the mortgage payments, which had left her empty-handed. But the divorce had deprived him of his children. It shouldn't have come as a surprise to him given the preferential treatment habitually shown to mothers in custody cases. A woman practically had to turn up with a syringe dangling from her arm, a hash pipe in her mouth, a bottle of vodka in her hand, an aluminium cap on her head to ward off aliens, before she would be deemed less suitable to be granted custody than a man. Despite being an exemplary father and model citizen, he hadn't had a snowball's chance in hell of winning the custody battle over their two children. Æsa, who had been considered the more suitable guardian, was a nonentity who worked for the council. She had barely scraped through her school-leaving exams, while he had graduated fourth in his year. And although he'd had to forgo the postgraduate degree he had planned, he would have passed that with flying colours too.

He was gifted; she was average. He was comfortably off; she would struggle financially as a single mother. Yet she had been given custody. Unbelievable. Of course, it hadn't helped that she had brought up what she described as his excessive drinking, and because he was a man his lifestyle had been subjected to extra scrutiny. Never mind that her claim was absolute rubbish. The magistrate had swallowed it hook, line and sinker, despite Thorvaldur's objections and a character reference from no less a person than the State Prosecutor herself.

His e-mail bleeped. He had received another message from *reckoning*. What the hell was going on? He had half a mind to take the matter to the authorities. Or at least report it in-house. Surely the guys in IT would be able to find out who was behind it? Enough was enough. Thorvaldur rubbed his chin thoughtfully. But what if they were from Æsa? Did he really want to remind his superiors of how messy their divorce had been? Naturally, his boss was a woman. They mostly got along fine; he knew how to mask his opinion that she had neither the expertise nor the experience that would have been required of a man in her position. But a shadow had fallen over their working relationship as a result of the custody battle and he was aware that she had taken a dim view of him. Women tended to stick together at times like that. It was a law of nature and therefore futile to try to change it.

Could the messages be from her? From his boss? Thorvaldur shook his head over his own absurdity. Of course not.

Not from his boss, or Æsa, or any old girlfriends or criminals he could think of. So who then?

No one could have any reason to wish him harm. So why didn't he hurry up and have the origin of the messages investigated? Was it the gnawing suspicion that this was not in fact a mistake? Was it the fear that an investigation might expose something he would rather keep hidden? Of course that was it. The sender made no bones about the fact that he had something on him. But Thorvaldur couldn't imagine what it could be. Something he could easily shrug off, perhaps. It would take a lot to threaten a prosecutor with a long and, though he said it himself, bloody successful career behind him.

It was nobody's business if that success was in part down to his habit of taking on the least challenging cases. No one ever appeared to notice. Unless his colleagues were whispering about it behind his back.

Was he becoming paranoid now on top of everything else?

Thorvaldur took a deep breath. He ran his eyes down the sleeves of his expensive jacket, resting them for a moment on the crisp, white cuffs of his shirt peeping out at his wrists, then flexed his neatly manicured fingers. This pleasing sight had a calming effect on him. An effect that was only enhanced when he tweaked his shirtsleeves a little to reveal the gleam of the expensive cufflinks he had recently treated himself to, when no one else had given him a suitable birthday present. His children's crudely drawn cards didn't count. Such naive creations held no charm for him.

The cufflinks glittered and Thorvaldur felt his spirits rising. He had no need to look down at his gleaming leather shoes and silk socks to recover his sangfroid and remind himself of who he was. A winner. A man who knew what it took. A man who inspired fear and respect, perhaps not from everyone but from most.

These e-mails were absolutely pathetic. He'd bet his life that the person responsible for the threats wrote them sitting at a crappy computer, wearing a grubby T-shirt and creased tracksuit bottoms that had never been near a gym. Loser. One thing was for sure, he was twice the man the sender was. Nothing got to him. So there was nothing to stop him clicking on the attachment and looking at the picture, then opening the latest message. He was strong. A winner. Thorvaldur smirked as he moved the cursor to the file *betrayal.jpeg* and clicked on it.

The photo almost filled the screen. He frowned. What nonsense was this? Two children, a girl and a slightly older boy, stared back at him, their expressions anything but happy. He didn't recognise either child, but then he wasn't particularly keen on other people's kids, and neither of them was in any way memorable. They looked pale and rather scruffy; there was no colour in their cheeks or sparkle in their dull eyes. Where his own children's untroubled glances revealed their irrepressible joy at being alive, these held a quite different, more adult emotion. He could have sworn it was accusation.

Thorvaldur stared at the photo, powerless to close it and resume his work. The longer he studied those nondescript faces, the stronger the feeling grew that there was something familiar about them. Where did he know these unfortunate creatures from? How were they connected to him? Think, damn it, think. It was bound to come back to him.

He shifted his attention to the rest of the picture. The surroundings told him nothing: the children were outdoors, the corner of a building and a street just visible behind them. They could have been anywhere in Iceland. Nor could he date the photo; he had nothing but the clothes to go by and they appeared to have been chosen with no purpose beyond shielding the children's nakedness: some things were too large, others too small, all of them threadbare.

All of a sudden it fell into place. Shit, shit, shit.

The terror that had seized him gave way momentarily to relief. Thank God he hadn't reported the messages. Thank God.

With trembling fingers he opened the latest e-mail. After reading it, he snatched up the telephone and selected Æsa's number.

What beautiful children you've got. Make sure you take good care of them. There are people out there who might betray them, as you know only too well.

Chapter 4

'It's the same handwriting. Without a shadow of a doubt. The writer doesn't seem to have made any attempt to disguise it.' The handwriting expert raised his eyes from the blown-up letters on his screen. 'There's no sign of hesitation or unusual care either, so we can conclude that he wasn't trying to copy the writing of the other boy. This Thröstur.'

'Great.' Huldar straightened up. He had been leaning eagerly over the man's desk. In the past he would never have wasted time on something like this in person, merely sent the man the letters and asked for his opinion over the phone. But even though the station had been turned upside down by the discovery of the severed hands, he was lucky to have the time capsule to keep him busy. Erla still hadn't assigned him any role in the new inquiry and he was beginning to wonder if she ever would. From what he had overheard, the case had made little progress. The hands had been sent to the Identification Committee, but there was no news as yet. And when it came to police investigations, no news did not mean good news.

'Is this really worth wasting police time on?' the handwriting expert had asked sceptically, after Huldar had explained where the letters came from. 'A fourteen-year-old boy's not likely to stick to a ten-year plan, surely?'

'No, fortunately not, but we're still obliged to look into the matter. There are always exceptions.'

The man grunted, though whether in agreement or derision was unclear. Not that Huldar cared either way.

'Thanks. Then I can go ahead and talk to the boy.'

'Young man, you mean. He must be in his twenties by now.'

Huldar didn't bother to respond. He declined the proffered photo-copies and left. There was no wind for once; the storm that had been raging earlier had blown itself out. He lit a cigarette, having long abandoned any attempts to give up, though he wasn't advertising the fact. His five sisters mustn't find out – they had a tendency to go overboard with the anti-smoking lectures, and right now he was in no mood to be harangued.

His mobile rang as he was putting away his lighter and he answered without checking the caller ID. There weren't many people likely to call him. It turned out to be the school secretary, who informed him with due solemnity that she had cleared a space in the headmaster's diary and that he could see Huldar later that day. At ten minutes past nine. A little surprised by this very precise time, Huldar thanked her and said he'd be there, possibly with a child psychologist in tow, just to be on the safe side.

Freyja had said the matter was worth looking into, and there was nothing wrong with living in hope.

He decided to head back to the office, though he knew there would be nothing to do there but surf the net. After the meeting at the school, he would hopefully know the pupil's patronymic and therefore be able to go round and see him. And once that was done and he'd established that everything was fine, the case would presumably be closed. And his in-tray empty again. He took a final drag on the cigarette, buried his hands in the pockets of his parka and set off.

The police station was a hive of industry but Huldar's desk might as well have been on a different planet. No one came to see him and those who did pass by never gave him so much as a glance. The only person to speak to him was Gudlaugur, who sounded as if he was going out of his mind with stress. The task he'd been assigned was clearly beyond him. Now and then Huldar caught sight of his sweat-beaded forehead above his monitor. The situation was a joke: here he sat, one of the most experienced detectives on the team, twiddling his thumbs, while the rookie cop was buckling under the pressure.

The breaking point came when Huldar found himself watching cat videos on YouTube. He marched over, knocked on Erla's door and opened it without waiting for a response, aware that she could see him through the glass wall and was unlikely to invite him in.

'I need a word. I promise to be quick.' Out of the corner of his eye he noticed the picture of the Reynisdrangar sea stacks that he had bought to liven up the office when it was his. It had been taken down and propped against the wall. To be fair, it had spent most of its time on the floor during his incumbency; he hadn't been able to bring himself to hang it for fear of tempting fate. Sure enough, shortly after the picture had taken its place on the wall, he had lost his job. If the towering black pillars of rock had the power to jinx anyone who dared use them for decoration, Huldar hoped that Erla would leave them where they were.

Erla tried to act nonchalantly but a flicker in her eyes suggested she was expecting a scene. Huldar was quick to dispel her fears. 'I need something to do. I can't sit there playing Patience while other members of the team are drowning in work.'

'Drowning? Who's drowning?' Erla's look of astonishment was designed to give the impression that things were unusually quiet. But her desk, buried under a ton of files, belied her words.

'Gudlaugur, for example.'

'Gulli?'

'Gudlaugur. The kid who sits opposite me. He doesn't look like he can cope and I'm itching to lend him a hand, apart from anything else.' Huldar pulled up a chair since Erla obviously wasn't going to offer him one. 'And I want to know how the investigation's going. That's hardly unnatural, is it?'

'No, of course not. I'm just a bit tied up at the moment. I wasn't deliberately sidelining you. Only I thought you had enough on your plate with that . . . what was it again?'

'The time capsule.' Huldar sat tight, ignoring her claim to be busy. 'I'm expecting to close the case tomorrow and after that I'll have nothing to do.'

'Oh dear.' Erla didn't look or sound particularly sorry. How times had changed – she used to be embarrassingly eager to work with him and her crush had been obvious to all. He didn't miss those days, but wished she would acknowledge that he was still one of the team. He couldn't understand why she had turned against him unless she was afraid that he was bitter and wanted to avoid an unpleasant scene. But he would never instigate one. She could keep her promotion; all he wanted was his old job back.

He smiled but it didn't reach his eyes. 'OK, well, I'll just talk to the Assistant Commissioner. If you have no use for me, I'm sure he'll find something for me to do. He'll probably take it as a sign that your team's underemployed and rustle up some forms for you to fill in. I know there are plenty he'd be only too grateful to offload.' Huldar's gaze flickered over Erla's desk, taking in several tedious documents that had a familiar look about them. He prepared to stand up. This wasn't the result he had been hoping for but he had no intention of letting himself be made a fool of at work. He was perfectly capable of doing that all by himself.

'Sit down.' Erla's face wore a new expression. She was regarding him, not like a boss or someone who was nursing a grudge against

44

him, but like an old colleague. It was a while since Huldar had last seen her look like this. 'You can help the boy. Gulli, I mean.'

'Gudlaugur.'

'Yeah, whatever.' She stared at him, her blue eyes bloodshot and weary. 'Things aren't exactly going well. It's been three days, and we still have nothing on those hands.'

'Has nobody rung to report them missing?' Huldar bit back the urge to add a flippant comment about the person in question having trouble dialling the number. It was taking him a while to get used to being on his best behaviour around Erla.

Erla glanced at her computer as if expecting an e-mail that would contain all the answers the inquiry so badly needed. 'No. No reports. Not yet. Which doesn't bode well.'

'No.' Huldar wondered if the owner of the hands would rather die than live without them. He was grateful not to be confronted with a choice like that himself. 'Are we looking for a corpse then? A corpse without any hands?'

'We're not exactly looking. I mean, where are we supposed to start? Any ideas gratefully received.'

'So you've still no idea whose hands they are?'

Erla shook her head. 'The Identification Committee's compared the fingerprints to the database but found no match.' She stole another glance at her monitor but the result was just as disappointing as before. 'Anyway, that would have been too easy.' She surveyed the documents on her desk, her gaze pausing on the most exasperating forms, then grabbed a sheaf of papers stapled together in one corner. Huldar recognised the layout of the boxes and the official header on the top page. 'I've just been sent the pathologist's report. It's not pretty.'

'No. They rarely are.' Huldar didn't even try to hide his curiosity. 'What does it say?'

Erla picked up a page of notes that had been lying beside the report. Huldar recognised her writing. So she was still in the habit of jotting down notes on everything she saw, heard or read. He had long envied her this facility but had never been able to get into the habit himself. Erla recited the conclusions almost without drawing breath. 'The hands belong to a male. Past middle age. Never performed any manual labour, unless it was a long time ago. There's a mark left by a ring on the fourth finger of his left hand, presumably a wedding ring. The ring itself is missing, removed either by the person who disposed of the hands or by the owner. There's the trace of a slightly thicker band on the fourth finger of the right hand, also missing. The mark indicates the type of ring people receive on graduation from some foreign universities or a Freemason's ring, for example. There's no way of establishing what kind it was. The traces of both are so faint that the pathologist thinks it possible the man may not have worn either recently. Not regularly, anyway.' Erla looked up. 'The man was alive when his hands were cut off. Or so the pathologist believes. Though he's added all kinds of disclaimers.'

Huldar nodded, his face impassive. He had heard his colleagues speculating on this point, though without any solid evidence. The rumour that the victim had been alive had probably been triggered by the grisly nature of the discovery. 'Do they know what was used? Was it a knife or a saw?'

'A chainsaw.'

'Shit.'

'Yeah. Shit.'

'Presumably there's no way of telling whether their owner died as a result?'

Erla shook her head. 'No. But the pathologist thinks it's likely. The chances that he bled to death as a result of this . . . procedure . . . are pretty high. He says here that, alternatively, the man's body

46

could have gone into shock, resulting in multiple organ failure. Which would also have led to death, although he would have lived longer than if he'd died from the blood loss.'

'But it's not certain? The man could still be alive?'

Erla shrugged. 'Yes, theoretically. But in that case where is he? I'm betting he didn't suffer this in silence.'

'No. Unless he's being kept unconscious or drugged.'

'That's a possibility, of course.' Erla heaved a sigh and ran her fingers through her hair, leaving it standing on end, which made her look slightly mad. As she was, thought Huldar. 'But the blood test came back normal.'

'Where would someone get hold of a chainsaw?'

'At a DIY store. Or a tool-hire company. I'm going to have checks run on all recent purchases and rentals, and I'm hoping that'll give us a lead. Chainsaws are mainly used to cut down trees and branches, so there's not much call for them in winter. Anyway, once we've collected their names it shouldn't be too long a list.'

'What about the bloke who owns the hot tub? Has his background been thoroughly checked? There must be some reason why his house was chosen. I mean, the hot tub isn't visible from the street or the neighbouring gardens, so the culprit can't have been driving past and decided to dispose of the hands on a whim. Surely he must have some connection to the incident?'

'Benedikt Toft? We're looking into him. So far there's nothing to suggest anything suspicious, and the statement taken from him at the time is credible. He seemed genuinely shocked. He's a retired widower and doesn't have a police record, which is hardly surprising as he used to be a prosecutor.'

'Could it be related to one of his old cases, then? Revenge for a jail sentence, something like that?'

'Maybe. We've yet to get a proper statement from him. He keeps putting it off and now he's stopped answering the phone. If we can't get hold of him today, I'll have him brought in. But I doubt anything'll come of it. It's probably just one of those weird coincidences; maybe the perpetrator was escaping through the gardens and needed to get rid of them quickly. Something like that.' When Erla saw that Huldar wasn't buying it, the blood rushed to her cheeks. Perhaps she was remembering the tip-off; someone had wanted them to find the hands, so the location was unlikely to have been chosen at random. 'Anyway, Toft appears to be a perfectly ordinary citizen. And seriously pissed off as well.'

'I can understand that. I hope I never find anything like that in my hot tub when I'm retired.'

'Oh, he took that in his stride. No, he's after compensation for the lid, which got broken. Maybe I can trick him into coming down to the station by pretending I want to discuss damages.'

Huldar was speechless. People's behaviour rarely took him by surprise anymore, but this was an odd reaction, to say the least. 'I'd take a good look at him, if I were you. Any normal person would take a week to recover from the shock before they even started thinking about compensation.'

Erla's face hardened again. 'I'm well aware of that. Though I expect his years in court will have made him thicker-skinned than most.' Folding her arms across her chest, she leant back in her chair. 'I can handle this, Huldar.'

Instead of sighing he smiled at her. 'I didn't mean to imply you couldn't. But let me help, Erla. I have zero interest in this office and all the crap that goes with it.' They glanced simultaneously at the forms covering her desk. 'Believe me.'

Erla's phone rang and she turned away without commenting on Huldar's offer. It was impossible to tell if she had recognised his sincerity.

But when she waved him out without so much as looking at him, he guessed that his words had fallen on deaf ears.

Huldar returned to his desk and told Gudlaugur that he'd been ordered to help him. The young man leapt up, staring at Huldar with flushed cheeks. Despite the hint of suspicion in his eyes, there was no disguising his relief. He explained in a rush what he was working on and as he listed one tedious chore after another, Huldar had to remind himself that it was either this or videos of stressed cats.

Once he had started sifting through old cases in a futile search for links to hands or amputations, he couldn't help smiling at the faith Gudlaugur apparently had in him. The young man kept peering round his monitor as if expecting Huldar to come up with the solution any minute. Unfortunately, his wish was unlikely to be granted. Huldar had a hunch that this was going to be one of the few difficult cases that came their way. In Iceland, most violent incidents or murders were solved either the same day or within forty-eight hours. He had no doubt that they would crack this one in the end – but the end was a long way off.

Chapter 5

They were met in the school foyer by a sign that announced in large letters: *Education for all and for all abilities.* Huldar wasn't after that; he wanted the office. Freyja spotted another sign, in much smaller letters, which directed visitors there – and to the toilets. Following the arrow, they entered a long corridor leading to the inner sanctum most feared by the kids, the office of the supreme power, the headteacher. Perhaps it had been placed right at the end of the corridor to give the pupils time to build up a suitable level of fear and awe.

Huldar was only too familiar with that feeling from his own school days. Snatches of memory came back thick and fast: a pencil case full of dried-up felt-tip pens, pencil stubs, a sharpener and grubby erasers; a school bag stuffed with homework assignments that never got done; a lunchbox containing leftover pieces of apple and sandwich crumbs; dog-eared textbooks that got bumped around in his bag but were never actually opened.

Apart from the squeaking of the sticky vinyl floor under their feet, the only sound they could hear was the echo of teachers' voices from the classrooms. The walls were covered in amateurish drawings of cells and amoebas, on what looked like cheap recycled paper. Come to think of it, Huldar had once drawn something like that in biology. But unlike these kids he hadn't bothered to colour it in.

The smell in the corridor was a cocktail of wet anoraks, trainers, craft glue and cleaning products. The same smell as in Huldar's school out east. But now there was a new batch of children on the conveyor belt and it was their turn to stare out of the window while the teacher droned on about mosses, spores, adverbs and other such mysteries.

Huldar wondered if the same thoughts were running through Freyja's head. Unlike him she had probably been a model pupil, as conscientious as the girls in his class or his five sisters, and never had to take home a note that caused his parents to turn scarlet with rage and bawl him out for failing to listen and being disruptive in class.

The headteacher received them in his office. He was more or less what Huldar had expected: fiftyish, with spindly legs and a tastelessly wide tie that was intended but failed to distract attention from a large paunch. The man glanced at the clock on the wall and gave a little approving nod when he saw that it was ten past nine on the dot. After offering them a cup of what turned out to be disgustingly watery coffee, he ushered them inside.

Huldar and Freyja sat down in chairs that bore the indentations of countless people who had sat there before them, evidence of all the parents forced over the years to listen to descriptions of their unsatisfactory offspring's latest antics, and dire warnings about how they would have to pull their socks up. It was like sitting in a mould.

The headteacher placed his hands on the desk. His fingers were long and thin like his legs. 'I do hope the police don't think I'm wasting their time. Better safe than sorry was the way I looked at it.'

Huldar answered for both of them. 'It's always best to report anything suspicious. You did the right thing in the circumstances, regardless of whether there's any real cause for concern.'

The headteacher glowed with satisfaction. From the trace of milk froth on his upper lip, it seemed that while visitors were fobbed off with dishwater, the staff enjoyed cappuccinos. 'Anyway, how can I help you? I'm a bit pushed for time, so we'd probably better cut to the chase.'

Huldar didn't wait to be asked twice; it was an odd feeling to be sitting in a headteacher's office after all these years. 'I've received confirmation from a handwriting expert that the threatening letter, if you can call it that, was written by the same person as the letter signed by a boy called Thröstur in 9–B. So I was wondering if you could tell us this Thröstur's patronymic, and, if you happen to remember him, give us your opinion of the boy. As I told you on the phone, Freyja here is a child psychologist from the Children's House, who's helping me with the inquiry. She's bound by confidentiality, just as I am.' Huldar made to pat the arm of Freyja's chair at this point but her hand got in the way. She jerked it back as though she'd been burnt. The headteacher looked rather disconcerted, though he tried not to show it.

'I see.' The headteacher drew himself up a little in his chair, as if Huldar's mention of confidentiality had lifted the conversation on to a higher plane. 'I'll check the class lists for that year; I dug them out earlier.' The man turned to his screen and read something on it while carefully moving the mouse. 'Thröstur, you say. Thröstur, Thröstur. Here he is. Thröstur Agnesarson. Thröstur Agnesarson. Aha. Him. Of course.'

'Of course?'

'It's just that I remember the boy so well I can't understand why I didn't twig immediately. In hindsight, it had to be him. I'd just been appointed back then and kept getting complaints about him, though he was new at the school too. New pupils don't usually cause much trouble. Not to begin with, anyway. He was the exception and had the dubious honour of being the first difficult pupil I had to deal with in my capacity as head. There have been any number since then, of course. I'm not sure I'd have remembered the later ones nearly as well.'

'Did he have behavioural issues?' asked Freyja.

'No, I wouldn't put it like that. This was different. Not the usual ADHD or ADD. He wasn't diagnosed as dyslexic either, or autistic. Didn't have Oppositional Defiant Disorder. Mind you, many of these diagnoses were fairly new at the time, so it's possible the findings would be different today. People have more experience in identifying all kinds of syndromes and disorders.'

'Then why was he hauled in to see you so often?' Huldar wished the man would just get to the point. He had no interest in the history of ADHD, and even if Freyja had she was presumably better informed than the headteacher. Huldar's aversion stemmed partly from the realisation that he may well have been struggling with some such disorder himself in his youth but had never received any help. Who knows, if he'd been born later, maybe he could have been a doctor today? But perhaps that was aiming a bit high; improved concentration might have enabled him to sustain a relationship, at least.

'You may well ask.' The man's gaze swung from Freyja to Huldar and back again. 'He was perfectly capable of concentrating and didn't have any particular difficulties with his studies – when he bothered to apply himself. His problems weren't connected to his school work or clashes with other pupils or teachers. It was some psychological issue that we couldn't deal with. My staff and I soon ran out of ideas, so we brought in a professional. A child psychologist like you.' He subjected Freyja to an appreciative gaze. Huldar felt it had lingered quite long enough – no sign of ADHD in the headteacher's case.

'What came of it?' he prompted.

'I never got to hear. He saw the psychologist outside school. I received one report, if I remember right, which said the boy should soon start feeling better. It also included advice on how to handle him if we experienced any further problems. But the boy left before the end of the academic year, so he became the problem of some other school, some other head.'

'How did it manifest itself?' Freyja was leaning to the right, putting as much distance between herself and Huldar as possible.

'The boy was . . . well, how shall I put it? Sullen, perhaps? He was never happy; I don't ever remember seeing him smile. He was obsessed with death and evil. Any pictures he drew were of dead people and his essays were full of executions and killings. I had so many teachers trooping in here to complain about him it was like having a revolving door in my office. I can check later today if we still have any of his drawings. Or his writing. You can judge for yourselves. The drawings were particularly unfortunate. In fact, I very much doubt anyone here will have kept them.'

Clearly, Thröstur's pictures were unlikely to have graced the walls in the corridors. Huldar wondered if it was possible to draw a dead cell or amoeba. 'Did he get into fights? Did he injure any of the other pupils or his friends?'

'Friends? He didn't have any friends. Oddly enough, though, he wasn't bullied. At first I thought it was because the other kids were too kind-hearted, that they felt sorry for the lad and understood that he had psychiatric problems. But it quickly became clear that it wasn't that. They were just frightened of him. Too frightened to bully him. That tells you something. But he never hurt anyone. Not here or anywhere else, as far as I know.'

'You say the psychologist was optimistic that his condition would improve?' Freyja sat up so she could see the headteacher above his screen.

'Well, I don't know if the verdict was that positive. What they sent me wasn't a final report so much as progress notes for our information. Actually, I remember it said the boy's behaviour was related to some kind of family drama. But there were no details. His family situation was quite ordinary, as far as I can recall; his mother was a single parent and he had a younger sister who was at a different school, for some reason. Understandably, the reference roused my curiosity and I felt that it would be better if I knew more. I called the boy in to see me and questioned him about what was going on at home, but he completely clammed up. Shortly afterwards I was notified by his mother that he would be studying at home for the rest of the year, before changing schools in the autumn. As it was close to the end of term anyway, I turned a blind eye to the matter of his attendance. The school certainly functioned more smoothly without him for those last few weeks.'

Neither Huldar nor Freyja spoke; they were doing their best to hide their disgust. Merely to satisfy his own curiosity the man had dragged the boy in to see him and tried to pry out of him whatever had caused his distress. Such treatment could hardly have helped and it was easy to conclude that the decision to change schools had been prompted by the intrusion. Huldar was the first to break the silence. 'Did he move to a nearby school, then? And do you know how he got on there?'

'Oh, no. His family moved away and I completely lost track of him. They were obviously incapable of settling anywhere. From what I gathered, they'd only just moved to this area at the beginning of the school year.'

So perhaps the change hadn't been motivated by his decision to give the boy the third degree. Dissatisfaction with their local school was only one of many reasons people had for moving. The boy's mother could have got a job that required them to live in another part of town, or they could have lost their home. As a single mother she was probably renting and tenants didn't enjoy much security in Iceland.

'Would it be possible to see the report?' Freyja sounded confident, as if she had every right to ask.

'No, I'm afraid not. It was almost certainly marked as confidential, so I imagine I'd need the authorisation of the psychologist who wrote it. And of course I'd need to track down the report itself. I'm not a hundred per cent sure we've still got it on file.'

'Could I have the name of the psychologist, then?'

'Yes, of course. I expect that would be simplest. Save me the trouble of chasing up the report, which would be a relief. I'm completely snowed under, as you can tell.'

Huldar couldn't see any sign of this. The man's desk was bare and his phone hadn't rung once while they'd been in there.

The headteacher turned to his computer. 'Luckily, I take the precaution of keeping every single work e-mail I've ever received. I archive them by year so they're easier to search.' He hummed under his breath as he moved the mouse to and fro and tapped at the keyboard. 'What was her name again? Gudlaug? Gudný?' He appeared to be talking to himself but suddenly looked at his visitors. 'If you can just give me a minute or two, I'll find the name. Possibly the report, too, though naturally I can't hand that over. Anyway, you should definitely talk to her because I have a feeling she'd dealt with Thröstur before, when he was younger. There was a delay after social services received our request because this particular psychologist insisted that his case should be referred to her. So she's bound to know far more about him than I do.' He turned back to the screen. 'Now, where is it . . . ?'

'Just take your time. We're not in any rush.' This was only too true in Huldar's case and he suspected it was the same for Freyja. When he had finally got hold of her yesterday afternoon, she had leapt at the chance to accompany him to the school. And since she made no bones about how much she disliked his company, it was obviously the errand that appealed, not him. He tried to catch her eye but she kept looking stubbornly ahead. So he went on staring at her, determined to prove to himself that he didn't have ADHD. It wasn't hard: Freyja's lovely profile was easy on the eye and he derived a degree of pleasure from watching her squirm under his gaze.

'Aha! Here it is.' The headteacher looked up. 'Did you time me? How long did it take?'

Huldar removed his eyes from Freyja. 'Er . . . no. But you were very quick.' There was no denying that the man was a little eccentric; not on the scale of his former pupil, Thröstur Agnesarson, but eccentric nonetheless. Perhaps it was the effect of working with children for so many years, of having to teach them, even do their parents' job for them, with limited means for enforcing discipline. It would drive Huldar round the bend if he had to maintain public order without the full weight of the law on his side.

'Sólveig Gunnarsdóttir – that was the woman's name.'

Freyja showed no sign of making a note of this. Perhaps she had an excellent memory but Huldar knew the name would have slipped his mind by the time they left the building. 'Like me to write it down?' he asked her.

'No need. I work with her. She's a part-time psychologist at the Children's House.' She still wouldn't look at him.

The headteacher clapped his hands together. 'That's lucky. Are we done then? Was there anything else?'

'Would you like the original back? You mentioned that the letters were going on display and I don't need it. I made a copy.' Huldar placed Thröstur's unsigned letter on the desk and pushed it over. The headteacher recoiled as if it were radioactive.

'Goodness, no. No, thank you. That's not going in our exhibition. Are you mad? Just take it. Throw it away or whatever you do with evidence that turns out not to matter. I expect we'll leave out the letter he signed as well.'

Huldar shrugged and took the letter back. 'When's the exhibition?'

'It opens next week. We're putting the letters up now, including the photocopies from America. It'll be great fun. At least for the young people who wrote them ten years ago. They're all invited to the opening.'

'Thröstur too?' Freyja's voice was like ice. 'Won't he be surprised not to see his letter? The one he signed?'

'He didn't see out the term. I'm inviting those who were still there at the end of the school year.' The man's long fingers formed a steeple. The school motto *Education for all and for all abilities* obviously didn't apply in this case.

Freyja's voice had lost none of its ice. 'One more thing . . . what information did you receive from his previous school when he started here? Did you contact them when it became apparent that the boy had problems?'

The headteacher's long fingers had twined themselves into a knot. 'I didn't, no. If I'm busy now, you should have seen what my first year was like. I had to learn the ropes as I went along. By the time it became apparent that Thröstur was . . . that something was wrong . . . he'd been with us almost three months; by then he was our pupil, our problem. I saw no reason to ask how his old school had handled him; after all, it clearly hadn't worked.'

'So he seemed normal at first? For nearly three months?'

'No. It just took us that long to work out that there was something seriously wrong rather than a temporary blip. He was a new boy, after all, and exceptionally withdrawn.' The man's fingers suddenly stopped their fidgeting. He untwined them and placed both hands, palm down, on the desk in front of him, as if to examine his nails. 'And now I'm afraid I'll have to wrap this meeting up. I'm already late for something else.'

'What about his parents? What sort of people were they and what did they have to say about all this?' Freyja was not about to let the man off so easily. 'You must have met his mother at least.'

'Of course. I never saw his father, mind you. His mother was rather a mousy woman, if I remember right. She had difficulty finding the time to come in during working hours and we don't have the funding to stay open in the evenings. That's not how it works. But she did come in once. She seemed to have given up, rather. Apart from that our only communication was via e-mail.' He didn't offer to read them the messages or print out copies. 'Anyway, now I really do have to dash.' He stood up, pursing his lips as if to show that no more answers would be forthcoming.

Freyja and Huldar thanked him and got up to leave, their cups of undrinkable coffee sitting virtually untouched on the desk. When Huldar offered to take the cups, the headteacher waved him away, then resumed his seat, showing no sign of dashing off anywhere.

The children were being let out for break when Huldar and Freyja left. The noise was deafening and there was no point trying to talk while they were crossing the playground.

'What do you think?' asked Huldar once they reached the car park. As he surveyed the horde of children, his eyes lingered on a few pupils alone on the periphery, and he guessed that the oddball Thröstur would once have been like them.

'I don't know. I'm less confident now than I was when I read the letters. If the head remembered correctly and Thröstur had been to see Sólveig on an earlier occasion, before his depressive episode at this school, it's a bit worrying. Children don't go for regular sessions with a therapist unless there's a genuine problem. There must have been something wrong with the boy. Or with his immediate environment.'

'Enough to make it plausible that he might act out his threats? Or do something equally serious?'

Freyja wrinkled her brow as if she were having second thoughts. 'Probably not. But I'd like to talk to him. After I've spoken to Sólveig. But I won't be able to tell you what we discuss, only what comes out of it. Very broadly.'

He'd forgotten what a beautiful smile she had.

'If you're lucky,' she continued, 'though of course I may not be able to share any of what she tells me.'

'OK. I'll have to be satisfied with that.' Huldar watched her burrowing in her pocket for her car keys. It occurred to him that, unlike most women, she didn't carry a handbag. Whenever his sisters got together their bags adorned every chair-back and table. The most common request at such gatherings was: 'Pass me my bag, would you?', invariably directed at Huldar. He was the youngest in the family and they would never stop regarding him as their errand boy. Perhaps what attracted him most about Freyja was how different she was from his sisters. He'd rather spend the rest of his life as a hermit than get hitched to a woman like one of them. 'I'm going to try and track Thröstur down. I've got enough information now to find his ID number and the rest should be simple. Would you like to come along and meet him with me?'

He noticed that Freyja unlocked her car with a key rather than by remote control. It was such an old wreck that it probably predated the technology.

'Sure,' she said. 'I'd like to be there for that. In the meantime, you'd better check if he's got a criminal record. It could make for interesting reading.' Without explaining what she meant, she got behind the wheel and slammed the door.

Huldar watched her drive away, then returned to his own car, musing on her comment and her sober expression as she had said it.

Chapter 6

Back at the Children's House after the school visit, Freyja stared out at the weather. Another day, another storm. She had begun the day by letting Molly out into the scruffy back garden of the block of flats where she lived. The flat belonged to her brother Baldur and Freyja had only intended to stay there temporarily, but almost a year had passed and she was still having no success in finding a place of her own. At this rate she wouldn't be moving out before Baldur's release, which had been put back twelve months. This had its pros and cons: on the plus side, it meant she didn't have to struggle with a difficult rental market; on the minus, it meant continuing to live among people on the margins of society. Her fellow tenants had no interest in taking care of the garden or cleaning out the dustbin store, or the other communal areas. They had more urgent priorities, like sourcing their next high – or anything, really, apart from getting out a vacuum cleaner, duster or broom.

Recently she had noticed a yellowing sheet of paper pinned to the wall in the hall, which turned out to be a cleaning rota for an unspecified – no doubt long-ago – year. As the squalor was really getting to Freyja, she decided to tackle the cleaning on the days assigned to Baldur's flat, in the hope of shaming the other occupants into following her example. It might help to win them over, too, since few of them ever said hello, and she got the impression that most would be pleased to see the back of her. But her plan misfired. While she toiled away at the cleaning, her neighbours peered out, one after the other, to see what on earth was going on. Their faces registered astonishment, even indignation or pity, when they saw the hoover. She certainly didn't earn any brownie points for her efforts and few seemed to appreciate the clean corridor or unblocked rubbish chute. In spite of this, she was determined to stick to the ancient rota and carry on cleaning when it was her turn.

If she set about tidying up the garden in the spring, her fellow residents would probably lose any last remnants of respect for her. But at least she and Molly could be sure of having the patch of grass to themselves. The other occupants tended to stay indoors during daylight hours. She could put out a table and chairs and bask in the sunshine with a cup of coffee while Molly was nosing around for the perfect place to do her business. With her back to the building, Freyja would even be able to kid herself that she lived in different, more salubrious surroundings.

But the summer was a long way off, assuming they were ever going to have one, and no one would dream of trying to sit outside at this time of year. Freyja had been ready to jump for joy when Molly finally finished and she could get off to work. At least it was warm at the Children's House and the coffee was good. The windows in Baldur's place let in the draughts and the coffee-maker seemed incapable of producing a decent brew anymore. If the weather hadn't been so horrendous she would have taken herself down to the homeware store to buy herself a new one. Where on earth was she to find the energy to turn her life around if she was prepared to let a bit of wind and snow come between her and a good cup of coffee?

The door of the Children's House opened and there was a sound of voices, almost immediately cut off again. Freyja decided that now was her chance to make another attempt to speak to Sólveig. When she got back earlier, Sólveig had already been seeing a child, whereas Freyja had nothing to occupy her apart from minor tasks such as reading over the evaluation and summary tables for the centre's annual report. It was infuriating that being asked by Huldar to assist the police should feel like winning the lottery. He was the last man in the world she wanted to associate with, but anything was better than sitting here, staring into space. She needed to be busy, to have a purpose in life. Cleaning the communal areas of her block every other month just wasn't enough.

She managed to catch Sólveig as the other woman was sitting down at her desk again. The fact that a part-time employee had a larger, better-equipped office than Freyja spoke volumes, but, trying not to let it rankle, she reminded herself why she was there.

'I couldn't have a quick word, could I? It's about a boy who was referred to you ten years ago and possibly a few years before that as well.'

'Ten years?' Sólveig frowned, four deep grooves forming in her forehead. As usual, her greying hair was drawn back in a tight bun, but there was nothing else in her appearance to suggest severity. Her pale yellow shirt was buttoned up wrong and her long brown cardigan hung unevenly from her broad shoulders. 'God, I can't remember that far back.' She swivelled her hand to motion Freyja in. Bracelets jangled at her wrist. 'But take a seat anyway. I have to admit I'm intrigued.'

Freyja's shirt was buttoned up correctly and her clothes hung straight. Next to Sólveig she felt prim, the way she felt about the communal cleaning; like a square who took life too seriously and missed out on all the fun. Her inner psychologist couldn't help wondering if this was the truth. Perhaps it was time to let her hair down a bit more, even though her attempts to do just that had ended disastrously in the past. It was time to cut loose, if only to have a fling. The weekend was coming up and she resolved to drag her girlfriends out clubbing with her. Then the following day she'd take her hangover into town and invest in a new coffee-maker. The first step in her mission to get her life back on track. With a decent cup of coffee, she could curl up on the sofa and look up the courses on offer at the university next autumn.

'You may not be aware but I've been asked to assist the police with rather an odd case connected to the boy in question.' As Freyja told Sólveig the whole sorry tale, she saw the furrows deepening in the other woman's brow. Sólveig clearly hadn't got wind of the job, which suggested that the director had kept quiet about it. Freyja was surprised by this, as usually the projects the staff were working on were discussed fairly openly within the four walls of the Children's House.

Perhaps her cases were no longer important enough to merit discussion. The renewed self-confidence created by her plans for the weekend faded a little. Freyja forced herself to focus. 'According to his headteacher, Þröstur was sent to you for primary diagnosis, and he was also under the impression that you'd dealt with the boy some years previously. And possibly treated him too, though he had no information about that.'

'Oh, it's all such a long time ago.' Sólveig shook her head. She appeared to be racking her brains to remember the boy, screwing up her eyes and twisting her mouth. 'No, I don't remember any Þröstur.' She smiled suddenly. 'So at least it can't have been anything serious. The difficult cases have a habit of staying with me, whereas the trivial problems, if you can call them that, tend to slip my mind. It's a wonder we're not all on anti-depressants, really.' The woman smiled again, revealing a glimpse of less than perfect teeth. Her smile left a lot to be desired too, as it failed to reach her eyes.

Freyja bared her teeth with equal insincerity. 'Did schools refer a lot of kids to you in those days?'

'Depends what you mean by a lot.' Sólveig dropped the fake smile and assumed a world-weary air instead. Freyja had lost count of the times she had seen her colleagues do this and it drove her up the wall. It was the face they put on, apparently unconsciously, when talking among themselves, as if to underline how dreadful their caseload was and how badly they were paid. Perhaps she could take some of them with her if she enrolled on that course in financial trading?

'Of course, even one child with problems is one too many,' Sólveig added, still with that care-worn air.

'There'll always be problems,' Freyja said bracingly, refusing to play along. 'Were you treating a lot of children at the time?'

Sólveig didn't seem put out by Freyja's brusqueness. 'Yes, I suppose you could say that.' The insincere smile made a reappearance. 'I had my own practice and also provided psychology services for four schools. But I only conducted primary diagnoses of children and adolescents with problems. If they turned out to need treatment, they were referred, mainly to the Child and Adolescent Psychiatric Department. I only had very brief contact with them, so I'm not surprised I don't remember this Thröstur.'

'Really? I understood that you'd treated him on an earlier occasion as well. There was no mention of how old he was at the time, but in that case you must have conducted more than a primary diagnosis.'

'I'm afraid I've completely forgotten. I must be getting old.' Again Sólveig put on that irritating smile, but it vanished when Freyja failed to demur. 'If anything comes back to me, I'll let you know.'

'Please do.' Freyja prepared to stand up. 'Anyway, I assume the police will want to talk to you about the boy and that period in his life. There may be reports on file that you could look up. You still work part-time for the schools, don't you?'

'Yes. But I very much doubt the report still exists.' The answer came a little too pat. 'At least, I'd be very surprised if it did.'

'Really?' Freyja remained sitting. 'Are the records destroyed after a certain number of years, then?'

'No.' Sólveig avoided meeting Freyja's eye. 'I mean, I don't know.' She seemed flustered and made a clumsy attempt to retrieve the situation. 'It's just that ten years feels like a lifetime, never mind anything from before that. Of course it's quite possible that the report on the boy is still in the system somewhere. But given the sheer number of cases we deal with, I think it's unlikely. That's all I meant.'

'I see.' Freyja wondered whether to persevere with this conversation or go back to her office. Finish her tasks, then devote the rest of the day to surfing the net. She could sign up to Tinder, as her brother was always urging her to. That's how he'd become involved with a whole series of women who didn't seem put off by the fact that he was behind bars. So surely she, who was free as a bird, must be in with a chance? But instead of rising to leave, Freyja decided not to let the woman off the hook quite so easily. There was no way Sólveig was getting away with this bullshit. 'No. Actually, you know what? I don't quite get it. What have all these changes got to do with the report? They're all supposed to be kept on file, just like patient records. Just because a filing system's upgraded, that doesn't mean all the existing documents are destroyed.'

'No, of course not. I'm talking nonsense. Of course the records must be somewhere. I'm just not au fait with the system. I file my reports but I don't actually know what happens to them once they've been processed. Didn't the school have a copy?'

'The headteacher claims he never received a final report, only a very general summary. Doesn't that sound rather irregular? Schools have no right to view pupils' mental health records.'

'Of course they don't. He must just have received a short summary of the findings relevant to the school – if special procedures were required for dealing with the boy. My brain hasn't woken up yet today. Sorry to be so scatty. I've had rather a trying morning. So sorry I can't help.' Sólveig heaved a sigh and re-assumed her world-weary expression, but again Freyja refused to mirror it.

'You could authorise me to see the summary, since the headteacher thinks he should be able to track it down. Until the other records turn up, that would be better than nothing.'

Sólveig was wrong-footed, though she tried to cover it up. Freyja had the feeling she was casting around in vain for an excuse to refuse. 'Yes, absolutely. Sure. I suppose that would be OK. I just want to refresh my memory of the case to make sure I won't be in breach of confidentiality. Would later this week be all right?'

Freyja got up. 'I suppose that'll have to do. I expect the police will approach you directly about the other records. Or go straight to the Child and Adolescent Psychiatric Department. Somebody at the hospital must know how the archives work and how to access them. Not that the police are likely to read the report themselves – presumably they'll ask you to look at it for them. Or me, for that matter.'

'Either way, we'll see.' The woman's bracelets jangled again as she turned to the computer and placed her meaty hands on the keyboard. 'Thanks for letting me know.'

Freyja's attention was distracted by the storm raging outside the window. It was a fair reflection of her mental state at that moment.

Freyja hadn't had any matches on Tinder, apart from one that hope-fully didn't count. She'd swiped right on a man and he'd reciprocated. But the attractive thirty-year-old had turned out to be a boy of nine-teen, as he revealed in a message asking if she was a cougar in search of sex with a younger guy. If so, he was up for it.

This did nothing to improve her mood. Instead of sending back a snarky reply that thirty-something women weren't that desperate, she'd simply deleted his message. She had only herself to blame if the most eligible bachelors in Iceland weren't exactly queuing up to meet her. The profile she'd put up was pretty uninspiring – she'd nicked the wording more or less unchanged from another woman and had used her photo from the office intranet. The camera on her phone was broken and she'd just uploaded all the pictures to free up some memory. Why did everything have to go wrong at the same time?

At that moment she received an alert that someone had liked her picture. This removed her frown briefly, until she saw who it was: Huldar. How the hell did that happen? Why hadn't she checked to see if he had an account before she signed up? She should have known. Freyja sighed. What was the betting he'd be the first man she bumped into when she went out clubbing this weekend? Annoyed by the thought, she deleted her account and went offline. If only she could unplug her computer as well.

Rather than give in to this impulse, she stared grumpily at the screen in search of something to do that wouldn't rile her further. Her mind was blank. The landscape photo she'd set as her wallpaper could hardly be seen for all the files she had saved on her desktop, in defiance of the centre's IT officer. The files were of no use to her now, the cases they related to long since closed. She had a choice between another bout of online surfing, refreshing all the usual websites in the hope that they would be updated faster than she could read them, or staring at the screen, wondering why her life had gone down the drain. The third option was apply her mind to Sólveig's puzzling reaction.

This option won and without pausing to consider whether she was authorised to do so, Freyja accessed the Child Protection Agency intranet. First she looked up Thröstur Agnesarson's ID number. Although she had no idea if reports by school psychologists ended up here, there was no harm in looking. If her concerns about the boy had any basis, he would presumably have received further treatment, and in that case she ought to be able to find him on the system.

She knew full well that all searches were logged, so she could expect an enquiry as to why she had been looking up old files about a young man who wasn't one of her clients. The prospect didn't alarm her; there were advantages to being at the bottom of the pecking order – she didn't have far to fall. Besides, she could always use the police investigation as an excuse. No one need know that she hadn't been asked to look at the reports. If she'd read Huldar right, he would back her up.

Suddenly she regretted having quit Tinder instead of simply liking his picture and following up with a polite message explaining that she wasn't interested. Too late now.

The ID number instantly brought up Thröstur's name and a date indicating when his case had first been recorded on the system. That date fitted with the headteacher's account: December 2005, or the boy's first term as a pupil at the school. But Freyja raised her eyebrows at the second entry, initially assuming it was a mistake. This one dated from 2001 and concerned not Thröstur Agnesarson but Thröstur Jónsson. When she compared the ID numbers, however, they were the same. At some point between 2001 and 2005 the boy had stopped using his patronymic and begun going by his mother's name instead.

So the headteacher had been right: Thröstur had also come to the attention of the system in early January 2001, when he would have been eight. It would be interesting to know if Sólveig had handled his case both times or only on the second occasion. With a flutter of excitement, Freyja called up a list of records linked to Thröstur's ID number. Much to her annoyance, she drew a blank. It seemed that Sólveig had been right: old records, even digital ones, could go missing.

Freyja fidgeted with the mouse. How was she to track them down?

An uncharitable thought occurred, unfair and unfounded, but persistent. Could Sólveig have accessed the system after their conversation and deleted the records? Then done the same with the report she had written, wherever it was archived? No, surely not . . .

Freyja put on her headphones and called the Child Protection Agency's IT officer. While waiting for him to answer, she idly studied his photo on the website, part of an initiative to ensure that the agency staff would recognise one another, although they worked at different sites around the country. The theory was that if you reminded people that they were talking to a flesh-and-blood human being, their interaction would be politer. As if they could be in any doubt that they were talking to a real person. The IT guy appeared to have been taken unawares in his studio portrait. If he was on Tinder, she hoped he wasn't using this as his profile picture.

'Have you cleaned up your desktop yet?' the man launched in immediately.

'Yes,' she lied without a moment's hesitation. 'How does it work with client records on our system – could someone delete them remotely?'

'Yes, it's possible. But who'd do a thing like that?' The man paused. 'Have you deleted something by accident?'

'No, of course not. I was just looking for some records that should be there but appear to have vanished.'

'Are you sure they were there?'

'Yes, they must have been. The client's ID number's on the system and there are two cases linked to it, but no files. Not a single one. Isn't that a bit odd?'

'Yes, I suppose so. Unless they never existed.'

'I'm fairly sure they must have done.' Freyja paused briefly, then added: 'Could you check for me if the records were there? Yesterday, for example?'

'Yesterday?'

'Yes, for example. Or last week. Or last year, for that matter. It's up to you. But yesterday would be best.' She gave him Thröstur's ID number.

'OK. I'll have a look. Just a sec.'

Freyja was surprised at how easy it was to persuade him to help her. 'Thanks. I owe you one.'

'Keep it. I'm the IT officer. I get paid to deal with stupid requests.'

Freyja didn't rise to the bait. In revenge she surveyed all the files on her desktop, pleased that she still hadn't deleted them. Even petty little victories like that could raise the spirits.

'No. There was nothing there yesterday. Want me to check further back in time?'

'No, that's fine. Thanks.' She had done Sólveig an injustice. But that didn't alter the fact that there was something fishy about all this. Something didn't feel right.

Chapter 7

Cheap little plastic flower pots were lined up on the windowsills in the sitting room. Æsa had given up hope that any of the seeds would be tricked into thinking it was spring. When she peered in to check, it was as she'd suspected: no change, nothing but bare brown earth. Perhaps it was just as well. If the plants did decide to sprout, she wouldn't know what to do with them once they'd outgrown their little containers. The winter showed no sign of releasing its iron grip, so they couldn't be planted outside. Æsa knew next to nothing about gardening. She had got carried away after hearing two women she worked with at the council offices holding forth about how much money they had saved by growing their summer bedding plants from seed, and, infected by their enthusiasm, she had seen no reason not to start them off shortly after New Year. Her weariness with this gruelling winter had been partly to blame: the thought of pansies and marigolds was so cheering. Last summer she hadn't been able to afford any flowers to brighten up her little plot. But now it looked as if she had wasted her money.

Æsa rapped on the big window, then opened the smaller one a crack and called to the two children playing outside. 'Time to come in. Supper's ready.' They turned to look at her, bundled up in their hoods, hats and scarves. The little that could be glimpsed of their cheeks was bright red. Between them was a mound – presumably the snowman they had been planning to build, or the beginnings of one. 'Come along, or supper will get cold.' Æsa added the last bit for the benefit of any neighbours who might be listening. There was no hot food, any more than there usually was, unless toast counted as a hot meal. There was no point cooking anything more ambitious: the kids wouldn't appreciate it and anyway they got a cooked lunch every day at nursery. For supper their preference was for bread, *skyr* and cold liver sausage, and why should she change this arrangement when it suited them all? She'd had enough of obeying other people's rules during her years with Thorvaldur, who had expressed an opinion – invariably disparaging – on everything she or the children did. How he must enjoy being alone and free to have his own way in everything.

Karlotta and Dadi reluctantly picked their way across the small white lawn. Their arms hung at their sides, their mittens weighed down by clumps of snow. They headed for the door that opened into the sitting room. It was the garden that had persuaded Æsa to take the plunge and buy the flat, though it had been beyond her means. Her pay was nothing to write home about, and since becoming a single mother she hadn't been able to take on any overtime because of the kids. It would have been more sensible to buy a flat on the first or second floor, not only for financial reasons but also to avoid the ongoing fear that a criminal had only to smash a window to break in. Although she liked fresh air at night, since moving in she hadn't been able to sleep with the window open. Every time she closed her eyes she imagined an arm reaching in to undo the catch. Such worries hadn't occurred to her when she'd let herself be captivated by the garden. All she had thought of was Karlotta and Dadi playing outside where she could keep an eye on them.

When she opened the door to let them in, she was met by a wall of cold air. The mat inside was soon covered in snow as the children shook the worst of it off their outdoor clothes. Much of it ended up on the parquet thanks to their clumsy efforts, but Æsa didn't let this annoy her. In the past Thorvaldur would have been standing over her, grumbling about the pools of water on the floor. Without lifting a finger to help.

This reminded her that Thorvaldur had rung earlier. Five times, so it must be something important. She had been at work and it hadn't occurred to her to answer since calls from him rarely ended on a good note. She couldn't bear to let her colleagues overhear their bickering.

'Go and wash your hands, then come and eat.' Æsa carried the pile of wet garments into the hall and started hanging them up on pegs. She moved the shoes from underneath so the melting snow wouldn't drip into them. Her phone rang as she was looking around for some-where to hang the Manchester United bobble hat Thorvaldur had brought back for Dadi after attending a conference in the UK, a month before she had announced that she wanted a divorce. The hat was threadbare and faded, but Dadi refused to wear anything else.

'Mummy! Your phone's ringing! It might be Daddy.' Dadi sounded excited but it was hard to tell if this was pleasure that his father wanted to talk to them or tension at the prospect of having to listen to yet another quarrel. One side of a quarrel, rather, because neither he nor Karlotta could hear what their father said. Just as well. The poor kids had more than enough on their plate as it was.

'Don't answer!' Æsa stuffed the hat into the hood of the nearest anorak, then hurried into the kitchen to stop Dadi or Karlotta picking up. But she was too late. When she came in Dadi was standing with the phone held to his ear, looking as if Parliament had just passed a law to abolish his birthday.

'Give me that. Give me the phone, Dadi. Now.' She regretted raising her voice when she saw that she had only increased her son's distress. He handed her the phone.

'We're eating, Valdi. Can't it wait?' Æsa tried to keep her tone civil. The children's eyes were fixed on her. They stood there side by side, showing no sign of sitting down, though their meagre supper was already on the table. In her agitation she had accidentally used her old pet name for her ex-husband, though after the divorce she had resolved never to call him anything but Thorvaldur, even in her head.

'If you'd answered my calls earlier I wouldn't have to ring now.' Thorvaldur could afford to vent his anger since the children couldn't hear. Mind you, Æsa wasn't sure he would have bothered to hold back even if the kids had been in front of him. He never had in the past. Fortunately, he didn't seem to have noticed her slip-up over his name. The last thing she wanted was for him to think she was still carrying a torch for him.

'I was at work. You know I don't like taking private phone calls at the office.'

'You're not telling me you've only just got home?' The sarcastic note was all too familiar.

She wasn't going to give him the satisfaction of listing everything she'd had to do since finishing work: race to the nursery to avoid a ticking-off for picking the children up late, shepherd them through the crush at the supermarket after selecting the very cheapest goods, drive home, get them and the shopping into the house, take off their outdoor clothes, clear away the food, give them a drink, help them back into their outdoor clothes, let them out in the garden, put a load in the washing machine and fix something for supper. There hadn't been a spare minute to return his call. But any mention of her difficulties in keeping things going would be music to his ears, so it was better to bite her lip. 'What do you want, Thorvaldur?'

'What do I want? Just to know if you're all right. Well, not you, obviously. I couldn't care less about you. But Karlotta and Dadi. They are OK, aren't they?'

It suddenly dawned on Æsa that Thorvaldur sounded worried. Æsa couldn't remember ever having heard him sound worried before. It alarmed her. 'What do you mean? Of course they're all right. Why are you asking? Is something wrong?'

'No, nothing. I just wanted to know.' Thorvaldur lapsed briefly into silence, then continued in a pleading tone that could hardly have been less like him: 'You will look after them, won't you?'

'What's wrong, Thorvaldur? Tell me.' She should have watched what she said. Karlotta and Dadi opened their eyes wide and gaped at her anxiously. She tried to retrieve the situation by adding at a more normal pitch: 'There's nothing wrong here. Nothing at all.'

'Look after them. Promise me.'

What on earth had happened to the old Thorvaldur? To the arrogant man who was accustomed to doling out orders left, right and centre, and would never have dreamt of pleading with anyone?

'I always do. I don't need to make you any promises.' Turning away from the children, Æsa hurried out of the kitchen and whispered so they couldn't hear: 'What's going on? Has someone threatened them?' Her initial thought was that Thorvaldur must have been threatened by one of the criminals he'd put behind bars. 'If they have, you've got to tell me.' Now it was her turn to sound pleading, thereby restoring their relationship to its old footing.

'There's nothing to tell.' Thorvaldur tried but failed to sound normal. 'Nothing at all. Just make sure you tell them not to talk to strangers or go anywhere with anyone they don't know.' He paused and his naturally overbearing manner reasserted itself. 'And answer the phone next time I ring. It's not as if your work's so important that you can't spare two minutes to talk to me.' He hung up.

Supper was a silent affair. Æsa had cut short any attempt by the children to find out what their father wanted, and as they couldn't think about anything else, there was little to say. She herself was too anxious to be able to lighten the atmosphere. As always when Karlotta and Dadi were feeling insecure, their appetites suffered, and she had to nag them to clean their plates. They had been born skinny, never developed apple cheeks like other children, and since they had no puppy fat to fall back on, they couldn't afford to miss a meal. They were so like their father. You'd have thought he'd produced them on his own, were it not for their temperaments. They were gentle and rarely got cross. Unlike their father in that respect, then. But, who knows, perhaps he had been a delightful child?

'Good night.' Æsa reached for the light switch as she stood in the doorway. She had put a red bulb in the lamp on the table between their beds to give them a soft light to fall asleep by. The pink glow lit up the little faces peering out from under the covers, their eyes still wide and staring.

'Good night, Mummy. We promise not to get in a car with a bad man.' Karlotta gave her a watery smile. 'Dadi promises too.'

Smiling back, Æsa wished she hadn't warned the children about strangers just before bedtime. She wouldn't be surprised if they woke up with nightmares. But it would be worth it if they took her lecture to heart. 'It's not only bad men, darling. There are bad women too. You must remember that.' No need to mention that the chances of a woman trying to harm them were negligible compared to the bad man of their imagination. They must be careful of all strangers, men or women. 'You can't always tell if people are bad by looking at them.' Their eyes became even wider on hearing this. 'But that's enough of that. Night, night.' She left their door open a crack.

Once she was fairly sure the children were asleep, she fetched her phone and rang Thorvaldur to insist he tell her what was going on. It was only fair. But he didn't answer; no doubt he was punishing her for not picking up earlier. Her repeated calls achieved nothing. She went to bed as much in the dark about what was going on as when Thorvaldur had hung up on her.

Sleep eluded her and the more tired she became, the more she tossed and turned, the more her worries multiplied. Twice she got out of bed to reassure herself that the window was definitely shut and the catch was on. The second time, she caught sight of a car she didn't recognise parked outside. It hadn't been there when she'd got up half an hour ago. It appeared black or dark blue in the darkness, one of those models that are indistinguishable to people with no interest in cars. If she'd had to describe it she would say it looked like the cars children draw: four wheels, four doors, a bonnet and a boot. It wasn't the colour or shape that fuelled her growing unease, however, but her conviction that there was a figure sitting behind the wheel. She couldn't be sure but her imagination filled in the gaps and by the time she finally dropped off she had convinced herself that he had been staring at her window. Or, even worse, at Karlotta and Dadi's room.

When she woke up later that night and looked out for the third time, the car had gone.

Chapter 8

Two seedy-looking figures walked down the steps of the police station on to Hverfisgata, one a little sheepish in yesterday's rumpled suit, the other in ordinary clothes that had seen better days. Neither was dressed for the weather and they shivered in their thin jackets as they emerged. From his years in the regular police, Huldar knew that it was chucking-out time for those who'd spent the night in the cells. Though he knew neither man by sight, he guessed that the guy in the grubby jeans was a regular, whereas the smarter man was probably the type whose arrest was a one-off that would shock him into getting his drinking under control. At least, he appeared to be furtively checking to see if anyone he knew had witnessed his humiliation. The other guy clearly couldn't give a toss. He even lingered on the steps to fish a cigarette from his pocket and light up.

Both figures vanished into the thickly falling snow.

Huldar stubbed out his own cigarette and hastened up the steps. He had no need to ask the way from the policeman at reception, merely nodded to him and went inside. The man he had come to see, Gudmundur Lárusson, still occupied the same office as he had when Huldar first joined the police, and would no doubt remain there until he retired. Which must be fairly soon now. His door was open but Huldar knocked for courtesy's sake. 'Is this a bad moment?'

Huldar got a shock when Gudmundur looked up. He had aged. His blotchy scalp shone through the sparse white hair and his skin was covered in liver spots. The thick, dark eyebrows that had once lent his face its character were now bleached and straggly.

'Bloody hell! Huldar! No, not at all. Come in, come in.' Gudmundur leant back in his chair and threw down his pen.

'You get younger by the year.' Smiling at his old boss, Huldar took a chair.

'Bullshit. I can't say the same for you, either. What are they doing to you over at the Police Commissioner's office?'

'Wearing me out.' Huldar grinned. 'At this rate we'll end up the same age.'

Gudmundur snorted. 'Is this a friendly visit? Should I get you a coffee? Or are you here on police business? In which case you can fetch it yourself.'

'Police business. And I haven't been gone long enough to forget how shit the coffee is here. So don't worry.'

'I worry about a lot of things, but whether you want a coffee's not one of them.' Gudmundur clasped his hands behind his head. 'Out with it, then. How can I help you?'

'Good question.' It was a drag having to repeat the story of the time capsule and the reason for the police inquiry, so Huldar got it over with quickly. While he was talking, Gudmundur's white eyebrows rose higher and higher up his forehead. Huldar couldn't tell if this was a reaction to his story or to the fact that he was frittering away his time on such trivial cases. He hoped it wasn't the latter. '. . . And I noticed that although Thröstur doesn't have any previous, he does seem to have had a brush with the law back when he was a minor. Something from December 2000, when he was only eight years old, which is kind of odd. Or at least that's what it looks like from the entry in the Police Information System, which I can't access. I assume it's him, though there he's using his father's name, not his mother's as he does now. His ID number's the same, anyway. I've never been denied access like this before, so I must need special permission to view his files, perhaps because he was a minor at the time. And that means all kinds of red tape. So I wanted to ask if you could check his record for me, to spare me the hassle. As a senior officer, you should have clearance.' The favour he was asking wasn't as straightforward as it sounded, since members of the police had recently been hauled before the courts on suspicion of accessing the Police Commissioner's database without a valid excuse. Although they'd been acquitted, that didn't alter the fact that people were now reluctant to use the database unless it was unavoidable.

Gudmundur nodded, looking thoughtful. 'You could have done it yourself if you hadn't been demoted.'

'I'm well aware of that. But it can't be helped. It's only when something like this crops up that I miss being a manager, a little.' Huldar hoped his sincerity was obvious.

His old boss shrugged. 'I hope you won't be offended but I was a bit surprised when I heard about your promotion. Less so when you were kicked downstairs again. Though of course it would never have occurred to me that you'd last that short a time. Do you know you broke the Icelandic record? Probably the European one too. Maybe even a world record. That's pretty good going.' The smile faded from his weary face. 'Shame how much gloating there was among some of the old bastards here. Men you used to work with. But I wasn't one of them.'

'I never dreamt you would be.' Huldar might not have been a good manager but he was a decent judge of character. He didn't need to be told the names of those who had taken a gleeful delight in his fall. 'Anyway, what do you say to taking a look at those reports for me?'

Gudmundur considered the matter in silence, his head cocked on one side. 'You know that every time we access the system it's logged? What will I say if I'm asked why I was looking?'

'Just be honest. I asked you for help with a case. Everyone in my department's so rushed off their feet that no one with clearance had the time to spare. Which is true enough.'

'Are they occupied with that business of the severed hands?'

'Yes.' Huldar shifted in the uncomfortable visitor's chair that was well past its sell-by date. Gudmundur wasn't the type to ask for his office furniture to be replaced. Nor, by the look of things, did he have any truck with the new regulation police shirt that had recently been introduced. 'Does everybody know?'

'The cafeteria's abuzz with it.'

'I suppose it's inevitable.' Huldar sighed. In that case it wouldn't be long before the media got hold of the story. Which was both good and bad. Bad for Erla, who would be cast in the role of the incompetent investigator unless the case was resolved in the next few days; good, because the news might result in a tip-off about the owner of the hands. Perhaps they should appeal for members of the public to get in touch if they had something missing. 'Well, if the story's already leaked, no one'll have any reason to doubt our workload at the moment – if you're asked to explain your actions. If you're willing to do me this favour, that is.'

'Hadn't we better stick together? Us two against all the rest?' Gudmundur gave a short bark of laughter, though he didn't sound amused. 'I can't see how it would do any harm. But I'm not printing anything out. You'll have to read it on screen.'

That was good enough for Huldar. He read out Thröstur's ID number and watched as Gudmundur carefully typed it in. The name appeared but there were no records or anything else of use. Instead it said '*No access'*, the same thing that had appeared on Huldar's own screen. 'Try again.' This produced exactly the same result. Huldar straightened up, disappointed. 'That's the message I got earlier.'

'Strange. I've never encountered that before. You've checked the police register, haven't you?'

The register was a database of general information about all complaints that had come to the notice of the police. Its existence had drawn criticism from some quarters as it lacked the proper data-protection safeguards. Unlike the official Police Information System, there were no formal rules for its use; access was not logged and chance alone dictated what kind of information accompanied the entries and whether the cases were followed up. The register contained the names not only of criminals but also of witnesses and other members of the public who came in to give statements. Nothing was ever deleted. There were now over 300,000 individuals on the register, many of them deceased. Huldar had searched the database for Thröstur's name but drawn a blank. It looked as if Freyja's gloomy predictions about his criminal record were wrong. 'I didn't find anything there. Perhaps he isn't on the system after all?'

'That can't be right. In that case it would say "no record found". He seems to have been known to the police but the entry's got buggered up somehow. Maybe it happened when the information was transferred between systems. They've been upgraded several times since this Thröstur turned eighteen.'

'Meaning what? Has it been lost?'

Pursing his lips, Gudmundur tried limiting the search to Thröstur's first name only, but the same result came up. 'I expect a hard copy still exists somewhere. But for that you'd have to fill in the correct forms. No one, however senior, can just waltz into the archives and start digging around. At least, I can't.' He leant back in his chair, frowning, suddenly looking like his younger self again. 'Something smells odd about all this. I wonder if those records could have been deliberately locked.'

'Why would anyone do that?'

'No idea. The boy's name doesn't ring any bells. If he was notorious or implicated in something major that led to his being granted anonymity, I'd recognise the name. But I don't.'

'Nor do I.' Huldar ran his fingers through his hair and realised that it could do with a trim. He made a mental note to do something about it before Erla ordered him to get himself down to the barber's. He didn't relish the idea and doubted she would either. 'I suppose I'll just have to put in a formal request to view the files myself.'

'Yes. But it could take time, as you know. I'm beginning to think that lot in the archives are a bit slow – mentally, I mean.' Gudmundur closed the database. 'If I were you, I'd pay the lad a visit. Ask him a few questions, steer the conversation round to his past. That way you'll probably get your answers long before the files turn up.'

Huldar nodded. He would have liked to know more about the young man's background before he went to see him, but there was no chance of that now. 'Thanks for your help.'

'Pity I couldn't be of any use. Sadly that's becoming more common these days.' Gudmundur picked up his pen and hunched over the form on his desk. He didn't look up as he added: 'Keep me posted. It's not often that anything interesting lands on my desk anymore.'

Huldar assured him he would, then said goodbye and left. All was not yet lost: Freyja might have found something in the Child Protection Agency's records.

The dilapidated building reminded Huldar of the grotty block where Freyja lived, though he refrained from saying so. The similarity didn't seem to have struck her. No one would ever have guessed that she lived in such a dump. She certainly didn't look as if she were short of money. Her blonde hair was drawn back in a high ponytail and glittered with melted snowflakes. There wasn't a single dog hair on her clothes, which fitted her beautifully. So beautifully that Huldar had to make a conscious effort not to keep running his eyes over her. He knew this wouldn't be appreciated; his attempt to approach her on Tinder seemed to have prompted her to delete her account. He hadn't asked her about this and she hadn't referred to it either. Some things were best left unsaid. He contented himself with feeling pleased that she had agreed so readily to come and see Thröstur, rather than suggesting they put it off until later or tomorrow. It probably hadn't hurt that he'd begun the phone call by filling her in on the story of the missing records, since, as she then explained, Thröstur's records were also missing from the Child Protection Agency's computer system.

It seemed Gudmundur had been right when he said there was an odd smell about all this.

'And he lives here with his mother and sister?' Freyja surveyed the three-storey building. The question was rhetorical; Huldar had already told her about Thröstur's living arrangements. The young man hadn't been exactly keen to meet them, but had agreed in the end. It struck Huldar as a little odd that Thröstur hadn't asked what he wanted, merely volunteered the information that his mother and sister wouldn't be home – Huldar would be better off coming at suppertime if he wanted to speak to them. Why Thröstur should have thought that he wanted to see them too would hopefully become clear in due course.

'They don't seem to be doing too well, poor things.' Freyja turned to look at Huldar. 'Strange he didn't opt to come into the station instead. That's what I'd have done.'

Huldar smiled a little foolishly. She clearly didn't realise that her own block of flats was no better. 'He said he didn't own a car. I don't suppose he felt like taking the bus in the snow.'

Freyja tipped back her head to look up at the overcast sky. 'It's not snowing now.'

Huldar went over to the doorbells. The brass plate and small black buttons almost certainly dated from the sixties, and for a second he doubted the bell would work. Perhaps Thröstur had never actually intended to let them in. Most of the buttons were unmarked but by one there was a small, yellowing card with the names of Thröstur, his mother Agnes and his sister Sigrún. Huldar pressed the bell twice, then waited. He was just about to try again when the door emitted a buzz.

The lobby and stairwell were what you might expect: wrinkled linoleum and grimy walls. There was a faint smell of cat's piss that intensified the higher they climbed but fortunately faded a little when Thröstur opened the door to them on the second floor.

He didn't introduce himself or greet them in the conventional manner. 'You'll have to be quick because I'm about to go out.' His expression was neither friendly nor hostile. 'I'm leaving in fifteen minutes. You're not getting a second longer.' On the back of his hand was a black tattoo in decorative gothic script that Huldar couldn't decipher upside down, though he thought it was in Latin, some classical quotation that the author could never have imagined would adorn an Icelandic fist more than two thousand years later. As Thröstur let them in, Huldar noticed that he had a similar tattoo on his other hand. It was in keeping with the rest of his appearance: the tight black jeans and sweatshirt bearing the anarchist symbol, which only accentuated his skinny frame; the huge tunnel rings in his earlobes, the piercings in one nostril and through the middle of his nose. His black hair was trained forward to hang limply on either side of his face, comb marks clearly visible in the thickly applied gel. Huldar had seen enough variations on this fashion to know that it offered a way for the physically weedy to pose as tough.

Huldar didn't bother to hold out his hand, knowing that it wouldn't be taken. 'I'm Huldar. This is Freyja. We'll try and be quick.'

Thröstur led the way inside without inviting them to hang up their coats. Freyja and Huldar caught each other's eye and removed their shoes by tacit agreement, though looking at the brown floor-tiles in the hall, they'd have to change their socks when they got home. The patterned carpet in the corridor only confirmed their fears. It looked as old as the flat and the underlay was showing through in places, but on closer inspection it appeared to have been recently vacuumed. The cheap shelves and battered sideboard they passed had also been dusted not that long ago. Huldar was willing to bet that Thröstur's mother or sister took care of the housework: a hoover and feather duster didn't really go with the recycled punk image.

'You can sit here if you want, though it'll hardly be worth it.' Thröstur cleared a space for them on the sofa facing an enormous, new-looking flat-screen TV. He chucked the stuff in a heap on the floor, then seated himself in an armchair beside the sofa. 'I know all about it, but I don't know what you think you're going to achieve. Try and stop me from doing something stupid? Just how do you plan to do that? The answer is, you can't.'

As Huldar sat down, he considered how to respond to this. It hadn't occurred to him that Thröstur would remember the letter after all this time. Perhaps someone had reminded him. All Huldar could think of was that the headteacher or one of the school's office staff might have bumped into him and asked him about it. Surely Thröstur couldn't have remembered the exact date when the time capsule would be dug up? Unless he had regretted the letter and his conscience had been nagging at him all these years. It wasn't unheard of for someone who had lied in court to come forward and confess many years after the event. Perhaps this was similar. 'We were only going to ask why you wrote the letter and who the people on your hit-list were.'

'The letter?' There was no mistaking Thröstur's puzzlement. 'What the fuck are you on about?'

'The letter you wrote ten years ago, at your old school. The one you put in the time capsule, which has just been dug up. The letter listing the initials of people who are supposed to die this year.'

'I—' Thröstur broke off, opened his mouth as if to add something, then shut it again.

Freyja cleared her throat and glanced at Huldar before intervening. 'We're perfectly aware that you wrote those things all those years ago because you were angry and that the threats weren't serious. I'm a child psychologist and I know that children say, write and do things that—' She got no further.

Thröstur was gripping the arms of his chair so tightly that his knuckles whitened, throwing the black tattoos into sharp relief. Huldar thought he could decipher the word *ultio* on his left hand and *dulcis* on his right. This meant nothing to him.

'A child psychologist?!' Thröstur exploded with such fury that a spray of spittle accompanied his words. 'You're not from the Child Protection Agency?'

Freyja gave no sign of being disconcerted by this outburst. She was probably used to such things. 'I'm from the Children's House, which is run by the Child Protection Agency. I'm not here on their behalf, though, but to assist the police.'

This did nothing to appease Thröstur. 'Get out!' he yelled. 'I've nothing to say to you. You' – he pointed a long, thin finger at Freyja – 'and all the other psychologists and child protection shits are a load of fucking cunts. If I had my way, I'd chop off all your heads and piss down your throats.'

Huldar rose quickly. 'Come, Freyja.' He rounded on the young man who was frothing at the mouth now. 'One more word like that and I'll cuff you. Do you want to spend a night in the cells?' His voice was steely but controlled.

Thröstur's nostrils flared with the force of his breathing. 'Get out! I've nothing to say to you.'

Huldar judged that there was no point trying to pacify him. He would have to summon him to the station and continue the interview there. As Thröstur's rage seemed to be directed mainly at Freyja and her profession, Huldar ushered her out of the room and followed close behind, keeping himself between her and the young man. He wasn't afraid of receiving a punch or a kick from the skinny little sod, but it occurred to him on the way out that Thröstur might just be crazy enough to pull a knife on them. 'If your sword is too short, take one step forward.' Perhaps the Latin motto meant something like that. At any rate, it appeared there was good reason to take the threats in his letter seriously.

Not until Freyja had her shoes on and was out on the landing could Huldar relax. He stepped out to join her but when Thröstur made to slam the door, Huldar stuck out a hand to stop it. Still keeping his voice perfectly calm, he asked: 'What did you think we'd come to see you about?'

Thröstur shoved at the door but Huldar was bigger, heavier and stronger. 'I asked, why did you think we were here?'

His face dark red with rage and effort, Thröstur snarled: 'I was dumb enough to think the cops would be worried about us now he's out. I should've known better.'

Momentarily distracted by this reply, Huldar relaxed his pressure and Thröstur flung his thin body against the door, slamming it in Huldar's face.

What the hell did Thröstur mean? Who was 'he'?

Huldar's phone rang. A police number flashed up.

'Hello, it's Gudmundur. I just wanted to warn you: there's something going on in connection with that Thröstur we were talking about earlier. I've just been asked to explain my interest in him. It's only a couple of hours since you were here. If I were you, I wouldn't advertise the fact you're planning to speak to him. And be careful when you do. God knows why he's being given the kid-glove treatment, but I'm guessing the reason's none too pretty.'

'Thanks for the warning but it's a bit late. I'm standing outside his front door right now. He threw us out after we'd only just sat down. I think you're right; something smells very odd about this. I'll call you later, if that's OK.'

They rang off and Huldar shoved the phone back in his pocket. He stared at the flaking paint on the door for a moment, then hurried off in pursuit of Freyja.

What the hell was going on?

Chapter 9

Freyja and Baldur's childhood had been far from typical. For the first few years they had grown up with a young mother who was quite unfit for the role but did her best to split her energies between her two main priorities – her children and having fun. The latter had been the death of her in the end, long before her time, and Baldur and Freyja had been sent to live with their grandparents. But their grandparents couldn't cope either. Not only were they remote and inflexible by nature, they were both retired and therefore badly equipped to take on two kids. The children's fathers were both typical weekend dads who did their best to fulfil their duties, but it had quickly become apparent to Freyja and Baldur that a sense of duty was no substitute for unconditional love. After their mother died, they had no one to offer them that. Except each other.

And so they had grown up, each in their own way: Baldur reckless, with limited respect for rules and authority; Freyja determined to do well and not be distracted. The fact they had different fathers may have had something to do with it, but Freyja knew it wasn't that simple. People were the product of both nature and nurture, and their influence was impossible to predict. Nevertheless, she and Baldur were alike in one respect: they were both tougher and more resilient than most of their contemporaries, undaunted by whatever life chose to throw at them.

So Freyja was completely unprepared for her reaction now. She was still badly shaken after the visit to Thröstur. Despite having experienced a thing or two in her time, she wasn't used to violence, and she had expected Thröstur to follow up his explosion with kicks or blows. Her heart was still beating faster than normal and her small office seemed airless, though the window was wide open. She was sitting in a freezing draught, the Post-it notes stuck to her computer screen flapping like small yellow flags.

She could do with a drink. A stiff one.

The outburst had come completely out of the blue. She had barely spoken when the whole thing blew up in their faces. Before joining the Children's House she had often been present at interviews with troubled teenagers that had ended with the subject losing control. But by then alarm bells would already have gone off: they would start breathing faster, flushing, raising their voices and fidgeting in their seats. She was used to having time to prepare herself. Thröstur had been quite different. He had exploded as if at the flick of a switch. In view of the young man's volatile temper, she now believed there was every reason to take his letter seriously. Unlikely though it was that he would hunt down and murder the individuals on a hit-list drawn up ten years ago, she wouldn't like to answer for what he might be capable of if the opportunity came up.

The person Thröstur had referred to as 'he' had better take care, at any rate. Before they parted company, Huldar had said he would try and find out who 'he' was and let her know. Freyja had been checking her phone unnecessarily often and had twice made sure it wasn't on silent mode. She was finding it impossible to concentrate on the section she had written for the Children's House annual report and kept losing the thread mid-sentence, her thoughts straying back to the young man and his letter. Sólveig still hadn't given her the authorisation, which meant she couldn't request the report from the school. When Freyja had looked in earlier, Sólveig's office had been dark and deserted. Not knowing Thröstur's history frustrated her so much that she couldn't think about anything else.

If she carried on at this rate, she'd be here half the night. The report was due tomorrow morning and that was one deadline she had better meet. She was in enough trouble these days without being the one responsible for delaying its publication. To make matters worse, Molly was at home, waiting impatiently to be fed and walked. If she was late, the dog was perfectly capable of gnawing the other arm off the sofa. The first one had paid the price when Freyja had had to work late back in the autumn.

She sighed as she thought of Molly. This wasn't the life she had dreamt of as a child. Her youthful fantasies had featured no annual reports, no formal reprimands or difficulties in concentrating. And although there had been a dog, it had been a cute little white one, not a mottled brown beast bred to inspire fear.

The phone rang and Freyja almost dropped it on the floor in her eagerness. 'Freyja,' she said breathlessly.

'Does the name Jón Jónsson mean anything to you?' Huldar asked without preamble.

'Jón Jónsson? Is this a joke? Is there a more common name in Iceland?'

'No, probably not.'

'I know several Jóns, and even more if middle names count. But I don't remember their patronymics, though one of them's bound to be a Jónsson.'

'I don't mean personally. Do you recognise the name Jón Jónsson in connection with the Children's House or your other work?'

'What?' The question took her aback. 'No. I can't say I do.' She had no sooner spoken than it dawned on her. A shiver ran down her spine. 'You don't mean—?'

Huldar interrupted: 'Yes. He was released from jail less than a week ago.' There was a dry rustling as he exhaled heavily into the receiver. 'He's Thröstur's father.'

'What?' Freyja was so dumbstruck she couldn't think of anything sensible to say. The Jón Jónsson in question was a paedophile. A paedophile of the worst kind. He had on his conscience not only the sexual abuse of a little girl but her murder as well. It couldn't have been easy growing up as the son of a man like that. No wonder Thröstur had changed his second name.

'Are you familiar with his case?'

'No. It was before my time. I was still at university.' She added, after a pause: 'Is he really out? Didn't he get sixteen years?'

'Yes. Time flies. He served the usual two-thirds of his sentence – ten and a half years. He's out on parole.'

'Parole?' Freyja closed her eyes and rubbed them as she tried to suppress the rage that flared up inside her. Her brother was constantly being denied parole, unlike this disgusting monster. Yet the harm Baldur had caused involved missing assets, the impact of which couldn't begin to compare with the loss of a child.

'Yes. That's the system for you. Presumably he behaved himself during his time inside.'

Freyja snorted. 'He raped and murdered a child. Who cares how he's behaved since he was caught?'

'Believe me, I wasn't consulted.' Huldar sighed wearily. 'Thröstur must have been under the impression that we'd come round to let the family know and discuss how they should react if he got in touch, and so on. I'm guessing that's why he lost it when it turned out we were there for a completely different reason.'

'Is that what they do in these cases?' Freyja transferred the phone to her left hand. She wanted to refresh her memory of the Jón Jónsson case and the best way to do that was to look up old news reports. It couldn't wait until after they'd finished their conversation.

'No. When people get out, the Prison Service assumes responsibility for them. In parole cases they monitor the released inmates but as far as I know they do nothing for the family unless the family contacts them first.'

Freyja mumbled some reply as she typed in Jón Jónsson's name. She got about two million results, the top ones unrelated to the paedophile. It was a long time since he had made the headlines. She added the date 2004 and searched again. 'So you don't keep any tabs on these men? By you, I mean the police. You know how great the risks are that they'll reoffend? There's no cure for paedophilia, only treatments that have limited success in teaching them not to give in to their unnatural urges. And those treatments aren't even offered in Iceland.'

'I'm not an expert. I just assumed social services were involved when they were released. Kept track of where they lived and so on. After all, it's your area.' He added hastily: 'I mean the consequences of their actions – the victims.'

'We don't receive any notification. Believe me, I'd have heard.' Links relating to the right man had now appeared. Freyja clicked on an article in a weekly paper that no longer existed. She remembered the article well – it had been highly controversial. The consensus at the time had been that the newspaper should never have published an interview with the prisoner, and that it had done so in a cynical attempt to boost its failing circulation. Despite the scandalised public reaction, the issue had sold out, but the article hadn't performed the required miracle, merely deferred the paper's bankruptcy by a few weeks.

'Anyway, what happens now?' Freyja asked. 'Should we make another attempt to talk to Thröstur? At least we know something about his background now, and of course this explains why he had problems as an adolescent; when he wrote the letter. "JJ" obviously refers to his father. The murder was less than two years before that, which isn't much time to get over such a traumatic event.'

'There's no question of making another visit any time soon, I'm afraid.'

A photo of Jón Jónsson appeared on screen. He was sitting in one of the visitors' cells at Litla-Hraun Prison, which Freyja instantly recognised, gazing out of the narrow window, looking as if he bore all the world's sorrows on his shoulders. From what Freyja recalled, however, the interview had made it clear that he wasn't exactly burdened with remorse, and the pose had struck her as tastelessly contrived. It was hard to imagine how the girl's parents must have felt on reading this. Especially the part where Jón talked about the date of his release. The injustice of it was scandalous: he could count down the days until he got out, while little Vaka Orradóttir had been given a death sentence. She started out of her thoughts. 'Did you say there was no plan to speak to Þröstur again? But what about the letter? Aren't you supposed to investigate it further?'

'No. I've been told to shelve it for the time being. There's a more urgent inquiry in progress. Perhaps I'll be able to come back to it once that's resolved.' She couldn't gauge how Huldar felt about this decision, but supposed the big cases must be more challenging and therefore more satisfying than minor affairs like the letter.

'I see.' Freyja stared at Jón Jónsson's profile. The photo was grainy, as the article had been scanned, but there was no mistaking his expression. The word that sprang to mind was slimy. Repellently slimy. She tore her eyes from the screen in an effort to concentrate on the conversation. 'So it won't be taken any further?'

'No. Not at present. I'll be in touch once things have quietened down, if that's OK.' Huldar hesitated. 'Actually, I was wondering if you were busy this weeken—' He got no further.

'Call me if the case is reopened. Bye then.' She hung up before he could make another attempt to ask her out. She was going out this weekend all right, but not with him. Absolutely, definitely not. Without giving it a second thought or allowing herself to feel guilty about cutting him short like that, she immersed herself in the interview. Just because the police had sidelined Thröstur's letter, that didn't mean she had to. Perhaps reading the interview would kick-start her brain again, galvanising her enough to finish revising the annual report.

As she skimmed the text the contents soon came back to her. She could feel her face twisting with disgust. Nothing that had happened had been the man's own fault. He kept harping on about how he had been an alcoholic and warning readers of the dangers of drink. This elicited a cynical smile from her. Alcohol had its downsides but it didn't turn people into sex offenders, let alone paedophiles. Though from what Jón said, you'd have thought it had been the decisive factor: excessive drinking had made him do it; alcohol had deprived him of his self-control. He had never done anything like that before and would never do it again. According to his statement, he had no memory of committing the crime. Although he didn't go so far as to protest his innocence, he came close. No doubt he would have tried to deny all responsibility if the evidence hadn't been rock solid. There had never been any doubt, if Freyja remembered right: biological specimens and DNA retrieved from the girl's vagina, together with his fingerprints on her throat or her mouth from where he had throttled or suffocated her. She couldn't remember which method he had used.

But now he was in rehab, he said, and had found God. If he could share his experiences and help others when he got out, he would be content. Freyja felt sick. Not one word of regret, not a single hint of remorse for what he had done, not one mention of the girl's parents.

And naturally not a word about the victim, whom he had robbed first of her innocence, then of her life. Instead, there was a long description of how God had forgiven him and intended to use his energies in future, since by his own account he was now doing God's work. If that was really the case, God had better review His policy of forgiveness and get Himself a lie detector, pronto – and fire His personnel manager while He was about it.

In spite of the rage it stirred up, Freyja continued reading. She couldn't remember whether the man had mentioned his family. If he had, there might be some information about Thröstur, and she was also curious to know if Jón's wife had maintained any contact with him while he was in prison. But either the journalist hadn't asked about his family or Jón hadn't been willing to answer.

The article left Freyja with a bad taste in her mouth. She was convinced of three things: one, that he was faking his newfound piety. The way he kept banging on about God simply didn't ring true. He wouldn't be the first person to hide his real nature behind a sudden conversion to Christianity. All you had to do was memorise a few choice quotations and trot them out at regular intervals. It didn't hurt either to carry a Bible around with you and cast mawkish looks heavenwards, especially when there were rays of light piercing the clouds.

Two, little faith should be placed in his protestations of sobriety. How was he supposed to carry on drinking behind bars? He had no choice but to go on the wagon while he was locked up. Besides, attending AA meetings was a pleasant distraction in an otherwise dreary existence at Litla-Hraun, and even those who had no problems with drink turned up to the meetings simply to break the monotony of their days.

Three, Freyja was convinced it was a lie that this was the first and only time he had given in to his lust for children. Paedophile urges didn't suddenly manifest themselves in middle age. A man like him, constantly under the influence of alcohol, was bound to have abused a child before. And Freyja, familiar with so many other distressing examples, could guess with a fair degree of accuracy who that victim had been. The child closest to hand, of course, which meant either Thröstur or his sister Sigrún. Perhaps both. Presumably that was why social services had intervened in Thröstur's case when he was eight years old, but that didn't explain why the files and other paperwork had gone missing. Nor why Sólveig, who had treated the boy, had behaved so oddly. Given who Thröstur's father was, Freyja was sure the woman must remember him. The headteacher's ignorance was more plausible, since the boy's mother must have withheld his father's identity. She must have wanted a new start for herself and her children; to leave the past behind. That would explain their frequent moves too.

To acquaint herself with the details, she looked up the records of the trial. The annual report could wait. So could Molly.

Chapter 10

'I'm freezing to death. Can we please just leave?' Thröstur hugged his jacket tighter around himself. Though the zip was broken the jacket still had plenty of wear in it, so there was no need to shell out for a new one. Anyway, with the total lack of choice on this shitty island, he didn't know where he'd find another one this cool. His teeth were chattering and a punishing wind was seeking out the rips in his trousers. The rips had cost him extra; they weren't a sign of wear. But now all they revealed was gooseflesh.

He was such an idiot. He'd forgotten what day it was and dressed with his image in mind, not for hanging around out here. Not that remembering would have helped much, since he hardly owned any clothes that were suitable. He was wearing his only decent pair of boots – black, laced high up the calf – but even they were freezing as he didn't have any socks on. They weren't genuine Doc Martens, but similar enough to fool people from a distance. At least, he hoped so.

Resenting the weather was pointless; he should just call it a day. 'It's so fucking cold, Sigrún. We might as well come back tomorrow.' If only he could rekindle the heat that had flowed through his veins earlier when that bloody cop and that bitch of a psychologist had blurted out their errand, he could have stood naked in a blizzard without feeling a thing.

His sister shook her head. 'Let's wait. Coming back tomorrow wouldn't be the same.' She was wrapped up so warm that you could hardly see her face. His gaze fell on her hands. She was wearing an old pair of gloves and had cut off the last two fingers and sewn up the holes on the right hand. Why she couldn't just wear mittens to hide the stumps like she used to was beyond him. But he would never refer to her missing fingers, though whether this was to protect her or himself he didn't know.

He reached into his pocket for his cigarettes. He'd heard somewhere that your blood vessels contract when you smoke, which should theoretically make you feel warmer. This was as good a time as any to put it to the test. Besides, he was desperate for a fag; he hadn't had one since they were waiting at the bus stop. The habit was one reason why his dole money was so quick to run out.

'Don't smoke.' Sigrún flapped her hands in the air as if her brother had already lit up. 'If they see the smoke, they might guess we're here. It'll only draw attention to us.'

The cigarette was already half out of the packet but Thröstur pushed it back in. If he ignored her and lit up, it would only stress her out. And she was right, too; after all, his sister was an expert at avoiding being noticed. In contrast to his own 'fuck you' attitude, her aim was to be as inconspicuous as possible, almost invisible. She had been like this for as long as he could remember: desperate to pass under the radar, because the minute someone noticed her, disaster would strike. She wasn't safe anywhere: at school or at home, at clubs or games, any activity that involved other kids. Although the teasing and bullying had diminished as the years went by, she was still suffering the effects. Don't see me. Don't notice me. I'm not here.

This desire for invisibility was reflected in her clothes. Strangers, if they noticed her at all, would get the impression that Sigrún was going out of her way to be as dowdy as possible. You'd have thought she was Amish in those drab-coloured clothes that were too long and baggy to suit anyone. Her hair matched: long, frizzy and mousy. She had never owned any mascara or lipstick, and although he would be the last to admit it, he spent more time in front of the mirror than she did.

He knew why. So he let her creep along the walls without commenting on the fact. That was her method; his was the exact opposite. The tunnel rings now making his earlobes ache with the cold were a sign of that. 'How long have we been hanging around here anyway?'

'Not that long.' Sigrún peered round the corner of the large, white church. 'They must be about to leave.' She leant against the wall again but he couldn't follow her example; the concrete was too chilly. In her intact left hand she was holding a bunch of flowers they had bought at a supermarket before catching the bus to Fossvogur. The flowers were a bit limp and as uninspiring as you'd expect from such a cheap bunch. It didn't matter: bouquets from the florist's cost three times as much and it would be ridiculous to waste all that money on a dead person. It was the thought that counted. Sigrún stole another look round the corner. 'As soon as they've gone we can head over.'

Þröstur bit back a protest. The annual visit to the grave was important to his sister, though personally he thought it a waste of time. The dead were dead, and wouldn't be any less dead however many people flocked to their graves. But it wasn't often that she asked him a favour, so to refuse would be out of the question. He had nothing better to do, anyway. He never did. He had been unemployed for the last six months and although he was getting a bit bored, anything was better than spending one's days in meaningless drudgery. All his jobs to date had been boring, pointless and badly paid. He wasn't that much worse off on the dole, all things considered, and not having to get out of bed in the mornings was a big plus. He wasn't exactly rolling in it, though: the last job he'd had was part time and he hadn't realised that would reduce his entitlement to benefits when he lost it. But it was easy to be wise after the event, and the money just about covered the necessities, so it could be worse. Still, there was no denying it would be nice to be able to afford a proper pair of DMs. And a new jacket.

'I'm freezing my balls off here.' The instant he'd said it he regretted complaining. The look she gave him through the scruffy mane of hair blowing over her face was hurt and anxious. She was so desperately vulnerable. The slightest hint of criticism that most people wouldn't even notice could assume huge proportions in her eyes. He should have known better.

Thröstur hastily backtracked: 'Anyway, whatever. They must be leaving in a minute. How long can they hang about in this weather?' He noticed Sigrún relax slightly. Unfortunately, though, the couple were as well prepared for the weather as she was: the woman in a shiny, metallic-coloured down jacket with a leather collar; the man dressed just as warmly, if not as colourfully. What a bugger. They could lie down and take a nap on the gravestone if they felt like it without suffering any ill effects. In which case he would die of cold out here and end up with a stone of his own. Flippant though the thought was, it sent a strange shudder through him. It must be the effect of the cemetery. Though he was only twenty-four and unlikely to die any time soon, it was an unsettling thought that one day there would be a headstone with his name on it.

The realisation that Sigrún would be the only person to visit his grave just made the idea even bleaker. Their mother was unlikely to have the time. She worked flat out and when she did come home she mostly shut herself away in her room, completely knackered. That wasn't going to change any time soon. She was hopeless – in his opinion, not Sigrún's. His sister loved their mother as a child should, whereas he could never forgive her. Sigrún argued that there was nothing to forgive. In her opinion, their mother couldn't have acted any differently. She was a victim of circumstance. Well, Thröstur had no sympathy for her kind of victim; he kept it for the real ones, like him and his sister.

He didn't hate his mother, though he didn't love her. For years he had felt nothing but anger, but as time wore on and their horrific past grew more remote, he found himself pitying her. It was the nearest he came to affection.

You couldn't help feeling sorry for her when her life was so shit. It didn't even matter that her present wretched existence was self-imposed. It was her own choice to isolate herself and work herself to death in a futile attempt to atone for what could never be undone. She didn't have the guts to set fire to herself, perform hara-kiri, or flog herself with a whip like people in other cultures. Her penance was to turn herself into a human doormat. And she dragged him and his sister down with her, though perhaps she didn't realise it. She probably thought she was sacrificing herself for them and settling her debts that way. But that couldn't have been further from the truth.

He was hit by the craving for nicotine again as he contemplated their miserable, rootless existence. Everyone else seemed to have some kind of security in their lives, some kind of anchor, but not him and Sigrún. After their so-called father had been put away, they had moved house every year for the next five years. Every time people worked out who they were, they had to pack their bags. The moment the other staff where their mother worked started whispering, she would change jobs, moving from one low-paid occupation to the next. So it had gone on until she was hired by a fish factory and discovered that the foreign women who worked with her on the conveyor belt hadn't a clue about her background. Once she'd made it clear that she wasn't after their friendship, they had left her in peace.

As her wages from the fish factory weren't sufficient to support the three of them, she cleaned offices in the evenings after everyone else had gone home. The empty buildings offered another kind of respite from the glances and whispering, and she seemed content enough with this, though her chronic fatigue was clear to see in her haggard face and drooping shoulders. When Thröstur quit school after year ten and started work, she could have taken it a bit easier, but didn't, telling him to put his wages in a savings account for the future instead. Ever the martyr. He had jumped at her offer but squandered his money as quickly as he earned it.

Although Sigrún did well at school, she had also left after completing her compulsory education and initially joined their mother at the fish factory, where she was miserable. Hampered by her two missing fingers, she couldn't keep up and was forever being told off, though she worked as hard as she possibly could. Yet, typically, she had lasted a whole year before finally handing in her notice.

Next she took a job as a filing clerk at the insurance company where she still worked now, happily tucked away in a back office, alone among the papers that needed archiving. She performed her job so well that she had made herself indispensable, though her wages didn't reflect the fact. But then she had never requested a pay rise or made any other demands. What she did with her money was a mystery. She didn't seem to spend anything. Presumably she paid it into a savings account, as their mother had advised Thröstur to do, which meant she must have built up quite a tidy sum by now. He was always urging her to treat herself and stop this ridiculous penny-pinching, but she just looked shamefaced when he asked what the hell she was saving up for. Perhaps she dreamt of a round-the-world trip, of travelling as far from her roots as humanly possible. He could understand that.

Thröstur stamped his feet in a vain attempt to get the circulation back in his toes.

'Shh! I think they're coming. Shall I take a look?' Sigrún pulled the hood away from one ear and listened. Once he had stopped his stamping, Thröstur could hear the crunching of snow and the faint echo of a conversation. It must be them. At last. With any luck they would hurry to their cars and take themselves off. They were unlikely to stand around having a long chat.

When he and Sigrún had arrived, one of the cars had already been parked there and the other was just pulling in. The drivers had got out, nodded to each other – rather coldly, it seemed – and briefly shaken hands, after shifting their flowers from their right to their left arms. Their bouquets were large and cumbersome, unlike the pathetic bunch Sigrún was holding. Neither the woman nor the man had so much as glanced in their direction, and Thröstur and Sigrún had edged into the shelter of the church so as not to attract their attention.

Thröstur would hardly describe himself as sentimental but even he couldn't help reflecting on the sad fate of the parents' relationship. The first time he and Sigrún had visited the grave, the couple had arrived in the same car and held each other tight as they walked into the cemetery. He didn't even like to think about the funeral, at which the parents had seemed, if anything, even closer. As they followed the small white coffin, looking absolutely shattered, their faces had taken on identical expressions of horror when they spotted Thröstur, Sigrún and their mother. The three of them had sneaked into a back pew, where their mother had thought they could pass unnoticed.

Every single head in the congregation had turned in their direction when the couple stopped dead, staring at them, transfixed. That moment had felt like a lifetime. Then the woman had slumped against her husband, her eyes smudged black from the tears that kept pouring down her cheeks. Her husband's face was red and angry. The wet eyes of the other mourners stared unwaveringly at them. The intruders' terror had been plain to all when the mother of the little girl in the coffin began to howl, and all eyes had followed them through the crowd as they forced their way out, fleeing that grief-stricken keening.

Thröstur pushed away the memory.

It did nothing but stir up grief and anger. Why wasn't it possible to rewind life and change the past? If only he and his mother had been home that day, he wouldn't be stuck with this unbearable memory now, not to mention the consequences of it.

As with so many things, he held his mother responsible for the incident at the funeral. He and Sigrún had only been kids, but she should have known better. It hadn't occurred to him that the girl's parents would blame them, but an adult should have foreseen it. When Sigrún insisted on going, their mother should have refused, but as usual she had caved in at once. There wasn't a hint of steel in her nature, as if somewhere along the way her entire backbone had been extracted in one piece. He was quite different. Although what happened at the funeral was unspeakably awful, it did have one positive result. That night, as he lay in bed listening to his sister's muffled weeping, Thröstur had decided that from then on he would stand up for himself and whenever he encountered an injustice he would tackle it head-on. No one had any time for martyrs. Not until hundreds of years had passed, and even then people's admiration was lukewarm.

Without warning the wind dropped and the couple's emotionless farewells carried clearly to where Thröstur and Sigrún were standing. He snatched a glance round the corner and saw them clasp hands briefly, apparently without meeting each other's eye. They climbed into their separate cars and drove away. He saw the rear lights through the cloud of exhaust fumes as they slowed down, turned right and vanished. The prospect of finally being able to move warmed Thröstur up a little. 'Come on. They've gone.'

Sigrún had to check for herself before she could be persuaded to venture round the corner, and kept glancing behind her as they walked into the cemetery, as if expecting the couple to come back. They might have forgotten something by the grave. Thröstur said nothing, though her neurotic behaviour annoyed him. Why did she always have to act like that? But he knew there was no point criticising her; her nerves would only become worse if he showed that he'd noticed.

They knew the way by heart, having trodden this same path for the last eleven years. The first time a year after the girl died, then every year since on her birthday. Like reluctant party guests. She would have been twenty this year, if she'd lived. On the way here this fact had suddenly dawned on Sigrún; she had abruptly turned to him and said the number aloud. Much louder than was normal for her; loud enough for the only other passenger on the bus to look round and stare at her in surprise. She had flushed and waited for the old lady to turn away again before explaining. She hadn't remembered that it was a milestone birthday or she would have invested in a more expensive bunch of flowers. She had been seized by an urge to go back and buy a different bouquet, but Thröstur, who was enjoying the heating on the bus, had managed to dissuade her, idiot that he was, with the result that they had arrived at the same time as the parents and he had almost died of exposure. He'd argued that they had already forked out for flowers and bus tickets – it was quite unnecessary to make a fuss about the imaginary twentieth birthday of someone who was dead. Perhaps that explained Sigrún's jumpiness now, though it wasn't always easy to guess how her mind worked.

She stationed herself at the foot of the grave and stood there in silence, her eyes lowered. After a while, she lifted her chin from her chest and laid down the flowers, which looked small and cheap next to the two large bouquets propped against the headstone. Thröstur had to look away: the tatty little thing was somehow symbolic of him and Sigrún.

Unlike his sister, he followed no fixed routine on these annual visits but wandered around, reading the inscriptions on nearby graves, lighting a cigarette or kicking up snow. Anything to occupy himself while Sigrún was meditating, or whatever she was doing. He had never been able to bring himself to ask what she was thinking about.

This time he stood a little way off, silent and unmoving like her. Thinking how alone they were and how everyone had failed them. Always. Wondering how Sigrún would react when she learnt that their father was out. How best to break the news to her so she didn't overhear it at work or bump into the bastard in the street. How to stop him forcing himself back into their lives. Which brought him back full circle to the thought that had haunted him ever since he could remember: no one would ever help them.

It was up to him to protect his sister. And he wasn't going to let her down.

Chapter 11

The underground car park was deserted, in stark contrast to that morning when only a few spaces had been free, and then of course only the most inconvenient ones. Kolbeinn, late for work due to heavy traffic on the way in from Hafnarfjördur, had been forced to park right up against a pillar. It had required extraordinary skill to reverse in, but then he'd become pretty adept at this since acquiring his expensive new car. If the weather had been better, he would have parked outside; he was always a little uneasy about leaving his pride and joy packed in tight down here. Many of the other garage users drove around in beaten-up old wrecks and a small scratch would be neither here nor there to them. He couldn't bear the thought, though he no longer went so far as to note down the licence plates of the cars parked either side of him, in case he found a dent in his paintwork at the end of the day. He had abandoned the habit after one of his colleagues had caught him at it, and looked at him askance. Later that day Kolbeinn had come across the man by the coffee machine, sniggering about the incident with his cronies. Kolbeinn couldn't abide being laughed at. It was even worse than the fear of scratches on his smart new car.

His footsteps echoed and a sound of dripping came from one of the pipes that ran along the ceiling. Apart from that there was silence. The ceiling lights flickered into life one after the other as he walked past the sensors, except where the bulbs had gone. He could have sworn more of them had been working this morning.

Six months ago the caretaker's hours had been reduced to part time as a cost-cutting measure and the building was beginning to suffer the effects, especially in the areas where cleaning was considered low priority. The underground car park was unquestionably one of these. The accountants clearly hadn't factored in the lighting deficiencies, pervading smell of damp and piles of rubbish collecting in every corner. But it didn't occur to Kolbeinn to comment on this. During his almost fourteen years at the firm he had learnt that although the management encouraged people to speak out, in practice those who did complain seldom lasted long. For those seeking promotion, flattery was a far better policy. Certainly, this tactic had facilitated his own rise through the ranks, despite the fact he had no formal qualifications in accountancy or law. The CEO had even complimented him recently, saying that when he'd hired him on the recommendation of an old friend he had been a little doubtful of Kolbeinn's fitness for the job, but that he had been proved quite wrong. Pity the CEO was approaching retirement. There was no guarantee that his younger successor would be as appreciative of Kolbeinn's talents. And what would happen to him if there was a shake-up in the organisation?

The lights stopped coming on as Kolbeinn approached the far end of the car park and he shook his head disapprovingly. But when he peered up, he saw that the fluorescent tubes had been smashed. He halted and listened. The dripping was now so continuous it was almost like rain. As he stood there straining his ears, he thought he heard a faint scraping noise coming from the direction of his car – assuming it was still there. He didn't like the look of this. Who but thieves would have any reason to smash the bulbs? There was no other source of light in the windowless car park and darkness would provide the perfect cover. If he was right, his car was bound to be the target. It was the only desirable vehicle in here. Senior management parked in marked spaces near the entrance or beside the lifts.

And anyway they invariably went home early. But now the place was as deserted as a tomb.

What if the thieves were still down here? What if he interrupted them in the act of breaking into his car? Would they go for him? The answer was obvious: yes, of course they would. They would hardly just walk away as if nothing had happened. *Whoops, sorry.* Again there was a sound of scraping. Kolbeinn coughed, ridiculously loudly, in the hope of scaring any potential thieves. It would be best if they fled. He wouldn't give chase, and they were bound to be caught later. If they paused in their flight to beat him up, he could direct their attention to the CCTV and hope that would deter them. Kolbeinn coughed again, even louder. He could have sworn the scraping noise grew louder too. He was about to cough a third time when it dawned on him that the thieves must already be aware of his presence. They could hardly have failed to notice the lights coming on as he entered the car park.

Are you a man or a mouse? Kolbeinn puffed out his cheeks and exhaled slowly. He had no choice but to walk over to the car. There was no security guard in the lobby any longer – another result of the economy drive. The caretaker would have gone home hours ago, and Kolbeinn would never dream of asking one of the few remaining people in the building to accompany him to his car. That would really give them something to snigger about. If he turned up with two black eyes and a broken nose after an encounter with thieves, he would at least earn their respect.

Kolbeinn started walking again. His heart was thudding in a way that could hardly be good for him but in spite of that he quickened his pace. Best get it over with. The bonnet came into view, jutting out from behind the damned pillar that provided the perfect hiding place for thieves – if there were any. His heart was battering against his ribs now, as if a sparrow were trapped in his chest, fighting for its life. Of course there was someone, maybe more than one person, lurking there in the dark. Something must be making that noise. The closer he got to the car, the louder the scraping became, combined now with a metallic squeaking and what sounded like mumbling. It occurred to him that the thieves might be murmuring to each other, plotting how to ambush him. But the closer he got, the less it sounded like human voices, and more like an animal. Perhaps, after all that, the thieves were only mice or rats.

Nobody leapt out at him during those final few steps to the car, nor when his trembling fingers pressed the remote control to unlock it. Shaking with trepidation, he eased himself cautiously round the bonnet and was relieved to find nobody on the other side. But he wasn't out of danger yet, so giving himself no time to relax, he hurried to the driver's door. Before sliding behind the wheel and groping for the button to lock the doors, he hastily scanned behind the car to make sure no one was lying in ambush there. Immediately behind the boot was a waist-high concrete wall separating the parking space from the ramp to the lower level. The thieves could easily be hiding behind it, which seemed only too likely since the scraping, squeaking and mumbling were coming from there. The wall was topped by a handrail of steel bars, which the criminals would have to clamber over before they could get their hands on Kolbeinn, but the thought wasn't much comfort. He jumped into the driver's seat. The click of the electronic locks was one of the most welcome sounds he had ever heard. Without giving himself time to enjoy it, he inserted the key in the ignition. Not until the satisfying throb of the engine and the blast from the radio drowned out the muffled sounds did Kolbeinn allow himself to breathe easier.

For once he didn't bother to take care as he drove out of the space, perhaps because the rattling behind him seemed to grow louder as soon as he moved off. Instinctively, Kolbeinn stamped on the accelerator, ignoring the risks of driving too fast in an underground garage. In a moment he would be out in the open air and on his way home.

But his joy was short-lived. There was a violent impact, as if the car had been struck from behind at full speed, which was impossible because he was barely clear of the space. He was hurled forwards, only prevented from headbutting the windscreen by the seatbelt locking. Kolbeinn automatically braked, though the car was behaving oddly and hardly making any headway.

Ready for anything, he checked the mirror, then, after a moment, twisted round to peer through the rear windscreen in an attempt to work out what exactly he was looking at.

Erla had Huldar's full sympathy, though he didn't say so. Her nerves were so frayed that there was no telling what might set her off. It seemed nothing was going to go smoothly. The media had got wind of an incident and photographers were already laying siege, their camera flashes hurting his eyes every time the door opened. To make matters worse, the police were still waiting for the portable floodlights as the section of the underground garage they most urgently needed to examine lay in semi-darkness. The ceiling lights had been smashed and no one was in any doubt that this was connected to what had happened there.

Huldar leant against the wall and lit a cigarette. Like most smokers, he classified garages as outdoor areas. He had given up trying to conceal that he had lapsed; the smell had already given him away and anyway none of his colleagues could care less about his health. He took the first drag, then blew out a stream of smoke in the direction of the closed exit. Nobody was likely to object as they had more than enough to occupy them. Besides, he had an excuse ready – if he set foot outside he would be mobbed by the press and members of the public, who had gathered in the hope of witnessing some excitement. Strange how people were so drawn to horror and misfortune. He had a feeling they would quickly lose their enthusiasm if they were exposed to a scene like this one. He filled his lungs with smoke again. For once it was a beautiful, windless evening, just when a storm would have come in handy. Bad weather deterred both photographers and onlookers from hanging around crime scenes.

In a perfect world he would be sitting at home right now, beer in hand, watching the match. But he didn't really mind too much about missing it; there were plenty of other matches and these days pretty much all his evenings were free. To be at work outside office hours was the exception now, rather than the rule. He had been called out this evening because he was one of the few who hadn't done any overtime for months. Erla had told him as much, so he wouldn't start thinking he was back in favour. Out of the corner of his eye he spotted Erla stalking towards him, her face grim. He hastily took another puff before stubbing out the cigarette, although he'd only smoked it halfway down. It would give her less reason to nag.

'Isn't smoking banned down here?' Erla glanced round irritably in search of signs but, although there were plenty, they were all concerned with directing people to the exit or the lifts.

Huldar could tell this wasn't about smoking. Ignoring her comment, he asked instead: 'How's it going? Any sign of Forensics yet?'

Erla sighed and leant against the wall beside him. 'On their way, apparently.' She shook her head. 'What a bloody mess. The doctor's refusing to turn up until the sodding lighting's in place; the caretaker's being a pain in the arse and saying he's not paid to come in, and that Kolbeinn Ragnarsson's one of the biggest twats I've ever encountered.'

'Oh?' Huldar glanced at the man, who was standing looking over the shoulder of the police officer taking down his statement. The man's

attention was directed at something towards the rear of the garage –
his car, probably. 'Isn't he just in shock?'

'Not so much shocked as worried about whether his insurance
will cover the damage to his car. The back axle was almost torn off.'

'I'm not surprised. It must have been a hell of a yank.' A chain had
been looped around the axle and the other end wound around the
waist of the dead man lying in a heap in the parking space. They were
working on the assumption that the victim had been on the other side
of the concrete partition and that when Kolbeinn drove off, the man
had been flung into the air, only to jam against the steel bars on top
of the wall. Only for a moment, though. The force had been so great
that the victim had been bent double and dragged through. Huldar,
who had undertaken the job of measuring the gap between the bars,
felt sick when it proved to be no more than thirty centimetres wide.
He hoped the man had been dead at that point, but doubted it. The
gag indicated that the perpetrator had wanted to make sure he couldn't
alert anyone to his plight. It wouldn't have been necessary if the man
had already been dead. Dead men don't make a lot of noise.

'Any chance it could have been suicide?' Erla's tone made it clear
that she knew this was wishful thinking.

'I think the answer to that has to be no. There are countless easier
methods if you want to top yourself. Almost anything would be better
than this.' Huldar sucked air through his front teeth and clicked his
tongue. He would rather not have to think about it, but felt obliged
to reply since Erla was actually talking to him for once. The folded
corpse was one of the nastier sights he had ever had the misfortune
to see. Thank God the man's face was hidden. 'Can you imagine what
the waiting must have been like? Nobody would do that to himself. I
bet the poor guy would have given anything to suffocate while he was
waiting.'

'Maybe. For his sake I hope he didn't know what was coming. But I have the feeling that whoever did this would have gone out of their way to tell him. This stinks of sadism. There are plenty of simpler ways to kill someone, so the intention must have been to make him suffer. Let's hope the post-mortem will clarify things.' Erla reached in her pocket for her phone and checked the time. 'Where the fuck is everyone?'

Huldar wondered idly how many of her questions were purely rhetorical. Quite a large number, probably. Erla was perfectly aware that he couldn't answer this. 'The first thing I checked was whether the man had both his hands,' he said. 'This murder's so grotesque that it would have fitted with the hot-tub incident. I don't know if I was relieved or disappointed when I saw he still had at least one of them. My gut feeling is that the two cases are connected. They're both equally sick. And I don't like the idea of there being two psychopaths on the loose. What do you think?'

'No idea. Perhaps things'll be clearer once the pathologist and Forensics get their arses over here and we can get an ID on the poor guy. Hopefully he'll have a wallet or a credit card or something. It's a pity the body's lying like that so we can't get at it to check.' Erla sighed so heavily it was almost a groan. Then, pushing herself away from the wall, she walked back to the scene without another word.

Huldar stood there for a moment, wondering if he should relight his half-smoked cigarette, but in the end he followed Erla, fighting back a powerful sense of reluctance. This had nothing to do with her but with the horrific vision that lay folded up like a napkin, tied to the car with a heavy chain. He could hardly bear to look at it.

The situation didn't improve when Forensics finally put in an appearance and set up the floodlights. In that unsparing glare it was hard to stop oneself looking away. Only when the doctor arrived did Huldar steel himself to watch. He instantly regretted it because the doctor asked him to help straighten out the man – or 'unfold him', as he put it. With gloved hands, they each took hold of one side of the torso lying forward over the legs and gently unbent him to lie flat. Even through the man's clothing, Huldar could feel the broken ribs, crushed vertebrae and mangled flesh, as distinctly as if the body were naked and his own hands were bare. He fought down his nausea and had almost succeeded in mastering it when the doctor removed the gag and padding from the man's mouth.

Huldar stood up and tilted his head sideways to get a better look at the face. 'Erla. Look!'

Erla stared down thoughtfully at the dead man. 'There's our proof. The cases are linked.' Her anxiety was obvious. 'Shit. Shit. Shit. Fuck. Fucking shit.' She ran her fingers through her hair. 'What a total cock-up.'

Huldar was glad he wasn't in her shoes. This wasn't going to go down too well with the top brass, to put it mildly. The sole witness in the case of the severed hands was dead. Lying on the concrete floor of the underground garage was Benedikt Toft, retired prosecutor and owner of the house where the hands had been found. He sure as hell wouldn't be coming in for interview now.

Chapter 12

The argument was still ringing in Huldar's ears, though the raised voices had fallen silent some time ago. All activity on the floor had ceased as every word, every insult and expletive carried clearly through the glass wall of Erla's office. The row had ended as badly as it had begun, with the two senior officers storming out, slamming the door and leaving Erla sitting there alone. Huldar wasn't near enough to see her face but guessed she would want to give her fiery cheeks time to fade before she emerged to face her team.

Nobody had said a word yet. Most of the detectives were pretending to work, while darting furtive glances in the direction of the office. No doubt many of them expected her to bury her head on the desk and burst into tears, but Huldar knew her better than that. She would rather throw herself out of the narrow window and plummet four storeys to the ground than betray the slightest hint of weakness.

'Do you think she'll be sacked?' Huldar looked up to see Gudlaugur peeping over his computer screen.

'No.' Huldar leant back, glad of a chance to nip that idea in the bud, at least for one member of the team. 'It's often like this when an inquiry's not progressing as well as it should. The guys upstairs get jittery and come down here to take it out on somebody. They'll be bawling out us foot soldiers next.'

'Oh.' Gudlaugur clearly didn't relish the prospect.

'It could be a lot worse.' Huldar stood up, looking across at Erla's office. Without another word to Gudlaugur, he went over. Someone had to take the lead or an impasse would develop, with Erla too proud to break the ice and the others too scared to speak to her, or to each other for fear she would think they were talking about her behind her back.

Huldar tapped lightly, then opened the door without waiting for an answer. Sticking his head round, he encountered Erla's glare. Her voice, like her demeanour, was off-putting. 'What do you want?'

'Nothing really. Just to say don't let those bastards get you down. They've probably just received a similar bollocking from the next level up and needed to let off steam.' Huldar stepped inside and closed the door behind him. 'I'm here to offer myself as a punch-bag if you need one.'

Erla regarded him through narrowed eyes. 'And who are you going to kick? Your dog?'

'I don't have a dog. Gudlaugur will have to do.' Huldar's grin wasn't returned.

'No need to feel sorry for me. I can handle it.'

'I'm well aware of that, Erla. You know I am.' Huldar paused but Erla made no move to fill the silence, so he carried on. 'Regardless of what the top brass think, we both know that it was impossible to see this coming. Benedikt Toft was totally bewildered when the hands turned up – no one could have guessed that he had any connection to them.' Erla seemed a little less tense; her shoulders had relaxed slightly and her jaw no longer gave the impression that she was chewing gravel. 'Anyway, I didn't come here just to talk about that crap. I wanted to know if we're making any headway and if there's anything I can do. I've got as far as I can with that list.' He had offered to run through the names of all the people they could find who were connected in one way or another to the dead man, to check if they were still alive and in possession of both their hands. He hadn't managed to reach everyone, but there was no point ringing back the remaining people yet. The plan was to send Gudlaugur round to their houses to peer through their letterboxes to try and work out if they were away.

When Erla spoke again she sounded more like her normal self – still gruff and humourless, but not as bad as when he had first walked in. 'Should we maybe expand the list? It's got to be someone he knew. It stands to reason.'

Huldar shrugged. 'Unless Benedikt spotted the culprit putting the hands in the tub.' The old man hadn't admitted to that when questioned. According to Erla, the statement he gave that evening had sounded convincing. He'd insisted that he hadn't noticed anything out of the ordinary, but of course the perpetrator couldn't know that. 'Say he was telling the truth when he swore he hadn't seen anything – is it possible he could have witnessed something without realising it? A car outside, for example? Perhaps the perpetrator decided to dispose of a potential witness because he didn't want to take any chances.'

'Maybe. But the method of killing's weirdly elaborate in that case. Wouldn't it have been simpler to break into Benedikt's house and stab him or batter him to death? This garage business carried a huge risk of being caught. It would be bloody stupid to kill the man like that unless the intention was to make him suffer.' Erla sighed. 'Then there's the letter I got originally, tipping us off about something of interest in Benedikt's garden. The only way I can read it is that the person who put the hands there didn't trust Benedikt to notify the police when he found them. What other reason could there have been? The implication being that Benedikt had a guilty conscience. Any normal citizen would ring us straight away if they found a pair of sawn-off hands in their hot tub. So he must have had an idea who put them in there, despite his show of being all shocked and innocent.

But of course that's just a theory, like everything else in this bloody case.'

Like everyone involved in the inquiry, Huldar had given a lot of thought to the method of killing. His only conclusion was that the case was utterly bizarre. They were waiting impatiently for the results of the post-mortem, though Huldar had no hope of being among the first to see them. 'Have you been sent the CCTV footage from the garage yet?'

Erla snorted. 'There won't be any. An unbelievable fucking balls-up.'

'Oh?' Two CCTV cameras had been visible in the garage, though neither was pointing directly at Kolbeinn's car. One covered the entrance, the other the area in front of the spaces where Kolbeinn had parked. Assuming the killer hadn't popped up out of the sewers, it would have been impossible to reach the car without being caught on film. Huldar assumed the killer had hidden his face, but his image would nevertheless give an idea of his age and build. The video might also show how he had entered the garage. The consensus was that he must have driven in, since how else could he have brought the victim there? And while they couldn't rule out the possibility that he had tricked the man into entering the garage, it was difficult to imagine how. Huldar had assumed the CCTV footage would answer that question once and for all. But if there was a problem with the recordings, the prospects looked bleak: they would have a job on their hands if they had to question everyone who had used the car park that day and might conceivably have spotted the killer. 'Weren't the cameras hooked up?' He knew it wasn't that paint had been sprayed over the lenses as he had checked them himself and been profoundly relieved to see that the glass was clean.

'They were hooked up all right. But the computer that was supposed to store the recordings broke down months ago and, according to the caretaker, the building committee decided there was no need to replace it as the cameras were a good enough deterrent by themselves.' Erla scowled in disgust. 'Part of the same cost-cutting drive that made them reduce the caretaker's hours to part time.'

Huldar tipped his head back and closed his eyes. Everything seemed to be conspiring against them. 'Are we any clearer about when Benedikt went missing? Or where he was snatched from?'

Erla shook her head. 'No. We're going over his house with a fine-tooth comb but haven't turned up anything useful yet apart from his mobile phone. It hadn't been used for two days, but no one knows how significant that is. The old man was a retired widower and his son lives abroad with his wife and children. The log of his previous usage makes it very clear that he rarely made or received any calls. And we haven't managed to track down anyone who can tell us his movements in the twenty-four hours preceding the murder. The one piece of evidence we do have is that the morning papers were in the living room, which suggests he was at home on the morning of the murder.' She gave a loud groan, then buried her face in her hands and rubbed it vigorously. 'This is one big fucking mess. The analysis of the chain and gag had better produce some fingerprints. If not, everything's against us. Everything. Nobody remembers selling or hiring out a chainsaw recently, so the next stage is to test all the chainsaws in the country in search of blood from the hands. Just the work of establishing who owns a chainsaw and where they're all kept is enough to tie up the entire team for days.'

'What about Kolbeinn? The owner of the car. What emerged from his interview?'

'Nothing.' Erla snorted dismissively again. 'He says he hasn't a clue why his car was targeted; he'd never seen the victim before and didn't recognise the name. We still haven't managed to uncover any connection between them.' Erla rooted around among the papers that littered her desk. 'I've got his statement here somewhere. It's almost exactly like Benedikt's. He knows nothing and can't begin to understand why this should have happened to him. Which is worrying, given what happened to the old man.'

'Maybe there isn't a connection. His car was parked at the back of the garage and it's a very powerful model. If I'd been planning something like that, I'd probably have chosen it. Anyway, the perpetrator must have waited for most of the cars to leave before setting the whole thing up. The question is how long he waited. Are we any clearer about when he might have arrived?'

Erla shook her head. 'No. I'm hoping the post-mortem will give us a time frame. It must be possible to tell from the wounds on the victim's hands and feet how long he was tied up.'

'The report's due any minute, isn't it?' Huldar hoped this unusually long conversation was a sign that they were back to being confidantes, that he would finally be accepted as a fully paid-up member of CID again. He'd been out in the cold long enough. 'Perhaps you'll give me a heads-up about what it contains?'

Erla frowned slightly. 'We'll see.'

Huldar judged that now would be a good time to make his exit. The conversation could only go downhill from here. 'I'm going to grab a coffee. You coming?' He threw her this offering in the hope she would accept: the moment she emerged from her office, the bollocking she had received would begin to fade from the memories of her underlings. It would be a difficult step but she had to take it sooner or later. However low his own standing with the team, it would be better if she went with him, if only so she could concentrate on what he was saying and ignore the rest of the office.

'No, thanks. I need to get on with preparing for the progress meeting later.'

'No problem.' Huldar watched her turn back to the documents on her desk. He added in parting: 'We'll catch him, Erla. It's only a matter of time before we stumble across a lead.' He meant it; more often than not this was how cases were solved. In conventional killings, this usually happened as soon as the police arrived, since few Icelandic murderers made any attempt to cover their tracks. Some were still at the scene with the murder weapon in their hand. However different this case was shaping up to be, Huldar didn't doubt that they would eventually chance on the solution.

Gudlaugur dropped into his chair. He was red in the face, from the cold this time rather than embarrassment. 'Nothing. There's no one left on the list.'

Huldar shifted so he could see the young man's face. 'Were they all in?'

'Three answered the door when I knocked and seem to have been too slow to answer the phone when you rang. One turned out to be in hospital, according to the woman in the flat next door, and the last one's at sea. His wife was home.'

Huldar rolled his chair back to his place. His eye happened to fall on the photocopies of the letters from the time capsule and his thoughts flew to Freyja. Grateful though he was to have a proper case to work on, he regretted not having an excuse to call her. Perhaps he would come across a child witness soon and she would have to conduct the interview. But it felt unrealistic. And he certainly wouldn't wish for any child to be involved in these horrors. Pulling the photocopies over, he read the threatening letter again. The garage murder would be solved eventually and after that he could return to the mystery of the time capsule, call Freyja in for a meeting and try to win her round. Who knows, it might actually work this time. She didn't seem to have started a new relationship, which was a definite plus.

'Why are you smiling?' Gudlaugur's head appeared over Huldar's monitor.

'No reason.' Huldar quickly rearranged his features. 'What are the names of the two men you still need to confirm are alive and well?'

The head vanished, then reappeared. Gudlaugur read from a scrap of paper. 'Ævar Einarsson and Haraldur Jóhann Gudnason. Why do you ask?'

'No particular reason.' Huldar didn't feel like explaining, and in any case neither name fitted the initials on Thröstur's hit-list. It had occurred to him that there could be a connection. Benedikt Toft's initials had got him thinking: BT cropped up in the letter, but that could be pure coincidence. He hadn't raised the matter with Erla for fear of being laughed at, especially if he added that K could stand for Kolbeinn and JJ for Jón Jónsson. No one was taking the time capsule investigation seriously, and in the absence of a link between Thröstur and the murder victim, he would have an uphill struggle persuading the team. He was sceptical enough himself. But hopelessly far-fetched though the idea was, he couldn't get Thröstur out of his head, or the way he had freaked out when he realised why they had come round to see him.

As Erla hadn't given him any new assignment yet and it was still half an hour until the team briefing, Huldar decided to take a quick look at Thröstur's father.

Reading about the murder of Vaka Orradóttir left a bad taste in his mouth. The man, if you could call him a man, had raped the little girl in his daughter's bed, then smothered her with a pillow. He had been unable to provide any explanation except that he had been too drunk to know what he was doing. His daughter Sigrún, who was in the same class at school as the murdered girl, had shut herself in a cupboard where she was discovered by the police when they turned up. Despite all their attempts, they had failed to extract a coherent account from her. It was thought that she hadn't directly witnessed the rape or murder but had hidden in the cupboard either before it occurred or as soon as it became clear what was going to happen. The psychologist who treated Sigrún believed she would open up eventually but that she was so afraid of her father it was unlikely to happen before the case went to court. In contrast, her brother Thröstur, who was twelve years old at the time, had not been backward about giving his side of the story, though he had been at school when the tragedy happened. He had come home, gone straight to his room and shut himself in, completely unaware that there was a little girl lying dead in the room next door. Around suppertime, feeling hungry, he had gone downstairs to the kitchen, poured himself some Cheerios and eaten them alone, which wasn't unusual. His mother was a cleaner and receptionist at an old people's home; her shifts began at midday and finished at eight in the evening. Since she went to work by bus, she was never home before nine. His father hadn't been about, which, according to Thröstur, wasn't unusual either. He was always drunk, either comatose on the sofa in the living room or hunched, shaking, over an overflowing ashtray in the kitchen.

His mother Agnes had returned home around nine, unusually tired, or so she claimed, as she was coming down with a cold. A medical examination carried out two days later could neither confirm nor refute this claim since by then her temperature had been normal and she wasn't displaying any symptoms. In her statement she said that her husband Jón had been awake downstairs when she arrived home.

By then Vaka had been dead in their daughter's room for over five hours and rigor mortis would have been setting in. He stank of spirits and seemed in an unusually foul temper, which she understood was because she hadn't bought him any alcohol, though she had never promised to do that – as if this detail had been of any relevance. Her husband had reacted furiously and hit her so hard that she had fallen, banging her head on the wall and almost losing consciousness. After that he had stormed out, leaving her on the floor. The same medical examination that had been unable to confirm her cold had shown that the woman had a large swelling on her right temple and a bruise extending from her left cheek down to her jaw, consistent with her statement. After he had gone, the woman had struggled to her feet and looked into the children's rooms. Her daughter appeared to be lying asleep under her duvet, so she had shut the door, then exchanged a few words with her son. After that she had gone to bed and hadn't woken up until the police arrived at eight the following morning. Thröstur had called them after finding Vaka's body. He had gone to wake Sigrún and found her lying with a pillow over her face. When he removed it, he discovered that the girl underneath was a stranger. During the phone call, the boy didn't seem to have grasped that she was dead; he said there was a sick girl lying in his sister's bed and he couldn't wake her up. She felt cold and strange to the touch, and although she was asleep her eyes were open. Sigrún was nowhere to be seen.

The photographs from the scene were sickening. They showed the girl lying among torn, dirty bedclothes in a messy, shabbily furnished room. In the pictures taken before the police touched anything, the covers were pulled up to her neck. She was gaping up at the ceiling with the glazed, bloodshot eyes typical of asphyxiation victims. Her light brown hair was spread out like rays around her head, as if it had been arranged with a hairbrush. Her lips were blue, and at the corner of her mouth there was a small white feather from the pillow that had been used to suffocate her. The pillow lay beside her head, though according to the brother it had been over her face when he found her, so she couldn't be seen from the doorway, which corroborated the mother's story.

The photos taken after the duvet had been removed were a lot more disturbing and Huldar shifted inadvertently backwards in his chair. The little girl had been stripped below the waist: her trousers were hanging inside out from one ankle, along with her colourful childish knickers. The girl's legs were splayed and between them was a dark patch of dried blood. It looked to Huldar as if there were other, older stains of the same kind on the sheet, which indicated strongly that Sigrún had also been abused by her brute of a father. Huldar recalled Freyja's comment that Vaka was unlikely to have been Jón's first and only victim. From the case file it was apparent that attempts had been made to question Thröstur and Sigrún on this very subject, but neither would respond. Their reluctance was attributed to fear of their father.

Huldar closed the files on the investigation, and turned to the records of the trial, but these supplied no new information. Jón had been sentenced to sixteen years in prison at the district court and his sentence had been confirmed by the Supreme Court. Nothing unexpected about that. But Huldar's search turned up the record of another, older court case. On that occasion the man had been acquitted. Neither the details nor the grounds for his acquittal were recorded. The only information provided was that a charge had been brought for sexual abuse of a minor and that the trial had been held behind closed doors. Huldar searched in the police filing system but could find no record of the investigation leading to the charge. He knew little about court cases tried in private, so couldn't tell if the summing-up was unusually brief. It was all very puzzling and he returned to the uninformative verdict in case he could read between the lines.

In the event he didn't need to. His eye fell on the name of the prosecutor and he leapt to his feet: Benedikt Toft, the man who had died in the underground garage.

Chapter 13

Smoke was rising from the large barbecue in the Family Park and a crowd of children were swarming around it. As Æsa drew near, the smell of grilled meat brought on her hunger pangs. She wasn't the only one: on her way through the zoo she had seen the animals standing pressed against their fences, sniffing the air.

The path offered a good view of the throng and she scanned it for Karlotta and Dadi. Everywhere she looked there were small heads in colourful bobble hats. The celebration of the nursery's anniversary with a barbecue at the Reykjavík Family Park and Zoo had generated huge excitement, as she knew to her cost. That morning her children had taken forever to choose what they were going to wear. Karlotta had changed three times and Dadi twice. But so genuine was their delight over this simple outing that Æsa hadn't liked to chivvy them. After all, it wasn't as if all work would cease just because she was a little delayed.

The hubbub of screeching children's voices grew louder as she approached until Æsa felt as if she were in the middle of a seabird colony. Calling Karlotta and Dadi's names would be pointless over this racket, so she picked her way carefully through the crowd, scanning the faces. There was a constant flow of children back and forth, going to the barbecue empty-handed and coming away with their hands full. Her attention was distracted by trying to make sure they didn't accidentally smear ketchup or remoulade on her clothes. She made a beeline for the nearest teacher and managed to reach her without incident.

'Hi!' The young woman beamed so broadly that all her molars were on show. This was the standard greeting whenever Æsa went to pick up or drop off the kids; an effusive friendliness out of all proportion to the occasion.

'Hello.' Æsa tried to respond in kind. 'I've come to collect Karlotta and Dadi. You haven't seen them, have you?'

'Oh!' The over-the-top jollity was replaced by a look of equally exaggerated sorrow, with a comically down-turned mouth. 'They can't leave yet! The barbecue's only just started.'

'Oh no, they can have a hot dog. I'm not in a hurry. I just wanted to let them know I'm here.' The last part was almost drowned out by the shrieks of a child whose Frankfurter had fallen out of its bun. The young woman went to comfort the child, then guided him back to the barbecue. Æsa was left standing there, still none the wiser about Karlotta and Dadi's whereabouts. She turned in a circle but couldn't see them anywhere. She began to feel anxious, unable to get Thorvaldur's odd message out of her head, though he hadn't been in touch again and she hadn't tried to contact him since that evening. Desperate as she was to know more, she didn't want to give him the satisfaction of begging. It was his turn to ring back.

This showed in a nutshell how toxic their relationship had become. Even information that could affect the children's welfare mattered less than coming off best in their petty little war. Æsa cursed her own stupidity as she carefully elbowed her way out of the crowd to get a better view. Perhaps Karlotta and Dadi had found a bench or some rocks where they could eat sitting down. But she couldn't see them anywhere. Her anxiety was turning to dread when she spotted Beta, a playmate of Karlotta's, racing towards the barbecue from the toilets. Æsa gave a sigh of relief. Of course, they must have gone for a pee. Whenever one needed to go, you could be sure the other would be just behind.

'Beta!' Æsa called to the girl who waved a mittened hand as she hurried over to her. 'Is Karlotta in the toilets?'

Beta sniffed. Although there was no wind the day was chilly and the children's noses were running. 'No. She's gone.' The little girl sniffed again.

'Gone?' Æsa wanted to grab her by the shoulders and shake her. 'Gone where?'

'Away.' Beta smiled, clearly unaware of the impact this news was having.

'Away where?' The longing to shake the child grew stronger and Æsa had to thrust her hands in her pockets.

'Just away. She said they were going to see some puppies.'

'Puppies?' Æsa realised she was repeating every word the child said. At least it gave her time to think. 'Where are these puppies?'

'I don't know. I wasn't allowed to go.'

'What do you mean you weren't allowed to go?'

'Karlotta said so. The man only wanted them to see.' It seemed to be dawning on Beta that all was not well. Her eyes flickered from side to side, as if searching for an escape route.

Æsa made an effort to appear calm. It was a strain. 'Was the man working here at the zoo? Are the puppies here?'

'No.'

This ambiguous answer was her own fault for asking two questions at once. 'So the man doesn't work here at the zoo?'

'I don't know. I didn't see him. Only Karlotta did.' Beta hesitated. 'And maybe Dadi. But there aren't any puppies at the zoo. The man had them in his car.' Beta then leant confidingly towards Æsa. She was clearly oblivious to the gravity of the situation. The school was having a party: nothing bad could happen. 'He said they mustn't tell the teachers.'

Æsa gave silent thanks that her hands were in her pockets as the urge to shake the child was becoming unbearable. But she couldn't disguise her desperation when she spoke again. 'Where did they go? Which way?'

'Over there.' A bobbly mitten pointed back in the direction that Æsa had come from. 'They went that way.'

Aware that it would be futile to ask a small child how long it had been since her kids had disappeared, Æsa set off at a run. She didn't waste precious minutes alerting the teachers either. They wouldn't be much help in the circumstances. The most urgent thing now was to reach the car park in case her children were still there. Or in the car of some man who must surely be up to no good. Her only hope was that the man hadn't managed to abduct them yet. Or harm them. She couldn't bear to think in what way.

Over the shrieking of the children Æsa heard someone calling her name. It must be one of the teachers puzzled by her behaviour. She ran faster. If they wanted an explanation, Beta would have to provide it. The thought of how bad they would feel when they realised they had lost Karlotta and Dadi gave her a little burst of extra energy but such was her frantic haste that she tripped over a stone, landing hard on one knee. Two horses watched her without interest. She cared nothing for the pain or the rip in the trousers she had only just bought and could ill afford to ruin. The hot blood trickling down her leg didn't matter either. Climbing to her feet, she limped the rest of the way.

When the car park finally came into view, Æsa was too breathless to shout. The children's names emerged as feebly as if they had been standing in front of her. Unsurprisingly, there was no answer. She hobbled, still panting, into the half-empty car park, calling their names again, louder as she recovered her breath, peering into one car after another. She couldn't see any sign of her children, let alone a man with puppies. There were only three cars left to check when she heard a voice calling her name. Not an adult this time but her daughter: 'Mummy!'

Æsa spun round disbelievingly. She must have misheard; there were countless children in the park and it must be some other little girl calling her mother.

To her indescribable relief, she saw Karlotta and Dadi come half running along the path beside the entrance to the car park, evidently returning from the road. They waved to her, beaming happily. Clearly nothing bad had happened to them and they hadn't a clue that they had done anything wrong. Yet she had told them over and over again that they must never go anywhere with strangers. Fury overwhelmed her. Though they seemed to have escaped unharmed, it could have ended in disaster.

Æsa limped towards them and they met by the entrance. The children, too young to read the situation, asked if they could get a hot dog, as if nothing were more natural.

She was so beside herself with rage that she stumbled over the words: 'Where have you been? How many times have I forbidden you to go anywhere with strangers? What were you thinking?'

Karlotta and Dadi stared at her, bewildered, their smiles fading.

Taking a deep breath, Æsa managed to speak more calmly. 'How could you dream of leaving the others like that? Especially when I've told you not to. Over and over again.'

'Yes but . . .' Karlotta didn't finish the sentence. She screwed up her face as she searched for the words to explain. Dadi stood beside her, keeping his eyes fixed on his sister for fear of meeting his mother's gaze. He was only three years old and could shelter behind the five-year-old Karlotta when things went wrong.

'No "yes but". Tell me what happened and why you disobeyed me.' Æsa's rage was subsiding with every word. Karlotta's eyes, so terribly like Thorvaldur's, gazed up at her from under their fair lashes, glittering with tears which swelled until they were heavy enough to spill down her red cheeks.

'It wasn't . . . a . . . bad . . . man,' she said, fighting sobs. 'He . . . had . . . some puppies. It wasn't . . . even . . . a man . . .'

Now that her anger had evaporated, Æsa regretted having spoken so sharply. She crouched down, ignoring the stinging of her knee, and wiped her daughter's cheeks. Her gentle caress opened the floodgates and Karlotta's tears began to flow in earnest. Æsa hugged her and drew Dadi into her arms as well.

It could have been so much worse.

Æsa stood up, herded the children into the car and set off home. It didn't occur to her to make a detour to let the teachers know that everything was all right after all.

The atmosphere was subdued on the way home. Slowly but surely Æsa had managed to prise the story out of Karlotta, though Dadi didn't say a word. Rather than constantly interrupt her daughter with questions, Æsa had let her tell it her own way, which took time. All she could think of was that this must be connected to Thorvaldur. He'd obviously had good reason to ring and ask her to take extra care of the kids.

To make up for the abrupt end to the festivities, Æsa stopped to buy them each a hot dog. Having seated them on bar stools at a high table, she stepped outside. She wanted to speak to Thorvaldur out of the children's earshot. At home there was a risk they would overhear any raised voices. To make sure he would respond, she sent him a text: *If you dont ring me now im calling the police – its about karlotta and dadi.*

He rang immediately. 'What the hell's going on? Have you completely lost your mind?'

Æsa ignored this pathetic attempt to pretend nothing was wrong. The fear in his voice gave him away. 'A man just lured Karlotta and Dadi into his car. You have to tell me why you rang to warn me against exactly this sort of thing.'

'What do you mean? Didn't you listen to a word I said? Are you crazy? Can't you even look after your own children?' His reaction wasn't so different from her own when she had found the kids earlier.

'Shut up, Thorvaldur.' Æsa paused to see if this had an effect. All she could hear at the other end was his breathing. 'Of course I've warned them. A hundred times. But your friend was too cunning for me. He dressed up as Father Christmas and told them he had some puppies. In their eyes Father Christmas doesn't count as a man, let alone a bad man. They thought it was safe to go with him. Despite what I'd told them.'

Thorvaldur continued to breathe heavily for a moment, then asked: 'Didn't they see his face?'

'No. I've just told you. He was wearing an American Santa Claus outfit. With a white beard and everything. That was all they could describe. For all I know it could have been a woman, though I think that's unlikely.'

'Jesus.'

'Yes, Thorvaldur. Jesus. I need hardly explain how badly it could have turned out. Luckily, he didn't do anything to them, but who knows what he'll try next time.' She cleared her throat and continued in a strangled voice, 'If he tries again.'

'What exactly did this Father Christmas do?' Thorvaldur sounded angry, frightened and bewildered all at once.

'He lay in wait for them during the nursery outing to the Family

Park. They'd got out of the coach and were waiting for the others when he lured them over to his car, parked by the entrance. He told them to come back out again when no one was looking and he'd show them his puppies. He forbade them to tell anyone else or bring any other kids with them. They were the only ones he would show the puppies to.'

'And they did as he said?'

'Yes. They did as he said.' Æsa rubbed her forehead. Unsurprisingly, the events of the day seemed to be bringing on a migraine. 'They're children. He was Father Christmas. Father Christmas with puppies. Of course they obeyed.'

'They must be able to describe the car?'

Æsa gave a mocking laugh. 'Sure they can. It was a car. Not a red one. That's as detailed as it gets. Believe me, I've tried.' She closed her eyes and rubbed them as well. It wouldn't help; the migraine was taking hold and nothing but strong painkillers could save her now. 'They got into the car and he drove off, saying the puppies were nearby but it was too far to walk. He drove around for a bit before bringing them almost all the way back. Then he stopped and said he couldn't remember where the puppies were. They'd just have to see them later. After that he let them out.'

'And?'

'No and. They got out, said goodbye and walked back to the park where I was almost having a heart attack looking for them.' Æsa wanted to end the conversation. If she left it any longer, her headache would be too bad for her to drive. 'When he said goodbye he asked them to pass on a greeting. To you.'

'To me?' Thorvaldur sounded hoarse.

'Yes.' Her own voice was no better. 'Karlotta was to say hello to you from Vaka.' Thorvaldur's gasp was audible. 'Who the hell is

Vaka, Thorvaldur?' When he didn't answer, she continued while she was still able to speak: 'I'm going to call the police. No matter what you say. You can explain to them how you know this man and who Vaka is.'

Æsa hung up. Inside the shop she could see Karlotta and Dadi sitting holding their half-eaten hot dogs, their legs dangling from the high stools. They looked as if they had no appetite. She felt the tears begin to run down her cheeks but didn't know if it was the headache, or her sore knee, or the relief at having recovered them safely against all the odds.

Chapter 14

Baldur was as cocky, carefree and optimistic as ever. Almost insanely so. He was lounging on the narrow bed, bolted to the floor, which took up most of the room. The inmates of Litla-Hraun received their visitors in old cells that were no longer in use. Freyja hoped the accommodation her brother occupied day in, day out, was larger, more modern and better equipped than these claustrophobic little shoeboxes, but she didn't dare ask, for fear of being disappointed. The prison buildings were unimaginatively designated House 1, House 2 and so on, so her expectations were low.

She tried unsuccessfully to make herself comfortable on the only chair that would fit in the cell. Baldur was no better off, constantly shifting his long legs as he tried to find a less awkward position. Having visited him here more times than she cared to remember, she knew he wouldn't succeed. Sometimes, like now, she took the chair, sometimes the bed. She always let him choose.

'Shouldn't you be eligible for day release soon?' Through the narrow window she could see the low-rise settlement of Eyrarbakki. She wondered whether his cell faced the village, the sea or the main road, but didn't ask. It was preferable to imagine him enjoying a view of the sea than to find out that all he had to look at was the thin stream of traffic travelling to and from Selfoss.

'I think so. I haven't really been keeping track but they said it would be sooner rather than later.' Baldur yawned, apparently unexcited at the prospect of this limited freedom. Then again, his reluctance to discuss it might have been because his extended sentence had led to the temporary loss of this privilege. Freyja had the feeling he found the subject even more embarrassing than she did. She had frequently used up their precious visiting time by repeatedly saying how sorry she was, forcing him to waste as many minutes reassuring her that he didn't hold it against her. 'At least I've got plenty of time to plan how I'm going to spend my day.'

'Let me know the moment you hear, so I can take the day off,' said Freyja. 'To give you a lift and so on,' she added hastily, so he wouldn't think she intended to cramp his style.

Baldur nodded. 'Will do. Don't want to have to walk into town.' He winked at her and yawned again, his interest in the subject now exhausted. You'd have thought he was oblivious to the fact that he was banged up for years on end and only allowed outside for two hours a day. What he did with himself for the rest of his waking hours was a mystery to Freyja. Though of course he filled up the quota of visits allotted to every prisoner, and would have no problem drumming up more visitors if the rules were ever relaxed. Freyja had been lucky to get a slot at such short notice; normally she had to resign herself to a two-week wait. His current girlfriend always took precedence as, naturally, he had rather more to look forward to from her presence than he did from a chat with his sister. But she had flu and couldn't leave the house, which Freyja interpreted as a sign that their relationship would soon be history. Baldur's enthusiasm and insouciance were irresistible while you were in his presence, but the spell soon wore off when he wasn't there, and the less time you spent with him, the shorter its influence lasted.

'What can you tell me about a prisoner called Jón Jónsson, who's just been released? He was convicted of the rape and murder of a little girl.'

Baldur's eyes opened wide. 'Why are you interested in that piece of shit?' He unwrapped a toffee from a bag he had brought in with him. Sending food or sweets to prisoners had recently been banned: instead, the inmates were allowed to order them and pay out of their own pockets. This had made Freyja's life easier since she found it impossible to keep up with Baldur's fads. One day he was a vegetarian, the next a vegan, then he was into raw food, then he became a sports fanatic and ate nothing but protein powders, while at other times all he wanted was meat and sweets. Now the parcels she brought him were restricted to inedible items like books, clothes, computer games and other forms of entertainment, some of them less than salubrious. She never came empty-handed, though her parcels weren't delivered to Baldur until long after she'd left. Choosing a present was rarely a problem because he was always obsessed with something, though like his girlfriends, these obsessions never lasted long. Baldur popped the toffee in his mouth and asked as he chewed: 'Has he reoffended already?'

Freyja shuddered. 'God, no. At least, I hope not.' She declined the proffered bag. 'I've been asked to help the police with a case that his name's cropped up in. I read the account of his trial but it doesn't say much about Jónsson himself, so I thought of asking you. You must have come across him in here. He's only just got out.'

The toffee seemed to get in the way of Baldur's tongue. He said indistinctly: 'Jón's toxic. I don't know how else to describe him. When he was around I used to catch myself holding my breath.' His handsome features contorted in disgust. 'Luckily I wasn't on the same corridor as him for long.'

'Was he really that vile? I read in an interview that he'd found Jesus in prison. Or claimed he had.' Freyja remained as convinced now as she had been years ago that the man's piety was a sham.

Baldur clicked his tongue dismissively. 'He's not the only one who's played that game. But he's one of the few who became even creepier as a result. I've never seen worse acting. People's eyes usually move when they read the Bible, but his didn't budge. I bet he was just sitting there having sick fantasies about children.' He grimaced again.

'No doubt.' Freyja wasn't surprised by Baldur's description. Since it was unlikely that anyone had actually bought his crap about finding religion, she couldn't understand why the man had bothered to put on such an act. Convicted murderers weren't eligible for release after serving only half their sentence, so that could hardly have been the motive. 'Are men like him left in peace in prison? Or did he do it to avoid violence from the other inmates?'

Baldur laughed. 'Seriously? It's a big misunderstanding that paedos and rapists are given a hard time inside. No one can be arsed to make their life a misery. Maybe they're a bit more isolated than normal, but that's all. Why should we take it on ourselves to punish them? If we're caught, our privileges are cut and we risk having our sentence extended. No, if the public wants tougher penalties for these bastards, it's up to them to sort it out.'

The ensuing silence was made awkward by the sound of a couple having sex next door. Baldur rustled around in the bag of toffees and Freyja shifted on the battered chair in the hope of making the legs creak. She couldn't wait for him to get out; she wanted to meet her brother where there was room to breathe. On a bench in the town centre or even, for that matter, out on the moors. But there would be no chance of that any time soon. 'Why the charade, then?'

'You should be able to answer that better than me. I thought you worked with men like him every day?'

Baldur had never really grasped what Freyja did for a living, or why she had chosen to work in an area so full of grief and misery. It was as alien to him as a career in crime would be to her. He went out of his way to avoid conflict; it didn't sit well with the unbridled optimism that was his overriding character trait. 'I don't work with men like that,' she explained patiently. 'I work with their victims. I never see the abusers, thank God. You could say I clean up after them.'

'Keep it that way. And stay away from that evil fucker Jón.'

'Don't worry.' Freyja had no intention of going anywhere near the man. It was his son she was curious about. Now that his violent outburst was no longer as vivid in her memory, Freyja was inclining to the view that Þröstur posed no risk. Except perhaps to his own father, since the initials JJ in his letter presumably referred to him. As for the other initials, it was hard to say, unless they alluded to paedophile associates of his father's. Or simply to other kids the boy had regarded as his enemies at the time. She didn't think the individuals in question had any reason to be on their guard now, apart from Jón. Þröstur and his sister Sigrún had almost certainly suffered appalling abuse at their father's hands, and now that Jón was free they must both be anxious about his next move. Perhaps not on their own account but in relation to other potential victims. How long before their father started drinking again and lost any self-discipline he might have developed in prison? No doubt they dreaded having to re-live the experience of being the children of a monster whose name was splashed all over the media. It was probably no coincidence that Þröstur had said the murders would be committed in the year his father got out. The family would have been warned at the time of his sentencing that Jón could expect to be released after serving only two-thirds of his sentence. Perhaps Þröstur had gone around with some crazy notion of becoming an avenging angel and taking out paedophiles. Freyja made a mental note to check the initials in his letter against the names of child abusers known to have been active ten years ago.

It would be tragic if Þröstur acted on the threats in his letter. He would receive no mercy from the courts. The system didn't like it when people took the law into their own hands. 'Do you think Jón'll reoffend?' she asked.

'I deliberately avoided getting to know him, so I haven't a clue what he will or won't do. But it wouldn't surprise me.'

'Or me.' Freyja decided not to mention how low the success rate was for the rehabilitation of those sexually attracted to children. It might lead to a conversation about how difficult it was to rehabilitate offenders in general, and before her sat a prime example of a man who refused to mend his ways, though of course his offences were very different in nature. 'Do you know if he's at Vernd?' It occurred to her to contact the manager of the halfway house and ask where Jón spent his days.

'Didn't you know? He never went to Vernd. The part of his sentence he'd normally have spent there, he served inside, because the halfway house committee didn't feel he was eligible to finish his sentence there. And their decision is final. In other words, they didn't like the look of him, though he's supposed to be so holy nowadays.'

She could understand their decision only too well. 'What about visits? Did anyone come to see him? His wife or children, for example?'

'I don't know. As far as I can remember, no one came to see him while we were on the same corridor. I never remember bumping into him here in the visitors' wing either. Of course that doesn't mean he never had *any* visitors, but they can't have come that often.' Baldur ferreted around in the apparently bottomless bag of sweets. 'He used to get letters, though. I do remember that.' He unwrapped another toffee, popped it in his mouth, and carefully folded up the paper. 'Who gets letters these days?'

'Me. You. Everyone, I imagine. But they're mostly bank statements or official circulars. Are you sure they were personal? Not just notices from the tax office or something?'

Baldur shook his head. 'No. These were handwritten.'

'From his children, maybe?'

'They must have been very good at writing then. It looked like an adult's handwriting.'

'His children are grown up now, of course,' Freyja said, half to herself. Baldur sat up and rested his back against the wall, his legs projecting over the side of the bed. As usual he was impeccably dressed. Thanks to Freyja he was more on trend than most free men. Since the rent she paid him was pitifully low and he wouldn't hear of raising it, she compensated by buying him clothes and other gear she thought he needed. They were alike in always wanting to present an immaculate appearance, and being in prison made no difference. It didn't require a psychology degree to work out that this was a legacy of growing up hearing themselves constantly referred to as 'poor motherless kids'. No child wants to be a 'poor kid' and they had both discovered that the best way to persuade those around them that nothing was wrong was to come across as strong. And look the part. This method still worked now that they were adults. 'I was curious about the letters because he always seemed weirdly tense when they arrived and I wanted to know why. Though not enough to have another go at snooping. After that I was moved to a different corridor, so I don't know if they kept coming.'

'When was this?' The letters could have been from Þröstur, though Freyja thought it unlikely. Unless he'd written to his father to threaten him. But in that case the bastard would probably have shown the letters to the prison authorities in the hope of eliciting sympathy or being given protection after his release. No way was he the type to sacrifice himself for his children.

'About eighteen months ago, I guess.' Baldur fell silent for a moment and his gaze suddenly became shifty. 'Speaking of letters.' He bent forward and reached into his back pocket. 'I got this.' He handed a folded sheet of paper to Freyja, then looked out of the narrow window at the grey sky beyond.

Freyja read the contents, and although she didn't understand all the details of the test results supplied, she got the gist. All the questions she had been longing to ask about Jón Jónsson seemed suddenly irrelevant, merely a symptom of her need to be professionally occupied. Here, in contrast, was something of tangible importance. 'This could hardly be more conclusive, could it?' The table showed the results of a paternity test. 'Ninety-nine point nine nine per cent.'

Keeping her eyes lowered, she reread every word and figure – not to acquaint herself more closely with the contents, but to buy time. She didn't know whether to feel happy or sad. She sat staring blankly at the paper. It struck her that here was a tragedy in the making. Although the child didn't seem real and she didn't experience any rush of family feeling, the thought of Baldur as a weekend father really hurt. A weekend father who spent more time in prison than out. A weekend father cast in the same mould as Baldur's own and therefore barely deserving of the title. Given how painful Baldur had found his distant relationship with his father when he was young, he would surely be determined to act differently himself. But how would he manage it from behind bars? It was extraordinary how often good intentions came to nothing. Freyja raised her eyes at last. 'What about the mother? Are you in a relationship with her? Is she nice?' The tone of her questions belied their seriousness. She experienced an overwhelming urge to grab her brother by the shoulders, shake him angrily and ask what the hell he'd been thinking of. Would it have killed him to use a condom?

'We're not in a relationship. Never were, really. She only came here twice. But the dates fit.'

'Has the baby been christened? Does she have a name?' All the sheet of paper revealed was the child's sex and ID number. The little girl must be about ten months old, though Freyja was too distracted to be sure.

'She's called Saga.'

'Saga.' Freyja handed the sheet of paper back to Baldur and their eyes finally met. 'Pretty name.'

'Yeah, sure. Though I didn't have any say in the matter.' Baldur looked away. 'I didn't know she existed until three months ago when I was asked to take a blood test. Apparently there were two of us in the picture, so it wasn't a question of just acknowledging the baby. Pity for her that the other guy didn't turn out to be the father.'

Freyja sensed that Baldur shared her concerns. What kind of father would he be? The answer to that would be decided not by luck or the vagaries of fate: the responsibility lay squarely with him. He would have to finish this bloody jail sentence, start a new life and try his damnedest to be a good father. Perhaps this would be the spur Baldur needed to turn his life around. Stranger things had happened.

'I'll help you both as much as I can. For as long as you're in here.' Freyja forced herself to smile. 'And after you get out too, of course. It's not like I'm about to add to the human race myself any time soon. If I was willing to help you with Molly, you can imagine how much more willing I'll be to help with your daughter.' The words sounded odd. Baldur was a father. The whole thing would seem more real once she had seen the child. Then it would no longer be a faceless baby but a flesh-and-blood little girl. A girl called Saga. 'You can rely on me, Baldur.'

The first creeping doubts began as she was driving with slow care up the desolate, icy road over the Threngsli Pass. The spell Baldur had cast didn't even last as far as Hellisheidi. She had meant every word when she promised her support, but it wouldn't be that simple. What about the child's mother? Baldur had been reluctant to discuss her, which suggested there was no love lost there. That wasn't a good sign. But even if all was sweetness and light between them, would she welcome interference from the father's sister?

The sky darkened as Freyja crossed the mountains. In the blizzard that followed, she was reduced to driving at a snail's pace. She had promised to call Saga's mother as soon as she got home. At least the hold-up delayed this excruciating task.

Chapter 15

Freyja zigzagged her way between the desks in the open-plan CID office, all the way to the far corner where Huldar sat. Several of the detectives glanced up; it wasn't every day that a young woman dropped in. A few, recognising her from the case that had led to Huldar's fall from grace, dropped their eyes again. Huldar could have sworn he saw a malicious smirk on some faces. He stood up and waved, glad for a chance to look at someone other than Gudlaugur, whose head was forever popping up to ask questions. Erla had ordered Gudlaugur to speak to a mother claiming that her children had been abducted by Father Christmas, and he was obviously dreading the conversation. He kept rehearsing his questions aloud and was driving Huldar up the wall. Freyja's appearance was a welcome distraction.

'Good that you could drop by.' Huldar bestowed his widest smile on her and wished he had gone for that haircut he kept having to postpone. As always, Freyja looked well rested and neatly presented, unlike him. His broad grin shrank a little when he caught sight of Erla. She had been bending over someone's desk but straightened up when she saw Freyja and stared at them both grimly. Huldar had managed to extract her permission to investigate a possible link between the time-capsule letter and the murder in the underground garage, but he had failed to add that he was planning to involve Freyja again. Erla had shown little interest when he drew her attention to Benedikt Toft's participation in the first trial of Thröstur's father, Jón Jónsson. Instead of being fired up with excitement as he had hoped, she had responded coolly that Iceland was a small country and connections turned up everywhere. It was the argument trotted out by politicians when they appointed friends and relatives to public office, and it was as infuriating when someone said it to your face as it was to read in the press.

Erla hadn't said a word about this possible lead at the progress meeting yesterday, merely listed the angles currently under investigation and those that had proved unproductive. He supposed he should count himself lucky that she had decided to allow him to pursue it, though she had only done so because the inquiry was still mired in darkness. It was obvious that Erla didn't believe for a minute that it would provide any answers, and now that she had spotted Freyja, there was every chance that she would revoke her permission and give him the list of chainsaw owners to plough through instead.

Ever since their first meeting a year ago, the two women had been at odds. At the time Huldar had suspected Erla of regarding Freyja as a rival for his affections. Although, for all Erla knew, nothing had happened between them, this didn't seem to help; she remained stubborn in her dislike and Freyja clearly couldn't stand her either. On second thought, their mutual antipathy probably had nothing to do with him; they were simply too different. He cursed himself for not having arranged to meet Freyja outside the office.

'Shall we take a seat in the meeting room?' Out of the corner of his eye, Huldar saw that Erla was showing signs of heading in their direction and it was all he could do not to drag Freyja away. Not that the meeting room would provide much of a refuge. It would be better to leave the building, but he couldn't think of a convincing excuse off the top of his head. 'It's quieter there,' he added lamely. He grabbed some papers from his desk and a pen that he only remembered too late had run out of ink. Never mind – he had to get them both to safety before Erla reached them. Freyja was clearly unimpressed when he almost shoved her down the shortest route between the desks to the smallest meeting room.

Holding the door open, he hustled her inside with the same haste. As he did so, he sneaked a glance over his shoulder and, much to his relief, saw Erla in the middle of the office, engrossed in a phone call. He closed the door behind him. 'Sorry about that. Things are a bit hectic.' Seeing that this apology had done nothing to mollify her, he added: 'There's been a fresh twist that's really put the cat among the pigeons. As you know, I was ordered to drop my investigation into Thröstur's letter since they thought it could wait. But the situation's changed.'

'What happened?' Freyja chose a chair as far away from Huldar as possible. He would have preferred to sit closer to her but, seeing Erla through the glass wall, changed his mind.

'It's possible it's linked to another case. Unlikely, but possible.' Huldar brought her up to date with the murder in the garage and the link between the victim Benedikt Toft and Jón Jónsson, and also with the severed hands that had turned up in Benedikt's hot tub. He asked her to keep it confidential, but that was only for form's sake as the media had already got hold of the story. The coverage was lurid, as he'd guessed it would be, and no wonder. Freyja could hardly add anything to the existing stories and speculation in the press. 'I was hoping you'd come with me to have another go at talking to Thröstur, and to his sister and mother as well this time. I'm also interested in talking to Jón Jónsson and would appreciate it if you were there to provide your psychological insights – is he likely to be violent on top of everything else? That sort of thing. It's not impossible that he's connected to the murder, or even that he's the killer.'

'As I've told you before, I'm no expert on sex offenders. I work with their victims.' She loosened her scarf and put it in her lap. 'I can come with you, but I doubt I'll be much use. I decided to read up on Jón and found the record of his judgement by the Supreme Court, but it wasn't very enlightening. There are no files about the case at the Children's House, but then the centre had only recently been set up and it took a while to persuade the courts and investigators to take it seriously. They seem to have completely bypassed us, which was a common problem in the early days. It's a pity, since if we'd been involved both Jón's children would have been given medical exams. I can't see any evidence that this was done. They were questioned in court but denied that he'd ever abused them.'

'Would it have changed anything? The judge has to stay within the narrow parameters of the charge and since the abuse of Jón's own children wasn't the issue, he wouldn't have seen any reason to complicate the trial further. I'm guessing the question was only allowed because the man's defence counsel wanted to demonstrate that the attack on Vaka was a one-off. He must have known the children claimed their father had never touched them, and trusted that they wouldn't change their testimony when he confronted them in court.'

Freyja made a face.

'There's another judgement,' Huldar added, 'dating back a couple of years earlier, from the Reykjanes District Court. I can give you a copy. You won't find it online because Jón's name was removed after he was acquitted. There's not a lot to be learnt from the version I have – all the details are missing. I've put in a request to see the full records. All I know is that he was charged with the sexual abuse of a minor.'

'Well, there's a surprise.' Freyja snorted. 'By the way, I went to see my brother Baldur. He says Jón Jónsson received few if any visits but quite a lot of letters, handwritten, from an adult. Perhaps from his children, or his wife. Though it's difficult to imagine why they'd have been writing to him.'

'When was this?' Huldar reached for his pen to make a note, then remembered that it was out of ink. 'Letters to prisoners are censored – especially letters to paedophiles, I'd have thought. I'll ring and ask if anyone remembers what they contained and who sent them.' Through the glass wall, Huldar noticed Erla shoving her phone back in her pocket. Their eyes met, and she looked anything but happy. She was about to move when her phone rang again. Saved by the bell once more.

'The prosecutor who was found dead, this Benedikt Toft, is he the one who got Jón convicted for murder?'

'No, he was the prosecutor in the earlier case, when he was let off.'

Freyja raised her eyebrows. 'And you lot think Jón Jónsson killed him? Rather than his son, Þröstur?'

'We don't think anything. We just want to decide if there's any reason to investigate Jón further. Benedikt Toft had a long career as a prosecutor and was involved in countless cases that could have prompted some nutter to seek vengeance. We're working through them all but I find this one the most plausible. The man is left in peace until shortly after Jón Jónsson gets out. It's a strange coincidence and I make it a rule not to believe in coincidences.'

'But why should Jón attack the prosecuting counsel in a case where he was acquitted? Wouldn't it have been more appropriate to go after the person who sent him to jail?'

'You'd have thought so, but when you stop to think about it, it hardly matters who prosecutes in a murder trial. Your dog, Molly, could do it. Defendants in murder trials are never acquitted in this country.' Outside the meeting room Erla had finally finished her phone call and was advancing in their direction. It was too much to hope that a higher power would intervene with a third call to prevent her.

She flung open the door and stood there with a nasty glint in her eye, taking care not to give any sign that she was aware of Freyja's presence.

'We've just had a call from the cemetery in Hafnarfjördur. A grave has been vandalised and there's quite a bit of damage. You'd better get over there.'

'Me?' Huldar was wrong-footed. He'd been prepared for an earful about uninvited guests, but not this. 'Can't someone else handle it? Someone who's not involved in the murder investigation?'

'Everyone's involved in the investigation. As you should know. The difference is, they're following up real clues, not wasting their time on a wild-goose chase.'

Huldar's face darkened. He didn't often lose his temper but when he did, he had trouble controlling himself. Or rather, he had no desire to. When he was angry, he was really angry. 'A wild-goose chase that you gave the green light for, remember?' He bit back a comment about the other leads turning out to be blind alleys. No need to reveal that kind of detail in front of an outsider.

'Get over to Hafnarfjördur.' Erla's lips compressed into a thin line. 'And, by the way, I'd rather you didn't drag every Tom, Dick and Harry in here without consulting me.' She jerked her head angrily in Freyja's direction, still without looking at her, then barked again: 'Hafnarfjördur Cemetery. Now!'

On the way to the cemetery Freyja barely paused for breath in her condemnation of Erla. Huldar had persuaded her to go along with him, partly so they could continue their discussion of Jón and Thröstur's case, but also in the hope of talking her out of storming back to the Children's House and making a scene. Pissed off though he was with Erla, he'd rather she didn't get into even more trouble.

'What is that woman's problem? I mean, what have I ever done to her? She was rude to me the first time we met, before I'd even said a word.'

Huldar hummed and hawed noncommittally as he pulled into the empty car park. It seemed the dead had few visitors on a weekday. He parked by the service building where he had arranged to meet the caretaker. Unwilling to give the man the impression that he wasn't taking the incident seriously, he tried not to fret about the foolishness of this errand at a time when far more urgent matters were awaiting his attention. But he couldn't shake off his resentment. Why couldn't Hafnarfjördur Police handle this? No doubt it was just Erla being vindictive.

Freyja followed him out of the car, still ranting. Huldar nodded from time to time but was privately grateful when she shut up on entering the silent service building. She didn't say another word about Erla as Huldar made the introductions to the caretaker, nor as the man led them to the desecrated grave, inhibited partly by his presence but also, Huldar suspected, by the sobering impact of the endless rows of crosses and headstones. When confronted by these symbols of life's transience, he couldn't help thinking how trivial their everyday problems seemed.

'Here it is. As you can see, the damage extends well beyond the grave itself.' The man gestured to the vehicle tracks that had torn up the turf, flinging earth over the snow all around the disturbed grave. The headstone had been knocked flat and its inscription now faced heavenwards: the person it commemorated could look down and read it if they so wished. 'I can't begin to understand why anyone would have done such a thing. This almost never happens. Even the worst vandals tend to leave us alone.'

Huldar bent down to take a closer look, though there was nothing to see but a mess of soil and gravel. He straightened up again. 'Who discovered this?' The snow on the path leading there had been almost pristine, the only tracks a line of footprints that the caretaker said were his. Since very little snow had fallen in the night, the vehicle that had caused the damage must have come from a different direction. The paths criss-crossing the cemetery were wide enough to drive down. Scanning the surroundings more carefully, Huldar spotted caterpillar tracks leading from the opposite direction.

'I did. I always do a circuit of the cemetery in the mornings to check that everything's in order. I don't often see anything. You get the odd cross leaning a bit, but it's usually just vases knocked over by the wind.'

'Do you have CCTV?' Huldar asked, though he could already guess the answer. He hadn't spotted any cameras in the graveyard or car park. He took a few pictures with his phone in case the police took any action, unlikely though it seemed.

'No. They didn't think there was any need. As I said, things are usually quiet here.'

Huldar nodded: 'Right.' He wondered what he could do beyond scribbling down a description and taking the man's statement. 'In other words, the vandalism you wanted to report is this disturbance here? A headstone knocked over and, what, superficial damage to the terrain?'

The man looked surprised. 'No. Not only that. The digger we use to excavate the graves has been damaged too. The vandals can't have shut the door properly when they finished and it blew open, breaking the glass. We never lock it; the keys are usually left in the ignition, but we won't be making that mistake again. It seems there's no limit to what people will stoop to these days. I'll take you to see the digger; it's parked behind the building. It was returned there, strange as that sounds.'

A damaged digger. Huldar caught Freyja raising her eyebrows and wasn't surprised. This was turning out to be an utter waste of time. 'I'll take a look, if only to make a note of the damage. I'm sorry to say it, but it's unlikely this incident will be solved. I'm guessing some drunks thought it would be a laugh to go for a joyride around the cemetery last night and collided with the grave. Perhaps they got stuck in the mud and tore up the ground while they were trying to free the digger.'

The caretaker looked around, frowning. 'I don't believe they just careered off the path by accident.' He pointed at the next-door grave that was now buried in soil and gravel. 'They obviously used the bucket here.'

Huldar stared at the marks left by the digger's bucket attachment, trying to keep a straight face. This mess didn't make it into the top hundred list of criminal damage he had seen. 'There's no telling what put them up to it or what exactly they were trying to achieve. But it'll certainly be almost impossible to catch the hooligans responsible.'

'You think so?' The caretaker looked disgruntled. 'Can't you take fingerprints from the digger? If they had bare hands, that should help you trace them.'

Huldar coughed to smother a sigh. 'Forensics take care of that side. But they're a bit tied up at the moment so I doubt they'll have time to send anyone along. They do have to prioritise. The fact that the vandals put the digger back where they found it suggests they're not the kind of petty criminals we have on record. If they were, they'd have either stolen it or abandoned it where it was after they'd tired of the game.' Huldar took a few more pictures to satisfy the man. 'Like any help straightening up the stone?'

The caretaker wavered. He was clearly dissatisfied but Huldar's offer of help was tempting. 'I was going to fetch the digger and pull it up. But the three of us together can probably right it. Seeing as you've come all the way out here without doing any actual investigating.'

Ignoring this, Huldar said, still in a friendly tone: 'Shall we get on with it then? In case anyone comes to visit the grave.'

'It doesn't get many visitors. The man lying here's been dead for years. Grief fades with time, just like everything else.' The caretaker donned a pair of work gloves. 'But you never know.'

They went over to the stone and positioned themselves as best they could. Freyja didn't seem too thrilled at being made to stand in the middle of a mud-bath and heave up a gravestone. She had pulled on a pair of bright red gloves that weren't designed for such dirty work. 'Do you think there's any point?'

Neither Huldar nor the caretaker replied; they were too busy pushing and grunting with the strain. It was an impressive block of stone; the dead man must have been a person of consequence. No simple wooden cross for him. When Freyja eventually joined in, they managed to right it, but they had to scrape away a bit of soil around the base before it would stand up straight.

Panting, they contemplated a job well done. Huldar remarked that this Einar Adalbertsson owed them a favour, though it probably wouldn't be repaid any time soon. Neither the caretaker nor Freyja seemed to appreciate his humour and they walked over to the digger in silence. There Huldar took a few more photos before they said goodbye and returned to the car.

Huldar's phone rang before the cemetery had even disappeared in the rear-view mirror. It was Erla, sounding a little agitated but other-wise normal, as though no cross words had been exchanged in the meeting room earlier. 'Are you at the cemetery?'

'No. In the car, just leaving. It didn't take long, you won't be surprised to hear.'

'Turn round.'

'Why?'

'Turn round. There's been a development.'

Huldar listened, then did a U-turn at the next junction. When Freyja asked what was going on, all he said was that he needed to check something before they went back to town. She didn't ask any further questions, just said she'd wait in the car while he ran in.

So she wasn't with him when he asked the caretaker how deep the coffins were buried. Nor when he asked if he could borrow a metal stake to prod into Einar Adalbertsson's grave.

Chapter 16

Over three hundred tonnes of rubbish was transported daily to be turned into landfill at the Sorpa site on Álfsnes, according to the digger operator standing at Huldar's side. The bulk of it arrived in the form of weighed bales, which were stacked up in mounds that would eventually be covered with earth. Those who didn't know would never guess how the resulting landscape had been created, though at the moment it was glaringly obvious. A swarm of screaming gulls circled over the colourful slope in search of food. At its foot stood two mechanical diggers, their huge yellow arms in the resting position, forced into inactivity by the discovery. Meanwhile the bales from the sorting centre at Gufunes were piling up. It wouldn't be possible to process them until the police had finished examining the area, and the digger operator predicted gloomily that it would take forever to make up for lost time.

The citizens of Reykjavík wouldn't stop throwing out rubbish just because a coffin had been found at the landfill site.

'Someone must have brought it here last night. There's no way we could have missed it yesterday. We were working in that area and I assure you that we never saw any coffin and none of us put it there.' The digger operator who'd reported the discovery, whose name was Geiri, folded his arms, resting them on his protruding gut. His massive bulk was stuffed into a hi-vis jacket that barely met around his middle. He looked as if he had been vacuum packed. 'We didn't notice it to start off with because it was covered in snow, but as soon as the wind picked up, we spotted it.'

'Who saw it first?' Huldar shoved his hands in the pockets of his parka to protect them from the biting wind.

'Him. Stebbi.' Geiri pointed to a man watching them from where he was leaning against a Portakabin with a steaming mug of coffee. He was the man who had come storming towards them, waving his arms urgently to chase them off the site, when Huldar's unmarked police car drove down the access road. He had relaxed once Huldar explained who he was, though he had flashed a doubtful glance at Freyja in the passenger seat, since she could hardly have looked less like a police officer. She was still in the car, having refused to get out because of the stench, though in fact one soon ceased to notice it. As the digger operator had informed Huldar, every effort was made to keep strong-smelling waste to a minimum at Álfsnes due to complaints from the nearby residential area, and in summer they used chemicals to reduce the smell. No such luxuries were available in winter, however. Perhaps that was why the gulls were making such a racket.

'Stebbi stopped work immediately. His digger's still where he left it.'

Huldar nodded. 'You're quite sure no one brought it here this morning – no unauthorised person or Sorpa employee? Could it just be a coffin someone was throwing out?'

The rows of bales mounted up in a series of steps like a ziggurat. The coffin was impossible to miss; it perched on one of the ledges, standing out black and filthy against the multicoloured rubbish. Geiri turned from the mountain of refuse to Huldar. 'All the waste is sorted before it arrives. Coffins aren't disposed of here, so it can't have come from our centre. And there's no way anyone unauthorised could have lugged it in after we started work this morning.'

Geiri looked as if he was about to add something, then closed his mouth again. Huldar was relieved: given half a chance, the man had a tendency to ramble on about solid-waste statistics and the importance of his and Stebbi's work.

'Is there a security guard here at night?'

Geiri snorted. 'A security guard? Whatever for? No one's likely to steal this rubbish. The sorting centre's removed anything of value.'

'What about CCTV?' Huldar hadn't spotted any cameras, either on the site or on the access road, so Geiri's answer came as no surprise. The man or men who stole the coffin from Hafnarfjördur Cemetery last night must have driven it here and deposited it on the waste mound, all without being caught on film.

'What time do you close?'

'Five. We open at eight.'

The grave robber must have done the deed in the middle of the night rather than just after closing time. First he would have had to dig up the coffin, taking care not to be seen, though since the grave wasn't visible from the surrounding streets, he wouldn't have needed to worry about passing traffic. Huldar didn't doubt that the coffin was the one that had disappeared from Einar Adalbertsson's grave. It was unthinkable that they could be dealing with two unrelated cases – a vanishing coffin and a different coffin turning up the next day. The caretaker at the cemetery had been unable to find a stake, but after scraping away at the soil in the grave with the mini-digger, he had swiftly established that it was indeed empty. The vandals had been grave robbers: they had stolen the digger, dug down to the coffin, hauled it out, then filled in the hole to conceal the fact. Goodness knows what could have motivated them. 'Do you think the coffin was dumped up there to be found or disposed of?'

'Eh?' Unsurprisingly, since Huldar had been thinking aloud, Geiri didn't immediately grasp what he meant. But he cottoned on fast. 'All

I can say is that if I'd done it myself, it would have been because I was hoping it would be found. There's no way it could have disappeared among the bales. But it wasn't me, and I'd bet my life it wasn't anyone else here. I can't begin to guess what the people who did this were trying to achieve.'

The sun peeped out from behind the clouds and low in the sky though it was, Huldar had to shield his eyes. 'And you're sure there's a body inside?'

'I wouldn't say sure. But me and Stebbi lifted it a little and it's definitely not empty. The lid's still intact so we thought we'd better call out the police rather than break it open. Before this I worked at the sorting centre. I'm used to people throwing out some weird shit but this beats everything.'

'I can believe it.' In more than a decade in the police, Huldar had never been called out to a cemetery, let alone for a coffin with a body in it. He was itching to look Einar Adalbertsson up. This must be more than a prank. Dumping the man at the municipal tip had to be symbolic: plainly, somebody thought he didn't deserve to lie in consecrated ground. Though it was odd that he had been allowed to lie undisturbed for so long; according to the inscription on his headstone he had died eleven years ago. Why wait all this time to disinter him?

'When do you think we'll be able to get back to work? Overtime's frowned on here.' Geiri nodded towards yet another lorry tipping out a load of bales.

'Ring them and put a stop to any further deliveries.' The bales slid off the back of the lorry and landed in a heap. Some rolled off and one almost hit Huldar's car on the passenger side. Freyja's expression was anything but amused. Huldar reflected that the day that had begun so promisingly was rapidly going downhill and could hardly get any worse. Instead of taking Freyja to interview Thröstur and possibly Jón as well, Huldar had dragged her first to a cemetery, then to a dump. The only thing needed to complete this disastrous day would be to take her to meet one of his sisters. He had long since given up introducing prospective girlfriends to them because his sisters invariably managed, by some mysterious means, to bring up the subject of what a huge head he'd had as a baby. A pumpkin was their favourite simile. None of the girlfriends who'd heard the story of his birth could be persuaded to sleep with him again.

'That'll only shift the problem on to them. And they haven't got a big enough warehouse to store the bales in.'

At this rate Huldar would have to order the inhabitants of Reykjavík to stop throwing away rubbish until further notice. He repeated his order, politely but firmly: 'Stop the bales. The Forensics team are on their way and they won't be long.' He glanced back at the battered coffin. The beads of moisture on the worn lid glittered like diamonds. 'It's not like they'll waste much time looking for clues.' Loose rubbish lay scattered over the entire area. It would be impossible to tell what belonged to the grave robbers, even if they had left traces behind. This morning's gale had swept the thin layer of snow not only off the coffin but also off all the bales around it, obliterating any signs of footprints. The forensic technicians would probably do no more than put on their protective overalls and carry the coffin down off the stack. 'When you spotted the coffin, were there any tracks or other marks visible?'

Geiri shook his head. 'No. The snow had started to clear away by then. It blew off the coffin lid first, because it's smooth. But if I had to guess, I'd say it was put there before the snow started last night, or while it was still falling.'

'So you have no idea how they got it up there?' The ledge the coffin was perched on was about three metres off the ground. It wouldn't have been especially difficult for two or three people to lug it up there between them.

'Well, I expect they used a rope. There are rope ends sticking out from under the coffin. It wouldn't have been difficult to haul it up there.'

'For two men? Or three?'

'I wouldn't know, but I'd think three would be more than enough; two would be ideal, but even one could have managed it alone, if he was strong enough.'

The vehicle belonging to Forensics approached down the access road and parked beside Huldar's car. Two men Huldar recognised stepped out and wrinkled their noses when the stench of the rubbish hit them. But they were used to worse and quickly shrugged it off. Huldar prayed that they wouldn't keep him there long. He'd had quite enough of this.

Freyja craned as far away from Huldar as she could. He himself was so inured to the smell by then that he didn't care. Besides, he was used to her keeping as much space between them as possible. It didn't require a bad smell. He had been dreading his return to the car, fully expecting her to have a go at him for wasting her time, but not a bit of it. Instead, she had bombarded him with questions and seemed to have been paying close attention to the forensic technicians. She didn't once ask how she was supposed to explain to her bosses what she had been doing all day.

But there was a catch. As soon as he got in the car, Freyja announced that he had to stop off at a children's clothes shop because she was going round to see someone straight after work and needed to take a gift. Huldar saw no reason why he shouldn't do her this favour, if that would make them quits. While she was choosing clothes he could grab the opportunity to ring Erla and bring her up to speed. He had ordered Forensics to take the coffin to the National Hospital pathology department. Naturally they would have to check whether there was a body inside and, if so, whether it belonged to the right man. For all they knew, the grave robbers might have put some incriminating evidence inside with the corpse, though there had been no indication that the lid had been tampered with.

'I did a search on Einar Adalbertsson while you were examining the rubbish.'

'And?' Huldar was forced to stop at a red light, just as the traffic was finally gaining momentum.

'He appears to have been a model citizen. Former chairman of Hafnarfjördur town council, president of all kinds of associations and so on. There's no sign that he did anything to deserve this humiliation.' Freyja fiddled with her phone. 'Though admittedly this is from an obituary, so you wouldn't expect it to dwell on his faults. For all we know, he could have been a complete shit. Other than that, there's not much about him online. Only short news items about long-ago council business, photos of him signing contracts or standing behind other men doing the same kind of thing.'

'Perhaps he was chosen at random.' Huldar moved off again. 'Though it seems unlikely. Moving a random stranger from the cemetery to the dump is an awful lot of hassle just for a prank. I can't imagine anyone thinking it was funny or clever.' The traffic continued to inch along and he puffed out irritably. 'What about family? Was he married? Any kids? Perhaps they're involved, or someone did it to get even with them.'

Freyja brushed her finger over the screen until she found the right place in the obituary. 'Yes. One daughter and one son from a first marriage. And a childless second marriage to a wife who predeceased him. His son seems to have died too – he can only have been eighteen. But his daughter and first wife are still alive, or at least they were when the obituary was written.'

'Try doing a search on them.'

Freyja fiddled with her phone again and examined it in silence, then finally looked up. 'The daughter's alive but her mother, the first wife, died five years ago. The daughter lives in Norway where she runs a nursery. So neither of them are likely to have done this.'

'Unless the daughter's in Iceland at the moment. Maybe it's a belated act of revenge against her father for abandoning her mother.' Huldar had no real faith in this explanation, but after all, there was no obviously normal, logical answer to what they were dealing with.

Freyja turned her attention to the phone again. 'No. Her Facebook page is public and yesterday she uploaded a photo of herself with a group of children at the nursery. Is that allowed?'

'I don't know. I'm no expert in online privacy.' Huldar switched lanes to turn into the Kringlan shopping centre. The action almost made his arms ache. He avoided shopping malls like the plague, only visiting them under duress in the run-up to Christmas when he would wander around aimlessly in search of presents for his family. In the end he invariably threw himself on the mercy of the shop assistants, and he suspected that his sisters now owned things that hadn't been selling as well as anticipated and had thus been fobbed off on hapless men. 'I suppose I'd better ring her later. You never know, she might be able to tell us who had a grudge against her father. Presumably she'll need to be informed anyway. She's his next of kin.' Freyja didn't seem to be listening; all her attention was focused on the phone. 'Find anything interesting?' he asked.

'Hang on. I'm looking at the second wife. Perhaps we'll find something there.'

'Unlikely. If she's dead and they had no children.'

'She might have left her husband for Einar. Her ex could be involved.'

Huldar found it hard to imagine an old-age pensioner excavating the grave and doing the necessary heavy lifting. Who would have helped him? His roommate at the nursing home?

'Christ!' Freyja recoiled as if she'd encountered something disgusting. 'You'll never guess what.'

'I give up.' Huldar drove into Kringlan, inwardly shuddering at the thought of the booming music and endless displays of goods. Ahead of them was a line of vehicles queuing for the car park. The snow evidently hadn't deterred the public from their favourite pastime.

'Einar's second wife already had a son before they met. She doesn't seem to have been married to his father, at least there's no mention of any previous husband in her obituary.'

'And?'

'The son's name is Jón. Jón Jónsson.' Freyja lowered her phone to her lap. 'Her grandchildren's names are Thröstur and Sigrún.' She stared wonderingly at Huldar. 'Wow.'

Huldar's hands tightened on the wheel as he prepared to swerve out of the queue, but Freyja read his mind and insisted he keep his promise. She also insisted he come inside with her, no doubt fearing he would do a runner. She had good reason to distrust him on that score.

While Huldar's brain was crashing through all kinds of theories about Jón's possible role in the theft of the coffin, he was continually required to nod and fake an opinion on a succession of tiny girls' outfits that Freyja kept shoving in his face. All his answers were along the lines of: 'That's nice, I'd buy that', but nothing worked. Finally she chose something without asking his opinion and they were able to leave.

Once out in the open air again his thoughts crystallised.

Number one: track down Jón Jónsson and call him in for questioning.

Number two: he had no idea what would happen next.

Only that it would happen.

Chapter 17

You could have knocked Freyja down with a feather: Saga, Baldur's baby daughter, was the spitting image of the internet sensation, Angry Cat. Remembering the photos of her brother as a little boy, Freyja had been expecting thick blonde curls, blue eyes and a sweet smile, but nothing could have been further from the truth. She kept thinking about the 0.01 per cent possibility that Baldur was not in fact the father. Saga was dark and her rosy lips were turned down in a grimace that her mother assured Freyja was a permanent fixture. Her only resemblance to Baldur as a child lay in her adorable apple cheeks. But Freyja didn't dare touch them. The little girl's eyes followed her every move, her down-turned mouth indicating that she was expecting the worst. Freyja wasn't going to risk patting her in case she started howling. The visit had got off to a ropey enough start already.

It reminded Freyja of all the times she and Baldur had gone on visits with their grandparents and been shooed off to play with the other children so the grown-ups could talk in peace. The encounters would quickly descend into embarrassed glances once all the obvious, easy questions had been asked: What school do you go to? Do you play football? Have you got a dog? The point at which silence descended was usually the question about what sort of games console they had. The other children simply couldn't relate to kids who had never owned such a thing.

There had been no need for anything to trigger the awkwardness on the present occasion. It had started as soon as the door opened. Fanney,

Saga's mother, was initially hesitant about letting Freyja in, and, even when she did, seemed unable to make up her mind what to think. She alternated between being terribly nice and friendly one minute, then frosty and sharp the next. Yet she had agreed to this visit; it wasn't as if Freyja had turned up out of the blue and thrust a present at her in the hope of being allowed in. The dress she'd bought was too cheerful for a child who would probably look better in muted colours – in shades of grey or funereal black, for example. Certainly not something with a strawberry print and puffball skirt, which, now she came to think of it, had been Huldar's choice.

The dress clashed with their surroundings too. The flat was immaculate; every object placed just so, surrounded by a protective zone at least a metre wide. It reminded Freyja of some of her girlfriends' homes where, whether it was a cream jug or a lemon press, as long as an item was expensive and had a famous designer label, it would be placed in a conspicuous spot. One long shelf sported nothing but a single handbag. There was no sign of any children's toys and Freyja hoped for sullen little Saga's sake that there was a nursery somewhere down the hall. But she suspected that the same empty minimalism characterised the whole flat.

'You don't have any children yourself?' Fanney sipped her coffee from a Royal Copenhagen cup. Freyja could have sworn she had deliberately drawn out the movement to show off the stamp on the base.

'No. I'm single. At present.' She gave the woman a brief, on-off smile, wishing the conversation would move on from her private life.

'That's better, actually. It means I don't need to vet your husband or boyfriend as well.' Fanney replaced her cup daintily on its pretty saucer. 'You seem fine, and since you're a qualified child psychologist I assume you must be reliable and good with children. At least I hope so. And since there isn't a boyfriend, I'm only taking a chance with one person, not two. I must say that's a great relief. I feel much easier in my mind. Now that I've met you too, of course.'

Freyja smiled in embarrassment. She had no idea what the woman was on about and her mind kept drifting back to the case that Huldar had mixed her up in. She answered as vaguely as she could. 'Right, thanks.'

'Baldur assured me your flat was suitable and child-friendly. Can I trust him or do I need to come round and inspect it for myself?'

'Oh, I think you can take his word for it.' Freyja wouldn't dream of letting this woman see her place. In comparison to this apartment, Baldur's flat resembled a charity shop. But Fanney's question puzzled her, though the woman seemed sufficiently satisfied by her answer to forgo a visit, or rather inspection. 'Sorry, I'm not quite sure I follow. Why would you want to inspect my flat?'

Fanney looked astonished. 'You weren't assuming you'd be able to stay here?'

Little Saga sat on the floor, conscientiously turning her head to watch whoever was speaking, like a spectator at a tennis match. Suddenly she furrowed her brows in a frown, which made her appear even angrier. Although she was far too young to understand what they were saying, she was sensitive enough to pick up on the vibes: clearly, something interesting was going on.

'No. I didn't think for a minute that I'd be staying here. Though I have to admit I'm not quite with you.'

'Oh?' Fanney scooped Saga up off the floor and settled her on her lap. Freyja was struck by the lack of resemblance between mother and daughter as well. You'd have thought the child was a changeling.

'I'm talking about the daddy weekends,' Fanney explained. 'Which you promised to cover for Baldur while he's . . . you know . . .' Putting her hands over the little girl's ears, she whispered, 'in prison'. Then, removing her hands, she continued: 'I'll need at least every other weekend off to study. I don't know if Baldur went into details but I started a course after Christmas, which I'm doing alongside work. It's turning out to be far more pressure than I'd anticipated, so it would be a big help if I could have a few days free every month to concentrate on my coursework.' She tightened her hold on Saga. 'But you can't have her overnight. Only during the daytime, while I'm working.'

By some miracle Freyja managed to keep her thoughts from her face. Baldur had committed her without checking with her first. No surprise there. 'Yes, of course. Sorry, I wasn't thinking.' He clearly knew her better than she knew herself. She couldn't deny that she had made any such promise, since if she did she'd almost certainly be shown the door. And behind that door would be this odd little niece with the perma-scowl, who she wouldn't see again until after Baldur was released.

Besides, what did she have to do every other weekend that was more important than this? Life would be tough enough for the poor little mite even if Baldur turned over a new leaf, since it couldn't be easy growing up with a convicted criminal for a father. In his absence Freyja would represent the father's side of the family. Without hesitation – once she had torn a strip off Baldur for dumping his parental responsibilities on her without having the decency to consult her first. 'She's not allergic to dogs, is she?'

'No, she has no allergies. Do you have a dog?' Fanney sounded doubtful. 'A big one?'

'She's not that big.' In the sense that elephants are not that big. 'It goes without saying that I'll keep her away from Saga.' If this proved difficult, she would just have to put Molly in kennels for those weekends. 'Are you sure Saga will be OK coming to stay with me? Is she shy? She doesn't seem very pleased with me.' Perhaps the little girl was making a face like that because she didn't trust Freyja.

It would be a nightmare to be stuck all day long with a crying child. Maybe she was all smiles and giggles normally.

'Not pleased with you? She's delighted with you!' Fanney craned her head round to look into her daughter's face, then raised her eyes to Freyja. 'Can't you tell?'

Meeting Saga's stormy gaze, Freyja smiled. The scowl didn't budge. Here was a challenge. She'd get a smile out of that child if it was the last thing she did.

In the end, the tongue-lashing she gave Baldur wasn't nearly as blistering as she'd intended. She had left a message for him to ring her, then broke the speed limit in her haste to get home in time for his call. Once she had plugged her phone in to charge and flopped down on the sofa, she felt her indignation draining away. She did her best when he finally rang, but he kept butting in with questions about his daughter and Freyja soon ran out of steam. Instead, she described the little girl, leaving out the bit about the perma-scowl, and it dawned on her as she was praising the child to the skies that she meant every word.

Baldur soon began to run out of questions, betraying how little he knew about babies. Realising this, he changed the subject. 'Hey, I had a word with a bloke who shared a cell for ages with Jón.'

'Oh?' Freyja had sunk back into the shabby sofa but sat bolt upright on hearing the paedophile's name.

'I asked him everything I could think of that might be of interest to you. According to him, Jón was quite cagey; always careful, like he thought someone was listening or their cell was bugged. That's not unusual for men like him, though. They're so obsessed with trying to appear normal that they're permanently on edge. I don't suppose I need to tell you but they think their urges are natural and can't understand why the rest of us don't agree.'

Baldur was right: she didn't need him to tell her that. 'Didn't he find out anything of interest then?'

'Sure. Nothing earth-shattering, though.' Baldur yawned into the phone, as if to underline the fact. 'According to this bloke, the letters weren't from his wife. She cut off all contact with him the moment he was arrested. He was in custody until he was sentenced, and his divorce papers were sent to him in jail. His wife seized the first chance she could to dump him. She didn't wait to see if he was found guilty or innocent. After all, it was obvious. And she never visited him while he was inside.'

'Understandably. She must have been ecstatic to see the back of him. I bet he treated her appallingly. That's how it usually works. It's a complex process that involves breaking these women down psychologically. It's not until they're isolated from their violent partner that they start to see things in their true light.' Freyja closed her eyes for a moment, suddenly overwhelmed by tiredness. 'What about the kids? I assume they followed her example and cut off all communication? I know they both use their mother's name, not his.'

'Oh? According to Jón's cellmate, at least one of them came to visit.'

'What?'

'Only the once though, according to him. Jón was in a very good mood afterwards, so it must have gone well. It's possible there were more visits but the bloke I spoke to was released, and when he was sent down again later, he ended up on a different corridor.'

'Did he mention when this visit took place? Was it just before Jón got out or early in his sentence?'

'I think he said about two years ago.'

Jón's daughter Sigrún would have been eighteen then; Þröstur twenty-two. Perhaps ten years had been long enough for one of them to forget the true awfulness of what had happened and decide that their father wasn't all bad. Or perhaps they had wanted to ask him about his future plans, since in 2014 he would have been nearing the point when he would normally have been eligible to move into a halfway house. They couldn't know that he wouldn't be offered this option when the time came. 'What did his cellmate say about the letters? Could they have been from his children after all?'

'He had no idea what the letters contained or who sent them, though he'd been curious about them. Like me and everyone else. Maybe they were from his kids.'

Freyja decided not to mention that Huldar was going to ask the prison authorities about the letters. The police weren't exactly Baldur's favourite people. 'Did you ask if he thought Jón was likely to reoffend? Or go looking for revenge?'

'Revenge?' Baldur's tone suggested he couldn't make up his mind whether to be surprised or indignant. 'What the hell for? If anyone should be after revenge it's the parents of the little girl he killed. Or his ex-wife. It was his fault he got sent down and he can't blame it on anyone else.'

'I know that, Baldur. Everyone knows that. Except him, maybe. Maybe he feels he's the victim in all this.' It was a pointless discussion and, since she couldn't confide in him about what was going on, it would be best to end it. They had already gone over the set time limit for prisoners' calls. She thanked him and said goodbye, but only after he had asked her to describe one more time how sweet his daughter was. As she rang off, she offered up a silent prayer that Saga would have morphed into a cutie pie before Baldur was released.

Freyja put her phone back in the charger, then got up and went into the kitchen to feed Molly. She stood and watched the dog wolfing down the unappetising food as if it was prime rump steak. The moment Molly's dish was empty, she bounded to the front door, banging into everything in the little hall, beside herself with excitement at the thought of going outside. This was all part of the routine: after supper it was walkies time. Whatever the weather and however tired Freyja was feeling. Anything was better than having to clean up after the dog in the flat.

Freyja had her shoes and coat on when the phone rang in the living room. She made to go back inside but Molly growled menacingly. She'd better return the call later.

The phone call turned out to be from Huldar. His message said he wanted to ask her opinion on something and could he drop round? With a bottle of red. Or two. To her astonishment she very nearly answered yes straight away. She tried to kid herself that this was because she was excited about the case but finally had to acknowledge that she was actually quite keen to see him.

Just before she texted back, she came to her senses. Celibacy was clearly driving her nuts. She would have to do something about it at the weekend, as she had been planning to for so long. But then she remembered her new role as a weekend daddy. Sighing, she reached for the phone again. Some things just couldn't be avoided: exams, slush, tooth decay, tax and – it seemed – Huldar. But she wouldn't let her agreement be the first step towards renewing their intimate acquaintance. Oh no. She would make it absolutely clear that nothing like that was on the agenda.

Chapter 18

Since the Identification Committee were still no closer to discovering who the hands belonged to, the police had decided to appeal to the general public in the hope that someone would recognise the description. They were expecting quite a few phone calls as the information was so vague that it could apply to thousands of men. The victim was at least fifty but no more than seventy. His marital status was unknown because the mark left on his finger by a wedding band was faint, suggesting either that he was divorced or that he had simply lost or stopped wearing his ring. He probably did some kind of desk job. Alternatively, he could be retired or unemployed. There were no scars or tattoos on his hands. His blood group was O positive like half the country, but that didn't rule out the possibility that he was a foreigner. He was likely to be a member of an organisation such as the Freemasons. The description went no further.

The first Huldar heard about the appeal was at the end of Erla's morning meeting with the investigation team. The incident room was so packed that some of them had to stand. Erla briefed them on the progress of the various lines of inquiry, but omitted to mention the time capsule or the coffin found on the landfill site. However, she did mention the possible link to Jón Jónsson for the first time, though without going into details. Huldar would have preferred it if she had described the letter, Jón's connection to the murdered prosecutor Benedikt Toft, and the fact that the coffin belonged to Jón's stepfather. Instead she merely mentioned in passing that Jón Jónsson's name had unexpectedly cropped up in connection with the inquiry. Huldar tried to convince himself that this was because she was planning to devote tomorrow's meeting to this new lead. If not, it was hard to see how he was to make any progress. Investigating further possible links would be far too much work for him alone. He was particularly concerned about the lone initial K, which fitted with Kolbeinn, the driver of the car in the underground garage. Erla didn't share his worries.

The best way to find out whether the K stood for Kolbeinn or somebody else entirely was to force it out of Þröstur. He was the one who had compiled the hit-list, after all. That interview would be the number one priority if Huldar had his way, in addition to questioning Jón himself. The man had already demonstrated that he was capable of incomprehensible acts, and this surely made him the most likely candidate for the murderer.

Still, Huldar was in such an excellent mood that he couldn't summon up any rancour towards Erla. This morning he was predisposed to feel magnanimous towards all the world, since yesterday evening could hardly have gone any better.

Huldar had no idea what he had finally done right in Freyja's eyes. He didn't really understand women, or men for that matter; he couldn't work out what was going on in their heads. But, for whatever reason, she had been willing to meet him, and for once not to discuss murder or the mistreatment of children. She had invited him round to her flat and, to begin with, had been rather quiet, as if regretting her decision. But he had made sure she never had a chance to put a polite end to his visit. When it came to the opposite sex, he was a veteran of both marathons and obstacle courses. Eventually she had relaxed, thanks either to the wine or to his bottomless well of police anecdotes. He didn't care which. After they had drained two bottles of red between them and she had started slurring something about babysitting and weekend dads that he couldn't make head or tail of, he had shifted to sit right next to her, having been inching his way closer all evening. She hadn't pushed him away – and before he knew it there was no telling which of them was keener to fling off their clothes.

At that moment Huldar had been struck by a revelation. If he wanted something deeper with this woman than a one-night stand, then a drunken shag on a sofa that was missing one arm wasn't exactly a good beginning. So, instead of pressing home his advantage, he had pulled back, telling Freyja that he had better make tracks. She had gaped at him in bemused astonishment, all glassy eyes and smeared lipstick. For an instant his resolve had weakened but, ignoring the ache between his legs, he had thanked her huskily for an enjoyable evening and left.

While he was waiting for the taxi, he had glanced up at the block of flats and seen Freyja standing at her window, watching him. He chose to interpret this as meaning that for once he had done the right thing. More often than not the women he slept with would be flattened by a hangover the morning after, incapable even of lifting a hand to wave goodbye. The sight was invariably so unappealing that he didn't bother to get in touch again and neither did they, since his face would probably forever be associated in their mind with throwing up and a crashing headache, the night's pleasurable sex reduced to a hazy memory.

Erla drew attention to her presence by banging down the remote control of the overhead projector. 'Aren't you listening?' She frowned. Like Huldar she had pronounced dark circles under her eyes, but hers were the result of worry and overwork, whereas his were due to red wine and incipient doubts about the wisdom of last night's decision. 'If you can't keep your mind on the job, I'll find someone else to assist me.'

'Yes. No, I just got distracted for a moment. Sorry.' Huldar forced himself to focus. 'Could you possibly repeat that last bit?'

Erla tutted but did as he asked. They were the only ones left in the room. She had asked him to stay behind for a brief chat and Huldar had been expecting her either to apologise for her outburst yesterday or to give him a bollocking. Unpredictable as ever, she did neither. 'I'm going over to the hospital to take a statement from Kolbeinn, the guy who dragged that poor sod Benedikt through the handrail. The doctors have given us the green light. You coming?'

'Sure. Of course.' Huldar was a little surprised but didn't show it. The taking of Kolbeinn's statement was important; the first attempt, which had been made while Huldar was at the landfill site, had been such a disaster that Erla and her colleague had been booted out of the hospital and forbidden to come back until Kolbeinn had recovered. Although the man hadn't been physically injured, the experience had, not unsurprisingly, come as a terrible shock. When Kolbeinn got home later that evening he had suffered a heart attack and been sent for an emergency angioplasty. The very next day Erla had turned up to question him and he had almost ended up in the operating theatre again.

'Will we be allowed in?' Huldar asked.

'Yes. They understand how vital it is for us to speak to him.' Avoiding his eye, Erla started raking together the documents she had used at the meeting. 'I had to ask the guys upstairs to speak to the senior consultant. The doctors were refusing to take my calls. They only picked up once and that was so some nurse could read me the riot act. Like I'd gone to see Kolbeinn for the express purpose of giving him another heart attack.'

A light suddenly dawned on Huldar – so that was why Erla wanted him to come along. He'd once half killed a man during questioning – by mistake, needless to say – but it amounted to the same thing. That had been during the fateful investigation that cost him his job. Based on his past record, if something went wrong this time he was bound to get the blame. His good mood slipped a little but he did his best to cling on to it. Did it really matter why she was letting him go along? At least he would have the advantage of hearing the man's statement first hand, and it would also give him a chance to ask about any possible links to Jón Jónsson. Because they weren't obvious, as he had already established. If Erla imagined he was going to sit in meek silence on an uncomfortable hospital chair and take the blame if the guy dropped dead in the middle of questioning, she was in for a surprise.

For once it was a beautiful winter's day. The sky was cloudless, there wasn't a breath of wind and the snow glittered a pristine white. Although it stung their cheeks, the frosty air was fresh and invigorating. The remnants of Huldar's hangover dissipated when he opened the car window, stuck out his head and filled his lungs. He filled them again, to make sure the effects would last, then rolled up the window. On days like this he felt an urge to go skiing, though he'd never owned a pair of skis, never even hired one. When he was a boy he'd been offered his sisters' hand-me-downs, but they were pink and covered in bunny stickers, so he wouldn't be seen dead using them.

He and Erla had hardly spoken during the short drive to the National Hospital. He didn't dare start a conversation for fear of revealing that he had seen through her supposedly friendly gesture. And she had apparently sensed this, because she concentrated on her driving, but even so managed to hit every red light on the way.

As they got out of the car, Huldar contemplated the old white hospital building that had originally been designed to cater for the nation's needs for the foreseeable future. The ugly mess of more recent annexes was testament to how misplaced that confidence had been. He looked up at the triangular frieze by the artist Gudmundur from Middalur. His grandmother had pointed it out to him when she took him with her on one of her trips to Reykjavík for tests. She had told him the picture was called 'Caring and Healing'. As a child he hadn't quite grasped what this meant, but now he admired the artist's humility in recognising mankind's limited capacity to intervene in the difficult cycle of life. Not everyone could be saved; sometimes all one could do was alleviate people's suffering. Countless spells in hospital had achieved little in his grandmother's case.

Since Erla had visited before, they didn't stop to ask the way but made straight for the lifts. They were accompanied by a patient in a towelling dressing gown, hooked up to a portable drip. He wore a woolly hat on his head and stank of smoke. Huldar considered offering the man some chewing gum but he got out on the first floor, so there wasn't a chance. No doubt the guy would receive an anti-smoking lecture from the first member of staff he encountered.

Huldar could have sworn that the woman sitting in a glass cubicle keeping an eye on the comings and goings in the corridor stiffened when she saw Erla. Jumping to her feet, she disappeared round the back, perhaps to alert the doctor on duty that the detective who had almost killed one of their patients yesterday had returned. Huldar hoped the doctor in question would be aware of the authorisation Erla claimed to have received. Otherwise this would not only be a waste of time but embarrassing as well. He had no desire to be shooed back down the corridor, watched by nosy patients with nothing better to do.

But nobody came running after them and they were able to enter Kolbeinn's room unhindered. The hospital had thought it best to give him a room to himself, rather than leaving him screened only by a curtain, like most of the other patients. It was simply too disruptive to have him on the ward, screaming in his sleep as a result of his traumatic experience.

'Oof. You again.' Kolbeinn reached for the bell. He was pale and wan, hooked up to a drip like the man in the lift, and to several bleeping monitors as well. His heartbeat was a moving line on a small screen. 'Are you here to finish me off? I thought the police were supposed to investigate deaths, not cause them.' He sounded hoarse and had clearly spoken little that day.

Huldar went over and moved the bell out of reach before Kolbeinn could summon help. 'No one's coming. We have permission to be here. I promise we'll be more considerate than last time.' Bending down, he fumbled for the lever on the bed and raised Kolbeinn into a sitting position. It was impossible to question a man while he was lying flat on his back, staring at the ceiling. Especially not when it was crucial to detect any changes in his expression, however faint. Bearing in mind that Benedikt Toft had flatly denied that the severed hands in his garden had anything to do with him, they were quite ready for Kolbeinn to attempt to mislead them about his link to the man he had inadvertently killed in the underground garage. However outlandish this case was, no one would commit such appalling crimes for no reason. If they could discover what lay behind them, the rest would be straightforward, or at least more straightforward.

Erla took a chair beside the bed and Huldar fetched another from the corner and sat down next to her. She came straight to the point. Perhaps, like Huldar, she was afraid the staff might intervene at any minute. 'I'm afraid we have to do this. It's a pity your health's so delicate, but I'm afraid the investigation can't be put on hold until you recover. You're a key witness.'

'Me?' Kolbeinn rolled his eyes as he tried to make himself more comfortable. 'If I'm your key witness, you're in a real mess. I didn't see anything except . . . the man who . . . who, well . . . died. There was no one around when I went to fetch my car and no one there when I parked it that morning.'

'So you still think your car was chosen completely at random?' Sarcasm dripped from Erla's voice and Huldar decided to interrupt at the first opportunity. If the man suffered the slightest relapse it would be a long time before they could interview him again; a situation they must avoid at all costs.

'Yes. I don't just think that.' The cardiograph took a noticeable jump, the numbers on the screen rising accordingly. 'I know it.' The readings dropped again. Was it possible the monitors could work as lie detectors?

'Right.' Huldar shifted to the front of his chair. 'But even when people think they're sure, they can find on second thoughts that they're wrong. So we're going to ask you a few questions and we need you to answer as conscientiously as possible. Take all the time you need to think; it's not a race against the clock.'

Kolbeinn seemed grateful to be able to turn to Huldar. At any rate, the readings on the monitors dropped. 'I can't help you. I parked my car that morning and went to fetch it after work. I had nothing to do with what happened and don't know anyone who'd be capable of such a thing. I can't give any other answers – however hard I rack my brains. I'm the victim here. Picked at random.'

Huldar jumped in again the moment Kolbeinn finished speaking. 'Tell me something. Now you've had more time to reflect, I can't believe you haven't given a lot of thought to the man who died. Can't you remember anything that might link you to him? Could he have been an old client or a childhood acquaintance, perhaps? Benedikt Toft's an unusual name.'

Kolbeinn raised his head from the snowy-white pillow, just enough to shake it. 'No, no and again no. The man was a complete stranger;

I never knew him and as far as I'm aware he was never one of our clients. Though of course I don't know them all by name. We have over a thousand clients on our books.' Not one of those thousand clients had bothered to send him flowers or chocolates or even a card. The bedside table was bare, apart from a yellow plastic jug.

'He wasn't one of their clients,' Erla said to Huldar. She sounded annoyed; she had planned to conduct the interview herself. 'Naturally we checked that.' She turned back to Kolbeinn, who made a bit of a face when he realised that she had taken charge again. The line of his cardiogram became more irregular, though this might be caused by fear that she would bring on another heart attack, rather than triggered by the name Benedikt Toft. 'Forget the work angle. We've also checked if your paths crossed in connection with his job as a prosecutor and found nothing. On the other hand, we have no way of examining the part of your life that's off record. For example, the victim was a Freemason. Are you or have you ever been a Mason yourself?' At the briefing Erla had made a big deal of this since it was one of the only links between Benedikt and the owner of the amputated hands. That said, the connection was tenuous; it was far from certain that the mark on the finger had been made by a Freemason's ring. Still, any lead was better than nothing, and on this basis the police were now scrutinising Benedikt's fellow Masons in search of anyone who had recently gone missing. So far it had yielded no results.

A hint of colour touched Kolbeinn's otherwise pale cheeks. 'No. I'm not and never have been a Mason.' He coughed, then added scornfully: 'You're not serious, are you? You don't think the man ended up like that just because he was a Freemason?'

'No. Of course not.' Erla's voice had lost none of its tetchiness. 'We're simply trying to establish a possible link between you.'

'Or confirm to our satisfaction that there are no links.' Huldar smiled, pretending not to notice Erla's expression. 'What you should know – and this might encourage you to exert yourself a little more to help us – is that a few days ago the man who died chained to your car was in a similar situation to you. He claimed to be completely in the dark as well, and we believed him. Instead of questioning him immediately, we left it. And he was murdered. Perhaps you're not in any danger but it would be better to be certain. Don't you agree?'

'Who on earth would want to kill me? I've never done anything to anyone and—' Kolbeinn broke off. 'I swear it. I know absolutely nothing about him.'

Erla pulled a photo of Benedikt Toft out of her pocket. She held it up to Kolbeinn. 'That's what he looked like. When you saw his face in the garage it was a death mask, distorted with pain. I doubt his own mother would have recognised him. Does this help at all?'

Kolbeinn took the photo and studied it carefully. It seemed he was actually trying to work out if he knew the man. But Huldar noticed that he was holding the photo so that it blocked their view of his face. Perhaps this was accidental. 'No. I swear I've never seen him before. Though of course he's old in this picture. I suppose I could have run into him years ago. His face is so ordinary, so unmemorable.' Kolbeinn handed the picture back to Erla. 'Are you really serious? Do you think the person who chained him to my car is after me now?' The fear in his voice sounded genuine. Like the anger that flared up immediately afterwards. 'If I'm in danger, why isn't there a police guard outside my room? What the hell's wrong with you people?' His readings shot up again, even higher than before.

'Do you own a chainsaw?' Huldar had learnt that an effective way of calming people down was to wrong-foot them with a question they weren't expecting. It worked.

'A chainsaw? What do you mean? What would I want with a chainsaw?'

'To saw down trees in the garden perhaps. Do you own one or not?'

'Of course not. There aren't any trees in my garden. A few shrubs that need pruning, but you wouldn't attack them with a chainsaw. I wouldn't even know how to use one.'

'Fine. Then you won't mind if we take a look around your house?' Erla had taken the conversational ball again and at last they were working like a team. Interrogations were supposed to be a doubles game, though their opponent was usually alone. Hardly anyone they interviewed asked for a lawyer to be present.

'Search my house? You want to search my house?' Again the man's reaction seemed genuine, genuinely astonished this time. But you couldn't place any reliance on that. It wasn't only professionals who knew how to act. When people were backed into a corner, they had a whole range of hidden talents they could call on, even a physical strength that they wouldn't normally possess.

'We won't make a mess,' Huldar said reassuringly. 'You and your wife won't know we've been there. Especially not you, of course, since you won't even be home.'

'I have nothing to hide. But I really don't like the thought of strangers rummaging through my personal belongings. I don't like it at all.'

Erla clicked her tongue. 'No problem.' She flashed him a brief smile. 'We'll apply for a search warrant. Most people prefer to avoid that as it has to go before a judge and so on. But it's up to you, of course.'

Kolbeinn needed no further persuading. They could search his house as long as they promised not to involve judges or courts. He was clearly desperate to avoid the slightest shadow on his reputation. Perhaps this was due to his job: it would hardly be good publicity for an employee of an accountancy firm to be mixed up in a criminal case, whatever its nature. Huldar made a mental note of this weak spot.

They continued to grill him about anything they could think of, but learnt nothing of substance. Kolbeinn appeared to be a model citizen who led a rather humdrum existence, never taking risks or putting a foot wrong. He was one of those people who read the paper from cover to cover every morning, was guaranteed to be scandalised by at least one piece of news. But he would rather die than comment on an article online or raise his head above the parapet in any way. He drank tea for health reasons but craved coffee, was no doubt filled with prejudice against minorities but would never air these views in company. Any more than Huldar would air his view of him. His instinctive dislike of Kolbeinn wasn't based on anything tangible.

Erla was about to stand up when Huldar slipped in a final question. He kept his eyes trained on the man's face. 'Do you know Jón Jónsson?'

'Jón Jónsson? It's possible. It's a common name.' Kolbeinn's face showed hardly any reaction, only a slight frown as he tried to place the name.

'Jón Jónsson. He's just got out of prison after serving a sentence for the murder of a little girl. Do you know him or have any connection to him?'

Kolbeinn didn't answer. Above the neck of his hospital gown his Adam's apple rose and fell as he swallowed. Then he took a sharp breath and said: 'No. I'm not familiar with anyone by that name. Anyone at all.' But the colour in his cheeks, the rising numbers on his monitor and the jumping graph all told a different story.

This time it wasn't Erla who intervened. The door opened and a doctor and nurse barged in and informed them that their visit was over; they needed to examine the patient. When they saw the readings, they were in even more of a hurry to get rid of them. Kolbeinn's relief was palpable: the numbers on his monitor went into freefall as the two detectives headed for the door.

Huldar glanced back at the screen. The graph had returned to what it had been when he and Erla arrived.

The bloody man. He did have a link to Jón.

Chapter 19

The ticking of the clock on Sólveig's wall was driving Freyja mad. She had a blinding headache after all the wine yesterday evening and was having to concentrate hard on every word to follow the thread. She still couldn't work out what had happened, how the evening had ended like that, why Huldar had suddenly said goodbye and walked out just when she had finally wanted him to stay. She was glad she wouldn't have to encounter him at work after sleeping with him. But it hadn't been her decision. What was his problem?

'So in other words he injured his sister?' Freyja suppressed a sudden longing to cradle her head in her hands. 'When he was eight?' She had been surprised when Sólveig called out to her as soon as she walked in the door. Freyja had arrived half an hour late, looking as if she'd put on her make-up in the back seat of a car driven by a learner on their first lesson. Instead of saying that she was busy and would look in later when she was feeling better, Freyja had obliged. Now she was having to pretend nothing was wrong, despite feeling as if her head had sprouted a new heart that was throbbing in time with her old one.

'Yes. That's how he ended up with me.' Sólveig was looking even scruffier than usual. The T-shirt visible above the neckline of her hippyish pinafore dress was on inside out, showing the label. She must have dressed in a hurry or in the dark. But her jewellery was in place: the bangles, necklaces and heavy earrings that stretched her earlobes by several millimetres. Surely they couldn't be comfortable. 'I don't remember how it happened – if I ever knew – but the girl lost two fingers. Or three. I'm not quite sure. She was in hospital for quite a while, though, and there was even a risk she could have died.'

'And you just suddenly happened to remember all this?'

'Well, maybe not *suddenly*. I had to rack my brains, but with the help of some old diaries – I always make notes of the main points that emerge from my sessions – I was able to piece it together. I couldn't find the reports, though.' Sólveig met Freyja's eye, only to look away immediately. 'You can tell that to the police. If they'd rather speak to me in person I should be able to find a space in my diary, though I'm pretty booked up.' This was accompanied by a short sigh so exaggerated that it belonged in a radio play.

'The police don't make appointments. They just turn up.' Freyja couldn't work out why she was so annoyed with the woman. Perhaps it was the hangover. But no, it wasn't only that; it was her suspicion that Sólveig wasn't being entirely straight with her. 'Anyway, we'll see. I'm more interested in the kids. The brother injures his sister, clearly not by accident. Then what? You're drafted in to diagnose the boy and treat him. Have I understood that right?' Given her current state, Freyja was quite proud of herself for managing to come out with this without garbling it.

'Yes. At the time, I was working on child protection cases for Hafnarfjördur Council and when the incident occurred they referred him to me. If my diary's right . . . which it is . . . I saw him five times in the follow-up. That was the entire course of treatment. I started my own practice after that and won a contract to provide support services for schools, so I don't know what happened after I left. But he ended up back in my care as a teenager, for abnormal behaviour at school. That was a far less serious matter but I recognised the name and asked if I could treat him.'

'What emerged from your original diagnosis? What drove the boy to injure his sister?'

'As I said, I can't find the files on Þröstur from that period, so I can only go by what I remember.'

'That's better than nothing.'

'Yes. Quite. If I remember right, the boy was unhealthily jealous of his sister. He was one of those kids who's hard to warm to, but everyone loved her. Being younger she undoubtedly enjoyed more attention from their parents. The boy also had problems controlling his temper. The two things made for a bad combination.'

Freyja wasn't hung-over enough to let this one go. 'Is it possible you're forgetting something?'

'What?'

Freyja leant forwards. 'Now you know who their father was, don't you see any reason to doubt your analysis? Don't you think it's possible that the boy's anger resulted from something rather more serious than problems with self-control? I find it extremely unlikely that he injured his sister in the hope of attracting his parents' attention. Were his home circumstances ever checked?'

Sólveig didn't answer immediately. Her thick lower lip twitched as if she had a nervous tic. 'I wasn't responsible for that. Hafnarfjördur social services took care of that side. I was sent a report by them that – again I'm relying on memory – said his home life was absolutely fine.'

'No alcoholism or other problems of that kind? No abuse?'

'No. I think I'm right in saying that his parents were given the all-clear. And I was in no position to cast doubt on that judgement.'

'But you must have spoken to Þröstur about his family. Do you remember how he described his relationship with his father?'

'No. I've forgotten. It was almost sixteen years ago. It's amazing that I can remember anything at all.'

Freyja decided to leave it for the time being. All she could think about right now was cold water – she was so parched her tongue was literally shrivelling up. 'Well. Thanks anyway. I expect the police will put in a request shortly to Hafnarfjördur Council or the Child Protection Agency for the reports, and that'll clarify matters. In the meantime it would be great if you could sort out the authorisation so Thröstur's old headteacher can give me a copy of everything he's got.'

Sólveig said she would get it to her later.

Freyja felt a little dizzy when she stood up but managed to keep her balance and leave the office without accident. She gulped down a glass of water at the sink, filled it up again, then went to her own office. Shortly afterwards she heard the door of Sólveig's room closing, followed by the front door. She had gone home, though the working day had only just begun. Strange. And of course no authorisation had been left in Freyja's pigeonhole or in Sólveig's deserted office.

By lunchtime Freyja was feeling more herself. The ibuprofen provided by the Children's House nurse had helped, as had the hamburger she had washed down with a milkshake for lunch. By the time the phone call came from the police station at Hlemmur she was feeling ready for anything. The man who rang introduced himself as Gudmundur Lárusson and said he had been given her name and number by Huldar who hadn't had time to deal with the matter himself. The request was simple but urgent: could she come straight over to Hlemmur and help the police talk to someone who had walked in off the street and was, it turned out, connected to a case Huldar was working on. Huldar had said Freyja was familiar with the background and should be able to help calm down the apparently inconsolable woman. There followed a description of the fit she had thrown in the lobby, screaming at the receptionist until he rang upstairs for assistance.

When Gudmundur finally got round to telling her the woman's name and her connection to Huldar's case, Freyja shot out of her chair, into her coat and out to the car with the man's parting words still ringing in her ears. The woman who had created a scene at the police station was none other than Dagmar, the mother of Vaka, the little girl Jón Jónsson had murdered.

The traffic was light and there were few people about, but Freyja kept hitting red lights and sat there impatiently, her fingers drumming on the steering wheel. Would she make it to the station before Vaka's mother left? She wondered why Huldar hadn't rung himself and this brought her back to the bigger question of why he had walked out on her last night. She still couldn't work it out.

Freyja didn't waste time putting any coins in the parking meter by the police station – if she got a ticket Gudmundur could no doubt use his influence to have it waived. She sprinted into the lobby and introduced herself breathlessly to the officer on duty. Presumably he was the man who had been subjected to a tirade by Vaka's mother. He gave no sign of having been shaken. In fact, he was singularly uncommunicative, though he did manage to point her in the right direction.

Gudmundur Lárusson came out to greet her, looking white-haired and rather frail. But the huge fist resting on the door-handle was testament to his former physical strength. 'I've put her in here – it's a sort of waiting room that we don't use much. She refused to talk to me. She seems very deflated after her outburst, poor woman. Hopefully you'll be able to comfort her and get some sense out of her, if that's possible. Maybe she lost her mind after that terrible business with her daughter. It wouldn't be the first time that had happened to a parent in her position. I'm considering calling her husband to come in and fetch her. What do you think?'

Freyja nodded distractedly, eager to go in and see the woman.

Gudmundur opened the door and showed her in, making no move to follow, then closed it behind her. Freyja assumed he would go directly to ring Orri, Dagmar's husband.

The windowless room could hardly have been more austere. Two small sofas faced each other across a coffee table, on which lay a small pile of tattered glossy magazines, with the cover missing from the one on top. On the table in the corner was a tangle of computer leads, looking as if they'd been dumped there. The woman was sitting on one of the sofas, her face buried in her hands. She didn't seem to have noticed that she was no longer alone.

Freyja moved closer, sat down on the sofa opposite and coughed. 'Hello. Are you Dagmar?'

The woman looked up, her red-eyed, tear-swollen face registering surprise. 'Who are you?'

'My name's Freyja. I was asked to speak to you. I know a little about your daughter's case.'

'My daughter's case?' Dagmar narrowed her eyes angrily. 'My daughter's case? Are you joking? My daughter never had any case.'

'I'm sorry. I put that badly.'

Freyja remained silent until the woman's anger had subsided. Now she was staring blankly into space, as if she didn't know where she was. Her look of bemusement briefly transformed her into a younger version of herself, the deep worry lines between her eyes fading, her puffy eyes widening and her slack, half-open mouth hinting at an innocence of which she had long ago been robbed.

'Who exactly are you, Freyja? Why aren't you in uniform?' Dagmar scowled again, twisting her upper lip into a sneer. Her real age reasserted itself.

'I'm not with the police. I work for the Children's House but I sometimes help the police with cases relating to children.'

'Is that so?' Dagmar snorted in disgust, rolling her eyes heavenwards as if to ask the powers that be what they were thinking of to burden her with this crap. 'Great. Are you a sociologist then? Are they planning to write an article about what happens to people who lose a child?'

'I'm a psychologist and I'm not writing any article.' This was true, despite frequent exhortations by the Child Protection Agency to their staff to deliver papers at conferences and submit articles to academic journals. 'I'm only here to give you a chance to get things off your chest. I'm assuming you came here for a reason but you haven't managed to make yourself understood yet. Unless you simply wanted to vent your anger. This is as good a place for that as any. Better than taking it out on your husband, for example.'

'My husband? I'm single.'

So there was little point in Gudmundur phoning Orri. No one would be collecting Dagmar any time soon. Although Freyja had thought about Vaka's parents from time to time, she hadn't looked up what had happened to them after they lost their daughter. It wasn't particularly surprising that they had separated: the divorce rate among parents who had experienced a trauma of this type was higher than average, especially if they'd only had the one child. 'I don't suppose it'll help but I'm single too and I know it's not always easy, especially when you're feeling down and have no shoulder to cry on.'

'Please, spare me the sentimental crap. It's not like we're friends.'

Freyja was unperturbed by the harsh words. Dagmar wasn't the first person to react like this; the parents of the kids who came to the Children's House rarely had their tempers under control and often lashed out verbally. The thin-skinned tended not to survive as psychologists. 'Of course not. Then perhaps you'd like to tell me why you came here?'

Dagmar drew herself up, smoothed the lapels of her coat and rubbed the creases out of her trouser legs. It was a pathetic attempt to restore her pride, not unlike the methods used by Freyja and Baldur when they were young. She was probably regretting her behaviour down in reception. 'I came here to tell the police what I thought of them. And once I'd got started, I remembered that I'm disgusted with the whole justice system, including people like you; people who are labouring under the delusion that they can glue something back together when it's been smashed to smithereens.'

'I'm not here to give you counselling. Though I don't think it would hurt for you to seek help. There are various methods of dealing with grief that could work for you. The grief won't go away, as you know, but it is possible to make life a bit more bearable. It's never too late to try therapy, even many years after your loss.'

'I'm not interested. Haven't I made myself clear enough? You asked why I came here and I'm telling you. There's something wrong with the way this country's run and I wanted to say so. Somebody has to, or this disastrous, ineffectual machine will just keep grinding on, convinced that everybody's satisfied. Well, we're not all satisfied. I'm definitely not.'

'Could you give an example of what you mean?'

'How is it possible that a man who rapes and murders a child is allowed to go free after a few years, while the child's family is given a life sentence? How is that possible?' The woman's voice broke and she lapsed into silence, all the air going out of her again like a burst balloon.

'It's very unfair, I agree. But that's our justice system and we just have to hope that it serves society on some level. If people are given life sentences and have no chance to turn their lives around, there's a risk they'll commit even worse crimes when they feel cornered. Murderers might start killing witnesses, since it would make no difference to them; they'd be condemned to spend their life in prison anyway. Maybe these arguments don't sound very convincing but there's no perfect system when it comes to punishing people.'

Dagmar had listened. She hadn't interrupted or rolled her eyes but listened attentively, her head lowered. 'I should go. I don't know what I was thinking of.'

Before she could rise to her feet, Freyja seized her chance. She didn't want to have to tell Huldar that she'd extracted nothing of interest, merely spent the time debating the rights and wrongs of the Icelandic justice system. 'It's twelve years since your daughter was murdered. Have you been here before for the same reason? If not, what made you come today?'

'I saw him. The bastard. Walking along the same pavements as I do, breathing the same air—' Dagmar broke off and shook her head. She sniffed, then continued: 'He looked happy. As if the years in prison had meant nothing to him. Before we divorced, my ex-husband pointed out that I'd started walking with a stoop. I didn't mention that he had one too. I know I still walk like that. So does he.'

Freyja sat and watched the woman without speaking. Dagmar's shoulders shook and a few tears dripped onto her pale-coloured trousers. After a little pause, Freyja asked gently: 'Where was this?'

'Does it matter?'

'Maybe. Maybe not.'

Dagmar glanced up. 'Are you keeping him under surveillance then?'

'Yes and no.' Freyja kept her answer deliberately vague. She didn't want to get the woman's hopes up. Although Huldar wanted to speak to Jón, that wasn't the same as keeping tabs on him.

'Why wasn't I informed? Why? Would it have killed someone or messed up the budget?' Dagmar stared at Freyja, her eyes filling with tears again. 'I'd have liked a chance to prepare myself. Is that too much to ask?'

Freyja wished with all her heart that the door would open and Huldar would come in and take over. Even old Gudmundur would do. Anyone who could explain why the system worked like this. Was it really true that no one bore a responsibility to inform the victims or next of kin in cases like this? In Iceland it was almost inevitable that people would run into one another sooner or later. 'No, it's not asking too much. I'm afraid I don't know enough about it; I assume it's a question of protecting people's privacy.' She took a deep breath and quickly continued before Dagmar had a chance to freak out again. 'I'm not responsible for this legislation but in my opinion they should have let you and your ex-husband know. And Jón's family too, but they weren't informed either. Whether it was a mistake or standard practice, I don't know.'

Dagmar nodded slowly. 'Tell me about it.'

'Would you mind saying where you saw Jón?'

'Like I said, does it matter?'

'I don't know. Possibly.'

Dagmar pondered the matter as if it was a secret she was reluctant to share. 'He was walking along Borgartún. This morning.'

'Where exactly on Borgartún?'

'By one of the office buildings. He gave the impression he was snooping around for something. Maybe he was collecting cans for the recycling money.' She paused, then added harshly: 'I hope so.'

'Was this near the big accountancy firm, by any chance?'

'How the hell did you know that?' The fragile sense of trust that had been developing between them seemed on the point of shattering.

Freyja dodged the question, though she guessed the woman wouldn't let her off so easily. 'Do you know a man called Kolbeinn Ragnarsson who works in the building?'

'No. Should I?'

Again, Freyja avoided answering Dagmar's question. 'What about Benedikt Toft, a retired prosecutor?'

'No. What's going on? Who are these men? Paedophiles?'

Freyja was disconcerted. 'No, they're not suspected of anything like that.' She had compared the initials in the time-capsule letter with the names of paedophiles known to have been active ten years ago but had found no correspondence. Nor did she recognise the initials from any cases that had come through the Children's House.

At that moment the door opened and Freyja was saved from having to explain why she had mentioned these two men. She regretted having done so now and offered up a heartfelt prayer that Dagmar wouldn't go out looking for Kolbeinn because she suspected him of having some connection to Jón Jónsson. Gudmundur Lárusson was standing in the doorway.

'Your husband's here to fetch you.'

'My husband?' Dagmar stood up. She flushed, with fury, not embarrassment. 'What the hell's wrong with you people?'

A man of about forty pushed past Gudmundur. He was holding a car key in both hands, fiddling with it like a Catholic with a rosary. 'Come on, Dagmar. I'll give you a lift home.' The man avoided meeting his ex-wife's eye. 'They didn't know we're divorced and I didn't correct them. I just wanted to help.'

'Help?' Dagmar adjusted the bag on her shoulder and clutched at the collar of her coat as if to hide her bosom. 'I don't need any help from you.' She walked out without a word to Freyja, shoved at Gudmundur who had inadvertently got in her way, and stormed off down the corridor.

'Please excuse her.' The husband looked shamefaced, as if her behaviour was his fault. Perhaps he had walked out on her when things hit rock bottom, unable to live with a woman who would always remind him of what they had lost. Perhaps he had been prepared to put the past behind them but she hadn't. Or vice versa. Or perhaps the love they had once shared had simply dried up. 'She's not normally like that. Or she didn't use to be.' He nodded goodbye and hurried after the wife he had once loved.

Belatedly Freyja remembered what had upset Dagmar and brought her to the police station. She ran after the man, calling: 'Jón Jónsson's just got out of prison. That's why she came here in a fury. I thought you ought to know.'

Orri stopped dead, and slowly turned. His calm manner had vanished and there was a sudden crazy glint in his eyes, as if he were a hand grenade and Freyja had just pulled out the pin. He took a step closer. 'What did you say?' His voice slowed and deepened. Perhaps they weren't so different after all, Orri and Dagmar.

Freyja instinctively retreated two steps, closer to Gudmundur. She should have kept her mouth shut. Perhaps this was why people in their position weren't informed when prisoners were released.

Chapter 20

As so often, it wasn't one big thing but a number of smaller ones that finally changed Erla's mind about Jón Jónsson's possible connection to the murder in the garage and the severed hands. Huldar was too delighted to care what had brought about her change of heart. Erla was in charge and without her support his hands were tied; there were too many ill-defined strands to untangle, too many jobs to be done. Hard though it was, he hid his satisfaction. He felt like he had that time he scored the winning goal in the match against the other class in his year. His troubles were behind him; the way forward was clear. At nine years old he had been confident that his victorious goal was his passport to a professional career abroad, though, as it later transpired, his career as a footballer had peaked in that moment. Similarly he was now confident that his victory over Erla's obstinacy would lead to a breakthrough in the murder case. Although the goals were different, the sense of triumph was the same. He almost felt like going out and celebrating with a coconut truffle like he had when he was nine.

Huldar's hopes had first been raised as he and Erla stood in the corridor after being turfed out of Kolbeinn's hospital room. She may not have been particularly adroit at social interaction but Erla was a good detective and knew how to read people. Kolbeinn's lie hadn't escaped her. It was obvious that Jón Jónsson's name had switched on a light bulb somewhere inside his head.

The phone call from the pathology lab had been another contributing factor. After examining the body in the coffin, the pathologist was cautiously confident that the cause of death did not match that given on Einar Adalbertsson's death certificate. He wouldn't provide any further details over the phone but asked Erla to come over herself or send a representative. The officer who'd gone in her place had yet to return.

Yet another factor was Erla's telephone conversation with Einar's surviving daughter. Far from being upset when informed about her father's unscheduled trip to the dump, the woman had retorted that for all she cared his coffin could stay where it belonged, with the other rubbish. Then she had hung up.

The tipping point probably came when Erla tried to track down Jón Jónsson himself. She had taken the trouble to inform Huldar that this was only because she suspected him of having stolen his step-father's coffin, but Huldar knew better. She was beginning to have her doubts. He sat in her office while she made one phone call after another, always receiving the same answers. No one knew what had become of the man. His ex-wife and kids weren't answering the phone and the Prison Service was unable to help. It was the same story at Litla-Hraun, at Reykjavík social services and at all the homeless shelters: none of them had seen or heard from Jón or had any idea what had become of him. It was as if the ground had swallowed him up the instant he stepped out of the prison transport in the centre of Reykjavík, a free man.

While Huldar was listening to Erla's phone calls, he had received one himself from Gudmundur Lárusson. His old boss had wanted him to know that the mother of Vaka, the girl Jón had murdered, was making a scene down at the station on Hlemmur. Huldar decided he had better stick close to Erla so he could strike while the iron was hot. Nevertheless, curious to know what Vaka's mother had to say, he asked Gudmundur to give Freyja a shout. He hadn't heard from either of them since. He would ring Freyja as soon as things quietened down here. Deep down, though, he knew that the real reason he hadn't contacted her directly was because of last night. He had to find some way of explaining his abrupt departure that would show him in the good light that he felt he deserved. The trouble was, he couldn't plead in his defence that he had wanted to spare them both the usual outcome of his drunken one-night stands. Freyja was unlikely to be disarmed by any allusion to his long and varied list of conquests. Faced with the prospect of this conversation, he had begun to doubt the wisdom of his decision to walk out on her. In hindsight it would probably have been wiser to stay and spend the night with her. Not only wiser but a whole lot more enjoyable. Still, too late now. He pushed the thought away. He needed to focus on Erla and the investigation.

Morsel by morsel he had fed her every bit of information he had in support of his theory, like a mother feeding her young. He knew the battle was won when she told him to ring the Identification Committee and ask them to do another comparison between the fingerprints of the amputated hands and those of Jón Jónsson. Although no match had been obtained by running the prints from the hands through the police database – where Jón's details were presumably stored – Erla thought it worth examining his prints especially, in light of his disappearance. The Identification Committee and Fingerprint Department were no more infallible than anyone else. But, as it transpired, there was another, much more serious problem.

'When he called back it was to tell me that Jón's prints are missing. They're not there. If they ever were. I suppose it's possible they omitted to take them during the murder investigation. It was an open-and-shut case after all,' Huldar said.

'Are you shitting me?' Erla furrowed her brow. 'That just can't be right.'

'No, actually you're right, it can't. His fingerprints were found on the pillow he used to smother the girl. So they must have been recorded, but they haven't found their way into the database. It's the same story with various other records relating to Jón and his son Thröstur; they should exist but they don't. I still haven't received any material from the Reykjanes District Court about the case in which he was acquitted.'

'What the fuck is going on?' Erla reached for the phone.

'You can save yourself the effort. The guy I spoke to was positive – the fingerprints aren't in their database.'

'Great. So what the hell do we do now?' The question wasn't directed at Huldar; she was thinking aloud. 'What about Litla-Hraun? Perhaps we could lift his prints off something there? He must have left some belongings behind. The bugger of it is that they'll have cleaned out his cell by now and moved another prisoner in.'

'It's worth trying.'

Erla shook her head despondently. 'This whole case is a total shambles.'

Huldar could only agree. 'I'll talk to them. And while I'm doing that, I'll ask about the letters Jón received while he was inside. Perhaps they'll remember who sent them – the person who wrote them might have offered him a roof over his head.' Erla had been far from polite when she rang to question the prison staff about Jón, and Huldar doubted that a second call from her would be well received.

She made a dismissive noise that he chose to interpret as consent. When he got back to his desk, he was relieved to see that Gudlaugur wasn't there. He needed to concentrate and the young man was forever interrupting him. Recently his questions had mostly been concerned with how to identify possible retail outlets for chains like those used in the murder of Benedikt Toft.

In the event, the prison guards at Litla-Hraun didn't slam the phone down on Huldar, but the man he spoke to thought it unlikely that anything would be left with Jón's fingerprints on it. Another inmate had moved into his cell and the few items that had belonged to Jón had disappeared with him. But the guard promised to check. Before he could hang up, Huldar managed to slip in a question about Jón's letters. The man had to go and consult one of his colleagues and when he came back the answer proved to be yet another disappointment. The letters had been from Jón's lawyer and their contents were therefore confidential; legal correspondence couldn't be opened or phone conversations between lawyers and clients monitored. Jón had also written his lawyer any number of letters and their communications had continued almost to the last day of his incarceration. This news was better than nothing; perhaps the lawyer would know what had become of his client or, even better, would have organised his accommodation himself.

Huldar ended the call. He tapped the receiver against his forehead while pondering whether to ring the lawyer, one Sigurvin Helgason, next. Of course the lawyer wouldn't be able to answer any questions except those relating to matters he was sure Jón Jónsson wouldn't mind his revealing, but Huldar had to try. They were getting nowhere, yet the bloody man must have spoken to someone since he got out.

Before he could psych himself up to tap in the lawyer's number, his mobile rang. Freyja's ID flashed up on screen. He sat there staring at it, the ringtone seeming to grow ever louder and more insistent until the people at the nearby desks were looking at him and he could no longer avoid answering. He cast around frantically for an honest, sensible explanation of what had happened: he wanted to say of course he had been eager to sleep with her but, given his past experiences, he had wanted to wait until she wasn't drunk – while simultaneously avoiding saying 'sleep with', 'past experiences' or 'drunk'. Especially with his colleagues' ears flapping.

'Hi!' He sounded absurdly upbeat, like a salesman for a health insurance company. 'Thanks for yesterday evening.' It was the best he could come up with.

Freyja took a moment or two to reply. 'Yes, er, thank *you*.' She sounded embarrassed, which only made matters worse. A conversation where one person was dying of embarrassment was bad enough, but when both were in the same boat it was hopeless. His fears proved unfounded, however, as Freyja was quick to recover her composure. 'Anyway, I wasn't calling about that. I just wanted to give you the lowdown on my visit to Hlemmur. To see Dagmar, Vaka's mother. I assumed you'd want to know what happened.'

'Yes, absolutely. Absolutely.' He had to choke back a laugh in his relief at being spared the necessity of negotiating the minefield around their relationship – or non-relationship. How unlucky humans were to be the only animal that had to worry about such things. 'What was the problem?'

'She was furious that they hadn't let her know about Jón Jónsson's release. Her reaction was similar to Thröstur's. Her ex-husband came along too and he didn't seem much happier. Were you aware they were divorced?'

'No. I don't really know anything about them.'

'Nor do I, despite having sat with her for a while. Except that she's got a temper. So's he.'

'How did they hear about it?' Iceland was a small place but Huldar found it hard to picture a friend or workmate excitedly picking up the phone to let them know.

'She saw him. And guess where?'

'Where?' He couldn't possibly guess. Any more than he could when his little nephews posed ridiculous questions for him: *Guess what my teacher's called? Guess what I found in the road? Guess what I'm thinking about?*

'By the accountancy firm. The one where that man was murdered.'

'When was this?'

'This morning. Or so Dagmar claimed. But she didn't give an exact time.'

'Listen, I'll have to talk to you later. I'll call you.' He hung up and dashed over to Erla's office. If the woman hadn't been seeing things, Jón Jónsson was alive and kicking after all.

'I've already apologised and I agree with you about the system being hopelessly flawed. I'm not sure if I'll make myself any clearer by saying it all over again. What would really help now is if you'd answer the questions we came here to ask. The sooner you do, the sooner you'll be rid of us.' Erla reeled off this speech almost without pausing for breath. Ever since Dagmar had let them in, she had kept bringing the conversation back to complaining about how badly victims and their families were treated when violent criminals got out of jail. Erla had done her best to pacify the woman by agreeing with every word, but it wasn't enough.

They were seated in a living room that was no doubt the last word in chic; everything was in complementary shades of grey: walls, furniture, vases, cushions, rugs, even the pictures. Every time Huldar took his eyes off the two women he felt as if he were suddenly seeing the world in black and white. The overall theme must be depression. That would chime well with the classical music emanating from invisible speakers, from a compilation entitled, at a guess: 'Tearjerkers to Play at Funerals'. What surprised him was the total absence of pictures of Vaka. He had been braced to find them hanging on every wall and staring down from every shelf. Perhaps the woman found it hard enough to cope with her grief without being reminded of her daughter every time she sank into the grey sofa to watch a black-and-white film on TV.

'Sorry. Sorry.' Dagmar buried her face in her hands. She was a very different sight now from the description Freyja had given, her earlier state of agitation replaced by tiredness. She was an attractive woman; on a good day perhaps beautiful. Her features were unusually striking: those high cheekbones and large eyes with dark lashes. Her only flaw was her mouth; she could have been a model were it not for the thin, colourless lips that seemed incapable of smiling. And no wonder. Huldar was struck by her eyes, too: they were empty of life, as if her soul had died within her.

'I know it's not your fault. I'm not normally like this. Usually nothing gets to me. Nothing seems worth it anymore.'

Huldar's gaze had been wandering but now he snapped back to attention. At last they were getting somewhere. 'No problem.'

Dagmar emitted a dry, mirthless laugh, without breaking into a smile. Her lips didn't even twitch. 'I want to move to America. Ridiculous, I know. I'm not even good at English and I don't know anybody there. But at least the Americans don't let men like that disgusting animal out of jail.' She turned her head to stare blindly at the grey wall. 'It's just not fair.'

'Could you tell us a bit more about your encounter with Jón this morning?'

The woman looked back at them wearily. 'Why? Like I said to that woman earlier, what does it matter?' Then, without waiting for an answer, she continued: 'It was on Borgartún and it must have been about half past nine. I know that because I run a hair salon in the same street and we open at ten. He was loitering by one of those glass buildings, where the accountancy firm is. He was wearing an anorak and jeans. He hadn't changed much, though his hair was thinner and of course he was older. But the strange thing was that he didn't look any worse than he did at the trial. Prison seems to have agreed with him. Can you believe that?'

'Did he see you?'

'No, I don't think so.' Dagmar averted her face again. 'Funny. Orri and I sat through every day of the trial; we felt we had to hear every word. I stared at that man the whole time, imagining how I would tear him limb from limb if I ever got the chance. My thoughts weren't pretty, I can tell you, but they kept me going.' She emitted that same cold laugh and shook her head resignedly. 'Then what happens when I eventually do bump into him? I run away. I think that's why I lost it the way I did at the police station. I'm furious with myself. I just needed to get it out of my system, to blame somebody else.'

'Violence doesn't come easily to normal people. You should be glad you reacted the way you did. You wouldn't have been any better off if you'd gone for him.' Huldar's smile did not prompt one from her in response.

'I'm not so sure. To be honest, I think I'd be feeling a lot better now. I'd be feeling bloody great—'

Erla interrupted: 'How come you didn't go straight down to the station? You didn't get there until after twelve.'

'I couldn't get away before then. I had customers to style, cut and colour. But I got more and more worked up and when I finally got off at lunchtime I stormed straight down to the station. Would you like the names of the customers or the member of staff who covered for me? Am I under suspicion for some reason?' Dagmar's face brightened. 'Has something happened to Jón? Don't say he's been attacked?' There was no mistaking her delight at the prospect. Her thin upper lip curled back to reveal her front teeth in a snarl that reminded Huldar of the hyenas in wildlife documentaries, circling the prey brought down by a lion. He doubted she had ever made a face like that while her daughter was alive.

'Nothing's happened to him, as far as we know. Are you quite sure the man you saw this morning was Jón Jónsson? You couldn't have been mistaken?' Erla's words put an end to Dagmar's vindictive pleasure as effectively as a lioness driving away a hyena.

'I'm positive. A hundred per cent positive.'

'Are you acquainted with anyone who works at the accounting firm where you saw Jón? Kolbeinn Ragnarsson, for example? Does his name ring any bells?' Huldar bent forwards, watching the woman closely. He wanted to be sure he could read her expression, pick up the tiniest hint that she recognised any of the names he was about to mention.

'I was asked the same thing this morning. Who is this man?' Dagmar's face revealed nothing but suspicion.

'If you don't know him, it doesn't matter. What about Benedikt Toft?'

'Who exactly are these men? Why should I know them? Don't I have a right to know who you're trying to link me to?' When neither Erla nor Huldar replied, she leant back in her chair with a contemptuous expression. 'For God's sake, like I can't just google them. What century are you people living in?'

'We can't stop you. You're free to google them if you like.' Huldar sat back. He hadn't detected anything interesting in the woman's reaction. Nothing but her trademark contempt and resentment.

'Well, there we are.' Erla caught Huldar's eye. 'Was there anything else you wanted to ask?'

'Nope.'

'Can I say something before you go?' There was no mistaking Dagmar's fury. Her eyes narrowed and the muscles in her face tightened, throwing her cheekbones into even starker relief. 'Never, ever call my ex-husband again. He's not my next of kin; he has no connection to me any longer. None at all. We divorced ten years ago and I can't get over the fact that you had the nerve to involve him in this. You ought to be ashamed of yourselves. How would you feel if your ex was hauled in to fetch you from the police station? When you were at rock bottom?'

They shook their heads foolishly. Neither wanted to answer but as Huldar was slightly more to blame than Erla, he felt obliged to speak for them both. 'Again, we can only apologise.'

Dagmar glared at him, evincing not the slightest desire to forgive. 'Are we done here then? I've had enough of the police for one day. Enough to last me a lifetime.'

Huldar thought he had never in his life met anyone so full of violent emotions, all of them negative. She fluctuated between rage, hatred, vengefulness and malice. The only gentle emotion that seemed to stir in her breast was grief; a gut-wrenching grief that was presumably the source of all the other feelings. He wondered if her ex-husband was in a similar state. Had the loss of their child robbed his life of all pleasure too?

On his way out Huldar happened to glance through an open door leading to the master bedroom, as the large, neatly made bed revealed. It wasn't this that arrested his attention but the walls, which were covered from floor to ceiling with framed photographs. Photographs of a little girl at various ages. Presumably Vaka. Although he walked past too quickly to see for sure, he could have sworn there was also a wedding picture of Dagmar and Orri. There was no doubt, then, about which of them had walked out on the other. With the murder of her daughter this woman had lost everything she cared about: her family, her child and the man she loved. Jón Jónsson had an awful lot to answer for.

Chapter 21

Although it was Friday outside, Huldar had the feeling that inside this drab little flat it was still only Tuesday. Perhaps it was forever Tuesday. No Fridays or weekends here. No holidays or other special days to break the monotony.

All the curtains were drawn to prevent the feeble daylight from spoiling the picture on the large flat-screen TV. In spite of its size, the TV looked like the cheapest model. No question who had been responsible for its purchase: Thröstur looked like the type who went for size over quality. His sister and mother, on the other hand, seemed like the kind of people who endlessly weigh up prospective purchases to be sure of getting their money's worth, before eventually deciding not to buy at all. Huldar had also noticed that unlike him, this family seemed to be in the habit of repairing things that broke. The two glued-together china figurines on the coffee table were testimony to this spirit of thrift, though the person responsible for the repairs had done a clumsy job: the parts had been stuck together crookedly and the glue had dripped. He itched to take the statues with him when he left and chuck them in a bin.

This visit was turning out to be quite different from their first one. Last time he and Freyja had barely sat down before they were shown the door; this time they had already been there much longer, though still without managing to extract the answers he was after. Freyja was jumpy, constantly darting sidelong glances to check that the front door hadn't moved. But Thröstur gave no trouble, though he could hardly be described as polite or hospitable. When his mother Agnes had made a move to offer them coffee he had snapped at her, making her wilt. Now she was sitting, chastened, beside her children on the sofa.

The visit had been arranged at short notice. Erla had wanted someone to find out if the family had any news of Jón Jónsson. He seemed to have vanished off the face of the earth, like snow disappearing into the gutters in spring. Although the family had cut all ties with him, like lopping off an unwanted limb, the police thought it likely he would get in touch with them, perhaps in the belief that he would be forgiven now that he had served his time – and found Jesus into the bargain. They were also after some item with his fingerprints on it, as the police couldn't simply rely on Dagmar's claim that Jón was alive and in possession of both his arms. Finally, Huldar wanted to grill Thröstur about the initials in his letter, though he doubted the young man would discuss the matter in front of his mother and sister. No doubt they would have to summon him to the station for a formal interview at the weekend. When Huldar rang to request a meeting with the three of them, he had offered them two choices: either they could come to the station – if they didn't turn up willingly, a car would be sent to fetch them – or the police could come round and interview them at home. Thröstur, who had answered the phone, had plumped for the second choice.

Erla had agreed to let Huldar talk to the family as she herself was due to present senior management with a progress report. There was no chance of postponing a meeting with them; you were expected to attend even if you were in a hospital gown with a drip in your arm. But she showed no sign of dreading the meeting now that the inquiry was getting somewhere at last. It hadn't hurt when Huldar had let it be known that he wasn't bothered about taking the credit for spotting the connection between the murder of Benedikt Toft and Jón Jónsson.

If it turned out to be a false lead, though, he was willing to bet that the blame would fall squarely on him.

Huldar wasn't going to worry about that now. He was used to dealing with problems when they cropped up; there was no point fretting about them beforehand. All the same, he wasn't looking forward to the inevitable conversation with Freyja after the present visit was over. They had both been held up by the Friday traffic and only had time to exchange a few words in front of the building before coming upstairs. They'd been so keen to cut the embarrassing encounter short that they had bumped into each other in their haste to ring the bell. Now Huldar was regretting not having hung around long enough to get their little chat out of the way.

'So none of you have seen or heard from Jón since he got out?' The trio on the sofa shook their heads in unison. 'I'd prefer it if you each answered individually. Let's start with you, Sigrún.' One of the few things Freyja had said to him before entering the building was that he must never refer to Jón Jónsson as their *dad*. The word was inappropriately affectionate in the circumstances. She had also advised him not to ask the siblings if their father had abused them as children. That ought to be done in private, not out of the blue like this, in their home. 'Sigrún?'

The young woman raised her eyes and briefly met Huldar's before lowering them again. Her long, mousy hair fell over her face as she said in a small voice: 'I haven't spoken to him. Or seen him either.'

'He hasn't tried to reach you? Hasn't tried to call your mobile, for example?'

The young woman shook her head.

'I'd appreciate it if you'd answer, rather than just nodding or shaking your head.'

Sigrún looked up and although she didn't meet Huldar's gaze, he could at least see her face. He was struck yet again by how unmemorable it was. If he closed his eyes he'd have difficulty recalling what she looked like.

'I don't have a mobile phone.'

Huldar raised his eyebrows in astonishment. 'You what?'

Sigrún blushed and started fiddling with her maimed hand. Up to now she had kept her hands in her lap, as if to hide the missing fingers. 'I said I don't have a mobile phone.'

'I'm sorry, it's just so unusual these days.' Huldar ventured a smile, but it didn't help. Thröstur bristled and their mother looked as though she didn't know where to put herself. 'Anyway, good for you. Mobile phones are a terrible waste of time.' The trio on the sofa relaxed slightly. 'What about you, Thröstur? Have you seen or heard from your father?'

'No.' Thröstur managed to charge even this brief monosyllable with fury. He had painted his nails black since Huldar last saw him but the varnish had begun to chip, making his hands look dirty and drawing attention to his tattoos: *Ultio dulcis*. Huldar had looked it up and wanted to ask Thröstur why he had chosen to adorn his skin with this quotation, but there would be plenty of time for that later.

'You haven't received a call that you chose to ignore?'

'No.' Thröstur expanded his puny chest as far as he could. The action smoothed out his wrinkled T-shirt, revealing a picture of a man's head with a gun at one temple and a mess of blood and brains bursting out of the other. The man's face was distorted by a scream. Huldar felt a sudden urge to drag Thröstur along to the scene of a suicide; show him what it really looked like when someone blew their brains out. That would make him think twice about wearing the T-shirt again.

'OK. What about you, Agnes? Have you been aware of him at all?'

The woman looked up, apparently surprised that it was her turn.

She glanced nervously at her son as if he were controlling her answers, but Thröstur ignored her. 'No.'

'Does that surprise you? That he hasn't been in touch with any of you?'

'No. Yes. I don't know.' Mother and daughter were not dissimilar, both hunched and shamefaced, with restless hands. Naturally, Sigrún looked a good deal younger than her mother, but Huldar guessed that in thirty years' time she would be the living image of her. Agnes's age was hard to guess. Gaunt and round-shouldered, with all the spirit drained out of her like that, she probably seemed older than she was. 'I don't think so.'

'When did you last speak to him?'

'Oh, not for years.' Agnes opened her eyes wide and her grey face brightened momentarily. 'Not for years and years.'

'Could you say how many?'

'I haven't spoken to him since it happened . . . since his arrest. I don't know exactly how many years it is. I try not to think about . . . about all that.' The woman seemed incapable of meeting Huldar's eye; her gaze kept flickering to the side, up, down, anywhere but at him. Now, though, she was looking at Freyja, which Huldar took as a sign of good taste; in her place he would rather look at Freyja too. He suspected that Agnes was uncomfortable in the presence of a man, and no wonder: her husband, who should have been her life's companion, had treated his family worse than words could describe. They would have been better off with a python in the house.

Apparently reading Huldar's mind, Freyja now stepped in. She spoke in a gentle voice, without a trace of superiority. 'What about child maintenance and so on? You must have had to discuss that sort of thing at some point.'

'I never applied for child maintenance. I didn't want a penny from him; all I wanted was to get the divorce over with as quickly as possible.' Agnes sat up a little straighter at this, as if somewhere inside her lurked the ghost of her pride. 'The main thing was to cut all ties with him. Even if the money came via the Department of Social Security, it would still have been tainted by association with him.'

'I understand.' Freyja nodded, then went on, still in a gentle voice: 'We know that Jón received letters in prison, handwritten letters from an adult. Were they, by any chance, from you?'

'Are you joking? No, I never wrote to him.'

'I see. Did he try to stay in touch with you or the kids while he was in prison? In the early years, for example, before he realised you were serious about breaking off all contact? Did he send Christmas cards, birthday messages, anything like that?'

Agnes tutted indignantly. 'No. Nothing like that. I'd have been amazed if he'd remembered Thröstur and Sigrún's birthdays, let alone mine. He can hardly have failed to notice Christmas, but he left us in peace then as well.'

'What bullshit is this?' Thröstur thrust his head forwards and his mother instinctively shrank back. 'Christmas? Birthdays? Why the fuck are you asking about that?'

Huldar was about to intervene, but it seemed Freyja had no need of a knight in shining armour this time. All sign of nerves had vanished and he couldn't detect the faintest trace of fear when she replied. There was no accounting for women when they took offence. 'All right,' she said with a sudden edge to her voice. 'Then tell me something. You claim your father has never been in touch; you say you haven't seen him and no one informed you that he was getting out. So how did you know he'd been released when we came round the other day?'

Thröstur flushed dark red. His coarse skin was suffused; his face lost any last vestige of attractiveness. His nostrils flared, making the ring through his septum twitch. 'How did I know?' He glowered at Freyja in a vain attempt to intimidate her.

'Yes. You must be able to remember. He only got out a week ago.' Freyja stared back at the boy with icy equanimity.

'Of course I remember.'

'Oh, do tell us how.'

Thröstur clamped his thin lips in a tight line, but before Freyja or Huldar had a chance to press him, his mother interrupted. 'I told him.' A faint colour tinged her cheeks. 'I got a phone call from the Prison Service.'

'But it was our understanding that you hadn't received any warning?' Huldar tried to keep a simultaneous eye on the reactions of both mother and son but it was impossible. He chose to focus on Agnes instead as her nerves were more likely to betray her.

'They rang me. Not to tell us he was out or anything like that but because they wanted Jón's address. The one he gave them was wrong. At least, he wasn't living there.' Agnes smoothed her trousers and stared into space as if mesmerised. 'I told Thröstur about it afterwards.' Thröstur nodded and grinned, obviously pleased with this intervention.

Huldar turned to Sigrún. She came across as honest, if only because she seemed too much of an innocent to employ deceit. Then again, it could take more courage to speak the truth than to lie. Perhaps she was the worst of the three. 'What about you, Sigrún? Did you hear the news from your mother?'

Sigrún darted a glance at her brother, defenceless under this renewed onslaught. Her fingers twitched in her lap and she rubbed at the stumps. But before she could answer, Thröstur forestalled her: 'No. I told her. After you two came round. I didn't want some stupid arseholes blurting it out to her.'

No doubt 'stupid arseholes' was a reference to Huldar and Freyja. Neither of them batted an eyelid.

'Is that right, Sigrún?' Freyja employed her soothing voice again. Her whole manner was gentler than when she had been exchanging shots with Þröstur, like a dog lowering its hackles on encountering a harmless creature. 'Was it your brother who told you?'

Sigrún didn't look at Freyja but suddenly appeared fascinated by the two cracked figurines on the scuffed coffee table. 'Yes. I heard it from him.'

'Do you remember when?'

'A couple of days ago. I can't remember exactly when.'

Huldar didn't believe this for a minute and assumed Freyja wouldn't either. It was well known that people remembered exactly where they were when they received momentous news. And this news must have been momentous for all of them. But it was as clear as day that he wouldn't be able to get anything sensible out of the women while Þröstur was present. Much as Huldar disliked the thought of hauling them all into the station to be interviewed separately, there was no avoiding it. The family had already suffered a raw deal in life but sadly there was no upper limit when it came to suffering. 'I see. Changing the subject, you wouldn't happen to have anything in your possession that Jón could have handled?'

They all looked up as one and gaped at Huldar, nonplussed. Then the brother and sister turned to their mother and waited as anxiously as Huldar for her answer. Finding all eyes resting on her, Agnes realised she would have to reply. 'No. There's nothing of his in this flat. I got rid of most of his belongings when it was clear that he wasn't coming home again, and I chucked out the few remaining items when we moved. The odd thing of his used to turn up, but we've moved countless times since we lived in Hafnarfjördur.'

'Well, if you do come across anything, I'd be grateful if you'd let us know as a matter of urgency.' Huldar turned to Thröstur and Sigrún. 'I gather that one or other of you visited him in jail, on at least one occasion. Am I correct?'

Thröstur reddened as he shook his head. He wasn't much cop as a liar; none of them were. Perhaps it ran in the family. 'No. Sigrún never went there. Nor did I.'

'Is that true, Sigrún? Our sources tell a different story.'

Her voice emerged in a squeak. 'Thröstur's right.'

Huldar turned to Freyja. That was that then. He would have to call them in separately for questioning. If he carried on now, there was a risk the family would prepare their answers by synchronising their story. 'Shall we call it a day?'

Freyja agreed and they rose to their feet. The mother and daughter's relief was almost palpable, as if they'd received a visit from the Stasi and been given a stay of execution at the last minute. Thröstur did a better job of feigning indifference. He escorted them out, stood over them while they put on their shoes, then slammed the door behind them without saying goodbye.

They walked downstairs without a word, then stood outside on the pavement, shuffling their feet awkwardly, until Huldar broke the silence: 'About last night—'

'Do we have to talk about it? I should never drink liqueurs. Let's leave it at that.' Freyja zipped up her parka and pulled up the hood.

'OK. I just wanted—'

'Fine. Please don't say any more.' Snow settled on the fur collar of her parka and Huldar yearned to brush it off. Freyja's make-up had been applied unusually sloppily that day; one eyelid was smeared with mascara and there was a hint of lipstick at the corner of her mouth, but these imperfections only made her more gorgeous. If they were on that sofa now, there was no way he could get up and leave.

A car drove past, spraying slush onto the pavement where they stood. They moved back from the kerb and Huldar saw that she was fumbling in her pocket for her car keys. The moment she found them she would say goodbye, so it was now or never. 'Are you busy this evening?'

Freyja had her keys now. She smiled thinly. 'No. But I'm getting an early night. I'm still feeling the effects of that wine.'

'What about tomorrow evening?'

'I'm babysitting this weekend. My niece. You'll have to try elsewhere.'

'Have I ever told you how brilliant I am with kids? They adore me.' No need to mention that he only had nephews. 'Can I invite you both to the cinema?'

'She's not even one.'

'To feed the ducks, then? They must be starving in this weather.'

She jingled her keys. 'We'll see. Maybe I'll call you.' She neither smiled nor frowned nor gave any other clue as to whether he should get his hopes up. 'See you.' She walked away.

Huldar stood there watching until Freyja disappeared round the corner, then strolled back to his car. He took his cigarettes out of his pocket but before he could extract one, his phone rang. It was the guard he had spoken to at Litla-Hraun earlier that day.

'We found something that used to belong to Jón Jónsson. Handled a lot by him but no one else. Can you pick it up or should I send it over?'

'What is it?'

'His Bible. He left it behind. They usually do.'

Chapter 22

Æsa's children meant the world to her. They were all that mattered; without them life wouldn't be worth living. All the same, she couldn't help feeling grateful for the weekends they spent with their father. She could sleep in, binge on sweets, turn up the TV as loud as she liked without the risk of waking them, miss a meal or eat when she felt like it, order a pizza – something other than a margherita for a change – and lounge on the sofa, reading a book, with no need to feel guilty. In other words, it gave her the opportunity to be lazy, and to enjoy every minute of it. She could go out on the town too, if her friends were planning a girls' night out, though these had become much rarer since they got themselves husbands and children.

There was nothing arranged for this weekend. She was faced with the prospect of spending it alone in the flat with only her worries for company. Thorvaldur was due any minute to collect the kids but she didn't trust him to look after them properly. He was as bad as that idiot cop who had spoken to her after she rang to report the incident at the Family Park. Not only had he belittled her concerns but he had actually dared to imply that she was making the whole thing up. Well, she knew better and so, of course, did Thorvaldur. He had claimed not to know any woman called Vaka, but she could tell when he was lying. Perhaps this Vaka was the new woman in his life and the man in the Father Christmas costume had been a jealous ex. If so, she wished the man would leave their children alone and get it out of his system by punching Thorvaldur instead.

Who on earth would do a thing like that? Lure someone else's children into their car and drive off with them? She had been plagued by such questions all day yesterday; they had invaded her dreams last night and she hadn't been able to shake them off even after she woke up. The colleagues she had told about the incident had rolled their eyes when they thought she wasn't looking. Even the nursery teachers seemed sceptical, though of course it was in their interest not to believe her tale. If Æsa was talking nonsense, they needn't feel ashamed of having failed in their duty to keep an eye on the kids in the park.

The bloody man had known exactly what he was doing when he put on that costume. If she had left out the bit about Father Christmas, the police would have handled the matter very differently, not sent round an officer who seemed closer in age to Karlotta and Dadi than to her.

'When's Daddy coming?' Dadi looked away from the television to stare hopefully at his mother. The cartoon flickered on the screen behind him. Figures that resembled neither man nor beast were fighting in a Wild West saloon bar. She doubted Dadi had a clue what was going on. He looked ready to drop, exhausted by the week, as he always was on Fridays. 'We've been waiting and waiting.'

'You haven't been waiting and waiting, Dadi. We've only just got home.' She went over and stroked his head, then bent down and kissed him on the brow. His eyes were glazing over and she knew that any minute now he would fall asleep on the sofa, in spite of the noisy shrieking of the cartoon. 'Daddy'll be here very soon. Don't go to sleep, you know how hard you find it to wake up again.' It was pointless even to say it; if Thorvaldur didn't arrive shortly, Dadi would be out for the count.

Karlotta appeared in the sitting room. 'Is Daddy coming?' It was always like this; they would take it in turns to ask. Every other Friday she had to put up with a deluge of questions from the moment they stepped in the door until Thorvaldur deigned to turn up. When he was late she sometimes thought they'd drive her demented.

'Yes, Karlotta. He's coming very soon.' Really, she should be grateful that they looked forward to going to stay with their father. She'd heard stories of children who always cried when it was time for daddy weekends, clinging to their mother's legs so they had to be prised off by force. How would she feel if their parting was like that? Even worse than she did now, undoubtedly.

'He's going to buy us ice creams. With sauce. Big ones, not kids' ones like you always get.'

Æsa forced a smile. 'I bet that'll be fun.' Thorvaldur spoilt them rotten during the weekends they spent with him, filling them with sweets and taking them to the cinema. No rules, just constant excitement and doing whatever they liked. She couldn't compete; when it was her turn to have them for the weekend she was always too worn out from working all week, and besides she couldn't afford to provide them with a two-day children's paradise. She didn't blame Thorvaldur; she would do exactly the same in his shoes. If she had the money, that is. It was no joke getting them back from their weekends with him, their faces sticky with sugar and their sleep patterns all messed up, but at least she did get them back. Now she was terrified that Thorvaldur would fail to keep an eye on them, and that 'Father Christmas' would be on the prowl again and seize his chance.

The doorbell rang shrilly and Æsa jumped. 'Well, Karlotta, who do you think that is?'

'Daddy!' Karlotta raced to the door with Dadi on her heels, his tiredness temporarily forgotten. Æsa gave chase but they had already opened the front door by the time she reached the hall. For a second it occurred to her that it might not be Thorvaldur but the man from the park. But there in the doorway was the familiar face, the highly polished shoes and the jacket that looked as if it had only been taken off the hanger five minutes ago. Thorvaldur was like a cat: always neat and sleek, whatever happened.

'Fetch your things. I need a quick word with your father.' Æsa pushed them inside to fetch the bags they had packed the evening before, spending ages choosing clothes and toys that Æsa knew they wouldn't touch. They had another set of everything at Thorvaldur's place, things he had bought for them himself as he obviously didn't want them to be seen wearing the threadbare hand-me-downs they brought with them from home. Well, that was his problem.

Thorvaldur stepped into the hall, making a face as he always did when he was forced to enter the flat. He would rather wait out on the landing, wallowing in his sense of martyrdom. 'What? I'm in a hurry. I've booked a table – I don't want to be late. Do you have any idea how busy the restaurants are? It's all about tourists these days.'

Æsa didn't have any idea. She hadn't eaten out for months. But tourists were unlikely to be dining in large groups at this time of year. It was typical of Thorvaldur to make a fuss. She hoped for his sake that the menu wasn't all escargots and Kobe beef. If he'd had to book, it was unlikely that he was taking the kids for a burger and chips, though she wouldn't put it past Thorvaldur to book a table at a fast-food joint. 'Who's Vaka? Are you going to tell me?'

'I don't know any Vaka. Stop going on about it, will you?' Thorvaldur glanced over her shoulder as if checking where the kids were. They both knew he was doing it to avoid meeting her eye.

'If you won't tell me who she is, you'll have to tell the police. I rang and they'll be in touch with you shortly.' In fact, there was no chance of this. The youthful officer who had come round had kept interrupting her with ridiculous questions about whether she smoked dope or was in the habit of imagining things, so Æsa had left out the bit about Vaka in a desperate attempt to keep him to the point. But there was no need for Thorvaldur to know that. She had decided to ring the police again on Monday morning and demand to finish giving her statement. It had become abundantly clear that they weren't going to get back to her.

'I can't tell the police about some woman when I don't even know who she is. For God's sake, stop nagging.' Thorvaldur flung back his head and called: 'Come on, kids! We're going to be late for supper.'

If Æsa knew Karlotta and Dadi, they would come running, trailing their backpacks behind them, in a panic that their father would leave without them. After that there would be no peace in which to talk to Thorvaldur. Clearly, there was no point pressing him about this Vaka. She didn't care if he wanted to keep his girlfriend a secret. There were more important matters at stake. 'Will you promise to look after them and never take your eyes off them for one minute?'

'What's the matter with you? Of course I'll look after them. Has anything ever happened to them on my watch?' He answered the question himself before Æsa had a chance to bring up the occasion when Dadi had cut his hand on his father's razor, or Karlotta's hair had been singed when one of her plaits swung into a candle on his coffee table. 'Nothing's happened because I take good care of them. Better than you. Who were they with when they were supposedly abducted by "Father Christmas"?' He made invisible quotation marks around the words.

'I can't be bothered to argue with you. Though you won't admit it, I know this has something to do with you, and all I ask is that you take special care this weekend. Don't take your eyes off them for a second.' Æsa could hear Karlotta and Dadi's noisy approach behind her. The peace was over. 'Promise me, Thorvaldur.'

'What? What's he got to promise?' Karlotta tugged at her jumper.

'To look after you, darling. And you must promise never to run away from your daddy. You must stay beside him all the time. All weekend.'

'What?' Dadi squeezed past her and took up position beside his father. 'What if I need to go for a wee-wee?'

'Or if Daddy needs to go to the loo? Do we have to go with him?' Karlotta giggled and pushed past Æsa after Dadi. They had no idea of the gravity of the situation; they were too young to understand that there were people out there capable of harming others, even children. However hard she tried to impress this upon them, in their eyes other people were merely there to make life easier and amuse them. Other children existed to be played with and grown-ups were for making sure they had food on the table, were wrapped up warm and were allowed to play between meals.

'Listen to what I'm saying. Promise me.'

The happy expressions faded from their faces as they gave her their word. Thorvaldur immediately started dressing them in their anoraks and helping them into their boots. Æsa bent down to receive two goodbye kisses. Thorvaldur's parting shot was that she could have dressed them a bit more smartly – they were going out for dinner, for goodness' sake. Then he herded them out. Karlotta waved goodbye to her mother as her father closed the door behind them.

Æsa could still feel the imprint of their kisses on her cheek. She hurried into the bedroom and stood watching as Thorvaldur helped them into the back seat of his car and fastened their seatbelts. As his car vanished down the street, she felt overwhelmed with dread. Her fears redoubled when it occurred to her that Thorvaldur had never promised her not to take his eyes off them, as she'd asked. Why hadn't she just told him the children were ill? But then she would have had to ask Karlotta and Dadi to back up her lie, and that wouldn't be fair on them.

Oh God.

The weekend had begun. Now she could start pacing the floor.

Thorvaldur knocked back another dose of ibuprofen and gulped down some water, hoping it would ease his suffering. His head was killing him; the wine at the restaurant yesterday evening must have been of a lower quality than he was used to. Unless it had been that second glass of whisky after he'd got home. Christ. Now he just needed an ice-cold lager to perk him up. It wasn't as if he didn't have any – there was a whole six-pack in the fridge. But it was out of the question. He was looking after the kids and he had to consider them. It wouldn't look good if he turned up at the cinema later reeking of alcohol. He would have to rely on the ibuprofen to see him through this weekend, just like it had on all the previous daddy weekends.

Thorvaldur re-wrapped his dressing gown and knotted the belt more tightly. He would have to find something for the kids to eat; it was nearly half past ten and they hadn't had breakfast yet. When they had barged into his bedroom at eight he had managed to buy himself some peace by planting them in front of the television. That had worked until half past nine. Then a cartoon started that they found boring. Still feeling groggy, he had talked them into going outside in the garden to play in the snow. They were still out there, presumably starving. If he called them now, he would have time to get himself together while they were taking off their outdoor clothes and washing their hands. Get himself sufficiently together, at least, to be capable of putting out their cornflakes.

The sour sensation in the pit of his stomach intensified when he remembered the lecture Æsa had given him yesterday. The kids had been outside in the garden for an hour, alone and unsupervised. Was it possible that . . . ? No, of course not. The garden was fenced off.

His stomach gave a half-turn, like a washing machine at the end of its cycle. What had he been thinking of? The wooden fence wasn't much of a barrier; it hadn't been designed to keep an enemy out. If someone was determined to climb over, there was nothing to stop them.

Thorvaldur strained his ears, suddenly too afraid to look outside. What if the kids had vanished? The relief that flooded him when he thought he heard their voices was so intense that his headache faded and even his stomach temporarily behaved.

He went into the living room, the parquet icy under his bare soles. As he approached the window, he could hear their voices more clearly. There was no doubt about it, Karlotta and Dadi were squabbling. His worries abated with every step; there was nothing to be afraid of. By the time he was standing at the window, about to wave to the children to come inside, all his fears were forgotten.

It was then that both children started screaming.

Chapter 23

Erla was jubilant: evidently the meeting had gone well and she'd been given a pat on the back for achieving a result – if you could call it a result. Huldar suspected her of giving the impression that they were on the verge of a breakthrough. How she had introduced Jón Jónsson – as a suspect or as a victim – was hard to guess, but it had clearly had the desired effect. Erla was never any good at hiding her feelings: if her bosses had reprimanded her, it would have shown in her face. Huldar guessed that their judgement had been clouded by Jón's name and record. What could be better than a perpetrator who was already a villain? They would be given a more or less free hand to investigate; no one was likely to start finding fault with their methods or clamouring about the human rights of the suspect. If, on the other hand, Jón Jónsson was the victim – if he'd been deprived of his hands and possibly more – all the public would be interested in was how badly he had suffered. The identity of the culprit would be almost beside the point; after all, people would be inclined to sympathise with him or her, however reluctant they might be to admit it.

The news had evidently got out that she was back in favour and it was safe to be seen with her, because the members of CID had been flocking to her side, one after the other, hoping she would notice them when it came to handing out new assignments. A fresh lead called for a change in emphasis. But although they were all raring to go, no one wanted to be left with the crappy jobs that always formed part of any large-scale operation. Huldar found it wise to hang back; he was sure Erla wouldn't overlook him. That is, he was convinced she would allot him one of the shitty tasks. Well, there was no chance he was going to suck up to her, or to anyone else for that matter. He was still too much the proud country boy.

The only other member of the inquiry team who didn't join in was the man who had been sent to see the pathologist about Einar Adalbertsson's remains. He sat at his desk, staring at his computer screen, getting up every now and then to fetch another cup of water. Huldar, feeling sorry for the guy, left the gung-ho group who were convinced they were on the brink of cracking the case, and went over to talk to him. Personally he hated visiting the pathology lab – it was always an ordeal for the eyes, nose and ears. And the same, it seemed, applied to his ashen-faced colleague. The man had been compelled to listen to a lecture from the pathologist on the decomposition of human tissues following interment, before being made to view the contents of Einar Adalbertsson's coffin. The man almost gagged as he described the experience to Huldar and repeated what the pathologist had told him.

'Enzymes and microbes break down the organs, destroying them in a few years, so there was no chance of examining them.' The man made a face. 'Thank God. I'm not sure I could have coped with that. There were still tatters of skin and flesh on the bones, though. If it had only been a skeleton, I wouldn't have minded as much.' He closed his eyes, shuddered and took a sip of water. 'It was horrible. His eyes were missing, sunk into his skull maybe, but I didn't dare ask in case the pathologist tried to retrieve them. There were tufts of hair on his scalp.' He took a deep breath. 'I'm going to be cremated.'

'I don't think you're the only one to come to that conclusion after a visit to the lab.'

'Apparently I was lucky, though. It could have been a lot worse. The pathologist said that if the coffin had been airtight, the body would have been reduced to a putrefied black soup.'

'What else came out of your visit, apart from this delightful experience? What about the cause of death?' The least the man could do, after making him listen to this stomach-churning description, was to slip him some information.

'Well, it turned out not to be as clear-cut as he told Erla. He's going to insist on a proper post-mortem and he's hoping that will clarify the cause of death, as it definitely wasn't cardiac arrest.' He shuddered again. 'Even I could see that when he showed me the back of the skull.'

'What did you see?' *And don't start on about withered scraps of scalp again,* Huldar added under his breath.

'A hole. Almost perfectly round.'

'So? It was my understanding that he hit his head when he passed out in the bathroom. He suffered from an irregular heartbeat, didn't he?'

'Yes. There was a fracture in the back of his skull that was consistent with hitting the edge of the bathtub. But there was another wound that couldn't have been caused by that – a round hole resulting from a blow with a blunt object. Or that's what the pathologist thought.'

'Why wasn't that mentioned in the original post-mortem? There isn't any doubt that it's the right body, is there? I suppose it's not impossible that there's another empty grave somewhere and that Einar's coffin will turn up at a later date.'

'His body was never examined. They never held a post-mortem of any kind. At the time there was no doubt about how Einar had died. He was on a waiting list for a pacemaker; he'd been receiving treatment for arrhythmia, which can cause dizzy spells. It wasn't the first time he'd had a fall. The wound on his head was consistent with hitting the edge of the bath, and the death certificate mentions that there was blood and hair on the tub where he'd struck it. He lived alone and there was no indication that anyone else was present when he died.' The man shrugged. 'His daughter was his only next of kin and she saw no reason to demand an inquest. It seems people were content to describe it as an accident. But now that his scalp has gone . . . apparently it remained behind on the pillow when they lifted out the skull . . .' The colour drained from the man's face. '. . . it's almost certain that it wasn't an accident. But it's not clear whether the doctor who issued the death certificate could have worked out that there were two wounds without doing a post-mortem.'

Huldar's mind was working furiously. 'It's definitely him, then?' he asked.

'Yes. The proof's pretty incontrovertible. The name of his late wife was engraved on the wedding ring still hanging off his finger bone. The skeleton was also wearing a ring from his Freemasons' lodge. But the pathologist's going to request his dental records, if they still exist. He's also going to consult Einar's medical notes for evidence of old fractures or other injuries that can be used to confirm his identity. There's a chance that it's someone else, but only a very slim one.'

The group around Erla was thinning out. The interesting assignments had probably already been allocated, leaving only the most tedious ones. Those still awaiting their tasks would be keeping their heads down in the hope she wouldn't notice them.

Huldar stood up and returned to his own desk. He looked Einar Adalbertsson up in the police register and found an entry relating to his death eleven years ago. He had been fully expecting to draw a blank yet again – for the entry to have gone missing or been deleted. Perhaps the inquiry team's optimism wasn't misplaced after all and they really had reached a turning point.

The entry wasn't very detailed but it was sufficient to give Huldar a clearer picture of the incident. Einar's cleaner had turned up as usual at eleven o'clock on Monday morning, only to discover him lying on the bathroom floor in a pool of blood. She'd heard a tap running and gone to check if Einar was still at home. He usually went out while she was cleaning. The woman had panicked when she looked in through the open door and saw him lying on the bloodstained tiles. She hadn't checked for any signs of life or touched him at all, just rung for an ambulance. A doctor had pronounced the man dead at the scene and called the police, though he thought it was fairly clear what had happened.

The man had fallen and banged his head on the edge of the bath. He was not thought to have been drinking as there was no smell of alcohol. He was wearing a pair of pyjamas and still clenched in one hand was a toothbrush with toothpaste on it. The medicines in the bathroom cabinet indicated that he was being treated for high blood pressure, a fact confirmed by the doctor who had prescribed the drugs. The doctor had added that Einar suffered from arrhythmia, which had caused him to have a fall on an earlier occasion. There was nothing to suggest his death had been anything other than an accident.

On closer enquiry, it was found that Einar had received a text message from a grandchild on the evening he died. The grandchild in question was a boy of thirteen, the son of Einar's stepson. The boy had sent a message to ask if Einar would buy some toilet paper that he was selling to raise money for charity and, if so, could he come round to collect the money. Einar had texted back immediately to say yes. When the police got in touch with the boy and asked how his grandfather had seemed that evening, he said he had only stopped by briefly, for half an hour at most, as his grandfather hadn't been feeling very well and said he needed to lie down. The boy added that he'd had no idea his illness was that serious. The boy's name was Thröstur Agnesarson. When asked, he explained that his father was dead, and the police officer who handled the case apparently didn't check up on this. Jón Jónsson's name was never mentioned.

The conclusion was that Einar Adalbertsson had died of an accident caused by his illness. The case was closed without further investigation and a death certificate was issued.

Huldar stood up again. It looked as if he was going to have to book out the interview room for several hours in Thröstur's case. The list of questions was growing ever longer.

Erla hadn't budged. She was still standing there, talking to the only member of the group left. He looked rather dismayed. When Huldar approached, the man seized the chance to melt away.

'How's it going?' Huldar reached for a plastic cup, stuck it under the nozzle of the drinks machine and selected black coffee. The lettering on this button had worn off long ago, whereas those for latte and cappuccino were like new.

'Good. Bloody good. Things are really starting to happen. I can sense it. We'll have made an arrest by Tuesday. Worst case, Wednesday.'

'Is that what you told the top brass?' He watched the dark stream filling the cup.

'Yes. Maybe I didn't put it quite that strongly, but I said I was optimistic we'd be making an arrest shortly.'

Huldar sipped the scalding coffee. Erla had made a big mistake, but there was no point telling her that. 'Thröstur's interview is going to be long and tough. We need to decide how to tackle him.'

'That can wait. A few of us are going out for a meal. A celebratory pizza and beer. There's a special deal on the drinks if we get a move on and order before seven.'

'Who's going?' Huldar wasn't sure he felt like it. Then again, he had nothing else to do; most of his friends had partners and children, and although they still hit the town on occasion, it was never spontaneous. They always needed several days' notice, sometimes as much as a couple of weeks.

Erla ran through the names of those going, but Huldar stopped listening in the middle; he'd made up his mind. 'I'm up for it.' He was hungry and wouldn't say no to a beer or two. Perhaps this would help to restore his relationship with his colleagues, or with some of them at least. If so, it wouldn't be a complete waste of time.

Three hours later he was still in the pub. They were seated around a large table. A few bits of leftover pizza graced the middle. The beers had long ago exceeded one or two and showed no signs of drying up. By now they were all talking louder, laughing harder and behaving as if they hadn't a care in the world. With every round Huldar's relationship with the others was slowly, slowly returning to the way it used to be before his temporary advancement. The music struck him as better now than when they had first arrived, the conversation more interesting. It seemed he wasn't alone in this feeling as some of the others broke into tuneless singing whenever a familiar chorus was played, or drummed along noisily on the table.

They all agreed that they should do this more often. And before long it was decided that from now on this should be a regular Friday event. Even those Huldar knew to be family men wholeheartedly endorsed this excellent idea. The next step wasn't far off. They would begin to break up into pairs, each earnestly telling the other how great they were, and exchanging phone numbers so they could keep up their newfound friendship.

A waiter arrived with a tray loaded with beers, prompting a new round of rejoicing. They raised their glasses and toasted some concept that none of them quite grasped, not even the person who had proposed the toast. When the glasses were banged down again, slopping froth all over the table, no one noticed or made any move to wipe it up.

Erla, who had taken a seat next to Huldar, was much closer to him now than she had been at the beginning of the evening. It felt good and he sat tight, even resting his arm along the back of the wooden bench behind her. She didn't seem to mind this in the least. When he felt her warm hand on his thigh, it seemed to him the most natural place for it to be. Until she shifted it somewhere else that felt even better.

Huldar stroked her hand to make it clear that he didn't object, though she could hardly have failed to notice the fact.

And then there was no turning back.

Chapter 24

Kolbeinn had felt better but he had also felt a lot worse. He was floating in a state of numb detachment, but that was probably the lingering after-effects of the anaesthetic or else the painkillers they kept shovelling down his throat. While he packed his few belongings, he reminded himself to check that he would be given more of these pills to take home. Above all he felt comfortable; the worries that had been preying on his mind ever since the detectives were shown out of his room now seemed unreal and unimportant. Until the police had arrested the person who had chained that man to his car, it would be best if he was allowed to remain on this pleasant high. His wife Heida would be glad, at any rate. She had asked if he'd be very hurt if she went with her sewing circle on the planned weekend trip to London, despite the fact that he was a bit under the weather.

A bit under the weather.

Here he was, recovering from a heart attack, and she would rather go gadding off abroad than nurse him. She hadn't even had the decency to come to the hospital to break the news, just did it over the phone. Yet aware as he was of her unfeeling behaviour, he couldn't register any hurt through the fog of opiates. After their conversation was over, he had actually smiled like an idiot over the derisory state of their marriage.

He had to secure a prescription for more of these miracle pills.

There was nothing left in the locker or on the hideous bedside table. All his possessions apart from the clothes he stood up in were now stuffed into the orange plastic bag in which Heida had brought his things, when she'd finally bothered to show up. Kolbeinn had been lying woozily in bed when she held out the bag to him. And there he had remained throughout her brief visit. Heida had been too busy complaining to pay any attention to how he was feeling. And he was too doped up to comment on the plastic bag that she had unceremoniously plonked on his stomach. When she said good-bye she had bent over and kissed him on the brow, like an aged aunt with a nephew. As she did so her weight had pressed down on the bag, but she didn't seem to notice and left without removing it from his middle.

When he surfaced again after a nap, someone had emptied the plastic bag, hung up his clothes, put his toothbrush and toothpaste in a glass by the sink and placed his tablet on the bedside table. The battery was flat and Heida had either forgotten or couldn't be bothered to find the charger. The same applied to his mobile phone, which was lying on top of the computer.

Holding on to the bed for support, Kolbeinn slowly lowered himself into the chair. It was the only way he felt able to put on his shoes. As he pulled them towards him with his feet, he was confronted again by the sight of his odd socks. Through the haze of drugs a slight sense of resentment stirred against Heida. Was it too much to ask that she bring him matching ones? Not to mention some under-wear? How could she mess that up?

Instead of focusing on Heida's shoddy behaviour, there were plenty of nice things to think about. Like the fact that the CEO of his company had phoned the ward personally to ask after him. A young nurse had passed on his wishes for Kolbeinn's quick recovery when she brought him his pills. He had swallowed them cheerfully, though at that moment he hadn't needed any drugs to perk him up; it was enough for him that the CEO had called. He didn't usually show much interest in Kolbeinn, merely nodded when they passed each other in the corridor, and on the rare occasions he did address him it quickly became clear that he had confused Kolbeinn with one of his colleagues. He always asked after the football star. Kolbeinn and Heida didn't have any children, but the son of one of the departmental managers played for Iceland. Since Kolbeinn wouldn't dream of embarrassing the CEO by pointing out his mistake, he had let it pass and scooted off as soon as he got the chance.

He finished tying his shoelaces. Then he slapped his thighs, gripped the arms of the chair and propelled himself to his feet. No point in hanging about. He had been discharged: the hospital was like an oversubscribed hotel and there was no question of being allowed to stay any longer, however much he pleaded. The next patient was waiting outside and before Kolbeinn even left the ward he would have been wheeled into his place.

Bag in hand, Kolbeinn shuffled out into the corridor. The man who was waiting to take his place was snoring, mouth wide open – obviously still alive. Apart from that all was quiet. It was evening and the other patients were asleep, knocked out by the sleeping pills that were distributed like sweets. Perhaps he should ask them to add some to his prescription; he'd need to sleep all weekend if he was to go back to work on Monday. Though he'd better not mention that again. When he had done so earlier that day, the doctor had advised him against it, recommending that Kolbeinn rest and take it easy for at least the next two weeks. Out of the question. He had to go in to work, if only to put a kibosh on the gossip. He must be the most popular topic of conversation in the office right now and he didn't care for it.

Kolbeinn stopped by a glass cubicle where a nurse was poring over some documents. She didn't notice him until he tapped on the glass, then she glanced up and smiled. 'All set then?' He nodded and she smiled again: at last they were getting rid of him. 'How are you feeling?'

'Well. OK. Ill. I don't know.'

'That's not unusual. But you've turned the corner and you'll make a full recovery, as long as you follow our advice and take it gently.'

'Yes, will do.' Kolbeinn wondered if he would have to ask for the prescription. The nurse didn't seem about to give it to him unprompted.

'Are you being picked up?'

To his own surprise Kolbeinn answered without embarrassment: 'No. I'll take a taxi.'

'OK. I can call one for you if you like.' All of a sudden, the nurse remembered something. 'No, silly me, I'm forgetting. When your boss rang earlier he said he was going to send a car for you. It may be outside now – I told him when you were getting out. You'd better check before calling a cab.'

A foolish smile crossed Kolbeinn's face before he could stop it. Perhaps the stories circulating at work were sympathetic after all. He was quite happy to play the victim, *poor Kolbeinn* – far better that than have them suspect him of being involved in the atrocity. *The atrocity*. It was the word he chose to use for the incident in the underground garage. It helped to distance him from what had happened. The atrocity. The word conveyed his respect for the gravity of the event, without conjuring up the grisly image of the mangled corpse or the ghastly sound of snapping bones. Overcome for a moment with dizziness, Kolbeinn tried to focus on the woman in front of him and banish all thoughts of what couldn't be undone. 'Can I get a prescription from you?'

'Oh yes, that's right – the doctor who discharged you took care of that before he left.' She retrieved the prescription from a card-board pocket on the desk. 'Is there someone who can pick it up for you tomorrow?'

'Yes.' He was lying; there was nobody he could ask. He would just have to go himself in the morning. He took the prescription she handed him, together with a paper bag containing some pills.

'These should see you through tonight and tomorrow morning, until somebody can pick up your prescription.' The nurse watched him pocket the note, reminded him of his next appointment at the Acute Cardiac Unit, then fell silent, waiting for him to leave. He stood there without speaking for a moment, then said an awkward goodbye.

As he descended in the lift, Kolbeinn stared glassily at the man in the mirror, a stooped, lonely figure with a plastic bag in his hand, greasy hair and his shirt buttoned up wrong. His coat hung loose from his shoulders as if his body had shrunk while he was in hospital. He supposed he should be grateful he hadn't been chucked out in the middle of the night like some of the other patients. And that he lived in Reykjavík. It wouldn't have been much fun having to wander aimlessly around town with his plastic bag, killing time while waiting for the next flight to the other side of the country. He looked like a tramp and if the police spotted him they were bound to pick him up. The cops were good at that sort of thing; at dealing with minor offences. But they didn't have time to post a guard outside his hospital room while he was lying there defenceless, despite the perceived risk. Unless the guards were down in the foyer?

But there was no one at all down there; no staff, patients or visitors, let alone police officers. The shop was closed and apart from the rustling of his plastic bag, the only sound was the humming of the refrigerator units against the wall, loaded with all kinds of unhealthy snacks and drinks. Kolbeinn stared, as if mesmerised, at the gaudy sweet packets. He was met by his reflection again, this time in the windows of the horseshoe-shaped foyer. This was no improvement. You'd have thought he was a mental patient, standing there gawping at the illuminated vending machines like a child at a Christmas tree. The sooner he was home and in his bed, the better. There, no one would be able to see him in this state.

He went outside, hoping to spot someone from his firm waiting for him. He couldn't call for a taxi as his phone wasn't charged, and the last thing he wanted was to have to go back up to the ward and ask the nurse on duty to call one for him.

His worries proved unnecessary. There was a car waiting a short way from the entrance with its engine running. It flashed its lights at him. He couldn't see the driver over the glare of the headlights, so he didn't know which of his colleagues had been given the task of driving him home, unless it was just some taxi driver. He hoped it was the latter. It would be quite beyond him to make conversation with a colleague, who was bound to be eaten up with curiosity.

Kolbeinn walked very slowly over to the car and climbed into the back seat. It occurred to him belatedly that he should probably have got in the front, but he hadn't the strength to move. It couldn't be helped. The driver didn't say a word, just waited for Kolbeinn to close the door, then drove off. To Kolbeinn's intense relief, the man seemed to be absorbed in some boring political discussion on the radio. The driver wasn't one of his colleagues anyway, so it was unlikely their paths would cross again. Keeping quiet seemed to suit them both.

When the car pulled up in front of Kolbeinn's house he did at least make the effort to thank the man and say good night. The reply was a mumbled comment that he couldn't quite catch. It didn't matter. Kolbeinn slammed the door and hobbled up to his front door. When he bent down to retrieve the key that Heida had promised to leave under the mat, he thought it odd that he didn't hear the car drive away. Perhaps the man wanted to make sure he got inside all right. What a kind thought. It would be handy too if Heida had been as remiss about the key as she had about other matters recently. But there was a gleam of metal when he lifted the mat. As he inserted the key and unlocked the door, he thought he heard the car door opening, and turned slowly to see what the man could possibly want. He hadn't forgotten anything, except to pay. He had simply assumed that was all taken care of.

If the driver was after money, he was going about it in an odd way. As Kolbeinn watched, the man lowered his head and came charging towards him like a mad bull. Kolbeinn reacted in slow motion; he heard himself say, 'Oh,' with calm deliberation, but made no attempt to retreat. In the instant before the man shoved him in through the open door, the thought occurred to him that he would have been better off lying on a bench in the town centre with the plastic bag for a pillow.

Chapter 25

It wasn't the first time Huldar had woken up in these circumstances. Yet he was as helpless as ever, too hung-over to think of any plan to take the edge off the inevitable embarrassment. Instead, here he was, lying naked in a strange bed, with no idea what to do next, only that it would be excruciating. He had stirred earlier, disturbed by the ringing of his phone, but, unable to face the new day, had gone back to sleep. Now he was awake. Not in the best of shape – but awake.

Huldar cracked open one eye and surveyed his surroundings. He was alone in bed. That was good, but it meant he had no idea who he had shared it with last night. He wasn't particularly keen to remember the identity of his bedmate either. He wanted to enjoy his amnesia a little longer. But then he spotted a shirt on the back of a chair. It looked as if it had been flung there from the other side of the room. The shirt was familiar, so familiar that he couldn't suppress a deep sigh. It was a regulation police shirt, much smaller than his own, with shorter sleeves and a narrower cut. Huldar closed his eyes as memories of the previous evening came flooding back.

Erla.

He had beaten his own record in ill-advised shagging. He had only gone and slept with his boss. Her duvet was rucked up at the bottom of the bed, her pillow under his arm. Shoving it away, he tried but failed to roll over onto his back. He would be able to in a moment, but for now he would be glad if he could just pull the duvet up over his bare body. Although he was alone in the room, Erla couldn't be far away and might appear any minute. It was sheer wishful thinking to hope that she might have gone outside and be sitting in her car, full of regrets, waiting for him to take himself off.

He thought he could hear the distant sound of a shower. All his instincts screamed at him to seize the chance and make a run for it. But that would only give him a brief respite. He couldn't avoid her forever. Huldar sighed. How the hell was he going to get out of this one? They worked together, met every morning of the week. The investigation would probably require them to work today and no doubt tomorrow as well, even though it was the weekend. So he would have no chance to recover or prepare for what was to come next. If he couldn't face talking to her now, there would be no way out of this cock-up except to hand in his notice. What on earth had he been thinking?

The recollection that a number of their colleagues had been drinking with them at the pub did nothing to make Huldar feel any better.

There was a squeak and the sound of water stopped. He managed with difficulty to reach for the duvet and cover himself. It was a start. Warily he opened one eye again and the other followed suit. Then, summoning all his strength, he rolled over. Though his stomach seemed to have been left behind and his head was about to burst, he felt better. But when he surveyed the room and saw their clothes strewn all over the place and the empty wine bottle on her bedside table, he almost rolled back on his face again. Rather than give in to the urge, he concentrated on trying to locate his trousers. Of course they were as far from the bed as they could possibly be. He listened and heard footsteps in the hall. Lifting his head, he wondered if he could struggle out of bed, retrieve his trousers and pull them on before Erla appeared, but before he could come to any conclusion she was standing in the doorway.

Erla leant against the doorframe, wrapped in a white towel that she was holding up with one arm while rubbing her wet hair with another, smaller towel. Below, her legs were studded with beads of moisture. 'Good morning.'

Huldar cleared his throat. 'Good morning.'

'You should jump in the shower. You'll feel much better afterwards. And wash the smell of smoke out of your hair. It fucking stinks.'

'Yes, I should do that.' Huldar stroked his wild mane back, suddenly powerfully aware of the reek of cigarettes.

'I'll put on some coffee. Want some shit to eat?'

'No, thanks.' The way she put it killed any appetite he might have had. Though to be honest, he had to admit he had appreciated her foul mouth when they'd been in bed last night. It had really done things for him. 'What time is it? I can't see my phone.'

'It's in the living room. It's eleven o'clock. Time to—' Erla broke off mid-sentence when her own phone started ringing in the other room, so Huldar didn't get to hear what it was time for. She spun on her heel and shortly afterwards he heard her giving terse answers, her tone serious. The sound of her voice came closer and before Huldar could grab the chance to pull on his clothes, she reappeared in the doorway, her wet hair standing on end. 'We'll be there – I will, I mean. Round up the others.' She ended the call.

'Something up?'

'Yes, you could say that.' Erla wasn't any more forthcoming. Perhaps she wanted Huldar to beg but he wasn't going to give her the satisfaction. 'Hurry up and jump in the shower. I'll tell you on the way in.'

Huldar was sitting up now and didn't know what to do next. Erla wasn't budging from the doorway; her legs had dried – the droplets could now be counted on one hand. 'I'll be quick.' But he didn't move, hoping she'd get the message.

'You don't seem to be in much of a hurry.' Erla grinned. 'You're not shy, are you? You're kidding me.' Her grin widened. 'You weren't shy last night.'

Huldar wasn't used to feeling ashamed of his nakedness in front of the women he'd slept with, but then they weren't usually his boss. 'No, I'm not shy. Just hung-over.' He edged to the side of the bed. Best get it over with.

'Does this make it any easier?' Grabbing her towel by the corners, she whipped it off. Her body was revealed, naked, clean and athletic, the pink nipples stiff on her small, pert breasts.

If the intention had been to create a nudist vibe so Huldar wouldn't be so embarrassed, it was a total failure. Now he had a more urgent problem about getting up.

Most of the inquiry team were in bad shape. They avoided one another's eyes, all the absurd declarations and promises of the previous evening still vivid in their memories. There had been a steady stream of people to the soda-water dispenser until it ran out and produced nothing but cold water with an oddly metallic taste.

'Is it true?' Gudlaugur stood up so he could get a good look at Huldar's face. He was unbearably bright and perky himself since he hadn't gone out with them the previous evening; perhaps because he'd been busy, perhaps because they'd forgotten to invite him.

'What?' Huldar continued to stare at his screen, though he had a good idea what the young man was referring to.

'Erla. You know. Did you go home with her?'

'No. What on earth makes you think that?' Huldar didn't look up. He was pleased with his ability to lie while in such a rough state.

He'd almost succeeded in convincing himself that the night with Erla had never happened.

'Oh . . . I heard the others talking about it. Then you arrived together. And you're wearing the same clothes as yesterday – you've got the same coffee stain on your sleeve.' In time Gudlaugur would make quite a decent cop. You certainly couldn't fault his powers of observation.

'You shouldn't believe everything you hear. I was too tired to dig out a new shirt this morning. And it was a complete coincidence that Erla and I arrived at the same time. That's all.' Huldar raised his eyes to Gudlaugur at last. 'Have you got nothing to do?'

Gudlaugur sat down again, looking abashed. He had largely kept quiet since Huldar appeared, apart from confiding in him that he was expecting to have his wrist slapped over that Father Christmas business. It had taken rather an unexpected turn. From the little Huldar had heard, this was hardly Gudlaugur's fault. How had he been supposed to guess that the episode was linked to the murder case? The connection was still far from clear; all the police knew at present was that the children who had been abducted by a man in a Father Christmas costume had just come across two amputated feet in their father's garden.

Huldar had emitted an almost audible sigh of relief on learning that he didn't have to accompany Erla round to the children's father's place to view the evidence. The prospect of examining a pair of sawn-off feet lying in the white snow would have limited appeal for a policeman in full health, let alone for a man in his current state. It would also have meant being alone in the car with Erla and he had already said all he could without actually saying anything. She had made repeated attempts to steer the conversation round to their night together and the implications for their professional relationship, while he had kept pleading a splitting headache that made it almost impossible to talk. This was no exaggeration, though he was feeling a little better now after filching the last three painkillers from the office first-aid kit.

His phone rang. Erla's name flashed up.

Against his will Huldar picked it up. He decided to ask if he could move desks after the weekend. He'd rather sit in the gents than here under Gudlaugur's watchful eye. It shouldn't be any problem to get what he wanted, now that he was in his boss's good books. Though in reality their new intimate relationship would probably mean he wouldn't ask for anything. Not today, not tomorrow – never. Maybe it would make more sense to request a transfer to another department. Huldar closed his eyes for a moment and took a deep breath while ridding his mind of these thoughts. That would have to wait. Instead he concentrated on the phone call, only too conscious that Gudlaugur could hear every word.

'Hi.'

'Listen, I've just sent this guy, Thorvaldur Svavarsson, over to the station. The father of the kids who found the feet. We couldn't work with him in the way – he's an unbelievable tosser. I want you to meet him and kick off the questioning. I should hopefully be back before you finish.' Huldar silently hoped she wouldn't be.

'OK. Anything in particular I should bear in mind?'

'Yes. The stupid prick works for the State Prosecutor's office. Like Benedikt Toft. I don't need to tell you how slim the chances are that that's a coincidence. But you'll need to handle him with kid gloves. It's incredibly important to maintain good relations with the prosecution service.' There was a crackling in Huldar's ear as the wind blew into Erla's phone. 'Tread carefully until I get there.' She hung up without saying goodbye, in the middle of a curse that seemed to be directed at someone in Thorvaldur's garden.

Huldar hurriedly looked Thorvaldur up in the police register but drew a blank. That was to be expected: members of the prosecution service didn't usually come into contact with the police except in connection with the cases they were working on. An online search didn't throw up much either.

When Thorvaldur turned up a quarter of an hour later, Huldar saw that he wouldn't need much background information after all. The man wore his identity on his sleeve: his clothes and air gave him away as that familiar type who regards himself as superior to other people. Huldar introduced himself with a smile, taking the man's soft hand in a firm grip.

'Can I offer you a coffee before we sit down?'

'No, thank you.' You'd have thought Huldar had just offered the man a drink of urine. Plainly he was accustomed to something better than the police station brew. 'But if you have some sparkling water, that would be good.' Or maybe he was hung-over too.

'I'm sorry – it's tap water or coffee.'

Thorvaldur declined both and they took a seat in the small interview room. Huldar told the man that he was going to record the conversation and Thorvaldur waved his indifferent consent. 'Let's just get this over with. I don't know what you think I can tell you. Those feet have nothing to do with me. You'd be better off going out and trying to track down their owner, not to mention the person who did this. You can hardly imagine I'm responsible?' To underline the absurdity of this idea, Thorvaldur twitched his shirtsleeves to show the cuffs under his expensive jacket. He was wearing a tie but the knot was a little crooked, a sign of negligence that was almost certainly out of character.

'Were you on your way to a meeting this morning? For work?'

'No. Last time I looked it was Saturday. I've got the day off, like everyone else.'

'A funeral, then? Or a concert?'

'No. What kind of questions are these?'

This wasn't a very good beginning. Remembering his promise to Erla, Huldar abandoned the attempt to find out why the man was dressed so smartly. 'Could you describe how your children came to find the feet? It would help if you could state their names for the record.'

'Karlotta's five and Dadi's three, going on four. They were outside playing in the garden when they started screaming. I hurried out and saw what had set them off – there were two feet, cut off at the ankles, lying in the snow at the bottom of the garden.' Thorvaldur broke off and closed his eyes for a moment. 'It was extremely unpleasant.'

'Had they just gone outside?'

'No. They'd been playing outside for half an hour or thereabouts. Perhaps longer, but no more than an hour.'

'And they didn't notice the feet straight away?'

'No. They'd been staying close to the house. They were trying to build a snowman, something they're always trying to do but never manage. They'd used up most of the snow by the house so they went down the garden to find more. That's when they spotted the feet, but they didn't realise what they were. Not until they'd gone right up to them. Even then it took them a moment or two to work it out. It was the same for me. I couldn't believe my eyes at first.'

'I'm assuming you'll have heard talk at the Prosecutor's office about the severed hands? And the murder of Benedikt Toft?'

'Yes. Both cases have been mentioned.'

'Are you involved with them at all? Or hasn't the Prosecutor's office started preparing the case yet?'

'Yes, we've started looking into it. But nothing's been assigned yet.

It complicates matters that Benedikt worked for us. We don't want to be accused of a conflict of interests.'

'Good. Then you can let them know first thing on Monday morning that you're not to go anywhere near this case. You'll probably be required to take leave until the investigation's over.'

Thorvaldur looked down his nose in disgust. 'Out of the question. I've just told you that it's nothing to do with me. And it's unbeliev-able cheek for the police to think they can dictate to another institution.'

Huldar maintained a carefully blank face, allowing Thorvaldur's words to wash over him. Others would have to bring home to him the seriousness of this case. 'Were you acquainted with Benedikt Toft?'

'Of course. We worked at the same place. But he retired about three years ago and I haven't seen him recently.'

'Benedikt prosecuted in a case that we believe is the common link between all these incidents. It was fourteen years ago – a child-abuse case. The defendant was acquitted by the Reykjanes District Court and there was no appeal. Unfortunately we can't find out much about it but we've sent a request to your office to hand over all the documen-tation.'

'So? Do you imagine that I deal with that sort of thing?'

'I have no idea and I really don't care. My question is, did you assist Benedikt or work with him on the case in question?'

'No, I didn't.'

'Don't you need to know the name of the accused before you can answer that?'

'No. The name's irrelevant. Fourteen years ago I didn't work for the Prosecutor's office. I've only been there for twelve years. Or thirteen, rather.' The man glowed with self-satisfaction. 'So your theory's utter nonsense, if you can call it a theory. I can't wait to hear what possible link you think you've found between a case that ended in acquittal all those years ago and Benedikt's murder. Not to mention the hands and feet.'

Huldar would have given anything at this moment to be fresh and alert. He couldn't stand the thought of coming off worse in his confrontation with this obnoxious git. 'Had you started working for the prosecution service when Jón Jónsson was tried for the murder of Vaka Orradóttir? The trial took place eleven years ago.'

Thorvaldur lost some of his complacency. He licked his lips with the tip of his tongue and re-crossed his legs. 'I had started working there by then, yes. But I wasn't involved – it was a major case and I was fairly new at the time. I may have been given some minor tasks to do in connection with it, but nothing important.'

Huldar changed the subject, a tactic often used to make it harder for the interviewee to prepare his answers. Given his profession, Thorvaldur was bound to be familiar with the technique, but he had probably never been on the receiving end. 'The way it looks to me is that, wittingly or unwittingly, you're connected to this case. The pattern's beginning to look familiar. Benedikt claimed not to know anything when the hands were discovered. Then he vanished. And now you're sitting here, claiming not to know anything, and I suspect that the next thing we'll hear is that you've vanished too. I don't suppose you're particularly thrilled by the prospect?'

'No. I'm not.' Thorvaldur looked away. 'But I still think you're barking up the wrong tree.'

'Let's hope so.' Huldar was silent a moment, then added: 'For your sake.' Leaning forward, he gestured at Thorvaldur's right hand. 'Nice ring. Are you a Freemason?'

Thorvaldur jerked back his hand. 'I don't see that it's any of your business.'

'Benedikt was a Freemason. And one of the sawn-off hands had a mark left by the same kind of ring. Funny coincidence.'

He got no further. The door was flung open and Erla marched in. 'You can go, Huldar. We'll take over now.' Behind her appeared one of her superiors: Thorvaldur's position as prosecutor had clearly galvanised senior management to intervene. The tone of the questions would no doubt be friendlier from now on. Well, that was their problem. At least it was plain from the two men's expressions that they had no idea what he and Erla had got up to last night. She went on in a peremptory tone: 'You can bring in Thröstur, his mother and sister, and interview them separately. It's up to you what order you take them in.'

Huldar nodded. He had the brainwave of asking if he could have Freyja with him, calculating that Erla couldn't afford to fly off the handle in front of the other two men. This might be his last chance to benefit from Freyja's expertise. Sooner or later he would have to tell Erla that he wasn't interested in continuing their relationship because he had feelings for Freyja. But he couldn't do it today. Not when he was feeling this rough; not so soon after they had slept together. Once he had broken the news to Erla, there was no way she would allow Freyja anywhere near the case; she probably wouldn't let her in the building. 'Is it OK if I get Freyja from the Children's House to interview the brother and sister with me, just to be on the safe side? I need to ask them about their relationship with their father, to find out if he abused them.'

He had been expecting to have to provide further grounds to justify his request but Erla jumped in the moment he stopped speaking. 'Absolutely. Give her a call. Good idea.' For once she smiled at him, with apparent sincerity.

Huldar hurried out before she could change her mind. He tried Freyja's number. If she agreed straight away, Erla wouldn't have time to retract. But Freyja didn't answer. Disappointed, he sent her a text message. She'd told him she had to babysit her little niece over the weekend, so she might be busy. There would be no chance to go and feed the ducks together if the investigation lasted all weekend, but if she could be persuaded to come down to the station, he would at least see her.

The reply came before he even reached his desk. *I'm busy today. And tomorrow. And the next day, etc. Don't call me again. Hope you enjoyed yourself last night.*

Huldar closed his eyes.

Erla. So that's why she had looked like the cat that got the cream. Erla had told Freyja. The tiredness that Huldar had been keeping at bay with regular injections of caffeine now overwhelmed him. He couldn't even be angry with Erla; he was too livid with himself.

When it came down to it, the responsibility for this cock-up lay squarely with him. And he would have to sort it out. Though how he was going to do that, God alone knew.

Chapter 26

From what she had seen of her flat, Freyja had assumed that Saga's mother was into beautiful, expensive designs, but her taste for designer gear clearly didn't extend to buggies. Freyja was on the receiving end of so many strange looks from other mothers that she felt she might as well be pushing Saga around town in a dining-room chair. Although the glances were mostly directed at the pushchair, the glower Saga bestowed on anyone who happened to peer under the hood also played a part. Her mouth was still firmly turned down and Freyja had utterly failed to coax a smile from her. But there had been a crow of laughter from the pushchair when a man slipped and fell on his backside right in front of them. Freyja had been so surprised that, ignoring the man as he struggled to his feet, she had darted round to catch a glimpse of Saga's face. By then the perma-scowl was back in place.

'What shall we do now?' Freyja held out a spoonful of ice cream to Saga, opening her own mouth as she did so, in an age-old instinctive gesture – as if persuading children to eat was a problem in the West these days. Saga grimaced, then obeyed the signal and took a mouthful of ice cream.

This contravened Fanney's strict instructions that no sugar was to pass the little girl's lips. But reasoning to herself that ice cream was made from milk, Freyja felt they could just about get away with it. The gummy bears she had fed her earlier were a different story, of course. Still, it was their secret, and Freyja could trust a child who couldn't talk not to give her away. 'Shall we have another go on the swings and slides?' Saga swallowed. She gave no sign of being particularly excited by the prospect. Freyja had completely run out of ideas; she hadn't looked after a small child since one summer in her teens when she had babysat for a two-year-old boy. The playground had been a favourite in his case, but then the boy had been older than Saga, the sandpit hadn't been frozen, and the swings and slides hadn't been covered in wet snow. They couldn't go home to Freyja's place either. Molly had proved overly interested in their young visitor and kept trying to lick her face. Saga hadn't minded but Freyja had been so nervous that in the end she had taken to carrying the child around with her. Setting out on a walk with them both hadn't solved the problem. Molly kept sticking her head in the pushchair to sniff at Saga and lick her. Perhaps the little girl smelt of Baldur. Eventually, Freyja was forced to take Molly home before she and Saga could enjoy their walk.

Freyja wiped Saga's mouth and cheeks, then leant back and inspected the result. 'There!' Bending down to the small face, she sniffed. There was an unmistakable smell of ice cream on her breath, and a hint of gummy bears too.

It was getting on for two; she would have to return the little girl shortly. Saga's mother had said she didn't want to rush things; tomorrow Freyja could have Saga for the same length of time. That was fine by Freyja; she couldn't imagine what she was supposed to do with the child for a whole day, though that time would be here soon enough. She'd better consult her male friends who had personal experience of being weekend dads.

It might be an idea to ask the advice of the single father who had started chatting her up down by the lake. Freyja had been the only woman among a horde of fathers, and the man who had flirted with her had been the best-looking of the lot. He had been amused by Saga's perma-scowl too. He had asked what had happened to make the little girl look so sad and when Freyja replied that she always looked like that, he had nodded thoughtfully and said, 'Cool.' OK, he might not be the world's greatest wit, but he was handsome and well groomed. The child in his buggy had been a little older than Saga but of indeterminate sex. Freyja hadn't liked to ask if it was a girl or a boy for fear of offending him. But if she was going to pluck up the courage to ring the number he had slipped her, she would have to find out somehow.

Normally Freyja would have hesitated to accept a telephone number from a strange man on a Saturday morning, but it had come as a godsend at that moment. As she put the scrap of paper in her pocket she had almost got over her fury with that bastard Huldar. Almost. It would have taken a miracle to have been completely indifferent, so soon after that phone call. She had rung to see if he wanted to come down to the lake with her and Saga but instead Erla had answered Huldar's mobile, cool as a cucumber, and when Freyja asked if she could talk to him, assuming they must be at work, the bitch had informed her that he was asleep. She could try again later but not until lunchtime as he'd got so little rest last night. At that moment Freyja had wished she had a good, old-fashioned desk phone with a receiver that you could bang down with satisfying violence.

She bent down to Saga again, putting on her hat and tying it firmly under her soft chin, then lifted her out of the plastic highchair that hadn't been designed for Icelandic children in snowsuits. One of Saga's little boots got caught and fell off on the floor, leaving the woolly brown sock hanging off her toes. Freyja was stooping down to retrieve it with the child in her arms when her phone rang. Amazingly, the caller hadn't hung up by the time she had finally settled the little girl in her pushchair and put down her boot. In spite of this, Freyja still took a moment to check that it wasn't Huldar.

Luckily it wasn't. But then the text message she'd sent him that morning had been unequivocal, even for an idiot like him. 'Freyja,' she answered.

'Hi, Freyja. It's Elsa.'

'Elsa? Oh, hi.' The director of the Children's House didn't usually call her at the weekend.

'I'll come straight to the point. I've had a call from the Police Commissioner's office.'

'Oh?' Freyja trapped the phone between ear and shoulder while she bent down to put Saga's boot on. The little girl did nothing to make life easy for her.

'Yes. I gather you refused to assist in an investigation into a possible instance of historical child abuse. I just wanted to hear your side of the story and find out if it's a matter of crossed wires. You know how crucial it is for us to maintain good relations with the police.'

It didn't enter Freyja's head to explain what had happened between her and Huldar. 'I'm afraid I'm busy. I can't get away. The case in question relates to a murder. It's extremely inappropriate to link it to an old sex offence and try to put the blame on individuals who may have been victims. They're not children any longer either; they're both in their twenties.'

'That's as may be, but I'm not sure you have any say about it. If they want to investigate these alleged crimes now, they will. And if the case is sensitive, then all the more reason for you to be present during the interviews.'

'What about Sólveig? Can't she go? She actually knows one of the people they're planning to interview; she treated him when he was a boy. I'd have thought she'd be ideal.'

Elsa was silent for a moment, then said: 'That's a possibility.' She paused. 'I leave it up to you. Talk to Sólveig, and if you can persuade her to go, then fine. Otherwise, you're to go yourself. No buts. The interview's due to start at four.'

Freyja could feel herself tensing up with rage but managed to ring off without saying something she'd regret. She didn't want to find herself out on her ear this summer when the plan was to wait until autumn to start her new life. Perhaps she should enrol at the School of Navigation. At least there would be no shortage of hunky ships' captains to feast her eyes on during boring lectures. They'd be an improvement on that bastard Huldar. He'd obviously put in a complaint about her, on top of all his other sins.

The boot finally slid into place. Freyja pulled down the leg of Saga's snowsuit and slipped the strap under her sole. 'Remember, Saga?' The little girl looked at her with a frown. 'Huldar,' Freyja said. 'Huldar.' Freyja made a face at her and waited.

Saga produced a fearsome scowl and Freyja grinned. Attagirl.

As soon as Freyja had delivered Saga back into the arms of her mother, who behaved as if she were recovering her daughter from an expedition to the moon, she phoned Sólveig. The conversation began well: Sólveig was thrilled to be so sought-after all of a sudden – until she heard that the case involved Thröstur and Sigrún. At that point she suddenly discovered all sorts of reasons why she couldn't come out at such short notice. It wouldn't be professional, she said. After that nothing Freyja tried, neither pleading nor veiled threats, had any effect. It was strange she was so opposed to helping out. Freyja thought briefly of the S in the letter . . . but why would Thröstur want to harm someone he had hardly met, and who had nothing to do with his father's trial? And how many people in Iceland had names that started with S?

It wasn't worth walking home to fetch the car, so Freyja took the bus. Still in a foul mood, she sat at the back, wiping the mist from the window. The view was dispiriting. The anorak-clad pedestrians looked like zombies picking their way gingerly along the slippery pavements, heads down, hands thrust in their pockets. Every now and then Freyja's reflection appeared in the glass, her face red in all the wrong places, her hair wild from her battle with the elements. Still, it wasn't as though there was anyone she needed to impress at the dreary CID offices.

She got off the bus and joined the ranks of the zombies, pulling up her hood, burying her hands in her pockets and trying to shield her face from the stinging pellets of snow. She had nearly reached the Police Commissioner's headquarters when she passed a car parked outside. The driver was staring fixedly at the entrance and it was only as she was about to go inside that she twigged. It was Orri, Vaka's father, the man who had come to fetch his ex-wife from the police station.

Freyja turned back and studied him. He was peering at the doors, apparently without realising that she was watching him. What the hell did he want? Freyja continued inside and stamped off the snow. The big clock on the wall opposite showed that she still had twenty minutes until the interview started. As she had no intention of spending any longer than necessary in Huldar's company, she decided to loiter in the lobby. Taking up position by the door, she watched Orri through the glass.

The man was staring at the building as if transfixed. She thought he was holding something to his eyes – binoculars, perhaps. What on earth was he up to? There was something very poignant about the scene: the father of a long-dead girl sitting in his car outside police headquarters, binoculars to his eyes, on a freezing winter's day. If life hadn't treated him so badly he would be at home or at work right now, still married to Dagmar; Vaka would have moved out and perhaps been on the cusp of starting her own family. The melting snow dripped from Freyja's coat, as if weeping for the family's tragic fate. If Orri was awaiting his chance to attack Jón Jónsson, their fate would be even more tragic.

Zipping up her coat again, Freyja went outside, walked straight over to his car and tapped on the window. When he turned and met her gaze he looked horrified, like a man caught trespassing. Freyja gestured to him to roll down the window.

'Hi. My name's Freyja. We met when you came to collect your ex-wife from the police station on Hlemmur.'

'Yes, I remember you.' While he was speaking, Orri laid the binoculars on the passenger seat and pulled a newspaper over them. 'What do you want?'

'I just wanted to check if you were waiting for anyone in particular.'

'No.' The man paused, then added, sounding irritated: 'Is there some law against sitting here? I'm not in anybody's way.'

'You can sit here as long as you like. I just wanted to point out that this isn't the best place to ambush someone – if that's your plan. Think about it – it's police headquarters. You'd be arrested immediately.'

Orri looked a little sheepish and seemed at a loss. Freyja could almost hear him thinking: *Should I deny it or thank her for the tip and take myself home?* She hoped he would opt for the latter course. If he did something stupid now it would only exacerbate his and Dagmar's troubles. 'I don't know if you're aware, but people who take revenge don't get an easy ride from the justice system, however horrific the crime against them may have been.'

Orri remained silent. Apparently he didn't trust himself to look at Freyja.

'Can I tell you something?'

He nodded.

'I'm making assumptions here, but I'm guessing that you're hoping to run into Jón Jónsson, possibly because you want to kill him. No need to confirm or deny it, I'm not a police officer.' Seeing the man relax at this, she added: 'But you should bear in mind that it's extremely rare – *extremely* rare – for anyone to actually go ahead and do the deed. People may dream of revenge but when it comes to the crunch, they hardly ever go through with it. And there's a reason for that: your life would never be the same again. If you're sucked into the abyss, you'll never get out. So you'd be better off leaving the man alone. He's not worth it.'

'Easy for you to say.'

'I know what I'm talking about. I help children who've been sexually abused, so I've met countless parents who are coping with the same kind of thoughts that you're wrestling with now.'

'But you don't work with children who've been killed by men like that. Or their parents.' His voice emerged as a growl.

'You're right.' Freyja wondered if she should leave it at that and stop interfering. Whatever he was planning, when it came to the point he would probably stop at beating the man up. Perhaps that would do him good. Or perhaps Orri was one of those who would be unable to restrain himself from committing more serious violence. 'I do know for certain that you won't heal your grief by attacking this man. You'll only get yourself into terrible trouble.'

Orri grunted. 'Not that it's any of your business but, to be honest, I don't really know what I'm doing here.'

'Why not go home then?'

'Home?'

'Yes.' The snow had turned into sleet and her trouser legs were soaked. 'Or back to work.' She recalled Gudmundur Lárusson telling her that Orri was an estate agent. Quite a successful one too. 'When you're struggling it can help to immerse yourself in work. It can provide temporary relief.'

'Temporary, yes.'

'Think about it.' Freyja straightened up. She would have to go back inside or she'd be late. And anyway she couldn't untangle the man's emotional turmoil out here in the sleet. She pulled out her card and pushed it at him. He hesitated. 'Take it in case you want to talk to someone. My specialism is children but I might be able to recommend someone who can help you – if I turn out to be useless.'

Orri took the card. He examined it, then put it on the seat beside the binoculars. 'Thanks. Though I doubt I'll call.'

'It's entirely up to you.'

He rolled up the window without saying goodbye. Freyja headed back inside. The clock in the foyer showed that she was cutting it very fine. As she entered the lift, she glanced back and saw that his car was still there.

Chapter 27

Freyja's worries about being late turned out to be unnecessary. Huldar wasn't even there when she arrived. Gudlaugur greeted her, shy and sweaty-palmed. He informed her that Huldar had gone to pick up Thröstur's sister, Sigrún, since the plan was to interview her first. The young woman had rung to say she doubted she could come and he had thought it safer to jump in the car and go and fetch her himself.

The atmosphere was muted in the CID office, even though virtually every desk was occupied. The detectives were pale and uncommunicative. Perhaps there was a bug going around.

Gudlaugur, in contrast, seemed bright-eyed and bushy-tailed, despite his hapless attempts at conversation. He managed to offer Freyja coffee no fewer than three times but seemed unable to think of anything else to say. After an embarrassed silence, he invited her instead to come into the incident room. As he made to open the door, however, he hesitated, apparently recalling too late that she wasn't actually a member of the inquiry team. From where she was standing Freyja could see documents and pictures pinned all over the wall and comments scribbled on a whiteboard. She glimpsed some rather grisly photographs. No wonder Gudlaugur had hesitated. Hastily she assured him that she was already bound by confidentiality, so it was quite safe to let her in. Her curiosity was piqued; it wasn't every day that she came into contact with material like this.

Freyja examined the display, studying the photographs and reading bits of text, fascinated by the horror, almost forgetting about

Gudlaugur fidgeting behind her. Finally she looked round at him with a grimace. 'This is major-league stuff.'

'I know.' He smiled shyly. 'You must be pretty tough. Are you a doctor, by any chance? A psychiatrist, I mean, rather than a psychologist?'

'No. I'm a psychologist.' Freyja turned back and studied the photo of the hands. 'Perhaps the pictures don't affect me that much because they seem so unreal. I mean, I know they're real but my mind can't take it in. It just assumes they've been photoshopped.'

'I can assure you they haven't. Trust me, I was there when they found them.'

'What about these . . . feet?' Freyja pointed to a similar photograph. 'I didn't know about them.'

'They were only discovered this morning.'

'Do they belong to the same person?'

'Almost certainly, but we'll need to do a DNA test before that can be confirmed. The blood group matches, though, and the pathologist reckons they belong to a man of the same sort of age.' Gudlaugur stared at the photo. 'The feet were also cut off with a chainsaw, but it's thought the man was dead by then. I was extremely relieved to hear that.'

Freyja smiled at him. His confession was unusually honest, and she automatically assumed that he must be from the countryside. 'I see you've started taking Thröstur's letter seriously. The one from the time capsule, I mean.' She gestured at the whiteboard where the initials had been written in a single column. Names had been added after some of them. BT stood for Benedikt Toft, K for Kolbeinn Ragnarsson and JJ for Jón Jónsson. There were question marks after S and OV and also after the I. At the bottom was the name Thorvaldur Svavarsson, followed by two question marks. 'Who's Thorvaldur Svavarsson?'

'The man who owns the garden where the feet were found. He's a prosecutor but so far he doesn't seem to have any link to Jón Jónsson. Except that the other day a stranger lured his children into a car, then returned them with a message to say hello to their father from Vaka.'

'Vaka Orradóttir?'

'We think so. It only emerged this morning when their mother was interviewed again. She was asked to come and fetch the children when the feet turned up – she and Thorvaldur are divorced. The fact didn't come out during her original interview about the abduction.' Looking embarrassed, Gudlaugur added: 'That is, she didn't mention it then. The mother, I mean.'

'What about the man who took the children? Has he been caught?'

'No. He was wearing a Father Christmas costume and they can't describe him or his car. They're very young – nursery age.'

Freyja was well aware of how imprecise children could be when it came to describing things. 'Jón Jónsson's the obvious candidate. Have you had any luck tracking him down?'

Gudlaugur shook his head. 'No. Unfortunately.' He brightened a little. 'But we've established that the hands don't belong to him. We compared the fingerprints to those on a book he used to own and they don't match.'

'Didn't the police already have his prints on file?'

'No. There was a mix-up. And now the Prosecutor's office is having trouble digging up some records we wanted to see. But that's inevitable when you're dealing with historical cases. Nothing's kept forever.'

Freyja was sceptical. Losing one set of fingerprints might have been a mistake, but when so many of the official records relating directly or indirectly to Jón Jónsson had vanished into thin air, there had to be more to it. You'd have thought the files had been systematically destroyed. She couldn't imagine how one would go about this, who could have done it, or why, but she kept quiet as she didn't want to come across as some kind of conspiracy theorist. The police must have realised how irregular the whole thing was. Unless it was a common problem; what did she know about record-keeping in the public sector? 'Is he your main suspect for all this?' With a sweeping gesture she indicated the material on the walls.

'Yes and no. We don't have any specific suspects. Though, having said that, we believe it must be two individuals working together. It's hard to see how it would be possible for one person to carry a coffin, let alone lift it out of the grave.' Gudlaugur pointed at some comments scrawled on the whiteboard: '*1 person or 2?*' and '*1, 2 or 3 cases?*', which had been repeatedly circled. 'As you can see, we aren't even sure that the coffin, the murder and the sawn-off limbs belong to the same case. Let alone the letter from the time capsule. Perhaps it's all connected; perhaps not.'

'Connected? Surely it must be? Einar Adalbertsson, the man in the coffin, was Jón Jónsson's stepfather, and Thröstur, who wrote the letter, is his son. It can't be a coincidence. And Benedikt Toft prosecuted in one of Jón's trials.'

Drawing himself up, Gudlaugur announced rather pompously: 'We're hoping the situation will be clarified shortly. A number of questions remain but things are moving in the right direction. Having said that, the old letter's causing us a few headaches. Did Thröstur draw up the list himself or are these names he knew were on his father's hit-list? In that case, why are his father's initials there? Jón Jónsson can hardly have intended to do away with himself.'

'No. Hardly.' Though Freyja couldn't help thinking how convenient that would be. 'If these are Jón's intended targets, I suppose Thröstur could have added his initials to the list with the idea of finishing off his father himself.'

Gudlaugur didn't seem to think this worthy of comment. He rubbed his smooth jaw. 'Another puzzle for us is, if Jón Jónsson's the perpetrator, who's his accomplice? He doesn't have many friends. You wouldn't think he had many acquaintances either. He was in prison for over ten years. We've spoken to Litla-Hraun and most of the other inmates couldn't stand him; he kept himself to himself. So it's unlikely he made a friend there who could be acting as his accomplice now.'

'And his son's unlikely to be helping him.'

'I wouldn't know. I've never met Thröstur.' Gudlaugur folded his arms and perched on the table. 'But we can't rule out the possibility that he's involved. He's even a potential suspect for the murders, either of Benedikt Toft or of the owner of the hands and feet, or both.'

'But let's say he would have needed two accomplices?'

Gudlaugur shrugged. 'A friend, his mother – even the sister, though I gather she looks as if she wouldn't say boo to a goose. And personally I don't believe a woman could be involved.'

Freyja bit back the observation that women were no slouches in this area. In fact, they had shown themselves capable of extraordinary brutality, especially in relation to paedophiles. But nothing like this had happened in Iceland to date; no women – or men for that matter – had retaliated in anything like the horrific fashion illustrated on the wall. The victims didn't fit this scenario either; at least Benedikt Toft didn't. As far as she knew, he was no paedophile. 'Are any of these men – Benedikt Toft, Kolbeinn or this Thorvaldur – suspected of having abused children?'

'No. Their backgrounds have been thoroughly vetted, so they'd have to have kept it incredibly quiet.'

It was as she suspected. This simply didn't fit. 'What about Vaka's father, Orri? Have you considered him? Or her mother?'

'Yes, but we didn't get anywhere. As long as the hands could have belonged to Jón, Orri was a strong candidate, and if Jón's found dead the guy will go back to the top of our list. And his ex-wife will be number two. But we can't see what motive he had to murder Benedikt Toft. Or what could have prompted him to saw off somebody's hands and feet.'

'He's outside right now. Sitting in his car, watching the entrance. I think he's waiting for Jón Jónsson to appear. That's not to say I believe he'll actually kill him – but who knows?'

She accompanied Gudlaugur out of the room and over to a window, but the car had gone.

The atmosphere in the interview room was oppressive. The room itself was drab and cheerless; its yellowing walls were kept deliberately bare so there was nothing to distract the attention of the person being interviewed; the chairs were hard so they couldn't get too comfortable; the table was battered and stained. Freyja and Huldar's strained interaction did nothing to alleviate the tension either. She kept her eyes averted and he seemed to get the message as he never looked her way.

He seemed sheepish and at the same time depressed. When he turned up with Sigrún he had avoided Freyja's eye and merely offered her coffee. She quickly declined, having had plenty of practice by now as this was the fourth such offer she'd had since entering the building.

Sigrún completed the dreary scene. She sat facing them with the air of someone who has just been informed of the death of a close relative. Shoulders drooping, hands in her lap, though they seemed to be constantly fidgeting, judging by the twitching of her shoulders. Her long, dry hair hung down over her cheeks like two curtains. So far she had answered all Huldar's questions with monosyllables.

No, she didn't know where her father was. No, she hadn't seen or heard from him. No, she knew nothing about Thröstur's letter. No, she didn't know Benedikt Toft, Kolbeinn Ragnarsson or Thorvaldur Svavarsson. No, she had no idea who could have dug up the coffin of the man referred to as her grandfather, though he was no blood relation. No, she hadn't been involved; she didn't have a driving licence and didn't know how to operate a mechanical digger. No, she'd never touched a chainsaw and didn't know anyone who owned such a thing. Each answer emerged in a near whisper and Freyja's head ached from having to strain her ears every time Sigrún opened her mouth.

Freyja felt a vibration in her coat pocket. Her phone. It must be Baldur, eager to hear how she had got on with the babyminding. She regretted having turned off the ringer; it would have been a relief to have an excuse to step outside and chat to her brother. She had no contribution to make. She was just sitting here, listening to what passed between Huldar and Sigrún. Baldur's call was far more important; he couldn't just ring someone else. Freyja felt even worse than before, upset by the thought that she was letting down the most important person in her life. Patience wasn't one of Baldur's virtues and she knew the phone would only vibrate a few more times before he gave up. Sigrún's hands appeared from under the table and she brushed the hair back from her face. Again they saw her evasive gaze in her pale, expressionless face. Beside her, Freyja heard Huldar ask: 'What happened to your hand?'

The result was the longest continuous speech Sigrún had produced so far, and Freyja snapped back to the present. 'An accident. I was so young at the time, I don't really remember it.' Sigrún stared at the stumps where the little finger and ring finger of her right hand used to be, as if seeing them for the first time. Then she flinched and stuck her hands under the table again.

'I understand that it was your brother Thröstur who did this to you. Is that correct?' Huldar pushed a packet of Ópal liquorice towards Sigrún, who shook her head, though whether in reply to the question or to decline the sweets was unclear. Huldar persisted: 'So Thröstur had nothing to do with it?'

'No. Not as such. Not deliberately.'

'Not deliberately? What do you mean? What exactly happened?'

'Does it matter?' Sigrún met Huldar's gaze, then dropped her eyes again, her face filled with sadness.

'We simply don't know at this stage. But I can tell you one thing, the more we know, the more likely we are to find this murderer who's on the loose. He's already killed two people. So I'd appreciate it if you could answer all our questions.'

'Can this one wait?' The small voice sounded like that of a little girl.

'Er . . . yes, I suppose that's OK.' Huldar sounded taken aback: evidently this was an unusual request by an interviewee. 'Last time we met, we asked you about visiting your father in prison. We know now that you went there once; it's on record and you signed the form. Why did you visit him and why did you never go back?'

'I went to tell him I didn't hate him.'

At this point Freyja intervened for the first time. The question and answer had roused her curiosity. People like Sigrún didn't usually act on impulse; they weighed things up carefully. 'Why was that? What prompted you to go then?'

'I . . . I was reading a book. A self-help book.' Sigrún stopped talking, apparently with no intention of elaborating. She hardly needed to. Freyja had looked at a few of these works out of professional interest and could all too easily imagine the chapter on how people should face up to their fears; how attack was the best method of defence, and so on. In Sigrún's case such advice was highly questionable; she had every right to be allowed to live in peace and security, and shouldn't be forced to confront her traumatic past without help. Meeting their attacker face to face rarely helped the victims of sexual violence get over their ordeal. At best the effects were short-lived. Before long their distress would return.

'Did this book recommend that you confront your past? And did you interpret that as meaning you should meet your father and talk to him?'

'Yes.' Sigrún kept her eyes lowered.

'Do you feel it helped at all?'

Sigrún's curtains of hair swung to and fro as she shook her head. 'No. I just felt worse. I threw up in the bus on the way back to town.'

'Tell me something, Sigrún. Since you're obviously interested in working through your problems, have you never been to therapy? I promise you that it would be more beneficial for you than any self-help books.'

'No, I haven't.'

'Not even as a child? After your father was sent to prison?'

'No.'

'May I ask why not? You could have received free treatment on the state.'

'Mum didn't want me to. Nor did Thröstur. They're against that sort of thing.'

'I see.' Freyja looked at the abject creature in front of her, and allowed her righteous indignation to flare up, then subside again, before she went on. It would be futile to criticise Sigrún's mother or brother, who were just as broken and damaged as she was. 'I think we should have a chat later about the options available. It's never too late to overcome the kinds of issues you must be grappling with, and I can help you if you like.' For the second time that day Freyja dug a card out. She was turning into a walking advertising campaign. Usually her cards lay untouched until they were so creased she had to chuck them out.

'Yes. Maybe.' Sigrún put the card in the pocket of her anorak, which she hadn't taken off, despite the warmth in the room.

'Would you be willing to answer the question about how you came to lose your fingers?'

'Then can I go? Once I've answered?'

Huldar clicked his tongue. 'Yes. All right.' He had slumped down in his chair but now straightened up again. Reaching for the packet of Ópal that neither Sigrún nor Freyja had touched, he popped two in his mouth and went on, a little thickly: 'Tell me how Thröstur was involved.'

'He didn't do it. You mustn't think that.'

'I don't know what to think. That's up to you to fix. Go on.' Huldar's voice had acquired a harsher, more authoritative edge than before.

'It was an accident. A mistake.'

'You'll have to be more precise. There are different kinds of accidents and mistakes. But they don't usually end up with someone losing their fingers.'

'I don't really know any more than that. All I know is that he didn't do it on purpose.'

'Do what?'

'I don't know. I was too young to remember.'

'Surely your mother or Thröstur must have told you what happened?'

'He took me somewhere and it happened. Mum told me it was an accident; he was only a child, so he couldn't have known what could go wrong. I remember the policeman who found us, and our grandfather. He came to fetch us. Then I remember the hospital. And how strange I felt afterwards. For a long time I thought my fingers would grow back.' Sigrún abruptly went quiet, as if she had surprised herself with this long speech. 'I was only four, you see.'

'Really? No one's ever told you exactly what happened?'

'No.'

'And you never asked?' Huldar couldn't hide his astonishment. He leant forward over the table in an attempt to convey a solicitous interest. Although the harsh note had left his voice, Sigrún recoiled. His proximity obviously made her uncomfortable, as it had earlier when he had reached out a hand to guide her into the room. Freyja wondered if it would have been better for a female officer to conduct the interview. Unshaven, his hair a mess, Huldar gave off a powerful aura of masculinity, though it wouldn't have made much difference if he had been tidy and clean-shaven.

'I used to ask. In the old days. But I never got any real answers. Mum told me what I've told you. It was a mistake, an accident. It was better not to think about it. Only a pianist needs all ten fingers anyway.' Sigrún met Huldar's gaze with a firmness unusual for her. 'And we never owned a piano.'

The interview was going nowhere. But before they called it a day, Freyja decided to ask the question that had been preying on her mind ever since she'd first laid eyes on the girl.

'Your father claimed during his trial that he had never abused a child before that terrible day when Vaka died. Now, I'm familiar with cases like this and I have serious doubts about his statement. If he was lying, it's possible that he abused other girls or boys. I'd like to ask if you or your brother were ever sexually abused by him, though I believe I already know the answer.'

Sigrún stood up, looking shaken. She clutched her anorak round her thin body and fumbled in her pockets. 'No. Neither Thröstur nor I experienced anything like that. You should have that on record.' She pulled on her gloves with trembling hands and stalked out of the room.

Chapter 28

Freyja shoved her phone in her pocket, relieved that Baldur hadn't given up trying to reach her. It not only assuaged her guilt at having failed to answer his call earlier but it had also given her an excuse to put off talking to Huldar while they were waiting for Thröstur. She had done her best to spin out the conversation, repeating her account of her morning with his daughter three times. After that, Baldur hadn't been able to resist asking if she was getting any action. She made a meal of describing the handsome single father she'd met by the lake that morning and how she was going to call him. She didn't usually share this kind of information but she made an exception on this occasion, conscious that Huldar could hear every word.

While Freyja was laying it on thick to Baldur about the fairy-tale prince by the lake, she had stolen a glance at Huldar. She thought he was looking pained.

Night had fallen outside and the streetlights gleamed on the wet tarmac. The parking space where Orri had been waiting was empty. Although the sleet had stopped, the sky was cloudy, threatening more snow. Freyja cursed herself for not having fetched her car; the thought of waiting for a bus out there wasn't tempting, especially now that her clothes were dry at last. Crumpled and dirty – but dry.

'Sorry about this morning. I'd like to have gone and fed the ducks with you.'

Although the view out of the window was nothing to write home about, Freyja continued to stare out, as if fascinated. 'No need to apologise. It made no difference to me whether you came or not.' She did her best to sound like her normal self; she didn't want him to think she was pissed off about losing him to Erla.

'Maybe, but it made a difference to me. I'd like to have gone with you.'

Freyja had only to draw back slightly to see herself and the corridor behind her reflected in the glass. Huldar was propped against the wall, arms folded, eyes closed. If she hadn't just heard him speak, she'd have thought he was asleep. 'Oh, well,' she said and put her face to the glass again.

'I'm going to quit drinking.'

'Sounds a bit extreme.' Her breath formed a round cloud on the glass, which rapidly shrank as it evaporated. 'What's happened to Thröstur? I thought he was supposed to be here straight after Sigrún? I need to get home.' She didn't actually have any plans but anything was better than hanging about here. Molly would be starving, regardless of the fact that Freyja had given her a good feed before she took Saga out. The thought of the dog conjured up the image of her sofa and suddenly she felt ready to drop.

'Sigrún left earlier than expected. He should be here in ten, fifteen minutes at most.' Huldar's reflection had opened its eyes and was staring at her.

Freyja permitted herself a quiet sigh. Did she really have to stand here listening to Huldar whining for ten whole minutes? 'How long do you think the interview will take?'

'Not long,' he said unhelpfully. 'I'm not expecting him to tell us anything useful.' He sighed. 'Kolbeinn's wife rang from London to say she couldn't get hold of her husband. He's gone missing too. They're going to search the house. I wish I could figure out how all this is connected.'

'Then could I maybe slip off? Or will you report me again if I do?' Still smarting from the dirty trick he had played on her, she couldn't keep the bitterness out of her voice.

'You can't leave now. And I didn't report you. I rang the Children's House because you wouldn't speak to me. What else was I supposed to do?'

'Leave me alone.'

Neither of them spoke. Huldar closed his eyes again and Freyja continued to gaze out of the window. The odd car passed down the street in a spray of slush. She decided to take a taxi home; she was in no mood to be soaked to the skin on her way to the bus stop.

'Would you like an Ópal?' The question was so absurd that Freyja turned her head. Huldar's voice had sounded hopeful.

'No, thanks.' She was about to add a cutting remark but decided it was pointless. There was nothing to fight about. It was up to him what he did. It wasn't as if they were in a relationship.

'Can I apologise yet again?' Huldar closed the Ópal packet.

'Nothing to apologise for. It doesn't matter to me.' Her calm indifference seemed to have more effect on him than being angry or upset would have done. Perhaps he was more used to women being mad at him. He didn't reply, merely returned the packet to his pocket and nodded. His fringe fell over his eyes and when he pushed it back, his face was sad. Freyja relented and was about to ask for an Ópal after all when, hearing footsteps, they both looked round. She was grateful for the interruption. There was Thröstur, accompanied by a police officer. Huldar stood up straight, dismissing the sadness from his face.

He seemed almost his normal self as he greeted Thröstur, who acted as if he hadn't seen his outstretched hand.

Once again, Thröstur was clearly struggling to suppress his anger, to play the anarchist who couldn't give a damn. His hair was combed into a Mohican that had developed a sideways droop on the way to the interview. He was inadequately dressed in a thin leather jacket and ripped jeans. On his feet he wore high lace-up boots, obviously made of fake leather, their long laces filthy from trailing on the ground. His eye sockets were painted black right down to his cheek-bones. It wasn't clear whether this was deliberate or whether his make-up had run. His skin was blotchy, his left nostril angry where the stud had been, and the ring through his septum had vanished as well. Perhaps his nose had gone septic. Without his facial piercings, Thröstur looked almost childishly vulnerable, in spite of the warpaint.

'We're in here.' Huldar showed Thröstur into the interview room, automatically lifting a hand to place it on his shoulder, but the young man nimbly dodged it, as his sister had earlier.

To start with, the interview was almost a repetition of Sigrún's. Same questions, same answers. No and again no. He didn't know anything, didn't recognise any of the names they put to him. Freyja listened without speaking, waiting until her contribution was required. Thröstur was a completely different type from his sister: surly, his emotions hidden behind a thick layer of armour. For him to open up would be a miracle. The room was stuffy, the smell of the red Ópal liquorice that Huldar kept chewing the only thing that made it bearable.

'Tell me about your grandfather. Were you close?'

Thröstur sat further back from the table than Sigrún had done, lounging with his legs splayed and his arms folded. Again he reminded Freyja of a wild animal. He was spreading out to appear larger than he really was, in compensation for his puny frame. 'Yes and no. He died years ago. What does it matter?'

Huldar didn't answer this. 'I understand you don't have a driving licence – at least you're not on the register. Is that correct?'

'Yes.' Thröstur loosened his arms. As he had sat as still as a statue up to now, Freyja guessed that the question had unnerved him, though why was unclear.

'Your mother has a driving licence, though, doesn't she?'

'Yeah. Maybe. I dunno. She doesn't own a car.'

'No. She doesn't own a car.' Out of the corner of her eye, Freyja noticed Huldar smiling faintly. 'But she rented one the other day. Were you aware of that?'

Thröstur compressed his lips and folded his arms again. Freyja thought his hands were shaking and that he was trying to hide the fact. 'No.'

'So you can't tell us why she did that? You see, we've spoken to lots of car-rental places and none of them have any record of renting a car to her before. So it must have been a special occasion. She was having a clear-out, maybe? It was an estate car, plenty of room if you put the back seats down.'

'I dunno what she wanted it for.'

'Really?' Huldar paused. 'I expect it'll all become clear when we ask her about it later. Don't you think?'

'I haven't a clue. It's got fuck-all to do with me.'

'All right. Let's leave it at that. Turning back to your grandfather. You were the last person to see him alive, weren't you?'

'I saw him the day he died, that's right. But I have no idea if he saw anyone else after I left.'

'You were selling him toilet rolls to raise money?'

'Yeah. Something like that.'

'Can you remember what you were raising it for?'

'No. It was bloody ages ago. Something to do with school. I can't remember what. A trip, maybe.'

'Is that so?' Huldar adopted an exaggerated air of surprise. 'The thing is, we checked with your old school and they've had a rule for many years now that pupils aren't allowed to fundraise. How strange. Would you like to reconsider your answer?' Evidently, the police hadn't been idle.

'No. I told you, I don't remember. It must have been for something else.'

'Yes. Maybe.' Huldar nodded slowly. Thröstur brazened it out as long as he could, before eventually giving in and dropping his gaze. 'Your grandfather's coffin was dug up from its grave in Hafnarfjördur Cemetery on Wednesday night. Did you have anything to do with that?'

'No.' Thröstur's answer came too quickly. He showed no sign of surprise, though the incident should have come as news to him.

'It happened on the evening of the same day your mother rented the car.' Since Thröstur said nothing, Huldar carried on. 'You're taking this news very calmly. I know I'd want to know more if it was my grandfather. Had you already heard about it?'

Thröstur gave himself time to consider his answer. 'Yes.'

'Where?'

'I don't remember.'

'You're strangely forgetful for such a young man.' Huldar bored his eyes into Thröstur. 'I get the distinct impression that you weren't too fond of your grandfather.'

Thröstur looked up, his face dark with rage. 'Firstly, that man wasn't my grandfather. He was stepfather to my so-called father. And last time I looked it wasn't a crime not to like some bloke who wasn't even family. Are you going to arrest me for that?'

'No. If I arrest you, it'll be for something much more serious.' Huldar relaxed his clenched jaw a little. 'But I can't help wondering why you chose to go and see him when you were trying to sell that . . . what was it again? . . . oh yes, toilet paper . . . if you didn't like the guy.'

Thröstur rallied, recovering his former bravado. 'Are you some kind of moron? Do you think salesmen have to like their customers? I got in touch with him because I knew he'd buy some off me. That's all. Haven't you pigs got anything better to do than investigate ancient sales of bog roll?'

Freyja watched for Huldar's reaction but he seemed unmoved by the insults. It was probably a daily occurrence for the police. When Huldar spoke again it was at a normal pitch, his voice calm. 'Take it easy, boy.'

'I'm not a boy.'

'No? Then stop behaving like one.'

Neither of them spoke for a moment. Freyja found herself thinking how unfair the situation was. Thröstur hadn't been born bad, and if he was linked to these crimes, it was only because of what had happened to him. If he had had a normal childhood, he wouldn't be sitting here now. She longed to get out of this claustrophobic room, to go home, flop on the battered sofa and watch a film with a bowl of popcorn on her lap. Preferably a film in which the bad guys got their comeuppance and their victims escaped unscathed.

'Turning to the letter you put in the time capsule . . . You've had plenty of time now to remember the circumstances, so it would be interesting to hear what prompted you to write it and who the initials belong to.'

Thröstur sat there like a statue, although his tightly clenched jaw suggested he was grinding his teeth, like Huldar earlier. 'I've already told you, I don't remember.'

'No. Of course not.' Huldar seemed far from amused. 'Let me tell you what we think. We think BT stood for Benedikt Toft, K for Kolbeinn Ragnarsson and JJ for Jón Jónsson. Benedikt has been murdered, Kolbeinn's gone missing and so has your father Jón. The matter's looking a lot more serious than it did last time we spoke. I'm going to ask you to stop messing about and tell me who OV, S and I are. We need to get hold of them. Urgently.'

Thröstur remained stubbornly mute and Freyja wondered what was going through his head. She didn't for a minute believe that he couldn't remember the letter; his reactions betrayed the fact that he had something to hide. But what? Looking at the painfully thin young man in his punk gear, she found it hard to believe he would be physically capable of murdering several people, though she knew violent individuals came in all shapes and sizes. It would make life easier if they looked the part. Her thoughts led her back to where she had started: children were not born bad; not Thröstur nor anyone else.

'Answer the question.'

'I don't remember what I was thinking. It was ten years ago. Can you remember the school work you did ten years ago? What the fuck am I doing here?'

'You're here to be questioned in connection with a murder inquiry. You and your family are linked to the case in a variety of ways. Right now, you're up shit creek without a paddle. And if you don't start talking, you'll be up to your neck in it. Do you hear what I'm saying?'

'Are we done here? Can I go now?' Thröstur directed his words at Freyja.

'No, you can't go and . . . no, we're not done. Look at me when I'm talking to you.' Huldar's angry command had no effect. Thröstur kept his eyes trained on Freyja. She was forced to sit there and fake indifference to the young man's mocking leer.

Huldar tried again. 'OK. Have it your way. Next time we meet you'll most likely be under arrest. Forensics are busy examining the hire car as we speak. If they find anything to suggest that you, Benedikt, Kolbeinn or even just the coffin were ever inside it, no judge will deny us a detention order. For your mother too. And maybe your sister.'

The twitching muscle in Thröstur's cheek suggested that Huldar's words had hit home.

'This matter is no joke and if you persist in refusing to speak, we have no choice but to conclude that you've got something to hide.' Huldar paused for a moment to glare at Thröstur, who was doing his utmost to feign nonchalance. 'What can you tell me about those tattoos on your hands?'

'Nothing. They're none of your business.'

'*Ultio dulcis*. Doesn't that mean something like "Revenge is sweet"?'

Thröstur shrugged. 'I don't remember.'

'Of course you do. You have it before your eyes all day every day. Tell me, what revenge did you have in mind when you branded yourself for life with that motto? Does it have anything to do with the people whose initials you put in your letter?'

'That's none of your business.'

There was a knock at the door. Gudlaugur put his head round and asked for a word with Huldar. Freyja was left sitting there alone with Thröstur. If this was some kind of good cop–bad cop routine, they'd forgotten to inform her. Thröstur continued to stare into her eyes, deliberately trying to unnerve her. It worked. From the corridor the sound of voices went on and on. They sounded grave but that could be her imagination. She suspected that when Huldar came back in, the interview would be aborted. Either because they had found some evidence in the car and Thröstur was about to be led to the cells, or because they had nothing on him and he was free to go. This might be her last chance to ask the question she was dying to put to him.

'Tell me something, Thröstur, now that we're alone. Did your father abuse you or your sister when you were children? Before he attacked Vaka? If he did, there's no reason to protect him. It might win you sympathy for anything you've done, depending on how serious it is. I work at the Children's House, so I'm familiar with these cases; I know how difficult it is to discuss them.'

Thröstur snorted with rage. 'You stupid bitch.' Gripping the tabletop, he loomed over her, bringing his face uncomfortably close. Freyja wished Huldar would come back. The room felt smaller than before, the door further away. What would she do if he attacked her? Put her hands over her head to ward off the blows? Freyja took a deep breath. No. She drew herself up and refused to be intimidated. If he attacked, she would fight back. They were a similar weight and she was almost certainly in better shape than him.

'So you think I'm a stupid bitch. Could you answer the question, please?'

'I'll answer. The answer is no. Nothing happened to me, nothing happened to Sigrún. And you can shove that up your arse.'

Freyja almost burst out laughing. She hadn't heard that one since she was at school. Clearly there was no point continuing this line of questioning. 'What about Sigrún's missing fingers? We've been told that you're to blame. Is that true?'

'Jesus. You lot are so stupid. You don't have a clue. Not a fucking clue. You stupid fucking cunts.'

The door opened to admit Huldar, who informed Thröstur that he could go, but he was to remain in town as he would be called back for further questioning shortly. Thröstur jumped up and stormed out. He purposely banged his shoulder into Huldar whose face hardened, though he didn't react in any other way. Just as well. Freyja had had it up to here with the whole situation. There had been enough angry altercations for one day.

'Something's come up. I've been called out. We'll talk to his mother tomorrow, but you're free to go now.'

Freyja walked out into the corridor, where she felt revived by the fresh air. She muttered goodbye. She had gone a few paces towards the lift when she heard Huldar call: 'Sorry about this morning. It was out of order.' She raised a hand and waved behind her, without looking back. It seemed he wasn't going to give up. But as far as she was concerned it was over between them, before it had even started.

As she stood waiting for a taxi outside the police station, her thoughts returned to Thröstur and Sigrún. She was forced to confront the possibility that she had been wrong. They had both denied it so categorically, as if offended or outraged by the question. Perhaps their father had never laid a finger on them and his assault on Vaka *had* been a one-off. Perhaps everything she'd thought she knew about the case was wrong. And – and this would be worse – perhaps the same was true of Huldar and the inquiry team: perhaps they were all barking up completely the wrong tree.

The taxi drew up and Freyja climbed in, feeling more confused than she had for a very long time.

Chapter 29

Huldar was so shattered he was afraid that if he so much as let himself blink, he'd be out like a light. The dream of getting an early night, then waking at the crack of dawn and going to the gym for a workout was not to be. Sadly. He'd intended to put on a pair of boxing gloves and beat the hell out of the punch-bag in the basement, to find an outlet for all the pent-up frustration of the last few days and weeks. Frustration that was entirely directed against himself. But at this rate he'd be lucky if he got home at an even vaguely reasonable hour. And even luckier if he made it to the gym any time before the case was solved.

There was nothing to look forward to but relentless work, sleep deprivation and bottomless guilt. Still, he could be thankful for one thing: at least his stomach had more or less recovered by the time he'd arrived at the scene and laid eyes on Kolbeinn Ragnarsson's body.

'I'm going to order a pizza. What kind of topping do you want?' It was hard to hear what Gudlaugur was saying behind his gas mask. As the youngest in the group, he was invariably landed with this kind of task, but he gave no sign of regarding it as beneath his dignity. Eventually he would rebel, but by then there'd probably be a new, even younger rookie to take over the role.

'Anything with a bloody ton of meat and cheese. And a beer.' Huldar zipped up his parka and prepared to step outside. It was his turn to stand guard. People didn't usually fight for the honour, but in this instance it was by far the most desirable job. None of them were in any fit state to relish working in close proximity to a recently deceased man, especially when the body was a gruesome mess like that. Whenever Huldar happened to glance into the kitchen where Kolbeinn had met his end, he couldn't help thinking it would have been better if that heart attack had finished him off.

'OK, another meat feast and a beer.'

'I was joking about the beer. Get me a Coke. Two Cokes. No, make it three.' Huldar pulled on his woolly hat. He couldn't wait to get outside into the cold, fresh air. Even the gas masks couldn't block out the throat-catching stench. Erla had ordered them to open all the windows, though this contravened the guidelines. They had no choice. The team were reluctant to enter the house for fear of being poisoned, but they couldn't afford to wait until morning when the worst of it would have dispersed.

'Three Cokes.' Gudlaugur added three lines to a much-scribbled-on scrap of paper, then looked up, resembling a huge insect in his mask.

'You can take that thing off out here.' They were standing in the entrance hall; the inner door to the house was closed and the front door stood open a crack.

'Oh.' Gudlaugur's gaze widened behind the two large bug eyes. Instead of ripping off the contraption like Huldar, he considered for a moment, then methodically loosened the ties. 'Phew, it's good to get out of that.'

Huldar pushed the front door open wide, stepped outside and drew in great lungfuls of the night air. Gudlaugur, who had followed him out, copied his example, carrying the mask over his arm. Huldar had dropped his on the floor.

'How could anyone do that to a living person?' Gudlaugur took out his phone to call in the pizza order.

'Don't ask me. It's incomprehensible.' Huldar inhaled deeply again.

This was better than any cigarette. 'Do you know how long Forensics are going to be?'

'No. Erla's with them now but everyone's impatient for some news. She screeched at me when I opened the door to ask what kind of pizzas they wanted.'

Normally Huldar would have smiled at this but Erla's name provoked no particular amusement at the moment. 'How are you lot planning to arrange this pizza feast then? Are we supposed to eat in there? With our masks on?'

'No, we'll have to eat in the car.' Gudlaugur still hadn't dialled the number. He seemed keen to spin out the conversation for as long as possible to delay his return inside. 'It'll be fine. I don't suppose they'd have any appetite in there.' He turned abruptly and surveyed the small detached house that had been home to Kolbeinn and his wife. Huldar guessed the wife would seize the first opportunity to sell. According to the police officer who had spoken to her, the grieving process was unlikely to be a protracted one. When she received the news over in London, where she was holidaying with friends, she had cried down the phone for a bit, then started asking about the kitchen. Had the sulphuric acid that had been poured over her husband also destroyed all the furnishings? She was especially concerned about the floor . . . Callous though it sounded, this practical question was probably a sign that her mind was groping for something it could understand. Anyone whose spouse had suffered a horrific fate like that would have found it difficult to take in. It made sense to focus on the flooring.

Sufficiently revived by the frosty air to risk smoking again, Huldar rummaged in his pocket for what was left of yesterday's cigarettes, a crumpled packet that had been marinated in beer. When he lit up, the smoke tasted of it. 'Aren't you going to call? People are dying of hunger here.'

Gudlaugur selected the number. 'I'm in a queue,' he informed Huldar, who hadn't been asking for a commentary. 'We can talk while I'm on hold.'

Huldar took another puff and wondered what to say. He wasn't about to start whining about his women troubles to Gudlaugur, though it was clear that he would have his undivided attention if he so much as hinted at them. His night with Erla was the juicy gossip of the day. Since none of the team dared raise the subject with her, Huldar was the butt of all their jokes. He repeatedly denied his little adventure and reckoned he had got away with it so far, since no one was very focused right now. Once they had recovered though, he was afraid the teasing would carry on mercilessly. They were all trained to see through lies, but Huldar knew the pitfalls and might yet get away with it. 'Where does someone get hold of sulphuric acid?'

'Not from the shops, at any rate. It was a huge amount.' Gudlaugur made a face.

'With any luck it should be possible to trace the purchase through the importer. Or the shop where it was bought – if anywhere really sells it by the litre.' Then Huldar remembered the chainsaw – hardly standard equipment for your average Icelandic home or business. Yet so far the police had had zero success in tracking down the buyer. Nor had they managed to identify a suspicious purchase of several metres' worth of steel chain. Perhaps it would be the same story with the acid. The next step would be to check if the saw, the chain and the acid had all been stolen, once the police had figured out what kind of business would stock all three. He would guess at some sort of workshop or contracting firm, of which there were hundreds.

'I'll fucking kill you if you spill any of that dip in my car.' Erla was sitting behind the wheel with a slice of pizza in one hand and a can of Coke in the other. Since she had been in the kitchen most of the time, breathing down the necks of the forensic technicians and pathologist while they worked, she had become inured to the reek of sulphur in her clothes and hair. Huldar and Gudlaugur, on the other hand, were struggling not to hold their noses while they ate. Huldar got the full force of it in the front passenger seat. Despite his determination not to end up in the car with Erla, she had beckoned him imperiously to join her, giving rise to much nudging and winking among the other members of the team. So much for Huldar's efforts to quash the rumour. In a last-ditch attempt to avoid being alone with her, he had resorted to dragging poor Gudlaugur along with him. There was no way he felt up to discussing anything but the inquiry with her.

On the way to the car he had muttered to Gudlaugur that if he didn't keep up a non-stop flow of conversation, he would have him to answer to. His attempt to steer the boy to the front seat had failed, however, since the moment Gudlaugur opened the door, Erla had barked at him to get in the back. Poor Gudlaugur hadn't won any brownie points with his boss for that, still less with his constant chatter, but Huldar certainly owed him a big favour.

'Do they know when he died?' Gudlaugur asked with his mouth full.

'Late yesterday evening, or last night.' Erla selected another slice from the box perched between the front seats. 'We'll have a more precise time of death after the post-mortem. Though God knows how they think they're going to perform one. The bulk of the body will have to be scraped off the kitchen floor with a spoon.'

'No fingerprints?'

'No. Nothing. Plenty on the furnishings, of course, but nothing on the empty canisters or the ties used to lash him to the chair. The labels had been removed too, and I'm hoping that means the murderer was afraid they could be traced back to him. That's promising. We'll

find out where it came from. There can't be many possible outlets.'
Erla gazed out at the empty street; the inhabitants of the neighbouring
houses had finally given up trying to spot any clue that would explain
the police presence. 'Fingerprints would have been too much to hope
for. These days even a child must know how to avoid leaving them.'

The brief silence that fell was Gudlaugur's cue. 'Was it a mistake
not to post a police guard outside his hospital room?'

Erla twisted round and shoved her head between the seats.
Although Huldar couldn't see her expression, he doubted it was
benign. 'That wouldn't have changed a fucking thing. Just you
remember that. We'll be facing enough criticism without adding to
it ourselves.' She turned back to face the front. 'If anyone's to blame,
it's the hospital. How were we supposed to know that they'd discharge
him without alerting us? Late in the evening too. As long as he was
in hospital he wasn't in any danger.'

'Mmm.' Huldar had contributed little so far but felt he could no
longer leave poor Gudlaugur to bear the brunt. 'Is the hospital still
claiming that he was picked up by someone from his firm?'

'The nurse who was on duty is adamant about that. But the CEO
of the accountancy firm – the man she claims rang the hospital –
flatly denies having sent a car for Kolbeinn. It must have been the killer
who rang, posing as him. It's not as if the CEO's name is a secret, and
Kolbeinn didn't take the call himself. The whole thing's a total fuck-up.'

'Have we uncovered any link to Jón Jónsson?' Huldar looked at
the pizza crust in his hand: he had no memory of eating the slice.
He had been overwhelmed with drowsiness as soon as he had finished
the first and was now struggling to keep his eyes open.

'No. Not yet. The house search didn't throw up any evidence and
Kolbeinn's wife claims not to know a thing. There's no sign of any
child porn on his computer, so they can't have met through a paedophile
ring. But there's a link somewhere. You saw his face when you mentioned

Jón Jónsson's name to him. The bloody man would have done better to come clean to us. Maybe we should take a picture of his corpse and show it to Thorvaldur, since he's being just as pig-headed. That might loosen his tongue.' Erla drained the last of her Coke and crushed the can in her hand. 'It might help persuade the other people who've refused to talk as well. God, I'd do it like a shot.'

'You'd be fired.' Although he was almost too sleepy to speak, Huldar thought he had better nip that idea in the bud. There was an outside chance Erla might be serious.

'Bullshit. Name one police officer who's been fired.' When Huldar didn't reply, she said: 'Exactly.'

'What about Thorvaldur? Is anyone guarding him?' Gudlaugur chipped in as he reached forward for another slice of pizza.

'No. The stupid prick turned down the offer. He swears this has nothing to do with him and if we insist on a guard, it'll imply we don't believe him. And that could bugger up our relations with the Prosecutor's office.'

'I'd send someone anyway. This is almost certainly about revenge and you don't have to actually deserve it for people to want to get even with you. Especially if it's your job to prosecute people.'

'Who asked for your opinion?' Erla snapped. Gudlaugur had not only had the gall to cast aspersions on her leadership skills but had also forced his way uninvited into her car. 'We've spoken to the Prosecutor's office and this is what they want. If they get involved any further they could all end up having to declare a conflict of interest. In which case they'd have to appoint new prosecutors, and the office is having enough trouble staying within budget as it is. The same applies to us. We don't have the funds to provide that jumped-up twat with a twenty-four-hour guard. Besides, his initials aren't on the hit-list.'

Gudlaugur shrank back into the shadows and Erla turned to

Huldar. 'I told them in no uncertain terms that they'd better get all the files relating to the earlier trial to us tomorrow. Even if it means the whole office having to search all night. That sodding useless lot at Reykjanes District Court say they can't find any records, so there's no point putting pressure on them. Un-fucking-believable. So the Prosecutor's office had better get their arses moving.'

Erla's optimism notwithstanding, Huldar doubted any files would turn up that weekend. The police were unlikely to receive a single piece of paper before Tuesday or Wednesday at the earliest. By which time it might already be too late to save the next victim. 'What about Jón's lawyer? He may not have the files any longer but he's bound to remember the case. He might know the identity of the child or children involved. There's a possibility he might even be able to tell us where to find Jón. And if he won't talk to us, we could try the judge. I'll get on to that, if you like. I'm not bothered about disturbing them on a Sunday. They're unlikely to be at church.' This short speech had drained the last reserves of Huldar's energy and he broke off to yawn.

'If anyone's listening to the word of God tomorrow, you can bet it's the judge,' said Erla. 'But you'd need a psychic to communicate with him. I asked to speak to him when I talked to those fuckwits at the district court, but no go. He left years ago to become a judge at the Supreme Court, and now he's pushing up the daisies.'

Huldar was about to make some pertinent remark but couldn't remember what it was. He sank back, blinking rapidly, and felt the pizza crust slipping from his hand as he succumbed to sleep.

So he didn't hear when Erla chased Gudlaugur out of the car.

'Right. I give up. If this is the way you want it, this is how we'll do it.' Erla turned to Huldar and jerked her head. 'Take him down. The car should be on its way. Make sure he doesn't have a nasty fall on the stairs.'

Huldar took hold of Thröstur's arm and yanked him to his feet. He felt strangely heavy. Given his emaciated body, Huldar had expected it to be like manhandling a child. 'Come on.' Thröstur let himself be guided, seemingly resigned to his arrest. When they reached the hall, Huldar was even allowed to drape a scruffy jacket over his shoulders, after searching in vain for a warmer coat. He hoped they wouldn't have to wait too long for the car. Just in case, he shoved a woolly hat on Thröstur's head. The gesture clearly wasn't appreciated but that was tough.

'You know it'll be better for everyone if you tell us where your sister is. We'll find her in the end anyway. If we have to launch a manhunt, everyone will know she's mixed up in this.' Huldar addressed this to the back of Thröstur's head as he followed him downstairs, without loosening his grip.

'She hasn't done anything. You lot haven't a clue what you're doing.'

'We'll see about that. We need to speak to her. The sooner we do, the better for everyone.'

Neither of them spoke again until they emerged into the cold outside. There was no sign of the police car. 'Do you smoke?' Huldar fished a packet of cigarettes from his coat pocket. When Thröstur didn't answer, he added: 'If you do, I'd accept one now if I were you. It'll be a long time before you get another chance.' Seeing that Thröstur was wavering, he shoved one in his mouth and lit it.

Thröstur sucked avidly on the cigarette and blew out the smoke. Huldar followed his example. 'You're in deep shit, I'm afraid.'

Thröstur took another drag, trying to act nonchalant. He was

Chapter 30

Of those who had been ordered in to work that Sunday, Huldar was the last to turn up. He'd had to catch up on the sleep he'd missed the night before. His body kept an exact account of the hours he rested and if there was a deficit, its demands were merciless. The alarm on his phone was powerless in the face of this audit when it rang at the appointed time, long before sunrise. With a fumbling hand he had knocked the phone off the bedside table and now there was a crack right across the screen. When at last he surfaced properly he felt restored and even his sense of guilt was receding. After a hot shower and a shave, he felt almost human again.

His good mood didn't last long. At first he thought his colleagues were calling him Sleeping Beauty because he'd overslept. It wasn't until he'd sat at his desk for an hour that he realised they were referring to the nap he'd taken in Erla's car the day before. He had woken to find himself alone; Gudlaugur and Erla had gone back into the house along with the rest of the team. As he sat rubbing his stiff neck, he had a vague memory of her trying to wake him, hazy recollections of a hand stroking his hair and cheek. What a stroke of luck that he hadn't stirred.

'Hey, Huldar! Sleeping Beauty!' One of his colleagues was grinning at him mockingly from a nearby desk, coffee mug in hand. 'Erla's pissed off today. Did someone fail to do his duty last night? Too sleepy, eh?' This was accompanied by a snigger. Huldar didn't answer but could feel his patience depleting by the minute. The next person who made that kind of comment would get his head bitten off. A punch-bag wasn't the only way to let off steam.

Erla's decision to let him sleep in her car while the others were labouring away in the horrific stench had destroyed any chance Huldar might have had of pretending that nothing had happened. Normally she would be more likely to empty a coffee mug over the man who fell asleep on his desk than shush those present so they didn't disturb him. 'What are you looking at?' Huldar glanced up irritably from his screen, then, remembering that he owed Gudlaugur a favour, added in a friendlier tone: 'Sorry. I've got to make a phone call that I'm not looking forward to.'

'Oh, sorry.' Gudlaugur gave an embarrassed smile. 'I was just going to tell you that I think I know how that judge died, that Yngvi Sigurhjartarson. It's only a guess, but I'm fairly sure.'

'Spit it out then.' Huldar was grateful for an excuse to delay picking up the receiver; the conversation with Erla wasn't the only one he was dreading. Through a fog of tiredness yesterday evening it had seemed no big deal to disturb a lawyer on a Sunday, but now the moment had come, he was having trouble deciding what to say. He was in no mood to put up with being patronised or abused for having the presumption to ring outside office hours. But since the documents from the Prosecutor's office still hadn't turned up, there was no alternative.

'The death notice says he died suddenly. And the Supreme Court issued a brief press release, saying only that he had died, followed by a lot of stuff about his education and career. I also went through the obituaries. There are tons of them. But nowhere is there any reference to what he died of; most gloss over the subject or just refer to a premature death. The thing is, it was same when one of my friends killed himself: no one wanted to hurt his parents by referring directly to the fact that he'd taken his own life.' Gudlaugur paused for breath. 'So I reckon the judge committed suicide. Of course it's unlikely to have had anything to do with this case, but it's a bit odd all the same.'

'When was this?' Huldar didn't know enough about obituaries or death notices to tell if Gudlaugur's conclusion was correct, still less whether it was significant.

'Very recently. Only two months ago.'

So they had narrowly missed their chance to talk to the man. Suspiciously narrowly. Had he known that a storm was brewing and decided to make his exit? It was a strange coincidence, if nothing else. 'Was he married?'

'Yes.'

'Good. Ring the widow and ask her what happened. Find out how he died.'

'What?' Gudlaugur looked aghast.

'Go on. You can do it. Just remember how you spoke to your friend's parents at his funeral. And choose your words carefully. The woman will still be grieving. Tell her the truth – that her husband's name has cropped up during an investigation, though of course he's not suspected of any wrongdoing.'

Gudlaugur was looking pale. 'OK. I just need a moment to prepare myself.' He sat down, vanishing from sight.

Huldar reached for the phone.

The lawyer answered after three rings, sounding as if he had high hopes of this conversation. 'I was expecting a call from you. Does this mean he's been found?'

'I'm sorry – did you say you were expecting this call?'

'Yes. Didn't the police put out a wanted notice for Jón? I assumed you must have caught him and that he'd asked for me. What's he done this time?'

Huldar cottoned on. 'We're appealing for news because no one's seen him since his release. I was actually ringing you about another matter.'

'Is he out already? God, how time flies.'

'You mean you didn't know?'

'No. I just assumed he'd escaped and you were hunting for him. I haven't heard from him since the verdict was returned at the Supreme Court.'

'What?' Huldar rooted around among the scribbled pages of notes beside his computer. 'I was told you two had kept up a correspondence. About his case, I assumed. That's what the prison authorities said, anyway.'

'What? Me? I've never written to him or sent him anything. They must be mistaken.'

Huldar raised his eyebrows. The lawyer sounded not only certain but astonished. He doubted the man had sent a single letter. 'Then I must have misunderstood what they said. Anyway, that's not what I was calling about. I was wondering if you could tell me about the time Jón Jónsson was acquitted by the Reykjanes District Court. We're having a lot of trouble digging up any information on the trial and I was hoping you wouldn't mind filling me in on the details. I know it's Sunday but the matter's rather urgent.'

'I understand. May I ask why?'

'It's related to an ongoing inquiry into a serious incident.'

'Benedikt Toft.'

'Yes. He was the prosecutor in the case I just mentioned. We're trying to find out if his job could have had something to do with his murder.'

'So you think Jón Jónsson's the killer?'

'Maybe. It's one of the angles we're pursuing. Can you recall the trial? I don't suppose you still have the paperwork?'

'Of course I've still got all the paperwork. I never throw anything away. You're welcome to copy anything that doesn't touch on my confidential relationship with my client.'

'Thanks, we'd be very grateful for that, but a brief summary would be helpful too. All we really know is that the trial was about the sexual abuse of minors.'

'I see. That shouldn't be a problem. The case was so bizarre that it stuck in my memory, although it was a long time ago.' Huldar heard footsteps at the other end of the line, then a door closing and the creaking of leather as the lawyer sat down. Maybe even the clink of ice cubes. He had a mental image of the man sipping a whisky. That would be good, as the alcohol was bound to loosen his tongue. 'Jón was charged with having abused his own daughter and son. I don't remember their names. The story emerged when the girl started school at six and told her teacher. That alone was pretty unusual. The kids were supposed to tell the class what their parents did and she misunderstood the question. Before the teacher could stop her, the girl had come out with a description of certain acts that was explicit, to say the least. The teacher took her aside and after hearing the whole story she was convinced it wasn't made up, so she took the girl to the police.'

'There doesn't appear to be any record of this.'

'That doesn't surprise me. The teacher must have been a tough cookie, judging by her witness statement. The police in Hafnarfjördur wouldn't even listen to her, so she went to Reykjavík and reported the incident there. That finally got the ball rolling. But her reward was a letter from the school telling her she was dismissed. It beggars belief.'

Huldar rummaged among his papers again until he found the page recording the verdict of the district court. Having checked the date, he did some mental arithmetic. 'Am I right that the girl was six when the case was reported and the trial was held less than a year later? That's an unusually quick turnaround.'

'Yes, almost unprecedented. But that's what happened. The inquiry was a complete shambles and the whole thing was rushed through.'

'And he was let off? How was that possible if the child's testimony was that strong?'

'There was nothing wrong with her testimony, I can assure you. But her brother insisted their father was innocent – that he hadn't touched either of them. Naturally his statement undermined half the charge, but the prosecutor didn't seem to care. He didn't ask the boy a single question. The prosecutor was Benedikt Toft, of course. I had the feeling he wasn't particularly committed to winning the case, and no appeal was ever lodged. I kept having to restrain myself from inter-vening and doing the prosecution's job for him, he let so many points pass unchallenged. The whole process made me very uncomfortable. But the mother backed up the boy's statement, a representative from Hafnarfjördur social services gave the family a glowing report, the child psychologist appointed by the local authority said the girl had probably made it up, and after only half a day in court, the whole thing was over. The teacher's name wasn't even on the witness list, so her testimony was never heard. Two weeks later the verdict was announced and – what do you know? – Jón Jónsson was acquitted. I'm not particularly proud of that victory and it came as no surprise when he reoffended a year later. Much more seriously, of course. But, you know, trials were very different in those days.' There was a definite rattle of ice cubes and the faint sound of sipping.

'Have you any idea what was going on?'

'Well, I have my suspicions, but they're only a hunch. I'm not sure I should be sharing them with you.'

'Right now we'd be grateful for any information. Another man's been killed – Kolbeinn Ragnarsson – and there's a third we haven't managed to identify yet. We believe more people could be in danger too.'

'Did you say Kolbeinn Ragnarsson?'

'Yes. Did you know him?'

'I could have sworn the man who represented Hafnarfjördur social services at the trial was called Kolbeinn. What was his patronymic again? The prosecutor never queried his participation in the trial, though there was every reason to. He was some kind of departmental manager for Hafnarfjördur Council, and had no qualifications as a social worker. And there were plenty more irregularities like that.'

'What about the judge? Shouldn't he have asked the questions the prosecution failed to put?'

'Yes, but he didn't. Yngvi Sigurhjartarson showed as little interest in the case as the prosecutor. It was all extremely odd. I didn't know what to make of it when he was elevated to the Supreme Court shortly afterwards. Perhaps he already knew about his promotion and his mind wasn't on the job.'

'He died recently. Had you heard?'

'Yes. There were rumours in the courts.'

'Rumours? About what?'

'Oh, I hate passing on gossip.' The man exhaled and the phone crackled in Huldar's ear. 'You'd better take it with a pinch of salt, but the rumour is that it was suicide.'

So Gudlaugur had been right. 'How?' It wasn't unheard of for murders to be made to look like suicides, and the killer they were after would have no scruples about doing something like that.

'I gather he walked into the sea.' The man hesitated, then added: 'But as I said, I don't have that on reliable authority.'

'I understand.' Huldar wondered if he should leave it at that, then remembered that one question remained unanswered. 'You said you'd had your suspicions about why Jón's first trial was such a travesty. What were they?'

The lawyer laughed coldly. 'I think I'll declare a conflict of interests if or when Jón's arrested for these murders. I can only welcome his recapture. I've no desire to defend him again.' The ice cubes clinked against his glass and he took another mouthful and swallowed before continuing: 'At the time I got the impression that Jón's father – or stepfather, rather – had something to do with it. Though I had no evidence for that apart from his being a big fish in Hafnarfjördur – I have a feeling he might even have been mayor.'

'Einar Adalbertsson was chairman of the town council, not mayor. But he was influential in his day, president of all kinds of associations, not to mention his political connections.'

'Exactly. In light of that, one can't help asking oneself who was responsible for the odd decision to send Kolbeinn to represent the local authority in court. And what about the psychologist? How impartial was she? The accused was the stepson of a man who was to all intents and purposes her employer.'

'But if Jón was Einar's stepson, that means Sigrún was in a sense his granddaughter. What about her? And her brother Thröstur?' Huldar couldn't understand why Sigrún's grandfather would be more likely to help his stepson get off than save his granddaughter from being abused.

'Good question. Einar attended the trial and I remember watching him while the girl was giving her testimony and wondering how he felt. It can't be much fun listening to your grandchild giving a detailed account of the incomprehensible things your stepson, her father, did to her. If it had been me, there's no doubt whose side I'd have been on.'

'Same here.'

'One last thing. From what I could see, Einar and the judge were the best of mates. Einar and the prosecutor too. Yet another irregularity.'

'Shouldn't the judge have declared a conflict of interests?'

'You'd have thought so. But Jón was the son of Einar's second wife and never formally adopted, so the judge may have taken a different view. Of course that's not a valid defence, but who was supposed to draw attention to the point? I couldn't do it as it would have gone against the interests of my client. And the prosecutor seemed to share the same conflict of interests, so he wouldn't have raised any objection. Sigrún's mother and brother insisted everything was fine and so did all the other witnesses who testified at the trial. The only person who seems to have wanted justice was the little girl herself. But she was too young to realise that anything was amiss. And the rest is history.' The lawyer paused, then added: 'But I can't for the life of me see why Jón would want to kill Kolbeinn or Benedikt. Neither of them showed any desire to put him behind bars. Quite the reverse. I think you're after the wrong man.'

They said goodbye, both in a rather more sombre frame of mind than when they had begun their conversation. Huldar closed his eyes so he could concentrate better and sat like that until the idiots at the neighbouring desks started joking that he'd fallen asleep again. Then he sprang up and marched over to Erla's office, not to explain his feelings, but to talk about what really mattered – the inquiry.

'What were you and Erla discussing?' Gudlaugur had held back for all of five minutes after Huldar's return. To give the boy his due, he hadn't almost dislocated his neck trying to peer through the glass wall into Erla's office, like his colleagues had. What kind of spectacle they'd been hoping to see was hard to say.

'I was briefing her about my phone call just now. Which, I can tell you, was pretty interesting.'

'In what way?'

'First, tell me what the widow had to say. Unless you were ringing your mum while I was away from my desk.'

'No, of course not.' Gudlaugur reddened, conscious that Huldar had overheard countless conversations between him and his mother. 'I was right: he did kill himself.'

'Yes, I know that. And?'

'How did you know? In that case why did I have to call her?'

'The lawyer told me but I needed confirmation. And to find out how he did it.'

'He walked into the sea.'

'OK. I knew that too. Anything else?'

'His body was never found. Only his car, parked out at Grótta, and his clothes neatly folded up by the lighthouse, with a letter to his wife in his coat pocket. His watch and jewellery lay on top of his clothes.'

'Jewellery? What kind of jewellery?'

'A wedding ring. And a Freemason's ring.'

'A Freemason's ring?'

'Yes. He was a Supreme Court judge. They're all Freemasons. That's what his wife said, anyway.'

Huldar didn't waste time pointing out that this was unlikely to apply to any female judges. 'Ring her back. Tell her we're on our way over.'

Gudlaugur looked horrified. 'No, please. You do it. It was an incredibly awkward conversation.'

'Do it. I'll bring the car round and meet you downstairs. I promise you needn't say a word when we meet her. I'll do the talking.'

'But—'

'Call the woman. I'll fill you in about my phone call to the lawyer on the way over there. Chop-chop, we need to get there and back before the guy from Forensics leaves for the day.' Without giving Gudlaugur a further chance to protest, Huldar left. He decided not to notify Erla: there was no time to lose and no need to raise her

hopes unnecessarily. He was about to cause her enough disappointment as it was.

Less than an hour later they left the home of Yngvi Sigurhjartarson's
widow. Huldar was carrying a plastic bag. The visit had been excru-
ciatingly uncomfortable; the woman's eyes kept filling with tears as
though she was about to break down. She took so long to find
something Yngvi alone could have touched that they were both
twitching with impatience. Finally she located the tablet that only
he had used in a drawer in their bedroom. Huldar took it from her
with gloved hands and placed it in a clear plastic bag. Luckily the
woman was too dazed to repeat her question about why on earth they
needed his fingerprints. Once they had got what they wanted at last,
they almost fell over each other in their haste to leave before the truth
dawned on her.

By observing only limited respect for the speed limit, Huldar
managed to get back to the office before the forensic technician left
for the day. The man heaved a sigh when Huldar ordered him to take
off his coat and fetch his fingerprint kit, but he obeyed.

He compared the prints on the tablet with those of the hands
found in Benedikt Toft's hot tub. The instant the results appeared,
his complaints were forgotten.

They left Forensics in a triumphant mood and Huldar got a
particular kick out of bursting into Erla's office to break the news to
her. They had found the owner of the hands: none other than the
Supreme Court judge, Yngvi Sigurhjartarson.

No one would dare to call him Sleeping Beauty now.

Chapter 31

Thorvaldur was cold. God, he was cold. The floor of this hellhole was wet; the ceiling was dripping and the rough walls were icy and damp, even slimy in places. Although as a rule he despised people who claimed to have illnesses caused by mould spores, he was beginning to wonder if there might be something in it after all. His throat was raw from the mildew in the air and the soreness had now spread right down to his lungs. If he didn't get a grip on himself, his imagination would start running riot, picturing green spores spreading through his bronchial tubes, leading to years of chronic illness that would ruin his future prospects – as if they weren't bleak enough at this moment. It was certainly hard to see how he was to escape from his current predicament in one piece.

He mustn't think like that.

And he mustn't let his eyes stray to the shapeless mound under the tatty old blanket in the corner. He still hadn't dared look under it, put off by the ghastly stench. Whatever it was, it could hardly provide him with a way out of here. The concrete walls were windowless and the steel door was locked.

He had never been good with his hands or performed any kind of manual labour. He had difficulty even picturing the kind of tools that could help him break out of here. All that came to mind was a gun, but that wouldn't open the door. Though with a gun he could at least overpower the person who was keeping him prisoner here.

If he had asked himself yesterday whether he would be prepared to shoot another human being, the answer would have been no. Today, he would aim straight for the heart or head. Without flinching.

But he didn't have a gun. That was pure fantasy. There would be no chance of stepping over the dead body of the person who had brought him here; of wiping his shoes on their corpse as he walked out of the open door.

He had only a vague idea of how long he had been held captive here. His phone was missing and the expensive watch had vanished from his wrist. When he discovered this he had been strangely relieved, though the feeling hadn't lasted. His initial reaction was that he must have been robbed. But then he got to thinking. He knew his countrymen; knew that Icelandic robberies didn't happen like this.

It would have been nice to be able to console oneself with the idea that this was one of those conventional, lame, incompetent Icelandic crimes. But he couldn't indulge in that kind of fantasy any longer. This was something altogether different and far worse. Thorvaldur tightened his grip on the expensive-looking walkie-talkie that he had spotted lying on a reasonably dry patch of the floor. At first he had been over the moon, thinking that the person who'd brought him here must have overlooked this life-saver. But then he realised that the channel selector button had been removed. His repeated calls for help on the channel it was tuned to had resulted in nothing but crackling static. The walkie-talkie hadn't been left there by mistake. He had waited in desperation for a message from his mysterious jailor. When nothing happened, he had started to think that maybe the radio was just some old junk after all.

A drip fell from the ceiling directly onto his head, making him even colder, if that was possible. Thorvaldur tried to focus on the positives. At least he wouldn't die of thirst.

Thorvaldur stared at the blanket covering the thing, whatever it was, in the corner. If he wrapped that around himself, he'd be able to lean against the wall without being soaked through. Maybe even have a nap. Then again, when he woke up he would be faced by the sight of the thing itself and the stench was bound to be twice as bad. No, better leave the blanket where it was.

How could he have been so stupid? Why hadn't he taken more care when he left the police station? He should have known that the man watching him meant business. If his suspicions proved correct, the man had already killed two, possibly three, other people. He had been perfectly aware of that as he walked back to his car, congratulating himself on having resisted the police officers' whining requests for him to come clean.

He couldn't actually recall much after that blow to his head. He could remember opening the car door but after that only snatches: he was lying on the back seat, struggling not to throw up in his car. He had a hazy recollection of being dragged out and leaning heavily on someone who led him along a gravel path or driveway. Next he remembered standing in the middle of this room, fighting dizziness and a lingering nausea. Amazingly enough he had managed to stay on his feet.

The bulb hanging from the ceiling flickered and Thorvaldur craned back his head to look at it. He couldn't bear the thought that it might blow any minute, leaving him alone in the pitch dark. With that thing in the corner.

The walkie-talkie crackled and Thorvaldur jumped. He held it up to his ear so as not to miss anything, only to jerk it away when a loud voice blared out: 'Hi, Thorvaldur. How are you doing?' There was nothing wrong with the volume, though you couldn't say the same for the sound quality. The voice was harsh and indistinct, made worse by the fact that the speaker was obviously trying to disguise it. Thorvaldur took this as a hopeful sign: if the intention was to kill him, why would it matter if he recognised the voice again?

'Who is this? What do you want?' He realised he'd forgotten to press the transmit button and repeated his words. 'Who is this? Why are you doing this?'

'Don't you worry about that. You'll soon find out.'

'Who is this?'

'Shut up. One more question out of you and I'll hang up. Is that clear?'

Assuming there was more to come, Thorvaldur waited. The walkie-talkie crackled again. 'Answer me when I ask you a question, you piece of shit.'

Thorvaldur pressed the button. 'Yes. Understood.'

'Not *understood*. Answer either yes or no. No ifs or buts. Just yes or no. Got that?'

'Yes.' Thorvaldur only just stopped himself from adding 'understood'.

'I'm going to make you an offer. Want to hear it?'

'Yes.' His tiredness had vanished. Instead, Thorvaldur was overwhelmed with fury and frustration over being forced to communicate in this restricted manner.

'You can expect visitors. I'm going to make it up to you for cutting short your weekend with the kids.'

The cold seemed to intensify. Thorvaldur's fingers were almost too numb to press the button to answer. This couldn't be happening. 'No.' He had to bite his lip to stop himself saying more.

'It's the least I can do.'

'No.' He did his best to charge the word with meaning. His children mustn't be mixed up in this. Oh God, no. But he couldn't convey the message. He heard the word echoing in his head, sounding as if he were merely declining the offer of coffee.

'But so it's not just the usual family reunion, I'm going to invite another guest.'

Thorvaldur didn't know whether to say yes or no but opted for yes in order to save up his 'no's. They would carry more weight if he didn't answer no every time. 'Yes.'

'You should know him.'

'Yes.'

'What do you mean "yes"? Do you know who it is?' The response betrayed anger and for a moment the speaker forgot to disguise their voice. Thorvaldur realised suddenly that it was a woman. A woman with a deep voice. Or a man with a feminine one.

'No.'

'I didn't think so. Your visitor will be none other than Jón Jónsson. You'll have a great time. Aren't you looking forward to it?'

'No.'

'Oh, well. Now we get to my offer. Listen carefully.'

The words echoed round the room, harsh and tinny, each one piercing his ears like a knife. When the voice finally fell silent he lost control, pressed the button and screamed into the radio: 'No way, you fucking cunt! Don't think for one second that you'll get away with this.' He broke off to catch his breath, then added more calmly, refraining from shouting for fear his words would be too distorted to be understood: 'I'm going to kill you. When I get out of here I'm going to kill you.' He released the button and waited.

For a long interval there was no sound; no crackling, static or speech. Then the voice emerged again, as level as his own had been towards the end: 'You broke the rules. So I'll have to say goodbye. But do one thing for me. Look under the blanket. Then you'll see that I mean business. And do smarten yourself up a bit. You're expecting visitors, remember?'

The radio fell silent and nothing happened, though Thorvaldur pressed all the buttons and howled like a madman, both into the gadget and up at the concrete ceiling. When he finally gave up he was exhausted.

He stared over at the mound on the other side of the room. He would have to look under the blanket. It was pointless to resist. Best get it over with.

Stiff with cold and fatigue, he walked over to the mound. He was forced to hold his nose as he bent down and took hold of the woollen blanket. Gingerly he lifted one corner, just enough to get a glimpse of what lay beneath. Despite the grisly sight that met his eyes, as bad as the worst of his fears, it wasn't enough; he had to see more, and he lifted the blanket higher. And was violently sick.

The phone bleeped. Æsa wondered if she should ignore it and carry on watching the boring cartoon with the kids, or check who the message was from. She got up. It was time to find them something to eat anyway. Since being returned to her they had been quiet and listless, too distressed to have any appetite, too traumatised to come to terms with their thoughts. None of the child-rearing manuals she had consulted had contained any advice for the parents of children who had stumbled on a pair of sawn-off feet.

'You go on watching. I'm going to make some food.' Neither Karlotta nor Dadi appeared to be listening. They stared at the screen, their eyes weary and red from weeping. Since they were obviously in no hurry to eat, Æsa checked her phone. The message was from Thorvaldur and despite her anger at him she opened it: *Let me take the kids out for a meal. I owe them and it might cheer them up a bit. Please. You're welcome to come along too if you like.*

She read the text again, glancing briefly at the two small heads just visible above the back of the sofa. Despite her reluctance to go anywhere with Thorvaldur, she knew the idea wasn't such a bad one. Karlotta and Dadi would be delighted to get out of the flat for a while, so long as it wasn't into the garden. It would be a long time before they could be persuaded to go and play outside again. Doubtless it would also do them good to see their father as soon as possible. If they didn't see him for two weeks, as the schedule dictated, there was a risk he would be forever linked to the idea of amputated feet. Also, Thorvaldur would owe her a favour in return, which meant she might be able to force him to explain what was going on. One miserable meal would be worth it for that.

'Would you like to go out to a late lunch with Daddy?'

Karlotta and Dadi got to their knees and peered over the sofa, their faces hard to read. 'Where?'

'I don't know. Perhaps he'll let you choose.'

'I don't want to go in his garden.' It must have been hard for Dadi to say this. He worshipped his father: in his eyes Thorvaldur was superior in every way and anything that belonged to him was the best. Including his garden.

'You needn't go out there. Of course not. Just out to eat.'

'What about the police lady?' Karlotta twisted a lock of hair round her finger, as she often did when she was insecure. 'Is she coming too?'

'No. Why do you think that?'

'The lady said he had to go and see the police. They wanted to talk to him. But they could talk to him at home.' She released her hair. 'Perhaps he's gone to jail.'

'He hasn't gone to jail, Karlotta. He's inviting you out to a meal. Me too, if you want me to come along.'

'Yay!' Dadi beamed, his tiredness banished. 'We're going to eat with Mummy and Daddy.'

The moment Æsa saw his reaction she realised this was a mistake. Now Dadi was bound to think they were getting back together. Just when he had finally stopped asking if they were going to. Too late.

The children were wild with excitement. She picked up the phone and texted Thorvaldur to accept his offer. She had hardly put it down when it bleeped again. When she opened the message it said simply: *Outside*.

Frowning, Æsa began to have second thoughts. This was typical of Thorvaldur: to be sitting outside, confident of getting what he wanted. She went over to the window and there was his car. He had reversed up to the house so all she could see was his shiny boot through the cloud of exhaust fumes.

'He's here.' She dropped the curtain. 'Put your boots on. Hurry up.'

Chapter 32

Erla stood with legs apart and one hand on her hip. Viewed from behind, she could have been either braced for an attack or auditioning as a backing singer for a Eurovision band. Thröstur was sitting on the sofa in front of her, hands cuffed behind his back. His mother had been taken down to the station and they were waiting for the car to return for him.

The frozen image of a heavily armed soldier filled the large TV screen. He was in the act of running along a sandy alleyway, brandishing an automatic weapon. Huldar had negotiated the same alley when playing the game with a mate of his. *Call of Duty – Black Ops II*. A few more steps and the warlike figure would be taken out by a sniper on a neighbouring rooftop. The controller was lying on the coffee table where Thröstur had put it down when they arrived. Beside it were those glued-together figurines, looking as forlorn as they had last time. It would be a while before Thröstur could finish his game. He was looking uncharacteristically low key and conventional without his black eye make-up and piercings. It made him appear younger: his face was naked and innocent, his skinny frame more apparent. But his eyes gave him away: they were dark in his pale face, flickering from side to side in search of an escape route.

'I repeat: where is your sister?' Erla's tone made it clear that she wouldn't ask again.

'I repeat: I don't know.' Thröstur had to tip his head back to meet her eye.

shivering slightly. Whether it was from the cold or from his predicament was impossible to say. 'Fuck you,' he mumbled.

Huldar smiled and carried on smoking. 'How long do you reckon your mother'll hold out under questioning – before she breaks down and tells us everything?' He stared down the empty street, watching the traffic lights on the corner changing pointlessly from red to amber to green. 'I'd give her a quarter of an hour. Five minutes to sit down, listen to the questions and hear them repeated over and over, with increasing seriousness. Ten minutes to cry, then bingo – a slip of the tongue and after that there'll be no stopping her. Your sister's a bit tougher, maybe, so I give her an hour. Then the tears'll start to flow.' He took a drag and let the smoke curl out from between his lips. God, it was good. 'I've seen it too often, mate. Don't try and kid yourself that this'll be any different.'

'Fuck you,' Thröstur mumbled again, impeded by the cigarette between his lips.

Huldar smiled. Thröstur could swear at him until he was blue in the face for all he cared; nothing could touch him at this moment. The case was about to be solved, thanks in large part to him. He meant to savour his triumph as it would soon fade; other cases would follow and his achievement would be forgotten. Nobody could rest on their laurels in the police. He turned back to Thröstur. 'I'm just telling you like it is. It's up to you to shield them from this. If it weren't for you and your obstinacy, I'm sure they'd gladly tell us the whole sordid tale.'

Thröstur took another puff, then indicated that he wanted to speak. Huldar plucked the cigarette from between his lips. Perhaps all he would get was a fresh stream of abuse but never mind. 'They've got nothing to do with this. Absolutely nothing. Leave them out of it. Save the sadism for when you get home.'

Huldar shoved the cigarette back between his lips. It hadn't worked.

'They found soil in the hire car. Quite a bit of it, on the back seats too. They'd obviously been put back to make room for quite a large object. What could that have been, I wonder?'

Thröstur had turned his head away to hide his reaction from Huldar.

'The samples we took will be compared to the soil from the grave and I'm assuming the results won't look too good. Why the hell didn't you return the car? They'd have cleaned it and that would have made our life much harder. Was the deal for the week really that irresistible?'

Thröstur said nothing.

'But . . . you're unbelievably clumsy operators. Like that business with the time capsule. I just can't understand why the hell you put that letter in there. If it hadn't been for your list, it would have taken us a lot longer to work the whole thing out. That was such a bad move. Though you were only a kid at the time, I suppose.'

'You're a moron.' Thröstur inhaled, then blew the smoke in Huldar's face. 'A total moron.'

The squad car appeared and pulled up to the kerb. Huldar removed the cigarette from Thröstur's mouth, threw it in the nearest gutter and flicked his own after it. Then he pushed Thröstur into the back and took a seat in the front himself. Before they set off, he twisted round to study the young man who was gazing at the rundown building. Nobody dreamt of watching their home recede into the distance from the back of a police car. 'One more thing. There's a sniper on the roof at the end of that alleyway. You have to take him out before you can progress any further. There's a good line of sight from behind the cart.' He turned to face the front again, fairly sure that Thröstur would have forgotten this advice by the time he got back to his computer game. Because he wouldn't be going home any time soon.

'What kind of person doesn't own a mobile phone? Even three-year-olds have phones these days.' Erla couldn't let it go, though they'd received confirmation from every telecom company in the country. There were so many other aspects she should have been giving her attention to. It wasn't as if all the other details had been pieced together yet. Huldar wished Erla would pack it in. He was burning with impatience to start questioning Thröstur, who had been sitting waiting for them in the interview room for more than three-quarters of an hour now. 'Shouldn't we be heading downstairs?'

'Yes.' She turned, her expression excited and pitiless. Huldar recognised that look from goose hunting; from the instant when a shot hit the prey. She wasn't gloating over the fate of Thröstur and Sigrún; she was simply glad that the end of the investigation was in sight. It was the same with him and his hunting mates: they didn't get a kick out of the act of killing – that was just a necessary evil, an instant in time, over in a flash. 'We'd better get this right. You know what's at stake.'

Huldar nodded. Outside the room, two senior officers were lurking, their faces grave. The top brass had been rattled to learn that the murder victims included not only a prosecutor but a Supreme Court judge as well.

The professional status of the murder victims was immaterial to Huldar, Erla and the inquiry team. Right now all their attention was focused on the living, on Thorvaldur Svavarsson and his children, who might possibly still be saved. All available personnel were combing the capital area and points north, specifically the shores of Hvalfjördur and the countryside around Akranes and Borgarnes. There had been no news so far, and the police were growing increasingly concerned that they wouldn't reach the family in time. There wasn't a minute to spare for anything else, including Huldar's showdown with Erla. For the moment their interaction had reverted to normal, their communications brief and strictly to the point.

Erla took a drink of water and banged her glass down on the

conference table. 'I'm not releasing Thröstur till he tells us where those kids are. I'm prepared to sit over him all night if need be.'

'I'm with you.'

They hurried out but didn't get far before the senior officers flagged Erla down for a word. Huldar stood aside impatiently. He studied Æsa, the children's mother, who was sitting, head drooping, exhausted from weeping. She had called the emergency number while they were bringing Thröstur in to the station, out of her mind with terror, and reported that her children had been abducted. The emergency services had sent a police car to pick her up since the woman had been dumped by the roadside in Hvalfjördur, without her phone or handbag, and was calling from a nearby farm.

When she reached the station she had gone completely to pieces, one minute sobbing, the next screaming at the police to find her children. She had ugly grazes on one cheek and both hands, and blood was oozing from the back of her head. But she didn't complain, didn't even seem aware of her injuries.

When finally they managed to calm her down and heard what she had to say, the whole office was thrown into confusion. Suddenly the order of priorities had changed; they were in a race against time to find two little children before something terrible happened. The murderer had already shown that he was capable of the unthinkable and it would be naive to imagine that the children's youth would give him any pause. The police immediately attempted to reach their father, Thorvaldur, and when they failed, concluded that he had been abducted as well since, according to his ex-wife, the perpetrator was in possession of his car and phone.

Æsa said she had been tricked into entering her ex-husband's car. She had put the children in the back seat and been hit on the head while she was fastening their seatbelts. When she regained consciousness the car was racing through the darkness. Her hands and feet were bound and she had a balaclava pulled down over her face, back to front, so she could see next to nothing. The driver, realising she was coming round, stopped the car and dragged her out onto the road, then sped away. She couldn't give any description of her assailant, though she thought the person who bundled her out of the car had been a woman – either that or a man with small hands. For now, they were working on the assumption that it was Sigrún. Although she didn't have a licence it was conceivable that she knew how to drive, and her gentle, timid manner might mask a very different person underneath.

Erla finally came away from her bosses, rolling her eyes. Together she and Huldar strode downstairs without a word, their faces set in determination, to the room where Thröstur was waiting. Erla flung open the door, stormed in and yanked out one of the chairs opposite him with a loud screech. 'Now you're going to tell us everything. You've got no choice.' She slapped down a photocopy of the letter he had written ten years before. 'Who's who on this list of yours? Let's start with that. Who's still in danger?'

Huldar slipped into the seat beside her and watched Thröstur. He looked tired, all sign of cockiness long gone, his shoulders sagging, shadows under his eyes.

'Can I have a drink of water?'

'No.' As well as instructing the guards to keep Thröstur awake, Erla had banned them from giving him anything to eat or drink. He hadn't been allowed to go to the toilet either.

'You can't leave me to die of thirst. I need water.'

'You're not having anything to drink. Complain to Amnesty if you don't like it.' It was an ugly trick, but necessary in the circumstances. There were other, still harsher methods they could use to pressurise him to start talking, and they might yet have to resort to these. 'While you're remembering the names, you can tell me where your sister took the children. If you do that, you can have some water. If you don't, you can't.'

Thröstur looked up and stared at Erla. His astonishment was obvious. 'What children?'

'Thorvaldur Svavarsson's children. Your sister's abducted them and gone to ground somewhere.'

'I've already told you I haven't a clue who Thorvaldur Svavarsson is. I'm telling the truth, I swear. And Sigrún hasn't abducted them. She's just gone off somewhere – she disappears from time to time when she's feeling down, but only for a long walk or something. I swear she hasn't made off with any kids.'

'We weren't born yesterday, Thröstur.' Reaching across the table, Erla grabbed him roughly by the chin. 'We know how these people are linked to you and your sister; we know they failed you both when you were young. That was bad, but your sick campaign of revenge is totally insane. You two are no better than the people who hurt you.' She released him so abruptly that Thröstur's head rebounded. 'Where are they?'

'I swear, I know nothing about any kids. I don't know any Thorvaldur. He's not on the list.'

'Is that so?' Erla leant back in her chair. 'Well, who are these people? And what the hell is this list? We know the judge Yngvi was among the victims, but he's not here. And what about Thorvaldur? Were they a later addition? Can we expect more of those?'

Thröstur was staring down at the paper. 'No children were supposed to be snatched. That wasn't supposed to happen.'

Huldar reached over the table to point at the initials. 'Who are they, Thröstur? If you help us now, you'll be treated more leniently. But if the children are harmed, your life is as good as over. You'll go to jail and be branded for life. Just like your father. Do you want to follow in his footsteps?' Huldar drew back his hand. 'These are young kids. It isn't their fault that you were treated badly by the system. If you have a shred of honour, you'll tell us where they are.'

'I've already told you a hundred times, I don't know. I simply don't know.'

'OK. Let's say that's true. But you know who took them.'

There was a silence. Huldar and Erla studied the top of Thröstur's head as he pored over the list. Then he sat up. 'BT is Benedikt Toft. He studied law with that bastard, my so-called grandfather. He agreed to rush the case so the prosecution would be a total fiasco. Did it as a favour to an old mate who couldn't face the scandal of being associated with a paedo. K is for Kolbeinn. I couldn't remember his patronymic when I wrote this. He worked for Hafnarfjördur Council and made sure the social services' report on our home was good. In return, Granddad pulled strings to get him a better job at an accountancy firm he had a stake in. S is Sólveig, I can't remember her patronymic. She was the psychologist who betrayed Sigrún; she told the court my sister had an overactive imagination, though she knew it was bullshit. She'd done the same thing to me earlier. Her reward was a big fat contract with the town council. The thing that pisses me off most is that she hasn't been bumped off. She's such a disgusting bitch.' He glanced up as he said this, his expression leaving them in no doubt that he meant it. Then he carried on. 'I is for Yngvi, the judge.'

'Yngvi isn't spelt with an I. It starts with Y.'

'So what? It's not a spelling test. That piece of shit betrayed me and my sister in return for Granddad putting in a good word for him about his application to be a Supreme Court judge. A great deal for him; not so good for me and Sigrún. And Vaka. Let's not forget her.'

'No. We haven't.' Erla pointed at the photocopy. 'What about OV?'

'Valdi. Officer Valdi.'

'And who is Officer Valdi?'

'A cop I went to see, to ask for help.'

'When did you ask him for help? We were told the matter came out when Sigrún talked about it at school.'

'Before that. Long before. When Sigrún was four and I was eight.' Again Thröstur lowered his eyes. 'When our creep of a dad started showing an interest in her. He'd got bored of me.' He broke off, breathed in slowly, then sniffed. Neither Erla nor Huldar dreamt of interrupting him; they were too busy trying to take in the full horror of events they had thought they understood, though now it seemed that they hadn't had any idea. 'I decided to go to the cops. They're supposed to arrest criminals. This was in December, the day before school broke up for the Christmas holidays. I walked down to the station, scared shitless but determined to save Sigrún. The cop I talked to introduced himself as Officer Valdi. He took me aside and I told him the whole story. For the first time in my life I told someone what had happened to me. He listened and I thought the two of us would go home in his police car and arrest my dad. But that's not what happened. He said they'd have to investigate first and asked if there was anyone who could come and collect me. I gave him my grand-dad's name because of course I didn't want my dad to come, or Mum. Granddad came and he and Valdi went off and had a chat. Then Granddad drove me home and told me I should learn to hold my tongue and not spread lies about the man who'd done nothing but be a good father to me. He told Dad everything. That evening I had the shit kicked out of me worse than ever before. I never heard from Valdi again, never heard anything about an investigation. Granddad told me later that he'd talked the cop round and made sure he'd keep quiet. He was studying law at university and Granddad promised to fix him a good job once he'd qualified. He must have done that, because Valdi never said a word. Not at the first trial or at the second. So much for my attempt to save Sigrún.'

'Didn't you speak to anyone else? Your teacher, doctor, your mother? Another adult?' Huldar was careful to keep his voice neutral. This wasn't the right moment to betray any pity for the poor lad, though it was hard not to.

Thröstur looked up. The fury and hatred were back. 'Hey, I was eight years old. Stupid enough to think the cops were the people to turn to for justice. After they betrayed me, I had nowhere else to go. Mum was totally useless, under the heel of that violent bastard and unwilling to face up to what was going on. I kept trying to tell her but she wouldn't listen. Just told me to shush and looked around shit-scared in case Dad heard us. So I took what I thought was the only way out. I ran away with Sigrún.'

'I don't suppose you got far.'

'We made it a bit beyond the aluminium factory. I was trying to get to Keflavík. I thought we could get on a plane and go and live abroad. But it was freezing and the wind picked up and it started snowing. We nearly died of exposure. Sigrún got frostbite on her fingers because I didn't have the sense to bring gloves. Someone spotted us through the snow flurries and rescued us. It was too late, though. Two of Sigrún's fingers had to be amputated. She was taken to hospital and Granddad came to fetch me. In the car he belted me so hard that my eye started bleeding. But no one asked me what had happened. I was sent to a psychologist – to that bitch Sólveig – and she spent most of the time trying to persuade me that I'd imagined the whole thing or was making it up. I came from a good family and should be grateful.' He stopped speaking to grind his teeth. Then continued, growling now in his fury: 'I hate her and I wish she'd been first, not got off scot-free.'

'She won't get away with it.' Huldar could understand the hatred now, even the violence and brutality of the murders. That didn't make the siblings' crimes forgivable but it was better than if they had been motivated by pure sadism. 'She'll be made to answer for it, I promise you that.'

'Yeah, right.' Thröstur shook himself. 'I believe you. Not.'

'We're just going to step outside for a moment.' Erla stood up. 'We won't be long.'

They left Thröstur sitting there. Huldar was half expecting to have a strip torn off him for making promises he couldn't keep, but not a bit of it.

'Officer Valdi must be Thorvaldur,' Erla said. 'When those feet turned up in his garden, I looked into his background and he started working for the Prosecutor's office straight after graduation, which is pretty unusual. While he was at university he temped for the police, in Hafnarfjördur among other places. That's how he's connected to this, not through the Prosecutor's office.' She frowned. 'There's one thing I don't understand. Thröstur was very convincing when he swore he didn't know any Thorvaldur Svavarsson; the man to kill was Officer Valdi. So he can't have taken part in the attack on him.' Apparently she wasn't expecting an answer because she continued, sounding increasingly exasperated: 'It just doesn't fit. What the fuck do we do if it turns out he isn't involved? I couldn't give a shit about Thorvaldur but I want to find his kids. Safe and sound.' Two deep creases had formed in her brow. When her phone rang, she glanced at the number, then answered. Huldar could hear a man's voice and Erla's curt replies. She hung up. 'Sigrún's been found.'

'Where?'

'The police who were watching their house saw her come home. She's been arrested and is on her way to the station. Claims she's been at the cinema. Went for a long walk, dropped in at a bookshop, then went to see some film.'

'Is she telling the truth?'

'That's yet to be confirmed. I don't like the look of this. Not one bit.' She blew out slowly, then pulled herself together. 'Get him some water, then let's press on.'

Huldar did so without protest, finding the largest glass in the kitchen and filling it up. When he returned, Erla had resumed her seat opposite Thröstur. She started talking the moment Huldar walked in. 'So now we know what's behind these atrocities. But the question remains, where are Thorvaldur's children? Officer Valdi's children?'

'I swear I don't know.' Thröstur reached for the glass of water but Huldar drew it back.

'You can do better than that. Who took them? Sigrún?'

'No. Not Sigrún and not me. This isn't a list of people *I* was going to kill. Let alone of people *she* was.'

'What the hell is it then?' Erla snatched up the sheet of paper and shook it in Thröstur's face.

'They're the people Vaka's parents are going to kill.' Thröstur stared at the glass of water. 'Can I have that drink now?'

Huldar pushed it over to him.

Chapter 33

Freyja's phone had run out of memory. She had taken countless photos of Saga for her brother in the hope that at least one of them would be OK, but the little girl had a peculiar knack of turning away or closing her eyes just as Freyja snapped a picture. It didn't help that in the only photos that weren't blurred the perma-scowl was in place.

Freyja had taken Saga down to the lake on the pretext of feeding the ducks, though the real purpose was to bump into the handsome single father again. He hadn't shown up but there had been no shortage of other fathers with children in buggies and bags of bread. Obese ducks swam around in the hole in the ice, hoovering up the endless supply of food. They wouldn't starve as long as there were toddlers in Iceland.

Molly flopped down heavily by the sofa where Freyja was lying. She had just gorged herself on mince. It was supposed to last for two meals but Freyja had felt so guilty for leaving the dog alone all weekend that she had poured the whole lot into her bowl.

As usual on a Sunday evening, there was nothing happening. Her friends were busy posting status updates of breathtaking tedium: banal quotations about happiness or the importance of good values, photos of their supper or of themselves in such convoluted yoga positions that they must surely be faked.

Perhaps her bad mood stemmed from having no one to cook for but Molly. She snapped the laptop shut and grabbed her phone instead. She still had the single father's number but the timing wasn't ideal. Like her, he would have been entertaining a small child all weekend and was bound to be shattered. Better to wait.

In that instant her phone rang, a number she didn't recognise appearing on the screen. Could it be him? 'Hello?'

'Hello. Is that Freyja? The psychologist?' She didn't recognise the voice.

'Yes. That's me. Who am I talking to?'

'Sorry, my name's Orri. You gave me your card outside the police station.'

'Oh yes. Hello.' Freyja sat up. 'I wasn't expecting to hear from you.'

'I wasn't expecting to call you.' She could hear him breathing, but just when she thought he'd changed his mind about talking to her, he continued: 'I know it's Sunday evening and all that, but I'm in a terrible mess and I don't know where to turn. It involves mental illness, so after a lot of thought I decided to get in touch.'

'That's fine. Are you in a bad way?' She tried to recall the names of any colleagues who treated adults and would be prepared to take on an emergency case outside office hours.

'I'm in a bad way all right but that's not what this is about. It's my ex-wife, Dagmar. I'm afraid there's something seriously wrong.'

'Is she there with you now?'

He seemed affronted, as if Freyja was implying that he had a lunatic frothing at the mouth in the bed beside him. 'No. Good God, no.'

'Where is she then?'

'I don't know.' Orri hesitated as if having second thoughts about the wisdom of ringing her. 'But I have my suspicions.'

'OK. Leaving that aside for the moment, are you afraid she might harm herself?'

'Can I come round?' he blurted out.

Freyja glanced round the room at the mauled sofa, the dog hairs and the mess she had been intending to tidy up all weekend. 'No, I'm afraid that's not possible.'

'Oh. I see. Then could you come to my place . . . or meet me somewhere? I feel very uncomfortable discussing this over the phone.'

Freyja thought. What else did she have to do? Spend her evening on social media, bored out of her mind? 'Can it wait till morning? You could come over to the Children's House and I could help you find a psychologist who specialises in adult cases. How urgent is it?'

Orri gave a dry, mirthless laugh. 'If my suspicion proves right, it would be hard to imagine anything more urgent.'

'It sounds like she needs to be committed. I'd advise you to call the psychiatric department at the National Hospital. I can't be of much help in a situation like that.'

'I've tried. They won't talk to me. I'm not her next of kin, and I had the feeling they thought I was trying to get even with Dagmar in some kind of divorce drama. But you've got to believe me, that's not what this is about. We've had nothing to do with each other for over ten years now.' He paused, then resumed in a flat voice, his earlier agitation replaced by a note of defeat. 'I don't know what to do.'

'OK, I'll meet you.' Freyja mentioned a café in the area that would still be open and was likely to be neither full nor completely empty. She had no desire to meet this man alone: his request was odd and she didn't really understand what he wanted. But then she remembered how cruelly fate had treated the couple. Vaka's death had destroyed their marriage, yet Orri plainly felt a lingering affection for Dagmar. 'I understand that you still care about your ex-wife and, you never know, I might be able to help in some way.'

But in this her psychologist's insight had failed her.

'Dagmar? I couldn't give a shit about her. It's the others I'm worried about.'

Freyja stood outside the café, watching Orri, still inside, staring unseeingly at the pictures on the walls. The hand she held her phone in was trembling with cold and shock. Orri had talked almost ceaselessly, barely once sipping his coffee. Her own cup was standing untouched on the table. Now and then she had got in a word, but apart from that she had sat and listened to the man's emotionless recital. During her studies she had read articles about extreme cases of psychopathic behaviour on a par with what he was describing, but it had never occurred to her that she would be faced with such a situation, let alone that she would be expected to come up with a solution. After he'd finished, she had needed a moment to savour the quiet ordinariness of the café, the muted chatter of the few other customers. How she regretted having agreed to meet him instead of staying home and scrolling through pictures on Facebook of her friends' kids with their colouring books.

Orri hadn't seemed at all surprised or unsettled by her silence; he seemed to be glad of a moment's respite too.

Finally, Freyja pulled herself together, stood up and told him she was going to call the police. They might also alert the psychiatric department, but that wasn't top priority right now. She was ready for him to react angrily and remind her of a psychologist's duty of confidentiality but he did nothing of the sort. He merely nodded and said he would wait.

Huldar's phone rang several times. Freyja began to fear that he wouldn't pick up – ironically, since in addition to not wanting to call him in the first place, she would have preferred never to hear his voice again. When he finally answered she didn't beat about the bush: 'You've got to send a police car. I'm with Orri, Vaka's father, and he's just been telling me about his ex-wife and what he thinks she's done.'

'Where are you?' He didn't ask what Dagmar was supposed to have done. Either he trusted Freyja implicitly or he already knew something. She suspected the latter. It didn't matter. The main thing was that he was going to take this nightmare out of her hands. She named the café and he interrupted. 'I know where it is. I'm on my way. Don't go anywhere and don't let him leave.'

Freyja hung up and turned back to the window. Through the dirty glass she met Orri's tired eyes. She raised a hand and waved to him like an idiot. Then walked calmly back inside.

A cloud of cigarette smoke hung in the still, frosty air. One of the police cars had taken Orri back to the station. There he would be made to repeat his story and sign a formal statement. What would happen to him after that Freyja didn't know and didn't really care. He seemed to be under the impression that there was nothing wrong with him, but that was far from the truth. It would be up to others to judge how ill he was. Perhaps he was simply one of the worst enablers in history.

'Thanks for calling. You did exactly the right thing.' Huldar was lingering over his cigarette, apparently in no hurry to head off again. He looked in better shape than the last time she had seen him; not as sorry for himself either. In fact, he seemed bullish and upbeat. 'You never know, this might help us find Thorvaldur's kids in time.'

'Let's hope so.'

After speaking to Orri, Huldar had taken the time to bring her up to speed with the case. At first she had assumed there was a professional reason for this but he ended by explaining that this was why he hadn't been in touch to apologise properly. Her only response had been an icy stare. 'Can you send someone straight there from Borgarnes?' she asked now.

'Yes, they've already been called out. If they find the family, I'll head over. The question is, would you be willing to come along? The kids are bound to need professional help.' He took a puff, then added: 'Or let's hope so. The alternative doesn't bear thinking about.'

Freyja didn't answer immediately. A one- to two-hour drive in the dark with Huldar wasn't exactly what she would have chosen right now. 'What'll happen to the couple?'

'Hard to say. If he's telling the truth, he might get off with a caution. Of course he should have reported this a long time ago. It's possible he'll try and claim that he never believed Dagmar would actually go through with her plans, but after the events of the last few days that just isn't credible. The moment Benedikt Toft's name appeared in the media, he should have realised she might be acting out her revenge fantasy. If he'd come forward then, Thorvaldur and his children would be safe, even if it was already too late to save Kolbeinn.'

Freyja nodded. She drew her hands into the sleeves of her coat; the frost was beginning to bite. 'Do you think he's lying?'

'No. But the truth has many versions. This is how he sees it. She may see it differently.' Huldar sucked the last puff out of his cigarette, then stubbed it out. 'How did he describe it to you? That account might not be quite the same as the one he fed me. You can sometimes read a lot from the discrepancies; no liar has all the details worked out when he starts inventing.'

'It was such a long story – I'm not sure I can repeat it in detail. But I remember the main points.'

'Go ahead.'

'It started normally enough. He talked about how badly they'd both been hit by Vaka's death. At first there didn't seem to be any difference in how their grief was affecting them, but as time wore on it became increasingly obvious that Dagmar wanted to – how did he put it? – spend all her time looking in the rear-view mirror, while he wanted to look at the road ahead. What finally drove them apart was when Thröstur came round to see them after his father was convicted. They had encountered him and Sigrún when the kids turned up at court to testify, and although Orri was reluctant to say exactly what happened, he admitted that his and Dagmar's behaviour didn't do them any credit. They'd also treated the children badly at Vaka's funeral. He seemed to be ashamed and stressed they hadn't been themselves at the time. In their eyes Sigrún was to blame for setting off the train of events that led to their daughter's death.'

'That's pretty consistent with what he told me. There was less emotional crap, but in other respects it was similar. What did he say about the grandfather, Einar Adalbertsson?'

Freyja wanted to shove that reference to 'emotional crap' down Huldar's throat but found she didn't have the energy. It wouldn't serve any purpose; he was entitled to his opinions and could live by them – like the uncivilised brute that he was.

'He said Thröstur came knocking on their door after they met at the Reykjanes District Court, almost a year after the murder. He'd come to tell them that it wasn't his or Sigrún's fault. They'd both tried to stop their father but their grandfather had blocked their attempts. Thröstur claimed he had gone to the police when he was younger, but no one would listen to him, and Sigrún had confided in her teacher, which had eventually resulted in a charge being brought. But his father had been let off because everyone had betrayed them. Thröstur said that before the trial his grandfather Einar took him aside and bragged that he had them all – judges, lawyers, social workers – in his pocket, and that if Thröstur didn't swear that everything was perfectly fine at home he'd make him sorry. The old man said he'd murder him if he didn't do as he was told. So naturally

Thröstur obeyed. Apparently the grandfather gave Sigrún the same lecture but it doesn't seem to have worked. Not that her testimony achieved anything.'

'That fits more or less with what Thröstur told us. We've got him in custody. Did Orri say nothing about his and Dagmar's visit to Einar?'

'Yes. That's when I began to have my doubts about his version of events. He said they didn't entirely believe Thröstur. They forced the boy to accompany them to his house.'

Freyja took a deep breath, filling her lungs with the pure, icy air. 'At first, Einar denied everything, as you'd expect, and wouldn't come clean until Dagmar threatened him with a hammer she'd brought along. Orri said she'd been intending to use it to smash the old man's place up. But instead of threatening his property, she started saying she was going to smash his face in. Einar was too frightened to lie. Although I don't know for sure, I have my suspicions that Orri played some part in that. Thröstur might be able to tell us more about who threatened Einar and how. Anyway, the old man came clean and told them exactly who had taken part in the cover-up and what he'd bribed them with. Thröstur was forced to sit through the whole thing.'

'What about Einar's death? Did Orri explain how that came about?'

'Yes, though he insists he doesn't know exactly what happened. He was so enraged after Einar had admitted everything that he had to step out into the hall to try and calm down. Next thing he knew there was a crash and when he went back in the old man was lying with his head on the glass coffee table, which was covered in blood. Orri said he was fairly sure that Dagmar had lost control and hit the old man on the back of the head with the hammer. At the time, though, Dagmar swore that Einar had fallen and hit his head on the table. Of course that's rubbish and so's his claim that he believed her lie. Anyway, they acted in a panic, put a plastic bag over his head and dragged him, dead or dying, into the bathroom. There they took off the bag and bashed his head against the rim of the bath. That finished him off. Then they poured the blood from the bag around the bathtub, and cleaned the coffee table. As a final touch, they forced a toothbrush into Einar's fist, then fled the scene. Poor Thröstur witnessed the whole thing and according to Orri, Dagmar threatened to kill him too if he didn't keep his mouth shut. But this time they promised Thröstur a reward. If he kept quiet, Dagmar would kill all the people who had betrayed him and Sigrún – and Vaka of course – but not until his father got out of jail. Dagmar wanted to wait that long because she was dead set on murdering Jón Jónsson too. And that meant having to keep her vengeance on ice until he was released.'

Huldar zipped up his parka to the neck. 'Do you want to finish the story in the car? You can sit in the front.' He smiled. 'I'm freezing to death.'

The heater worked, unlike the one in her pile of junk, and although the blast was cold for the first few seconds, it carried a promise of much-desired warmth. 'Please, go on.' Huldar rubbed his hands and blew on them. 'I'm just waiting for news from Borgarnes.'

'Where had I got to?'

'Dagmar had murdered Einar Adalbertsson and threatened Thröstur.'

'Right. Orri said that after that, Dagmar became completely obsessed with vengeance. At first he tried to ignore it. He thought she wasn't serious, it was just a phase she was going through. But as time went on there was room for nothing else in her life and in the end their marriage broke down. He waited until the Supreme Court had given its verdict, hoping that she would feel Jón had got his just deserts, but that wasn't enough for her. She went on plotting how to kill all the people who had been implicated in Jón's first acquittal. In her eyes they were all equally culpable. Orri didn't agree and said that the final straw came when she started stockpiling all kinds of tools, sulphuric acid and other worrying stuff. She was determined to get hold of them years in advance so they couldn't be traced when the time came. The day she came home with a chainsaw, he says he walked out.'

'I can understand that.' Huldar held his hands over the heater grille. 'If my wife came home with a chainsaw, you wouldn't see me for dust.'

'Yeah, right. Dream on.' Freyja wasn't interested in discussing his love life. She wanted to finish the story so she could go home. 'After he walked out, he said he stopped keeping tabs on her, so he didn't know if she'd persisted with her obsession. He'd hoped the divorce would act as a wake-up call. But then several months ago she got in touch to ask a favour. She needed a house off the beaten track, with a windowless cellar, to borrow for a while. He's quite a successful estate agent so he had lots of properties on his books that had belonged to the failed banks, which were standing vacant. According to him, she threatened to tell the police about his part in Einar Adalbertsson's death if he didn't do this for her. So he gave her the keys to a huge place just outside Borgarnes. The property's not about to sell any time soon, so he was able to lend it to Dagmar without any danger of prospective buyers wanting to view it. A further advantage was that it came with a lot of land, which means there are no other houses nearby.'

'That's got to be where the kids are. It's got to be. Their mother was thrown out of the car in the middle of nowhere on the shores of Hvalfjördur. I'm guessing Dagmar chose to drive the long way round the fjord to avoid the cameras in the tunnel. She can't have been going anywhere else.' The look Huldar turned on Freyja was almost pleading, as if begging her to back up his theory, to reassure him that everything was going to be all right.

'Don't look at me. I know even less about it than you. All I know is what Orri told me, and I'm not convinced he's a hundred per cent reliable.'

'What did he say about the murders? Did he know anything about them?'

'He claims not. He said he got a shock when he saw Benedikt Toft's name in the papers but didn't want to believe Dagmar could be involved. I don't find that very convincing, given that he knew she owned a chainsaw. Then he went quiet and seemed to be waiting for me to ask him questions. But I just wanted to get rid of him, so I rang you. Of course I should have asked why he'd only come forward now, but I didn't.'

'That doesn't matter, because I did.'

'What did he say?'

'That he couldn't keep deceiving himself after Kolbeinn's name was released and the severed limbs seemed to be linked to both cases. When the police appealed for information about Thorvaldur and his kids, he couldn't stay silent any longer and rang you.'

'Why me? It's obviously a police matter. Why did he want to mix me up in it?'

'I doubt he was thinking straight by then. Perhaps he just wanted to shift the burden to act onto somebody else. You rang the police, not him. Could it have been an attempt to assuage his guilt about Dagmar? Convince himself that he didn't betray her and only had her interests at heart – wanted to get her psychiatric help, even though it was ten years too late?'

'You're not so bad at this "emotional crap" after all.'

'Ha ha.'

'One more question before I go.' Freyja huddled closer to the blast of hot air. 'Did you believe him?'

Huldar shrugged. 'Yes and no. You?'

'Same here: yes and no. After all, he's compromised himself by admitting to his part in Einar Adalbertsson's murder. Is he likely to be shown any leniency for that?'

'For the part he claims to have played – he could be. All he did was pervert the course of justice. And since the statute of limitations is ten years, court action can't be taken for the offence now and there's every chance he'll get away with it. I bet he'd have kept quiet otherwise.'

Huldar's phone rang and he snatched it up. He said little, but let the caller do the talking. The message was brief and Huldar rang off. 'That was one of the officers from Borgarnes who was sent to the property.' He put the car in gear.

'What? What did he say?'

'Mostly: *Shit, this is bad. Jesus Christ, Jesus Christ.* Then he said they needed experts on the spot asap.' Huldar roared off down the street before Freyja had a chance to get out of the car.

So she was on her way north to Borgarfjördur – please God – to help two terrified children.

Chapter 34

There was no doubt they were on the right track. A host of recent tyres had torn up the snow on the dirt road. As they drew nearer, they spotted lights and Huldar instinctively accelerated, sending gravel flying up on either side. They skidded on a bend and he slowed down a little, not for fear of losing control of the car but because Freyja screamed, gripped the door-handle for dear life and shrieked abuse at him the rest of the way up to the house.

The headlights of a whole fleet of vehicles lit up the area, throwing every flaw in the bare concrete walls of the building into stark relief. Nevertheless, it was easy to imagine how the house would look if the construction were ever completed: large and imposing in its arrogant simplicity. Summer palaces like this had sprung up all over the country in the period when people were deluded into believing themselves richer than they really were, and quite a few were waiting, half completed like this one, for the good times to return. Huldar, never having belonged to the rich set, didn't know if he would have been tempted by a prize like this. He hoped not.

Boards had been nailed across all the windows, but light was spilling out of the open front door from the powerful floodlights inside. It must be jam-packed in there, however ridiculously large the so-called 'summer cottage'. As well as the Forensics van, he recognised cars belonging to Erla and the pathologist, and a couple of other police vehicles from Reykjavík. In addition there were two ambulances parked in the drive and two police cars from Borgarnes. The silhouette of a hunched figure was visible in the back seat of each of the Reykjavík squad cars. One appeared to be a woman – Dagmar, Huldar assumed. The other was a man, his short, dark hair a greasy mess. Jón Jónsson or Thorvaldur?

Huldar and Freyja jumped out of the car. The mountainsides echoed with the slamming of their doors and the snow creaked underfoot. The frost was harder here than in town and their breath produced clouds of steam. A strange odour hung in the windless air. Sadly, it was one Huldar was all too familiar with – the stench of decomposition. Slapping his coat pockets, he discovered that he'd forgotten to bring the menthol cream for smearing under one's nose at times like this. 'Maybe you'd rather wait outside.' He glanced at Freyja but she shook her head. 'Pull your jumper over your nose, then. This is going to be extremely nasty.' She paused to follow his suggestion, then accompanied him inside, her eyes wide and staring.

Huldar found Erla talking to a policeman he didn't recognise, presumably one of the officers from Borgarnes. They were standing at the top of the stairs to the basement, which seemed to be the source of the appalling stench.

'How's it going?'

Erla turned. 'Fine. Considering. We've got one pretty horrific corpse. But it could have been worse.' Looking past him, she clocked Freyja. 'I hope she's here for the kids and not as your special guest.'

'She came for the kids. Where are they?'

Erla looked back at Huldar, a gleam of menthol cream under her nose. 'In the ambulance. I suggest she gets her arse over there. Now. Before she pukes all over her fancy shoes.' Erla had sharp eyes; Freyja's footwear was totally inappropriate for a crime scene.

Huldar went back to join Freyja, who must have heard every word. She pretended not to care but her eyes were narrowed angrily above her jumper.

'The kids are in one of the ambulances. You'd better go and see to them.'

She stalked off without a word, the clacking of her heels echoing in the bare concrete interior.

'Well, then. Want to take a peek downstairs?' Erla's mood improved the moment Freyja had gone. Perhaps she was mollified by his unquestioning obedience. 'Though I warn you, it's a sight you won't forget in a hurry. Would you rather skip it?'

'No.' He was lying, but then he had no choice. Huldar really didn't like corpses. The smell alone was bad enough, without having the grisly vision imprinted on your memory. He took the menthol from Erla and wiped it under his nose but it didn't help much.

Erla went ahead, apparently immune to the smell that grew more sickening with every step. She had been there longer than him and seemed to have become desensitised. But then she was tougher than many of her male counterparts – in this as in other areas. 'The pathologist has just finished. He went with Forensics to fetch a stretcher and other equipment for removing the body. That should improve the atmosphere a bit.' She didn't hesitate when they reached the bottom of the stairs but walked straight over to the open steel door, towards the source of the light.

Huldar followed. He did his best to empty his mind in the hope that he would be able to survey the scene dispassionately, without taking in what he was seeing. But it was no good. He halted in the doorway, staring aghast at the body that had once been the Supreme Court judge, Yngvi Sigurhjartarson. At least, it must be him because the corpse was missing its hands and feet.

'They held him captive here, Dagmar and Orri. He was here for two months, believe it or not, after they ambushed him. Dagmar said it didn't take much to encourage him to write the suicide note, just the promise that, if he did, they wouldn't kill him. People believe all kinds of bullshit when they have no choice. They left him food and water but the house is so remote that they couldn't get out here very often, so the food can't have been too appetising by the end.'

'Did you say *they?*' Huldar asked, his voice muffled by his elbow. He couldn't even pretend to out-tough Erla in a situation like this.

She turned her head, but didn't comment when she saw how he was taking it. He was hardly the first person who couldn't cope with the smell of decomposing flesh. 'She insists that she and Orri plotted the whole thing in collusion. The divorce was part of the plan, to stop anyone guessing that they were working together. I know he denies taking any part in it, but that's her story. The truth's bound to come out in the end.'

'Yes, let's hope it does.' Futile to waste time wondering about the details now. Tomorrow, the police would commence their interrogation of Dagmar and Orri, which would eventually extract the truth, or at least one version of it. In complex cases like this, the police never felt confident of all the facts by the end of the inquiry. Some details were neither right nor wrong; they came down to the perception of the individual.

The corpse's grey skin was like marble where it was visible under the bloodstained clothes. The stumps were an ugly mess. The arms looked worse than the legs; there had been a chance for bruises and gangrene to develop before the man died, whereas the cuts on his legs looked relatively clean. A film covered the open eyes, obscuring their colour, and the bluish lips were parted as if the man had emitted a sigh as he finally gave up the ghost. Of relief, perhaps.

'According to the pathologist, he'd have been unlikely to survive long even if he'd been allowed to keep his hands. There's a nasty abscess from the tight bonds on his wrists, where he must have injured himself trying to break free. The poor guy had nothing else to do. The doctor says he'd soon have developed septicaemia from the wounds – that's if he didn't suffer a cardiac arrest. He wasn't in very good shape to begin with.'

'What do you want me to do?' Huldar prayed fervently that it wouldn't involve lingering down here. His gaze fell on a small, petrol-powered chainsaw on the floor beside the door and he could almost hear the whine of the motor and the poor man's screams.

'Can you take over interviewing Thorvaldur? Remember how insufferable he was when we questioned him before?' Huldar nodded. 'Well, he's a changed man – for the moment anyway. So we'd better take advantage before he recovers.'

On his way out Huldar spotted a bloodied, skin-coloured lump on the other side of the room and paused. In front of it was a small, yellow, numbered marker, placed there by Forensics to show that it was evidence. 'What's that?'

'Oh, that's Thorvaldur's hand.' Erla walked over to join him. 'She sawed it off.'

'I don't understand why they can't reattach it. It has to be worth trying.' Thorvaldur was lying on a stretcher in the ambulance. The doctor had joined the driver in front while Huldar talked to the patient for the ten minutes he had been allotted. Thorvaldur was almost unrecognisable as the smartly dressed, supercilious prosecutor who had sat in the police interview room only yesterday. The same expensive suit could be glimpsed under the blanket but the collar of his shirt was now twisted and grimy, and his jacket had seen better days. His hair, too, was wet and unkempt, his face ashen under the filth. His left arm was resting on top of the blanket, wrapped in a white bandage and unnaturally short.

'The doctor says the cut wasn't clean enough and that too long a time has passed. When did it happen?'

'I don't know. Some hours ago.' Thorvaldur cradled the stump with his right hand. 'But not that many. Why won't they even try?'

'They know what they're doing. At least it wasn't your right hand.'

'I'm left-handed.'

'Oh.' Huldar looked away, ashamed that he hadn't noticed. 'It could have turned out worse. Try to hold on to that thought.'

Thorvaldur raised his eyes to Huldar's face. 'How are the kids? Are they all right? Karlotta . . .'

'They're being looked after. They're young. They'll get over it.'

'You think so? Really?'

'Yes, I do.' Of course he knew nothing about it but he allowed himself to hope.

'I tried. I tried and I lost my hand as a result. That was the end for me. I couldn't bear to lose the other one. I should've given in straight away . . . should've . . .'

'Should have what?'

Thorvaldur dropped his gaze to his arm again. 'I was given a choice. To end up like the man under the blanket . . .'

'Yngvi Sigurhjartarson. The Supreme Court judge.'

'Seriously? I should have recognised him. But that . . . this . . . the corpse looked nothing like him.'

'No. I don't suppose it did.' Huldar tried to shrug off a mental image of the man's hideously disfigured face. 'Go on – you were given a choice between ending up like him and what? What was the alternative?'

'To sacrifice one hand for Karlotta, the other for Dadi. If I sacrificed both my hands, they'd be spared. But in the end I could only save one of them.'

'Were you told they'd be killed?'

'No. They'd be raped. By Jón Jónsson. She said that shouldn't bother me because I'd shown before that I thought it was OK. She dragged him in to prove to me that he was really there.'

'I see. Was she referring to the time when Thröstur came to you for help years ago, when you were temping with Hafnarfjördur Police?'

'Yes.' Thorvaldur's eyes were suddenly swimming with tears. 'But it wasn't like that. I never thought it was OK. I just didn't have any choice.'

'We always have a choice, Thorvaldur. The way I understood it, you did nothing to help Thröstur because you received such a good job offer from his grandfather. Isn't that the truth?'

'It was much more complicated than that. His grandfather said he'd see to it that I was sacked if I took the matter any further and I couldn't face having that on my CV. And he claimed the boy was a pathological liar and that this wasn't the first time he'd gone to the authorities with a pack of nonsense. For all I knew, it might have been true – how was I to know the man was a liar himself? Then he added that if I kept quiet, he'd make sure I landed a plum position at the Prosecutor's office after I graduated. Because I'd have proved I could be relied on.' A tear ran down his cheek, into his ear. 'He kept his promise. It was my big chance. I didn't have any connections. I'd have been forced to work my way up, waste years at the bottom of the pile in some crappy, two-bit practice. It was an offer I couldn't refuse. And he said the boy was a liar. That's what he said.'

'Which was bullshit. Thröstur was telling the truth.' Huldar couldn't bring himself to pity Thorvaldur; the man was feeling sorry enough for himself. The tears kept on flowing. 'Tell me about Karlotta. We need to know exactly what happened so she can be given the help she needs.'

Thorvaldur sniffed. 'At first I didn't believe she was serious about cutting off my hand. The chainsaw seemed so unreal somehow. I apologised for failing Thröstur and indirectly failing her daughter as a result. I kept saying sorry over and over again. But she wouldn't listen, she just kept insisting I had to choose between letting Jón Jónsson abuse my children or sacrificing my hands. So I said I wanted to save Karlotta and Dadi, and held out my hand. The kids were out of their minds with terror – completely out of their minds – clinging to me while all this was happening. I'd got down on my knees so I could hug them, and I held out my arm, thinking she would chicken out. But she didn't. She grabbed it and lifted the saw. Then . . .'

'Go on.'

'I blacked out. When I came round, the stump was numb and some rags had been wrapped round it. She was still standing there. Karlotta and Dadi had fled into the corner, terrified. They were covered in blood. I remember feeling desperately thirsty. But she didn't give me any water. Just kicked me in the side and told me to choose: I'd saved one of my children, but not the other. And I gave in. I couldn't take any more.' He fell silent, closed his eyes, then carried on: 'Karlotta and Dadi started screaming – I don't think they understood what was happening but they knew it had something to do with them – that I'd betrayed them. But I had no time to comfort them because she said she was going to count to ten, then I'd have to choose which of them to sacrifice.'

'And you chose Karlotta?'

'I couldn't think. I was in shock. The only thing I could take in was the numbers – each one seemed infinitely precious because as long as she was counting I didn't have to say either name aloud. Then suddenly she reached ten. And I blurted out "Karlotta". I don't know why. It was only after she'd taken her out of the room that I wondered what I'd have done if I'd been given time to think properly. I still couldn't decide. Is it worse for a boy or a girl to suffer that? Is it better to be younger? Or older? Did I make the right choice?'

'Both choices were equally bad.' Huldar saw the doctor twist round in the front seat, his expression horrified. He tapped his watch to remind Huldar that his time was nearly up. 'You keep saying *she*. Did you see the woman's face? Would you be able to recognise her again?'

'Yes.' Thorvaldur closed his eyes. 'I don't suppose she ever meant to let me or the kids survive. Perhaps we were lucky after all.'

'There's no question about that.' Huldar put a hand on Thorvaldur's shoulder. 'One more thing before I let you go. Did you see anyone else apart from her? A man, for example?'

'I saw Jón Jónsson. She showed him to me. No one else, though. She was alone.'

Huldar clasped his shoulder in parting, then stood up. After he had climbed down from the ambulance, Thorvaldur called out hoarsely: 'What would you have done? Which one would you have chosen? Karlotta or Dadi?'

Huldar turned. 'I can't answer that. I don't have any kids.' He closed the doors behind him.

Freyja was sitting in the back of the second ambulance with Karlotta in her arms. The girl was wrapped in a blanket and had her face buried in Freyja's chest. A pink sock, the sole wet and black with dirt, poked out from under the blanket. Her thin little body was shaking with sobs. Her brother was lying curled up in a foetal position on the stretcher, apparently asleep. Huldar climbed in, pulling the door to behind him. 'How is she?'

Freyja shook her head. 'Not good. I'm going back to town with the ambulance. They've got a doctor and a nurse waiting at the Children's House, and they've called out a nurse from the emergency services for victims of sexual violence as well.'

'So he . . . ?' Huldar gestured wordlessly, hoping she would understand.

Freyja shrugged and gently lifted the blanket off the little girl. She was naked from the waist down apart from her socks. 'Unclear. We're about to head off; I'm just waiting for the doctor.'

Huldar nodded. 'I'll call you, if it's not too late when I get back. Otherwise, talk to you tomorrow.' He reached out a hand to the little head and stroked the dirty, sweat-stiffened hair. 'Good luck. The worst is over.'

After that he stood in the driveway for a while, puffing out his cheeks and taking quick panting breaths in an effort to contain his rage. He kept trying to get himself under control and was still trying when a second doctor emerged from the house and climbed into the ambulance to join Freyja and the children.

The two ambulances moved off. He watched the rear lights until they vanished behind a hill.

'Are you coming?' Erla called from the front door.

'Just going to have a smoke. Be with you in a sec.' His voice was deep and hollow with tiredness.

'Is everything OK?' Erla sounded worried. 'Make sure you don't throw up anywhere near the house.'

'I'm fine. I'll be along in a minute.' Huldar forced a smile and Erla disappeared back inside. He lit up and drew the smoke deep into his lungs. The nicotine did nothing to soothe his murderous anger; if anything, it intensified it. But the fury brought a certain clarity, freeing his mind from thirty years of indoctrination in good behaviour, in knowing right from wrong. Sometimes violent instincts had to be given their head.

Best get it over with.

Still smoking, he walked towards the police car where Jón Jónsson was being held. He halted by the rear door and took another drag while looking the man over. He recognised him from the photographs: his face was puffier and dirtier but still the same ugly mug, the same sly expression. Sensing that someone was standing beside the car, Jón Jónsson swung his head round and met Huldar's eye. His mouth hung open stupidly as he stared at the policeman. He was dead drunk.

Huldar inhaled again and the glowing end of his cigarette grew longer. Then he opened the car door, to be hit by a sour reek of alcohol that he was all too familiar with. It was what people smelt like after drinking for days on end. Jón was swaying slightly, trying to find his balance. When Huldar spat in his face, he didn't even seem to notice.

Huldar took a final drag, then stubbed out his cigarette right in the man's watering eye. Then he slammed the door and lit another. Behind him he heard a scream of agony.

He set off towards the car where Dagmar was sitting.

Chapter 35

'And you're sticking to this story?' The woman from internal affairs caught her colleague's eye, then they both looked back at Huldar. He was familiar with the expression, having seen it countless times in the mirror when he slipped into the gents in the middle of interviewing a suspect. It was an odd feeling to be sitting on the other side of the table. He knew what was going through the heads of his interrogators, recognised the glances and the tactics behind the repetitive questions, the changes in intonation. Always knew what was coming next – and they knew he knew. 'You really expect us to buy this?'

'Yes.' Huldar didn't look away and was careful not to shift in his seat or tap his fingers. 'Does anyone say different?'

The man's face tightened, he compressed his lips and deep creases formed between his eyes. 'There are two versions, as I'm sure you're aware. One's being bandied about by the coffee machine; the other's the one your colleagues are prepared to go on record about. And that one, which you unwisely insist on repeating, simply doesn't stand up to scrutiny. No one, regardless of whether he's a drunk, a pervert or whatever else applies to Jón Jónsson, no one would stub out a cigarette in his own eye.'

'Yet that's exactly what he seems to have done.' Huldar shrugged. 'Stranger things have happened. What's he saying? That I did it?' He knew this wasn't the case; Erla had whispered that much to him before he was called in for questioning. And also that they were all prepared to back up his story. When he came in that morning, several of his colleagues had actually slapped him on the back.

'He can't remember. He was too drunk.' The woman smiled sarcastically. 'As I'm sure you're aware.'

Huldar made do with shrugging again. There was no need to insult them by contradicting them.

'How did you hurt yourself?' The woman pointed to Huldar's grazed chin and hands.

'I fell.' He omitted to mention that Gudlaugur had knocked him down to prevent him from getting to Dagmar. The young officer had stepped out of the car for a breath of fresh air, witnessed his attack on Jón Jónsson and reacted with lightning speed. 'I slipped on the gravel at the crime scene. It's nothing serious, but thanks for asking.'

'Aren't you Mr Wise Guy?' The man drew over a sheet of paper that he had placed on the table but not touched since they'd sat down. 'How about telling us the truth? We give you our word that the matter will be dealt with fairly. We're well aware that this investigation has been gruelling for all concerned, and presumably the change in your status at work hasn't made life any easier for you.'

Sooner or later this was bound to happen: they'd start acting friendly, pretending to be on his side. It was all by the book. If he fell for their fair words he would end up in 'the Box', the basement room where those who deserved to be dismissed whiled away their days on pointless statistics. No one ever returned from the Box to normal assignments. Huldar lost it. 'I couldn't give a toss about my promotion. Erla's welcome to the job, for all I care.' It came out badly and he leant back and counted to ten under his breath. The *oh-you-poor-thing* look on the pair's faces made him hold back for another couple of beats. Then, having recovered some of his composure, he added more calmly: 'Erla's a better departmental manager than I ever was. I assure you I'm not disappointed about being demoted. Not in the least.'

'Yes, right.' The woman leant over to the man and read a note he'd written. 'Since you mention Erla, there's another matter we'd like to raise.'

'Oh?' Huldar's stomach clenched. He had prepared himself mentally for the interrogation but hadn't been expecting any surprises.

'It's a sensitive issue and we understand perfectly if you'd rather discuss it with a counsellor. We can make an appointment for you later. The same applies if you find it uncomfortable having one or other of us in here while you're giving your statement. Some people prefer to discuss this kind of thing with a woman, others with a man.'

'What?' Huldar wasn't sure he'd heard the woman right. 'I'm not with you.'

The woman held up the sheet of paper. It was too far away for Huldar to be able to read the small print but the heading was clear: *Responding to Sexual Harassment in the Workplace.* His stomach turned upside down. That could mean only one thing. Had Erla really stooped so low as to bring a complaint against him? Had he delayed too long before talking to her? 'What's that?'

'You're not familiar with the contents?' The woman placed it on the table and pushed it towards him. 'It's compulsory reading. You should know that.'

Huldar didn't touch the sheet. 'I have read it. I just don't understand what it's got to do with me.' He wondered if he should ask for permission to discuss this with a counsellor instead. That would at least give him a breathing space.

'Oh, I think you do understand. What's more, we're convinced that this was one of the factors behind the incident on Sunday evening. If you tell us the truth about that, it will be taken into account when we're processing the harassment case.' The man had taken over. 'Everyone finds it hard to discuss this kind of thing. We understand that. That's why it's so rare for people to come forward. You're one of the few lucky enough to have had it reported by a third party.'

'What?' Huldar was beginning to think they must be on drugs. 'Me? Lucky?' He was glad at least that Erla hadn't shopped him. But the idea that he was lucky didn't make any sense.

'Yes. You'd probably never have brought a complaint yourself. Men rarely take that step.'

Huldar was dumbstruck. Erla hadn't complained about him; he wasn't even a suspect. He was the victim. Never in a million years would he have expected that. Who the hell had done this to him? And to Erla? Alas, there were plenty of suspects: the department was abuzz with gossip about the night they had spent together. The person who had reported this must have done it in a spirit of vindictiveness. To get back at him or Erla. Or perhaps for a joke, but he wasn't amused. 'Can I ask who fed you that pack of lies?'

'You can ask, but we aren't at liberty to say. Though you can rest assured that our source is reliable.' The man gave him a sympathetic look. 'It's nothing to be ashamed of. The shame belongs entirely to the offender.'

'No. No, no, no. There's been some sort of mistake. I haven't been harassed by her. Either sexually or in any other way. Please, I'm asking you: throw out this report and don't raise it with me again. It's a total misunderstanding.' He paused for breath. 'Honestly.'

'Are you denying that she made advances? That she used her position as your boss to lure you into a sexual relationship?'

'Yes. I am denying that. Partly. It wasn't like you say, and I insist you drop this report or charge or whatever this bullshit is.' Huldar prepared to stand up. There were limits to what he would put up with. 'Someone's making a fool of you.'

For the first time, the pair on the other side of the table seemed less sure of themselves. They dropped their condescending manner. 'Well, we'll see. Take your time to think it over and we'll discuss it again later. The complaint will be followed up whether you like it or not, and so will the inquiry into what happened to Jón Jónsson. Neither matter is closed.'

Huldar jumped to his feet. He couldn't spend another minute in here. 'I've got to go. People are waiting for me.' He wasn't about to tell them that he was due to join Erla for the interrogation of Dagmar. They were quite capable of banning him from any further involvement in the case until the inquiry into Jón's injury was concluded. And internal affairs worked at such a glacial pace that the murder case would be resolved long before that happened. It was only thanks to Erla that he hadn't already been transferred. And he was desperate to hear Dagmar's story. He was bitter enough about having to miss yesterday's interviews. Erla had dispatched him straight back to town with Gudlaugur after the attack on Jón, and ordered him to stay at home on Monday and cool down. So he'd only heard second hand what had emerged so far.

'Before you go . . .'

Huldar paused in the doorway.

'If you're involved in an intimate sexual relationship with your manager, Erla, you're to end it now. Or she'll lose her job. Understood?'

Huldar turned back, unable to suppress a smile. 'Understood.' In one fell swoop his worries about how to break it off had been removed. All in all, this interview could have gone a lot worse.

Huldar tapped gently on the door of the room where Dagmar's interview was scheduled to take place. He opened it, apologised for being late and slipped into the seat beside Erla. Facing them were

Dagmar and her counsel, a youngish lawyer who Dagmar had picked at random from the list she was offered.

It was more than twenty-four hours since her arrest. The cells were overflowing in the wake of the weekend's dramatic events, with Jón Jónsson, Orri, Thröstur and his mother Agnes all locked up separately. The police had decided to release the mother and son that evening. There was no point detaining them any longer: Agnes had confessed to having helped her son dig up the coffin and take it to the dump; Thröstur had admitted to the same offence and also to having covered up the murder of Einar Adalbertsson eleven years earlier. The latter offence fell outside the statute of limitations. Besides, Thröstur had been a minor at the time. He and his mother would have to stand trial for the desecration of a grave and the unlawful treatment of a dead body, but these offences were punishable only by a fine or a few months in prison. Sigrún had turned out not to have been involved in either incident. She was the only person to emerge with a clean conscience, apart from Thorvaldur's children.

Thröstur wouldn't get off as lightly. He had perverted the course of justice by deliberately withholding information. Since he had finally agreed to cooperate, however, detaining him further would serve no purpose.

Orri was a different matter. They were having difficulty proving that he had played any direct role in the murders. Dagmar alleged that he had and most of the inquiry team were inclined to accept her version. They didn't believe for one minute, as Orri's experienced lawyer never tired of claiming, that she was suffering from psychotic delusions. But her word was of limited value given that no solid evidence confirmed Orri's involvement, and none of the witnesses had backed up her statement. If no proof emerged, Orri might well get away with a token sentence. It would be impossible to prove that he was an accomplice, let alone an equal partner in the murders, as

Dagmar maintained. Her tendency to inconsistency about the specifics weakened her statement still further.

Her counsel wanted her to undergo a psychiatric assessment, but she flatly refused and threatened to hire a different lawyer. Despite her refusal to budge on this, a judge might still insist on one. To complicate matters still further, the judges might have to declare a conflict of interests, since she was being tried for the murder of one of their colleagues. And no one from the Prosecutor's office could act in the trial because of their professional links to Benedikt Toft and Thorvaldur; an outsider would have to be brought in. Thorvaldur was on indefinite leave and probably wouldn't come back even after he'd recovered from the loss of his hand. The same applied to the psychologist Sólveig; she had been sent on gardening leave while the inquiry was in progress and was no more likely than Thorvaldur to be allowed to return to her job.

'Well, well, if it isn't the smoker?' Dagmar grinned. Remarkably enough, she was looking much better now than the first time Huldar had seen her. She looked happier, carefree. She had been allowed to tidy herself up, her hair was nicely styled and she was wearing make-up, as if she was expecting photographers. 'My favourite cop.' She had witnessed his assault on Jón Jónsson, but so far had not admitted to it. She had no idea that she had been next on his list and, even if she had, it probably wouldn't have changed her attitude. Jón Jónsson was the person she hated most in the world and nothing unites people like a common enemy.

Huldar pretended he hadn't heard, and Erla ordered Dagmar to carry on with her story. The woman turned back to her. 'I've already told you the whole thing, both yesterday and the night before, but as you seem to be so slow, I'll repeat it all over again.' She pushed back a lock of hair that had fallen over her cheek. 'Like I said, it was never my intention to let Jón Jónsson go all the way with that girl.'

'Her name's Karlotta.' Erla locked eyes with Dagmar. 'Try to remember that.'

'Karlotta. Rather a pretentious name, don't you think? Never mind. I just wanted that vile father of hers to hear her scream. Scream like Vaka screamed. The moment Jón got ready to . . .' The woman faltered, seeming suddenly uncomfortable, then shrugged it off and resumed as carelessly as before: 'When he got ready to do the deed, I shoved him off. He was so drunk he was no match for me. My deepest regret is that I didn't kill him then, while I had the chance. But I made do with knocking him out and I was going to wait until he woke up before fetching the chainsaw.'

'The chainsaw, yes.' Erla scribbled a note and the young lawyer blanched.

'Could I speak to my client in private, please?'

'Oh, stop interfering, will you?' Dagmar said to him. 'You're here to satisfy the formalities. It doesn't matter what I say or do. I'll get the usual sixteen years.'

'That's not necessarily correct. It's possible to get twenty years. Or life. Just because that term has never yet been imposed, that doesn't mean it couldn't happen.' The lawyer looked at Huldar and Erla in an appeal for support but in vain. It was up to Dagmar to protect her own interests. If she threw her counsel out, then so be it.

Dagmar rolled her eyes. 'Blah-blah-blah. Can I go on?'

'Yes, please do.' Huldar finally joined in. 'Tell us about your relationship with Jón Jónsson. How did you get him on side?'

'It was simple. I corresponded with him. Had envelopes printed with the name of his solicitor's and the address of the hair salon, to make it look official, and added the lawyer's name to our post box. No one noticed. I wrote to him saying that I understood him; I copied texts I found online where people claim that paedophilia is a valid sexual orientation. He fell for it, and I just continued bullshitting him, saying I could provide him with material that would satisfy his urges so he'd leave real children alone. If I'd said I was going to provide him with kids, he'd have seen through me. As it was, he believed he'd found a soul mate, a woman who was attracted to prisoners.'

Dagmar fell silent and looked complacently at Huldar and Erla in turn. She seemed to expect them to applaud her for her cleverness. When they simply stared back stony-faced, she gave up, shook her head carelessly and continued her tale. 'I was a bit worried he'd see through me but I needn't have been. I mean, he had no one else to turn to. A drowning man doesn't stop to question the quality of the life-belt that's thrown to him.'

'And when he got out?'

'We arranged that in our last letters. He was to phone me when he got to town. I'd look after him until he found his feet.' Dagmar laughed grimly. 'It went like clockwork. He rang from a public phone and I went and picked him up. I had a bottle of whisky on the front seat and told him it was to celebrate his release. He hesitated a bit and that got me worried. I was afraid if he was sober he'd recognise me from the trial. But I needn't have worried – he unscrewed the top and took a swig. After that it was plain sailing. I drove him to the holiday house where Orri and I had put a mattress, booze, food, an electric heater and some disgusting material we'd printed off the internet ages ago. That was all he needed, and we didn't have to think about him again until later. Though I did take his shoes away to stop him wandering off, and locked the room where we were holding Yngvi. Mind you, by then Yngvi'd stopped his screaming and was pretty far gone. Then he went and died.' Dagmar took a sip of water. 'That was a mistake, actually.'

'In what way a mistake?' Erla looked up from the notes she was taking while Dagmar talked.

'We'd been under the impression that Jón would get out earlier. But his release was delayed for some reason, so we were stuck with that bloody Yngvi for two months.'

'Why wait for him?' Huldar assumed this had been clarified the day before but he had only been briefed with the main points of her statement. 'Why didn't you just murder your targets two months earlier? You'd been planning this for so long that I don't see why two months either way should matter.'

'For two reasons, my favourite cop. Firstly, we always meant it to look like Jón had killed the lot of them. Secondly, all the murders needed to be carried out in a short space of time. That would reduce the risk that we'd be caught before we'd finished – as we were, sadly. I'd like to have taken out that bitch Sólveig, and of course it was a mistake for Jón to survive. That was the police's fault. If you'd arrived an hour later I'd have chopped him into little pieces. In front of Thorvaldur, so he wouldn't get bored.'

'In front of his children too?'

Dagmar shrugged. 'No. Probably not.' Her lawyer was visibly relieved by this answer. 'But I can tell you one thing, Mr Marlboro Man.' Dagmar grinned at Huldar but didn't seem to care when he didn't respond in kind. If anything, it seemed to amuse her. 'By then I was past caring whether the murders were blamed on Jón or not. I was past caring what would happen once it was all over. But Orri felt differently.'

'Are you sure about that?' Erla interrupted before Huldar could speak. She was annoyed by Dagmar's constant allusions to the business with the cigarette. 'I'm pretty sure you'd have removed all the fingerprints and other evidence of your presence, as Orri seems to have done, if we hadn't tracked you down when we did.'

'No. You're wrong. If we'd managed to kill the lot, I'd have been satisfied. I could have died content. Something broke, you see, when

Vaka was murdered. Before that I was happy. I loved her more than life itself. I loved Orri and we lived our lives without hurting anyone else. Then one day she wasn't there anymore. I saw her that morning when we were in a rush and there was no time to say anything that mattered, to drop a kiss on her head or tell her we loved her. We were too busy trying to calm her nerves about her first day at her new school. The last thing I said to her was to make sure she didn't lose the teaspoon from her lunchbox. Can you imagine? A stupid teaspoon.' Dagmar was silent for a moment. 'We never got her school bag back. Or her clothes. They must still be here in your property office. The teaspoon too, probably.' The woman's arrogant manner had almost gone, leaving her looking utterly deflated. 'Before Thröstur came to see us, we were both losing the will to carry on. We couldn't get out of bed in the mornings. All we could think of was what Vaka must have gone through. Our darling little girl. I used to have fits of retching, imagining that monster groaning and her crying. It's been like a soundtrack to our lives ever since. Orri wasn't sick but he used to go into fits of rage. Over nothing.'

None of them spoke. Of course no child should lose her life in such an appalling manner, violated, bewildered and terrified. But that didn't justify what had followed. Dagmar drew herself up and continued: 'Then Thröstur appeared. That evening was a turning point: it gave us a purpose again. Revenge. It became our mission to deal out a just punishment to all those who had put their own interests before the children they were supposed to be protecting. Could there be any more despicable betrayal than that? Not for me. Not for Orri. I don't know about you, but then you've never had to suffer what we've been through.'

Dagmar paused again and silence settled over the room. The lawyer was growing agitated but he seemed to have learnt his lesson about interrupting. 'As we listened to Einar churning out the whole story something snapped inside me. Inside both of us. At that moment it was like we were standing on the brink, staring down into the vortex. Knowing that if we let ourselves be sucked in, we would be free to satisfy our anger, our thirst for revenge. No more having to struggle to get over it; no more being told to move on and put a cheerful face on things. Did you know that that's what everyone expects?' When they didn't answer, Dagmar continued: 'Instead, we could devote all our energies to the opposite, to nursing our hatred. The instant I realised this, I swung the hammer and after that there was no turning back.'

'Where was Orri at this stage?'

'In the hall. He walked out after Einar had finished talking. But he wasn't exactly pissed off about what happened. Oh no. When he came back in he was pleased. Never mind what he says now. Pleased enough to react positively to the idea of doing away with the lot of them after Jón's release. We were determined to go through with it. Of course we discussed the pros and cons, but before long we started collecting all kinds of stuff that would come in handy. I doubt you've been able to trace a single item to us, not now, more than ten years later.' She searched Erla's and Huldar's faces as if hoping to be praised for her ingenuity but they remained impassive. She continued: 'We bought everything we needed, even the alcohol for Jón. We'd decided how each person was going to die. It wasn't going to be a case of alive one minute, dead the next. No, their deaths would be drawn out, preceded by something to unnerve them, to give them a hint of what was in store. Looking back, I reckon the sulphuric acid was the most spectacular. I bet Kolbeinn would agree.' Dagmar smiled proudly, then raised her eyebrows, apparently surprised by the unenthusiastic response of those present. 'Shortly after we'd sketched out our plan, we took the decision to divorce, to avoid suspicion when the time came. Because no one could carry out an operation like that alone. It was hard, so terribly hard. I loved Orri and he loved me. But those were the lengths we were prepared to go to. After the divorce had been finalised and everyone thought we were sworn enemies, we met up twice a year to discuss our plans. By Vaka's grave, on her birthday and on the anniversary of her death. Then, when Jón wrote to me that he was getting out, I rang Orri from a friend's phone, and we met one evening up at the Heidmörk Nature Reserve, to divide up the tasks and finalise all the details.'

'He seems to have left you with all the most important jobs. Is that right?' Erla pulled over the jug of water and refilled Dagmar's half-empty glass. 'Or did he just fail to do his bit?'

'He took responsibility for a variety of things. He provided the accommodation, helped me kidnap the judge and drive him to the holiday house, and we both engineered Benedikt Toft's death in the garage. But he suddenly lost his nerve. He claimed he was rushed off his feet at work and that if we ended up in the police's sights he would be under more suspicion than me. Then he started getting paranoid that Jón had been spotted outside the holiday home. I tried to rescue the situation by pretending I'd seen him in town. The intention was to reassure Orri that if they started looking for Jón it would be here in Reykjavík, not in the countryside. I reckon I did a pretty good job of playing a woman on the verge of a nervous breakdown. I used to be that woman once. But not anymore.'

Huldar clasped his grazed hands behind his head. It appeared that Orri had always played a careful game, making sure he didn't leave behind any incriminating evidence. Perhaps he had been as gung-ho as Dagmar in the beginning but, as she alleged, had second thoughts when he realised that Dagmar didn't care if they were caught once it was all over. His decision to approach Freyja suggested that he had wanted to give his side of the story before it was too late – indeed, it was thanks to him that they had managed to save Thorvaldur and his children.

'You'd better think long and hard about anything that could link your ex-husband to the offences. Did anyone see or hear him? Is there some tool that might have his fingerprints on it? Anything that could support your allegations? Because he's telling a very different story. He claims he thought it was all just fantasy on your part and that he lent you the building without realising why you wanted it. Now it's your word against his and it's quite possible that he'll get off far more lightly than he deserves to. You can't be happy about that. After all, he was the one who turned up late to collect Vaka from school. If he'd been on time, none of this would have happened.'

Dagmar leant towards Huldar. 'You know what, Mr Smoker? I couldn't give a damn. It's not Orri's fault he was stuck in a traffic jam. He can get off scot-free for all I care. Jón too. And Sólveig. And Thorvaldur. But they'll get what they deserve. I've nothing to do for the next decade or so but plan how their lives will end.'

The lawyer interrupted. 'I advise you not to say another word.' He looked at Erla. 'Don't write that down. She wasn't being serious. I insist on speaking to my client in private. Now.'

Erla gathered up her papers. 'No problem.' Huldar followed her out but glanced round when Dagmar called out to him.

'Hey, Marlboro Man. We're not so different, you and me. It's only a question of degree. In my shoes you'd have done the same.'

Huldar didn't answer. He felt a powerful urge to wash his face, to take a hot shower. Dagmar's words had caught him off balance. It was time to get his life under control.

He followed Erla upstairs. Once in the office he would tell her about his conversation with internal affairs, thereby putting an end to any further sexual relationship between them. Slightly to his surprise, he was aware of a tinge of regret. But it was too late for that. Now he would focus all his efforts on Freyja. She had been forced to sit in the car with him for over an hour on the way to the crime scene and they had got on fine. You never know, he might be allowed to go down to the lake with her to feed the ducks. He had a hunch that if he made it that far, the battle would be won.

Epilogue

They lowered the coffin into the grave. The men were obviously experienced; there was no danger it would tip on its side or land with a bump. They freed the ropes, then withdrew a little to stand, straight-backed and solemn, while the minister spoke a few words, Bible in hand. Thröstur didn't take any of them in. He was the only mourner in attendance at this reburial, in stark contrast to the original funeral. Few if any of the prominent figures who had filled the pews then would want to be associated with the deceased now. How they must be regretting the praise they had heaped on him in the obituaries. So they should.

Thröstur hadn't been intending to go along; it had been a last-minute decision. In his eyes this ceremony marked the end of a journey that had begun long ago at Hafnarfjördur police station. As it happened, neither he, his mother nor Sigrún had been informed that the burial was taking place, since no one had expected them to attend. He had heard the news from Einar's daughter in Norway. She had rung and he happened to pick up the phone. Her reason for calling had been to tell them about the re-interment but also about a number of other things. If what the woman said was true, her father had been an absolute monster. This wasn't news to Thröstur. But he was surprised to learn that she and her brother had been abused by their father as kids, and even more taken aback when she told him that Einar had in all likelihood abused his stepson Jón as well.

That explained everything. That explained nothing.

Why should a similar experience produce such different individuals? The woman's brother, Einar's son, had killed himself after a long battle with depression. She was in no doubt about its cause. She herself had managed to work through her childhood trauma, though she didn't think she would ever recover completely. Jón, Thröstur's own father, had taken to drink and ended up the same kind of monster as the man who had moulded him. The next generation had developed in separate ways as well: Sigrún had retreated from the world as far as possible, whereas he had always given it the finger, and now didn't know how to stop.

The only thing the woman's story had actually shed light on was why Einar hadn't turned his back on his stepson when Thröstur tried, as a little boy, to involve the authorities. It hadn't simply been a question of avoiding disgrace by association; he had been afraid that Jón would reveal the abuse that he had been subjected to as a boy. It was strange that Jón hadn't done so later on, during his murder trial, but perhaps he had realised that it wouldn't make any difference to his punishment.

The phone call was brief. Once she had got these things off her chest they had only exchanged a few more words, despite the painful experience they shared. That's just the way it was: he was alone with his sorrows, just as Sigrún was, and the woman in Norway too. They would each have to find a way of coping on their own; standing together wouldn't make them any stronger.

That's why he was here. In a pathetic attempt at a final reckoning with a dead man. The cemetery caretaker hadn't known what to do with himself once it dawned on him who Thröstur was. In the end he had, like most people, adopted the course of least resistance, pretending he didn't know that here was the grave robber himself, come to see the coffin returned to its proper place. The minister and pallbearers, on the other hand, had no idea who he was, asked no questions and seemed merely keen to get the ceremony over with.

The minister snapped the Bible shut and beckoned Thröstur to approach the grave, before moving back. Thröstur stepped onto the planks that had been laid on either side of the hole. He wondered if digging up the coffin had been a wise move, or if it had simply made his problems worse. He couldn't make up his mind.

The aim had been to ensure that Einar received a proper post-mortem, so the police would believe Thröstur when he eventually told them that Dagmar had dealt him his death blow. Since no one in the system had ever listened to him before, he had no reason to expect things to be any different this time. But he had wanted to reduce the risk that he or Sigrún would be accused of involvement in Dagmar and Orri's killing spree. They were obvious suspects since they both had every reason to wish the victims dead. On top of that, he was shit-scared of Dagmar and Orri, and had been ever since that fateful evening. After she had dealt with Einar, Dagmar had told Thröstur that she wasn't going to leave it at that, and he had been petrified that she would try to get rid of him and Sigrún too. The couple seemed to be capable of anything.

Only now was that fear dying down. It was nothing like as bad as it had been in the beginning. That first year after he witnessed his grandfather's murder had been the hardest. Whenever he tried to fall asleep at night he would picture the couple breaking in. The secret of his grandfather's murder and the woman's threat had gnawed away at him, feeding his anxiety. Suddenly he'd found it hard to concentrate at school. His entire life had been blighted by the events. It wasn't until it occurred to him to unburden himself in the time capsule that he'd felt a sense of freedom. There was a degree of comfort in knowing about the information sealed in the earth, waiting to see the light of day. If he was murdered before the couple dispatched their other victims, the letter might help to expose them. It was unbearable to think they might kill him and get away with it. Yet he didn't dare to foil their plans. Not then.

Of course Thröstur had wanted them to succeed; his desire for vengeance had probably been equal to theirs and it didn't cross his mind to try and kid himself otherwise. The difference was that he wanted the couple to get caught in the end. The problem had been to find the right moment to report them, not too soon and not too late. He had tried to find out what his legal position would be if he covered up for them for too long and realised that it wouldn't be good. That was why he hadn't dared to let them finish their mission. Sadly. He would have enjoyed knowing that Sólveig had suffered like an insect crushed under the heel of a pitiless child. But he didn't regret much else.

Thröstur contemplated the coffin at the bottom of the hole. It was the same coffin that he and his spineless mother had dug up several days ago. During the phone call, Einar's daughter had told him how she'd laughed when asked if she wanted to buy a new one.

He studied the battered coffin lid. Beneath it lay the beginning and end of all his troubles. Closing his eyes, he took a deep breath. He saw, hopefully for the last time, the moment when he had opened the door to Sigrún's room, the day Vaka had come round to their house to use the phone. He saw his sister, her face swollen with tears, sitting on the bed and tidying the girl's hair with her brush. He heard his own anguished cries when he pulled the duvet off the girl and took in the fact that she was dead. He only had to see the bloodstain on the sheet to work out what had happened. He knew those stains too well from personal experience.

Thröstur squeezed his eyes tighter shut. This would be the last time he allowed himself to remember. When he left here it would be to begin a new life. He allowed himself to remember Sigrún's voice as she told him between sobs that Vaka wouldn't stop crying. She had cried and cried, and Sigrún had to stop their father hearing her and coming back. But when she took away the pillow the girl's face was blue and she was lying quite still. Since then she hadn't been able to wake her up.

Thröstur re-lived the devastating sense of shock. He couldn't comprehend how he'd had the presence of mind to take the pillow from Sigrún, carry it into the bedroom where their father was lying in an alcoholic stupor and push the pillowcase against his limp hands in the hope that his prints would be transferred onto it. It had worked. In his memory he walked back into Sigrún's room, laid the pillow over the girl's face, gripped Sigrún by the shoulders and told her she hadn't done anything. Their father had killed her friend. She herself had hidden in the cupboard and now she was to get back in there and wait until someone opened the door. She might have to wait a very long time. While she was sitting in the dark she was to keep thinking about how their father had put the pillow over the girl's face. Not her. She had remembered wrong. She must never breathe a word of what she'd first thought had happened. Never, ever. Then he shut her in the cupboard and went into his own room.

Still to this day he didn't know if Sigrún had succeeded in brain-washing herself or if she remembered what had really happened. His most fervent wish was that she should believe that their father had been to blame. As he had been, all things considered.

And the man in the coffin, of course.

Thröstur glanced round at the minister and the pallbearers waiting impatiently.

Then he unzipped his flies and pissed on the coffin.

When he had finished, Thröstur walked along the boards and back to the path. The shocked disgust on the other men's faces meant nothing to him. He strode away towards the exit, feeling more reconciled to life than ever before.